The Execution Code
D.R. Rose

Sequel to THE SECOND TWIN

Also by D R Rose:

The Second Twin

The Binary Conversion

The moral right of the author has been asserted.

This is a work of fiction. Names, characters, places and events are products of the author's imagination or are used fictitiously. This includes places that are clearly in the public domain but in this story form part of the fictitious events and descriptions. Any resemblance to actual people, living or dead, or situations, is purely coincidental.

No part of this publication may be copied, reproduced, stored in a retrieval system, circulated, or transmitted, by any means or in any form, without the author's prior written permission. Nor can it be circulated in any form of binding or cover, other than that in which it is published, without a similar condition.

© D R ROSE 2017.

ISBN-13:978-1979918688

How many goodly creatures are there here!

How beauteous mankind is! O brave new world, That has such people in it!

Shakespeare, The Tempest, Vi

1

It was the middle of the night. I opened the window of the little balcony, trying to make out any shapes in the dark gardens of the Askeys mansion. Then I sensed something moving on the lawn below. One of the security lights came on. A man was running across the garden. I stepped back, instinctively, although in the darkness of the house, he was unlikely to have seen me. More lights flickered into life and I saw other figures, running towards the man. They brought him to the ground and I heard him cry out. He was saying "Wait!" or something like that, but soon fell silent. They had perhaps knocked him out. From the side of the house, another figure approached the group. He was in nightclothes, hastily tying up a dressing gown as he walked purposefully towards them. He looked up at the balcony, where I stood in the shadows.

    I knew at once that it was Gaston Ajax, the Binaries head of security. Darkness was no barrier to him: he had sensed me looking down. He merely glanced but I detected him thinking, "Cassandra! It would be you, of course."

    Clothed only in a flimsy nightdress, I shivered in the cool, late autumn air, but I'd been unable to sleep and was now unwilling to leave this unfolding drama. When Gaston reached the guards surrounding the man lying on the ground, I couldn't hear what he was saying, guessing he was mainly sending thoughts. I made no attempt to pick them up, not wishing to be detected as an eavesdropper. I was turning towards the curtained window of the balcony when it parted and Kastor appeared. He wrapped an arm round me, looking into the gardens beyond. The group was moving off, Gaston disappearing into the gloom at the side of the house.

"An intruder," Kastor said, thoughtfully, "Rare, here. Very."

"What will they do to him?" I asked.

"Oh, find out what he was after," he replied, in a disinterested tone.

"You'll help them do that?"

He gave a weary nod in response. Security was very tight in the Askeys mansion where most of the Binaries telepaths lived. This was the first time I'd heard of anyone getting as far as the gardens, let alone see an intruder. I wondered if my sleeplessness, and wanting to get some balcony air, had been a precognition that there would be an event out there. I wanted to ask more about how they would investigate this unlucky man, now in the hands of Gaston's security officers. I thought of old advertisements for 'roach motel' traps to entice cockroaches: *'they check in, but they don't check out.'* Perhaps, if he was just a burglar, they would find some way of making him forget his capture, so that he could be released. More likely, his body would be found a long way off when they had finished with him. These were matters that one learned not to enquire about at the Binaries, although I had an uneasy feeling that I'd hear more about this incident, or be involved in the investigation in some way. Meanwhile, Kastor was drawing me back into the bedroom, obviously unwilling to discuss either my thoughts or the disturbance in the garden.

"Cassandra - don't you ever just want to sleep a whole night?" he asked.

"Leo keeps me awake, with his thoughts," I replied, rarely missing an opportunity to remind Kastor that Leo did not live with us.

Leo, short for Leander, was now two and a half years old and although he was with the other Binaries children in a dormitory, I could tune into him easily. Kastor was proud of our only child, but he had been brought up in this way and accustomed to the separation from parents that was deemed best for their development. With my experience of the outside world, I found it cruel, despite all I'd learned about the telepathy training. Inducing or enhancing an ability to send or read thoughts was one of the central purposes of the organization.

"It will make him so very different from children outside," I protested, when I discovered that Leander wouldn't be allowed to live in our flat, an idea so preposterous to Kastor that he had laughed, before seeing that I was serious about it.

"But to bring him up differently from the others," he said, "would make him alien to his little friends, as well as to children outside."

The concession had been made for me to visit the nursery training centre as often as I liked, when my work allowed. It was also a major difference from the organization's living habits that Kastor and I had continued to share the same apartment. Most of the Binaries residents lived separately. It was easier for these telepaths, with their heightened sensitivity, to have somewhere to be completely alone. Soon after moving into his home, making it ours, I'd learned to sense when Kastor needed this solitude. Adapting a large adjacent storage room had extended our apartment. This provided an extra bedroom and a study, as well as a larger dressing area and ensuite for the main bedroom. If Kastor was working on a particularly difficult assignment, he'd come in late and sleep in the other bedroom. I was also happy that he had made the study his own domain. This was not to imply that our relationship had cooled. We were still bonded, mind and body, *'now and forever'* as Kastor had put it.

Tonight, we were in the balconied bedroom that I'd come to consider as largely mine. Kastor closed the window, drawing the curtains across. The room had a chill from the winter air seeping in. I projected an image of us warming up, once we'd got back into bed.

"I should think so, too," said Kastor, smiling. "But keep your feet to yourself," he added, "They'll be freezing after being out there."

Even under the covers, Kastor started at the sudden cold sensation of my night chilled hands.

"Well, warm me up then," I murmured. He responded with an image of a blazing fire, which I converted into a gentle fire, burning in the grate of a log cabin. I was remembering a ski lodge from a holiday in my former life outside, adding a deep woolskin rug before the fireguard and the scent of pine logs. As more details filled the scene, he joined me in a shared mental image, lying together on the rug, holding both my hands to warm them up.

"I love the way you can do this, bring up scenes from outside," he said, releasing my hands so that he could slide his across my warming skin. The intruder was forgotten as we cuddled on the imagined rug, as if it were quite real.

It was three years since I'd entered the strange Binaries organization, having been forced in by my twin sister. I still didn't like to think of the treacherous switch in identity, so that Helen could take over my life outside. Sometimes I'd dream of the first few days when I'd been in the medical centre, injured from my fall into a Binaries manhole, then detained and interrogated. I would be walking down endless grey corridors, looking in vain for a way out. Without my exceptional telepathic ability, I might have suffered the fate possibly coming to the intruder in the garden. Instead, I was now liked and respected in this secluded community. I'd even adjusted, although reluctantly, to the separation from Leo. He's mine, but also one of them now, I reflected. I remembered Theodora, head of Binaries assessment centre, telling me that they were good at detecting *"our own kind."* Apart from my dreaminess and odd experiences of apparently picking up thoughts or future events, I'd no idea that I was telepathic, growing up on the outside. Here I was admired as one of the very few high functioning natural telepaths, with the focusing and additional skills acquired through

Binary training. Because I lacked the early conditioning, my mind was different, less rigid: and I was definitely less obedient.

Kastor and I married during my pregnancy with Leo, although the Binaries called it 'bonding'. He wanted the ceremony to take place at the French centre, Binaires, where he'd spent his early years. Excited at the prospect, but nervous about travelling, I went to see the obstetrician, Miss Artemis Chiron.

"How good to see you, Cassandra," she said. "And thank you again for letting those students examine you. They're coming on well."

The students, Pax and Phyllida, had examined me a couple of times now.

"Will they become assessors?" I asked.

"Possibly. They're already studying on a pre-medical course. But only the most talented will be selected for our medical school in India. A few of those will become assessors. It's difficult work, obviously involving visits outside."

"India…" I murmured. "Why so far?"

"We have postgraduate centres all over the world, but our private medical school in India has proved the best. There seems to be particular talent, as well as sympathy, for our aims in many from the Indian subcontinent."

"Do non-telepaths study there?" I was ever curious about how the Binaries members developed.

"Not from outside our organization," said Miss Chiron, "but as you'll have noticed, not all our members turn out to be particularly gifted. We need… ," she paused significantly, "…ordinary nurses and doctors, without strong telepathy, just as anywhere else. In fact, the ideal assessors are those with a special talent for detecting our kind, without being too sensitive to all the hubbub out there. They're as valuable to us as the exceptionally gifted telepaths, like you."

"But outside," I said, "I didn't feel particularly gifted, or troubled by… hubbub."

"Yes, but now it may be different. Your channels are open, you're accustomed to detecting mental messages and so on."

I wondered, a little fearfully, if the seven months in Binaries had already made me unable to go outside again. Miss Chiron shook her head, encouragingly, flicking open my maternity case notes.

"You're planning a short visit to the French centre, next week? Don't worry. It means travelling outside of course, but privately with some of us – and when you arrive, you'll love it."

"We, Kastor and I, are planning to have our marriage there," I said shyly.

"So I understand. Such bonding unions are rare events for us."

"Why don't more of you marry?"

The obstetrician shrugged. "We form partnerships with many of our kind, including those that result in a pregnancy. But we're a close community. There's little point in formalising these relationships, as people often do on the outside."

"So…" I said, trying to shut off any thoughts about what partnerships Kastor had made, before meeting me, "it… this wedding, is because Kastor wants me to feel truly part of the community. I don't want to marry just because it would be more normal, out there."

I felt a wave of empathy from Miss Chiron, who paused and then said, "Kastor wouldn't do anything, I think, unless he had deep feelings about it. Nor would he do something he didn't care to do, except for work duties. You're worrying, that you're just one of many partnerships?"

It was hard to hide anything from the high functioning telepaths here, even with thoughts shuttered down. So of course Artemis, who could detect a potentially telepathic fetus in the womb from several feet away, had picked up on my worries.

"Yes, I suppose so," I replied. "I mean, I'm sure we love each other, but I don't think the ceremony will include words like ' 'til death us do part'."

Miss Chiron gazed at me. "I can't tell you how it'll all turn out. You're the one with precognition."

"I'm not so good at predicting things that deeply concern me."

"Well, if it helps, I think that Kastor was very lonely until he met you. Not that he lived apart from the community, but I sensed he was searching for something more. It seems to me that he's been looking for you all his life. Soul mates are as rare here as on the outside..." she tailed off, a little wistfully.

I glowed, gratefully. "Thank you – it's all a bit scary, here, sometimes."

Artemis Chiron nodded. "But now I have to get on. And you should get some rest. I hope they're not working you too hard?"

"No, I'm still getting used to it, but no, it doesn't feel like work at all, compared with the outside."

"I scarcely know that world," said the obstetrician. "I wish I had more time to talk about it. Perhaps another opportunity will arise."

After the conversation, I went to the station nearby, to board the underground train. I was glad there were a couple of others on board, still not confident at driving the carriage on my own. It was quite simple, just pressing a button to start or stop, but you had to time it correctly or the train would just move on. So I worried about missing my station. On this occasion, we were going either to Askeys Pagoda or the Staircase stop. Only the most accomplished or senior telepaths lived in the main mansion. Beyond the trees around the pagoda, there were a few small blocks of flats and houses, camouflaged and with most of the floors underground.

"*One of many partnerships*," I pondered, recalling also that Kastor had once said he'd lived as a monk before he met me. "*I think not*," I smiled to myself, adopting a speech mannerism of Theodora. But I could sense the truth in Artemis Chiron's description of him as lonely before meeting me, remembering also that Theodora had said that one day I'd feel my strength, perhaps becoming stronger even than the enigmatic Kastor.

2

While I rested, I thought back to those early months at Binaries and the extraordinary wedding arranged for us in France. My trip for the bonding ceremony was my first outside since that September day when I'd been thrust into the Binaries. The journey by private jet took place on an unseasonably warm day for late February. My passport showed me to be Lily West, a blonde woman born in Bristol. The mysterious Lily West, whom clients on the outside so wanted to meet, but had been told she only worked through intermediaries to make the predictions for their questions and products. I wore a blonde wig and heavy make up for the short trip through the border check. I'd wanted to dye my light brown hair to Lily's platinum shade, but Kastor looked so pained at the idea that I didn't pursue it. Manes and Theodora were accompanying us to attend the wedding ceremony, while the plane also contained other Binaries residents who would stay on afterwards to attend a course.

I gazed, entranced, through the window next to my seat. "I never liked flying, before," I said, as Kastor looked at me with affectionate amusement. "Of course, I love the mental flying," I continued, turning to him, "but I was beginning to think I'd never see the outside again."

He leaned across and pointed to the coast of France, showing me the location of the *Centre Binaires* just beyond some golden beaches and cliffs. Before we left, he'd told me what he knew of his early years. He'd been born in France, or so he'd been told, spending his pre-school years at Binaires. He had lived at the Woodstock centre after finishing at the Binaries boarding school in Scotland.

"You needn't worry about language problems," he said, when I admitted that my French was at a halting, schoolgirl level. "They're mostly all fluent in several languages - and thought images don't have a language barrier."

On arrival at Binaires, a jovial man introduced as Grégoire welcomed us, adding that Kastor was a lucky man. Although I felt enormous with my now all too evident bump, Kastor had told me that I'd never looked more full of health and luminous enthusiasm. He kept sending little messages of pride and affection. I rather enjoyed seeing him unusually nervous. He really wanted me to like this centre and its people. The introductions to the group of men and women seemed to go on forever, Kastor being well known at Binaires. At last the thought images turned to refreshments and we were taken to a terrace overlooking the sea. A momentary thought of Helen, sitting forlornly on her island terrace, came into my mind, but I'd vowed not to think of my twin and Kastor, picking up the image, smiled understandingly. The others were too busy chattering, catching up.

Binaires, like its English counterpart, was mostly underground with just a few buildings on the surface, such as the terraced lounge overlooking the private beach. This fitted the impression of a millionaire's estate resembling others in southwest France. I gathered that we were some way west of Toulon, just beyond the Côte d'Azur. Most of the visitors would be staying at a small villa near the terraced sun house, with a special arrangement for Kastor and me to share a suite. My unborn baby was of great interest to the company, people coming up to eye and discuss the bump in a way that made me uncomfortable. Just when I was beginning to feel like a mere vessel, a carrying pot for this excitedly anticipated wondrous child, Kastor sent a thought message that we'd been invited to the nursery.

"Oh good," I signalled, "Pity the bump can't go on its own, since it interests them so much."

He came to my side, glancing to check that others in the group hadn't picked up this thought.

"Babies born inside our community are always very special to us," he said very softly. "Remember we're mostly orphans, or think we're orphans, brought up without ever knowing our parents. And they've picked up his strong telepathy, which makes it all the more fascinating. It doesn't mean they don't want to know you, as well."

I sent across an image of the celebration at the birth of Rosemary's satanic baby in the Polanski film and he grimaced slightly, saying to the group that I was tired and needed to rest before the visit.

A pretty woman called Amélie took us over to the villa, talking excitedly about babies. "Wouldn't it be wonderful if Cassandra's son came early, while staying with us!" she trilled, in an attractive French accent.

I rolled my eyes, alarmed and annoyed at this suggestion. Kastor tried to signal that I should be patient.

"You're being rude," he muttered, dragging me quickly to one side and signalled to Amélie that I was exhausted by the travelling. Ironically, the best way of having a private conversation in Binary company was to use normal speech.

"Sorry," I replied. I could detect that Amélie meant no harm, feeling only welcoming thoughts from her.

"She needs to lie down," said Kastor in a louder tone, getting a sympathetic smile from Amélie in response

Like all the Binary accommodation, the suite was luxurious. Kastor fetched me some tea and sat quietly with me, repeating what he'd said before the trip about trying to understand how exciting a baby was for the Binaires, just as it was at home in our labyrinthine set up near Woodstock. I nodded; of course I understood that. But I felt tears welling up as I thought about these strange telepaths, who couldn't be expected to know that at that moment I'd much rather be in just an ordinary hotel with non-telepaths, people who had families, friends, experience of the outside world.

"It's not like *Rosemary's Baby*," said Kastor. "We're not demons, or devil worshippers. We're different, like you. And our baby will be different, brought up in a way that would seem very odd on the outside."

"I know," I murmured, "but on the outside, I could breast feed my baby and look after him, just by myself. Doesn't anyone here ever want that?"

He wrapped himself round me, sensing I needed physical contact, not the mental communion that suited Binary telepaths after a tiring trip. I felt ungrateful for his patience. He was always helping me to adjust, never criticising my occasional plaintive objections to this new life.

"This is all they know," he said simply. "How can they understand what you've been through, these past months, how you didn't choose to be here?"

"I did choose," I protested, but we both knew I'd been given no real choice. Once Helen had taken over my identity, my fate was decided, with no chance of return. Helen hadn't realised that I had good telepathic abilities, as great or even better than hers. She had perceived only slight transference of thoughts and gullibility. Yet she had abandoned me in the Binaries labyrinth, knowing that I could be eliminated, as Gaston might put it, if I were simply an outsider nuisance with insufficient talent to bother with. Very few knew of Helen's forced switch. The public story was that I'd asked to come into the community. With my exceptional ability, most Binary people would have considered my outside life to cause considerable torture. Nor did they know that my strong attraction to Kastor, in those secret meetings at Blenheim, had been such an influential factor.

"I feel so guilty, sometimes," said Kastor, picking up these thoughts. "If we'd never met, if I hadn't fallen in love with you…"

"Or I with you," I interrupted, gazing into his eyes and taking a daring little plunge into his mind.

"Hmm," he said, breathing in with pleasure as he felt me take this dip. "I love you with this baby, and I'd have loved you just the same without him. It's all you, this feeling that I have, not as a carrier of a new telepath."

He paused, sharing images of my disquiet.

"But I'll love the baby too," he added, with an image of us both holding our son. I didn't think that now would be the time to talk to him about the baby being taken into a communal nursery. I was still hoping that it would be different for me, that I could look after him in his early months, at least. He was focusing too much on trying to explain his feelings to notice this.

"After that picnic at Blenheim, then the next meeting," he said, "I wondered how I could get to know you without bringing you into danger. I suppose I thought we could have… a relationship, outside. Secret lovers…"

"What, in a little flat in Woodstock, something like that?"

I smiled at the thought of Kastor calling at the love nest, with me greeting him in a negligée, like a *poule de luxe*. Picking this up, he laughed, sending in turn an image of him standing with a bunch of flowers, twirling a non-existent moustache with a meaningful leer.

"We would've been found out." To add emphasis, I transmitted an image of Gaston, in black, bursting into our secret hideaway.

"Oh, it's been done," said Kastor, grinning but perhaps would have said no more, without a penetrating gaze from me.

"Tell me," I said. I was learning to be more authoritative.

"Well, Manny for example."

"Really?" I was all agog now, at this mention of Kastor's friend

Manes, who was one of the senior supervisors in the surveillance department. Kastor nodded, clearly embarrassed already that he'd said too much.

So I prompted him. "And?" He wasn't going to get out of this so easily.

"At one time he had to go frequently into Woodstock. He met a waitress there, Poppy. She only knew him with his outside name, of course, as a businessman who passed through Woodstock occasionally. Soon, they were taking a room at The Feathers. He would book it for the night, but sneak back to Binaries. Poppy would stay on…"

"She didn't get upset, him leaving?"

"Well, I guess she did, but he told her he was married. She thought he had to return to wherever he'd told her he lived."

"Was she telepathic?"

"Just a little perhaps, unknowingly. Enough to interest Manny for a while, anyway."

"So it ended," I said sadly.

"I don't know the whole story." He now felt disloyal to have even mentioned it. We often saw Manes socially.

"But now you have to tell me what you do know," I said, adding, "I promise I won't tease him about it, or send the slightest thought of it when I see him."

"Well, she wanted more, of course, wanted him to leave his wife, the one that he didn't really have. Manny would have been in deep trouble if this affair had been discovered. He couldn't risk her making enquiries, perhaps even following him and discovering the Binaries."

"So he switched off his charm, tried to make her want to end it?"

"Something like that. He said his wife was ill, he had to think of his family. Lots of regrets, very sorry and all that. Also, he told her that his business contact with Woodstock had finished."

"She must have been devastated," I said, picturing a pretty waitress, weeping as she served coffees in a café like the one I'd visited on my fateful trip to Woodstock.

"Yes, possibly. He just wound up that part of his duties, keeping clear of Woodstock as much as he could, making sure she never saw him again."

"But he told you."

"Yes, in private, obviously. Gaston would not have approved, although he thinks that many us have affairs and brief liaisons. I think he rather likes the idea of it, but he'd come down hard if he had proof of an outside relationship."

I thought about Manes and Poppy. "It wouldn't have been so easy to stop, for us."

"No, because I can't get enough of you," said Kastor, kissing me.

"So it was already ordained, you and me. We had to be here," I said, looking into his eyes. "We're like a couple from mythology, bound by fate to see this through."

"No regrets, then?" he asked, uncertainly.

"Oh, let me see," I began, conjuring myself back into that innocent, inquisitive, disarmingly honest woman he had fallen for at Blenheim Palace, with a mischievous look in my eyes. But before I could make a list, he plunged into my mind so that I gasped, taking breath before I did the same to him and we were lost in an ocean of enveloping waves of our sensual images.

D.R.Rose

3

The nursery at Binaires was small, just a dozen or so children, none looking older than 5 years. One of the older housemothers greeted Kastor with huge hugs and I guessed that she must have been one of those who looked after him, in those pre-school years. She also warmly welcomed me although, annoyingly, looking mainly at my bump. We toured the dormitory and classrooms, filled with unfamiliar toys, except for an occasional teddy bear or toy train.

"Of course," I thought sadly, "they wouldn't have little cars, since none of them learn to drive." If Kastor sensed this thought, he ignored it. He was plainly delighted to see his earliest home again. While they talked and the children bounced up and down around him, excited at the unusual visit, I walked around the building, of which only a small part and a play area stood above ground, with class rooms and dormitories below. I descended a staircase, peeping through glass windows into the rooms beyond. As a member of our sister community, no one seemed to worry that I wanted to explore a little.

At the end of a short corridor, I saw two double swinging doors, as in a hospital. A small sign announced that it was the *Premier niveau maternelle*, with a picture of a sleeping baby. Pushing the door, I spied a room with six infants, less than a year old, lying in identical cots. The room was filled with soft sounds, coming from a loudspeaker in one corner. The babies had little electric leads attached to them, like those used for measuring brain waves or heart rhythm. They seemed contented enough, some murmuring in response to the sounds, some sleeping. A nurse sitting in the corner got up. I started to apologise for intruding, but the nurse seemed pleased, quickly finding a chair for me and switching into English when she perceived I was one of their visitors. To my astonishment, she laid a hand firmly on the bump, without asking if she might do that.

"It's so good to feel one of them, before they arrive," she said, with only a slight French accent. "You must be very proud, this one is so… sentient."

I told myself not to rise to this constant reference to another telepath for their collection. "And this is where they come, at first?" I asked politely.

"Yes, this is their first dormitory – unless they need medical care, of course."

"What are they listening to?"

"Their early education," said the nurse, in some surprise. Then a thought image: *ah, this is the woman from outside, bonding with Kastor.* I nodded at this, shyly.

"I'm still learning about the education, thinking of my baby doing this."

"Yes, wonderful, isn't it," sighed the nurse. "Their first conditioning, making them aware they are not alone, but in a community of *télépathes*." She emphasised the French pronunciation. I knew that *télépathie* was after all a word coined by a French physicist.

"Do mothers here, I mean mothers at Binaires, look after their babies themselves, in these early months?"

The nurse looked shocked. "No, of course not. They know that this is best for their babies, being with the others."

"Not even sometimes?" I asked, "I mean, just for a few days, now and then?"

"Ah, so you are surely the *recrutée à l'extérieur* – from outside?"

"Yes, I was hoping that I'd look after my son, as I could if he were born outside."

"But he isn't one of them, he won't be born outside," said the nurse, with Gallic logic. "This is strange for you, I can see. They must be together, there can't be exceptions. Your baby would miss some of the early, very important conditioning."

The babies were of various ethnic groups, possibly brought here from different countries. To cover their tracks, maybe, I decided, in a shuttered off part of my mind. The scene also reminded me of the conditioning nurseries in the novel *Brave New World*, where babies learned to be happy with their Alpha to Epsilon grading, carefully prepared for the course of life that best suited a strictly organised society. *My baby will definitely be an Alpha*, I thought, before having the alarming realisation that I was beginning to accept the process destined for my son. The nurse looked at me, concerned, trying to pick up my thoughts, sensing that I was dismayed by this nursery scene.

"Think of it in another way," she said, kindly. "Here, in our communities, women are not expected to be just mothers, or spend their time washing baby clothes and changing nappies. They can be just like the men, having lovers, doing work. It's very equal."

"But we have to bear the babies, and getting to know the baby, while he or she is growing inside us."

The nurse made a noise like "Pifft," smiling with exasperation. "They're already researching ways of growing a baby completely outside the womb."

"Surely they can't do that, yet?" I knew of couples who had used in vitro fertilisation to achieve a pregnancy, but not a full-grown test tube baby. But if it could be developed anywhere, the Binaries would be onto it.

The nurse nodded, "Very nearly, soon, I think. That would be very good for us. We could make our own babies, twins too, we wouldn't have to…"

"Rescue them from outside?" I suggested. I knew better than to use the word 'abduct.'

"Yes, so then you wouldn't feel this unnatural connection, with your baby," said the nurse, laying a hand on my bump again and smiling.

I wish you wouldn't do that to my baby, I thought quickly, before having a chance to tuck the thought into an unreadable part of my mind. The nurse took her hand away abruptly, taking offence.

"It is not your baby, not really," she said. "Outside, yes, we know how they do it there. But here, the baby is part of a network. As they take in the messages, they learn that. They need to be with each other to learn more."

I shuttered my horrified thoughts at this way of raising children. Like an ant heap, or a hive of bees. Potential worker bees, or drones for the support services. Little workers, being conditioned to know their place. I made an effort to nod, as if understanding at last what the nurse was telling me, showing my acceptance. The nurse looked relieved.

"May I ask," I said, "if you can tell what any of these babies will be good at?"

The nurse seemed pleased at this shift in subject. "Not for most of them, this early. Some, you know, can be seen to have tendencies. Music, mathematical thought, good with their hands, that sort of thing."

"And do they change the conditioning, if they detect that some babies will have different skills?"

The nurse beamed. "Yes of course. All talents are fostered, as soon as they're detected."

"Is it just electronic stimulation and messages," I asked, "Or do you use chemicals as well?" I couldn't keep a slight judgmental tone out of my voice.

She stopped beaming and considered her reply. "Whatever is necessary, but always with health as the primary consideration."

"Yes, of course," I muttered, knowing that I'd upset her and worried that Kastor would hear about it. "I'm keeping you from your work," I added, noticing that the noises of the transmission had come to halt. *Possibly she needs to change the disk*, I thought cynically.

"Not at all, they do have some silence you know!" said the nurse, laughing. I blushed, wondering if she had picked up that closed thought, or was just responding to the suggestion of being distracted from her duties.

"But I hope you've found this visit some help?" the nurse asked.

"Oh yes," I said, concealing the deep chill I felt. I longed to have time alone with my unborn son, so that I could try some of my own conditioning on him. You don't have to be like this, I'd tell him, I want you to have a choice. But to the nurse I said, "You've been very kind. As a *recrutée*, I have so much to learn."

"*Une recrutée exceptionelle*," said the nurse, who had heard a little of the gossip. "In any case, Kastor would not settle for anyone less than exceptional."

Now I knew I was blushing and I nodded to acknowledge the compliment with a little smile. She escorted me to the swinging doors, trying to resist giving the bump another pat. "Please, do touch the bump," I said, trying to make up for my earlier tactlessness.

"Merci beaucoup!" she said, immediately placing her hand on me. "It's so good to feel the baby's telepathic force," she murmured. I stood awkwardly, then murmured that I had to get back to Kastor and the tour of Binaires. She nodded reluctantly, taking her hand off my bump with a little sigh.

D.R.Rose

4

The ceremony was due to be held that evening, some guests being unable to stay more than a night at the centre. When I rejoined the nursery tour, I gratefully accepted Kastor's suggestion that I should rest in our suite until the evening. A beautiful blue green gown had been laid out for me, voluminous enough to easily drape over the bump. There was a dark blue robe for Kastor too. Like a priest and priestess, I thought, stroking the silky material. The ceremony was to be held in the terraced lounge, overlooking the beach, followed by a wedding feast. I felt anxious on learning that the ceremony would be mainly in silence, just using telepathy. I was too tired to conduct a conversation just in thought: my particular gift was in image transfer.

Kastor's confidence was reassuring, but I wished I could talk it all over with someone who wouldn't be hurt or offended. I thought of Aunt V, who would have understood. Once she had got over the shock of my being here, I would have been interested to discuss the methods used to bring on telepathy and maybe she would have given me some advice on how to cope. I remembered talking to her about telepathy, feeling so excited at the adventure of seeking my twin. It seemed years ago, but only a few months in reality.

It was good to be a privileged member of the Binaries, with all the luxurious trappings, but it was still a kind of imprisonment. Seeing the babies with all those wires attached had upset me. Part of their conditioning was the instillation of absolute loyalty, as well as no doubt altering their brains, despite the emphasis from Kastor and others that the mind was so separate from the brain. Yet Helen had rebelled. I felt a sneaking admiration for her, then a chill when I considered that, probably, we were both natural telepaths, with all the risks of mental breakdown that this entailed if combined with the Binary conditioning. Telepaths who became disturbed or deranged, including some of the remote viewers who were at particular risk, were shipped off to the Binary psychiatric hospital in Scotland for 'treatment'. I didn't like the sound of that at all. Especially as remote viewing was one of my best skills and the training had enhanced this.

So I turned my thoughts to preparing for the bonding ceremony, idly leafing through a French phrase book hoping that some vocabulary would sink in and help me to follow the proceedings. A few hours later, I stood before a crowd of Binaires and Binaries, feeling over dressed in my flowing blue robe and full of trepidation at whether I'd meet their expectations.

I was right to be nervous. Standing next to Kastor, with Theodora on my side and Manes on his, I strained to understand the droning thought monologue of the group's leader, Dominique, wearing white robes like a princess from ancient times. It was in French, with echoes from the others standing in a circle round them, also in French. There were few images to help me. Watching their pleased, relaxed faces I suddenly realised that Kastor had made another major concession to help me adjust, by conversing mostly in spoken words. Likewise, Manes and Theodora also did this back at the Binaries, probably understanding that although I could now pick up silent speech fairly easily, it was too much to expect me to have adapted to their lifelong methods of communications in only seven months. But this ceremony made me feel an alien again.

With the additional difficulty of struggling to translate the French, I felt apart, thinking again that this was all to welcome the unborn baby rather than me. So I stood, smiling faintly and trying to project pleasant, excited thoughts appropriate to a bride. My mind drifted to other weddings I'd attended outside, how different from this ritual circle, with the sunset visible through the windows of the terrace lounge, the scene lit only by candles.

My reverie was interrupted when I sensed they were all looking at me, expectantly. They had fallen silent. Kastor was looking embarrassed, also waiting for something from me. Finally he whispered in my ear, "You must say a few words. Just a short speech. It can be in English, but not out loud."

I thought desperately of what to say. Kastor looked around the circle, sending a message that they should all be patient. He had an air of humiliation: I was letting him down in front of his oldest companions. I felt like a complete outsider again. The guests must be thinking, poor Kastor, falling for this inept *recrutée* and even the candles on the windowsills seemed to mock me as they flickered. Kastor had closed his eyes, trying to help, but letting me know that the words must be my own.

"*Try an image*," he signalled, as my brief transmitted thought about how grateful I was for the speech was clearly not sufficient.

I took a deep breath, seeking support from my deepest resources. Suddenly I had an image of Athena, as the giant statue in the old temple of the Acropolis in Athens, long destroyed. Athena turned, gazing at me and suddenly bent down. I was swept into the colourful statue, feeling the strength of the ancient beliefs in the goddess's powers. The temple melted away and I was standing on the hill of the Acropolis, looking at a moonlit scene of Athens. I'd been there, making it easier to construct one of my three dimensional images. My hair was blowing about my face and I sensed, for a moment, that image of my twin staring with fiery eyes at the cruise liner where Mum had died. This is what I can do, I thought, make images richer than any most of them have known. My experience of leading of group meditations at Binaries had shown me that this could give great pleasure.

Now, I threw the Athens image into the circle so that they gasped with surprise. They could feel the cool of the night, the wind that was tossing my hair, the feeling of awe as I strode across the hill in the image of a giant goddess. I whirled them up into the air, flying over Greece, then high above the Earth. Then I started to throw image after image of all the places I could remember from my life outside. Seascapes, streets, inside great buildings: also railway stations, crowded museums, taking coffee with a friend at Borough Market, running for a bus. Instead of the irritating noise that these telepaths would have experienced in the real scenes, I made them silent, with just the sound of wind rustling in the trees or a murmur like music from the people in these visions.

I found that I could place each image in the rim of a kaleidoscope, spinning it gently so that they had to concentrate to catch each one. Increasingly the scenes were of London, the place I knew best. They were lifted up into a capsule on the London Eye, looking at Trafalgar Square, Buckingham Palace and Whitehall, laid out in stunning detail. They could dip into streets, as if able to walk along them, just as in those Magic Eye pictures that were once popular, where a shift in focus allowed the eye to penetrate beyond a coloured pattern and explore the images below. This made me think of fairgrounds visited as a child. I made them travel with me through stalls and rides, giving them the taste of candy floss and the cold iron of the safety bar across the seats on the Big Dipper. A large cuddly bear was handed across, a prize from one of the games at a stall. This brought the idea of circuses, converting the lounge around us into a large tent, full of the smell of sawdust, elephants and popcorn as clowns did Catherine wheels and acrobats swung high above us.

Then I projected an image of the Thames, my favourite river. We were in a pleasure cruiser, sailing slowly along to Greenwich, with only the sound of the boat moving through the water. The boat turned and I took them in the other direction, disembarking at Kew Gardens, which were full of spring flowering. I swept them through the vast wrought iron conservatories, plants rustling as they passed. Between the greenhouses, we became tiny, dwarfed by an avenue of spring wild flowers. The scent filled the terrace air and the flowers nodded and bent to touch us as, like people in Lilliput, we moved through a forest of leaves. Finally I drew them into a field of poppies and we were beside Dorothy, becoming heady in a poppy field in *The Wizard of Oz*. I melted the field so that it became the coast of France, seen from the plane.

Now, as the images faded, I needed some music and tried to recall the Mozart Sonata in C, which I played to my bump so often. I could sense that my unborn son had enjoyed this exhilarating chase across scenes, so I wanted him to share this moment. I could only manage a simple version of the melody, regretting my lack of musical talent, but suddenly felt some help coming from beside me. Theodora was adding in the rest of the notes, so that it soared into this final image. The kaleidoscope collapsed into a simple child's music box, playing the recurring theme of the first movement of the sonata. When the tinkling softly died away, I bent my head, like a stand-up performer exhausted by entertaining an audience, and my thought voice sent 'thank you' in a half a dozen languages that I was unaware I knew.

Silence filled the room again and I felt faint and unsteady on my feet. Kastor took hold of me, just as he had when we took our first thought flight in Blenheim Park. I felt the gaze of everyone there completely focused on me and looked anxiously at Kastor, wondering if this bravura demonstration of my skills had been inappropriate. But this was only for a second, before a wave of silent applause enveloped me and the people in the circle rushed towards me. I was hugged and kissed and Grégoire lifted me high into the air. They were laughing with amazed excitement and Kastor was beaming with unconcealed pride.

"This is the wonderful woman I've brought you," I heard in his thoughts, *"This is my Cassandra, she's a goddess."*

The Binaires settled back into a circle again. The ceremony moved on to its next stage. Manes and Theodora produced identical rings for us to slip onto each other's fingers, while Dominique announced that we were now bonded. The ring placed on my finger was a gold band, with an intricate pattern punched out. At first I thought it was full of unicorns but peering more closely, I saw lots of little ones and zeros, some of the zeros set with tiny diamonds. Binary rings. They were obviously hand crafted and I guessed that Manes and Theodora had ordered them for this occasion, their gift to us. I smiled at them with thoughts of gratitude, then up at Kastor, who could not take his eyes off me. We both sensed the guests were waiting for the wedding kiss. I had never kissed Kastor in public before, but this felt exactly right and the room and people around us faded away as we embraced, coming back into focus only when I sensed a wave of celebration and thoughts of the wedding feast waiting for us. No one was surprised when we left the feast early, smiling bashfully as we departed, accompanied by knowing thoughts of those around us and glasses being raised.

We walked up to the villa arm in arm. I was still feeling unsteady from all those soaring mental flights and the effort of constructing the elaborate images. We had no need of speech or thought messages at that moment, looking forward to being alone. In our suite, Kastor seemed unable to let go of me, spinning me round until I collapsed, dizzily, into his arms. I couldn't remember how we ended up so quickly on the giant bed, our robes thrown onto the floor.

"Mind the bump," I murmured breathlessly, as Kastor squeezed me so tightly that I could feel the baby within wake up, kicking in protest.

"Oh, to hell with the bump," he muttered, "I just want you, Cassandra."

Sometimes when he said my full name, it was in formal moments, enquiring what I was up to. But this was quite different from the way my ex-boyfriend Roderick had used my name, as if it were a castigation. At this moment, Kastor made it sound like a murmur of passion and I whispered his in return, with a long, yearning sigh. There were no images, no silent thoughts, as if we were so in tune that little else was necessary.

Despite all my qualms about my new life, the *Brave New World* nursery and the sinister actions of some Binaries members, I lay next to him, secure in his arms, feeling completely happy. I thought that I wouldn't now wish to return to the world outside.

Neither of us wanted to lose the present sensation of being so completely together, by just falling asleep. "We must do this more often," I murmured and he laughed.

"Your images were astonishing, marvellous. You'll be the talk of Binaires for years."

"The poppy field," I said, a little nervously, as this had worried me for a second during that cascade of visualisation, "I hope Manny didn't think…"

"I'm sure he didn't think of Poppy. Most of us were just trying to keep up with you, not wanting to miss a moment. It was difficult even for me - and I've had much more practice."

"I wonder if I could have eventually learned to do that, outside."

"Not in a million years. For if you did, you'd have been just conjuring up fantasy mind pictures that no one could sense or fill with their energy." I looked pensive and he added, "You'd have been bored, aimless, like Helen must be, living outside."

"And if she had stayed…?" I was too happy to worry about raising the subject of my twin.

"If you were here as well, she'd have been so jealous of you."

"I think she rather liked you, I sensed that," I said, touching on my insecurity about whether Kastor and Helen had shared one of those brief Binaries partnerships that Dr. Artemis Chiron had referred to so casually. He looked at me more gravely.

"Ah, you wonder if my animosity to Helen was based on an unrequited love, something of that sort?" He smiled mischievously. "She suggested that we should get together, once. Helen's work sometimes involved… a sexual element, perhaps you guessed that?"

I had blocked any such idea, but knew how Helen had ensnared Roderick with a talent for seductive application of discipline.

"So," he continued, "she liked pleasuring men but got bored with it and thought I'd be a fine conquest for her."

"And what did you say, when she wanted to…?"

He gazed into my eyes. "I said no."

"I suppose," I said, uncertainly, "you were seeing someone else?"

"No, it wasn't that." He turned and lay back on his arms, stretching and I remembered a similar pose in those meetings in Blenheim Park. I moved my hand across his chest, waiting for him to say more.

"I think, apart from disliking her intensely for her hardness, her too eager interest in the crueller side of our skills, it was just that…"

"Yes?" I prompted, resting my hand.

"Well, obviously, I was just waiting for the much better twin. Perhaps I have a little of your predictive skills." I laughed and then at last we slept.

It was 11 a.m. on the next day, when, as we were considering getting up, a silent rap at the bedroom door signalled the arrival of a maid. She was bearing a tray laden with croissants, juice, jam, coffee and steaming milk. "*Bonjour*," she said pleasantly, nodding with approval at the honeymooners still being abed. With quickly shared mental communications, Kastor recognised her as one of his early nursery companions and I tried to draw the sheet modestly around me. Kastor and the maid spoke briefly about mutual friends and acquaintances. I noticed gratefully that at least the maid showed no particular interest in my bump. He asked for swimming costumes and she nodded. When she had gone, Kastor brought the tray over to the bed.

"We have the place to ourselves today. The others from Binaries have already left or are on the training course. So I thought you'd like to try a swim? The sea at this time of year shouldn't be too cold for" - he was about to say 'the baby' but finished with - "you."

I liked the idea, glad also that there would be few to see me looking ginormous in a swimsuit.

The rest of our short honeymoon was almost like that of any other couple, outside. We walked in the grounds of the villa, swam in the sea and had barbecues with some of the Binaires group on the beach. I was sad when I had to change back into my Lily West persona for the flight back, remembering the waves and encouraging thoughts from that small community long after we had returned. I hoped that the next visit would be with our son, when he was old enough to play on the beach. Kastor said that would be too extraordinary. Coming as a couple with a child would be considered odd, even deviant behaviour. He tried to reassure me that when our son was a little older, perhaps a few of the nursery children could be taken as a group to Binaires. He suggested that it was just possible that I could happen to be attending a course there at the same time. I saw that he was trying to make it less painful for me, this way of bringing up children. But I wasn't surprised that Leander reached the age of two and a half with no mention of this group visit. I remembered a dream of playing with a little boy on the beach, feeling sadly that this apparent prophecy was more a case of wishful thinking.

5

A few months after the birth of Leander, I was walking through the Binaries underground corridors when Manes appeared from a doorway and asked me to make a quick visit to the surveillance centre. I could tell that Manes was worried, although his manner was calm and efficient. He took me into his private office. Apart from the portholes giving semblance of daylight, it could have been an office anywhere. I noticed a small framed photograph on his desk. It was positioned so that only Manes could fully view it, but I glimpsed the likeness of the Binaires member Amélie. I smiled happily at the thought that possibly Manes had found a fulfilling relationship. Catching this, Manes also smiled, but he obviously had other matters to discuss.

He pushed a newspaper cutting towards me. Newspapers from outside were available to the Binaries community, but I chose not to look at them. Apart from reminding me about my lost outside life, I didn't like to see stories and images that made me realise I'd foreseen events in dreams or visions.

"I think you need to see this one, Cassandra. It's about Helen."

Two pictures accompanied the story. One could have been me, although more stylishly dressed, with a glitter of diamonds in the necklace she was wearing. The other photograph showed a group of people dressed in black, attending a funeral ceremony with incongruous bright sunshine illuminating their bent heads. I closed my eyes, remembering that I had foreseen this but had hoped it was just my imagination picturing the possible fate of my twin. The group had been photographed from some distance away, but I recognised, with a start, the figure of Aunt V, also Dad, looking older than when I'd last seen a photo of him. I'd never met Roderick's parents, but guessed that two smartly dressed mourners could be them. There was a younger woman who could have been my school friend Anne, it was hard to tell. I read:

"TRAGIC DEATH OF BRITISH WOMAN IN CARIBBEAN

From our correspondent in Antigua: A funeral last Friday marked the sad end to the tragic story of wealthy young widow Cassandra Sampler. She had made her home on a small private island near Antigua, following the death of her husband in an accident at the Styxie Falls in the West Indies. Roderick Sampler's parents said that she had never come to terms with his death, less than a year before her own. Despite visits from relatives and friends, she had become a lonely figure, rarely leaving her island. A few days after celebrating her 20th birthday in June, she was alone in the villa apart from three members of staff. They reported hearing a scream from the terrace where she liked to view the sunset over the sea and arrived to glimpse a figure, presumed to be Cassandra, tumbling into the darkness. Later, one shoe was found on the rocks below. While her body was not found, the police investigation concluded that it had been swept away by tidal currents and after six weeks of searching, she was formally declared dead.

It was not clear if her fall was accidental or a suicide. She had become more depressed following the tragic sudden death of her mother, shortly after losing her husband on their honeymoon. An empty packet of tranquillizers suggested that she might have taken these shortly before the fall, producing drowsiness and imbalance, possibly causing her to lose her footing on the terrace, which projected out over a cliff. Staff said she never normally went near the balustrade of the terrace, because of her fear of heights. An unfinished letter found in her bedroom, addressed to her aunt, Oxford academic Veronica Myers, described her despair. She had made a will, leaving most of her considerable fortune to a young entrepreneur, Lily West. Mrs. Sampler had been impressed by Lily West's enthusiasm and ability. She wanted the funds to be spent on training young women seeking to succeed in business, particularly as she and Roderick had not had the opportunity to have children themselves.

The Coroner returned an open verdict, although relatives were convinced that her deep depression was a factor. She had taken to dressing in the plain, sombre dress that she had worn just after her husband's death and also wearing all the jewellery he had given her. The jewellery was missing but investigation did not implicate her staff, who were devoted to her. It was assumed that, as usual, Mrs. Sampler had dressed for dinner with the jewellery that reminded her of her husband. Lily West, a sought after management consultant in the field of product placements and organizational improvements, was unavailable for comment but a spokesperson for her company said that a foundation would be set up in Mrs. Sampler's memory."

When I finished reading, I closed my eyes, trying to picture the scene on the terrace just before she jumped. I could see Helen sitting there, looking lost and lonely. I also saw the glitter of the jewellery, but I couldn't visualise the fall, wondering if my emotions were blocking it. When I opened my eyes, Manes was studying me thoughtfully.

"You could see her, but not the accident."

"No. Is there more information, I mean, something the newspapers don't know?"

"Her body hasn't been found and we've no trace of her," he replied.

"But, lost with all her jewellery…" I murmured.

"Yes," said Manes, slowly, "that is an interesting detail."

We exchanged a knowing thought. Could Helen have engineered this disappearance?

"It would be a remarkable feat," murmured Manes. "Getting the staff to hear and jointly visualise an apparent fall from the terrace."

I considered my own exceptional skill with producing images. With Helen's gift for group panic, a joint hallucination might be well within her abilities.

"Wouldn't you know, through surveillance, if she'd been seen or traced, even with a different identity?" I asked.

"One would think so," said Manes. "But Helen had experience as a field operative. She only went on short missions, always accompanied, but she was a quick learner, like you." He smiled at me, thinking how unalike we were in other traits. Helen so scheming, while I used my talents in such a different way.

"And yet, when she left the Binaries to try to find me, she didn't seem to have coped at all well, outside."

"That was different. It was her first time out alone, she couldn't use any of our contacts and had no money. She was also in a bad place, mentally. Finding you had become an obsession. She made sure, when she took your identity, that getting money was a primary objective. And while playing the role of you, she had security."

"Kastor knows about this, I guess?"

"Only today. Gaston heard about the accident, or suicide, when it occurred but kept it quiet while he investigated. Kastor wanted to tell you himself, but I thought it would be better to hear it first from me, then discuss it with him later, if you want to."

I put the article back on the desk. I remembered the words in the one letter that Helen had sent me. She had seemed worried how long 'THEY', the Binaries security team, would allow her to live. Could she have just decided to pre-empt the inevitable visit from a death squad, or perhaps they were even involved?

Picking up some of this in my thoughts, Manes said, "As far as I know, Gaston and his team had nothing to do with this. He's furious at even the faintest possibility that Helen has escaped the fate he had in mind for her."

"Do you, does he, want me to try to mentally contact her, to see if she is possibly alive?" I spoke hesitantly. I'd found it easier to block off all thoughts of Helen.

"Well, I don't," said Manes. "I can't imagine that Helen could get up to much, if she survived that leap. If she attracted attention by using her skills, Gaston's team would be onto her in a shot. She certainly wouldn't come here, or to any of our centres."

Helen had mentioned her will and also one or more Swiss accounts in her letter. So it was just possible that she had access to funds, in addition to the jewellery that would keep her going until she could withdraw money from bank accounts. I felt that I'd have known if Helen had been trying to contact me. Even if she had been able to fake that fall, she could have died later, in the escape. How would she have done it: swim a couple of miles to Antigua? Binaries members learnt how to swim, water being a good relaxation for them, but long distance swimming was not part of their training.

"I haven't felt any contact from Helen," I announced, finally. "I think she regretted what she did, that at least part of her wouldn't want me in further danger."

"Yes," said Manes solemnly. "So let's leave it at that, for the present."

I stood up, preparing to leave, but Manes was looking at my sad face sympathetically.

"I'm sorry, I should have been more sensitive," he said. "All this started for you when you wanted to find your twin - and coming here you've lost all the people you knew outside. Now, you've lost her as well."

"It's all right, I've found my real home here, even if it does seem a very strange one, sometimes."

"Oh, and the money," said Manes, as I was just about to open the office door. "That won't be released for some time, because her body hasn't been found. But the Lily West foundation could be anything you want it to be."

I shrugged. "We don't really need money, here, do we?"

There was a credit system, based on work earnings, but the highest-ranking telepaths, like Kastor and me, could more or less order anything we wanted from catalogues. There were no rent or maintenance costs for our living accommodation. In this respect, ours was a utopian community, with no one going without something they needed or really wanted to acquire.

6

I discussed the probable death of Helen with Kastor, of course, but neither of us wanted to dwell on it. As the months passed after the news, with no reports of Helen emerging somewhere else in a different identity, I made no attempt to reach Helen in my thoughts. Sometimes I had strange dreams, in which I'd find myself sitting on that terrace with my sister. In one dream, Helen and I were playing with Leo, watching him collect pebbles on a seashore. One of our few shared sights on the outside was that watercolour picture of the twins, drawn from Aunt V's imagination. But Helen rarely spoke in these dreams. There was no indication that she was trying to contact me.

Meanwhile I settled into Binaries life and improved my skills, now more confident of my precognitive ability. I'd be called in, for example, to help the organization identify possible company mergers or changes in direction. Usually I'd be given photographs and a little background information. Sometimes I asked to be shown more, or said I needed to sleep on it.

On the morning after the intruder had been caught in the Askey mansion grounds, I was sitting in one of the commercial centre offices, looking at three photographs of company headquarters. I felt tired, having not had much sleep, thanks to the events in the night. Simon Arbalest, one of the commercial leaders, explained that they knew a merger was being discussed, but had not been able to find out more. I had already narrowed their search down to the three pictures.

I tried to focus, saying listlessly, "I think it's possibly these two."

Simon took the third photograph away. "Yes," he murmured, "that fits. There have been meetings between all three, we just need to know where to concentrate the surveillance."

I knew that this information could be used to do what was known on the outside as insider trading. When I once raised this with Simon, he shrugged indifferently.

"They'd do it all the time, outside, if they could. We have to live as best we can, as exiles from their society."

Simon asked if I could be more definite. I frowned.

"I'm sorry, I'm not very good today. I keep getting other distracting images. There's a block somewhere. Can you let me sleep on this one?"

"OK," said Simon, looking concerned and trying to conceal impatience. "Every day counts with these matters, as you know. But take a break and see if anything else comes."

I was in no mood for chatter and found my way to the walled garden where Kastor had spoken with me, when I first arrived in the Binaries. I hoped it would be empty. It seemed to be, so I found the rose-bowered seat and sat, closing my eyes.

My mind filled with the image of the intruder lying on the Askeys lawn, with Gaston peering up at me on the balcony. Then I found I was visualising an interview room, with Kastor and Gaston facing a man. He was slumped in a chair, looking pale and exhausted. I guessed this could be the intruder. Focusing more intently, I started to view the room like a roving camera, as I'd done during a remote viewing experience at the Ashmolean Museum, days before my descent into the Binaries.

"Are you going to let me go?" the man was asking. "It's just as I told you, I wanted to find out about Askeys. I knew nothing about all this, this underground place. There were rumours about a reclusive millionaire. I was only chasing a story."

"Chasing secrets can be dangerous, you must have known that," said Gaston, sourly. Kastor was silent, studying notes. He communicated something to Gaston, who nodded.

"I've told you, I won't write the story, I swear," said their prey, looking round the room. I was filled with pity. I couldn't do this work, wondering how Kastor could deal with it.

"Yes, yes," said Gaston, "But you would say that, wouldn't you?"

Kastor spoke, less menacingly. "You say they won't have missed you, yet?"

The man looked up, with pathetic eagerness. "No, I was due to phone in some time today. So they'd never know, I could just say it was a dead end. That would be all I'd say."

"We can arrange for you to phone and say that," said Kastor. "So when do you think they'd expect you in?"

"Well, tomorrow perhaps. Yes, I'm sure I could clear that with the editor."

"We can give you some sort of story about the reclusive millionaire," said Kastor, "a false lead, if you like. That would help to cover your back?"

"Oh, that would be great," said the man, "Yes, anything. Just please, let me get out of here." Kastor turned to Gaston: more silent communications. I felt this interview was no future vision. It was taking place somewhere in the surveillance centre.

"All right, Patrick," said Gaston, with the faintest glimmer of a smile. "We'll arrange for you to make that call, then have a rest, before just a few more questions about your life."

"Why are you so interested in that?" said the man now identified as Patrick.

Gaston sighed, but not sympathetically. "The more we know about you, about those who may care about you, the less likely it is that you'll be tempted to talk about your experiences here."

"How do you know I'm telling the truth about my family or my friends?"

Gaston gave a little laugh. "Surely you realise we don't make mistakes, by now? After all, we already know the name of your wife, your girlfriend, the friend you meet in the pub…"

I watched this vision with unwilling fascination. I guessed that Patrick's mind had been easy to read, to check these kinds of details against what he had told them. A guard came into the room. Kastor or Gaston must have called him in. The man was taken away. He was limping, perhaps from falling in the grounds, and could scarcely keep his head up. Gaston turned to Kastor, making a sinister nod. And I thought instantly, they are going to eliminate him. How could he be trusted not to tell, once out of this place? That nod was like an order. The execution nod, once they had extracted everything they could. But why did they need so much additional information – perhaps, to arrange a death that would be a feasible accident, given his various activities?

I had become adept at keeping thoughts in a deep, closed part of my mind. This now came as almost second nature. Only with Kastor could my deepest thinking be found, likewise his thoughts were now more or less open to me, when we lay together in intimate mind sharing. A flicker of a glance from Kastor at the position of my imaginary camera made me start. I closed that off immediately. I was going to ask him about it all later, anyway. He hated talking about this aspect of his work, but I felt involved in this case.

I opened my eyes, looking at the now dormant rose stalks around the garden seat, pruned for next year's growth. One or two buds remained, withered in the November chill. In the distance, I could hear the fountain where Kastor and I had sat, back in the summer. I was about to get up and go in search of a coffee, to focus again on those boring company photographs, when another image shot into my mind. First it seemed to be just an image of Kastor, sitting in that interview room. But it quickly transformed into different surroundings, with Kastor now the one looking bowed and weary. I saw a barred window, with a lamp shining onto his face. This vision showed Kastor being the prey, the subject being interrogated. My heart raced. This could be a future scene, with Kastor in danger. It was linked to that reporter, but I couldn't tell why. The image faded, leaving me shivering despite the wintry sunshine in the garden.

I returned to the underground labyrinth, having to pass through the surveillance centre level to reach the commercial offices. I wasn't feeling any better, willing myself to forget those troubling images and concentrate on something that didn't involve emotions. I sensed that Kastor and Gaston were looking for me and so it was no surprise that Gaston opened a door as I passed, calling me in. I noticed it was a different room from the one in my vision. This made me hope, unrealistically as it turned out, that their wish to see me was unconnected to the unlucky reporter.

Gaston was almost pleasant. "Ah, Cassandra," he said, "I hope you've recovered from that little disturbance in the night? I might have known that my favourite prophetess would glean that something was afoot."

"I'm fine, in a better state than I suspect the intruder is," I murmured.

Kastor nodded at Gaston and I caught something like, "get on with it." Gaston's face creased into a rare genuine smile.

"Yes, quite," he said, "But that's where I think you can help us."

I looked questioningly at Kastor, whom I sensed had no

enthusiasm about me helping on this case.

Gaston ignored this, continuing, "You see, quite by chance, we've discovered that the intruder has a twin in our wider organization."

"By chance," I said, thinking this highly unlikely.

"Yes, from one of our American centres. He's been on a visit here, which is how we made the connection. They're identical twins, like you and Helen."

Kastor shifted uncomfortably. He knew I'd quickly guess what might be coming next.

"You're thinking of doing a switch?" I said, getting directly to the point.

"Yes, as it happens, that has occurred to us as a solution to this little problem. The intruder was a reporter for one of the biggest London based newspapers, one Patrick Lynch. We've been thinking for some time that it'd be very useful to have one of ours working more closely in the media."

"A fortunate coincidence, then," I said, despite sensing Kastor was warning me to say as little as possible.

"Yes, indeed," said Gaston. "So what we'd like you to do, is just talk to this visitor. He's good at accents, in fact, one of his reasons for coming here was to spend time in the language labs, perfecting his British accent."

"And he's telepathic?"

"Yes, of course – not in your class, I'd say, but fully trained."

"And his twin, the intruder, is he trainable?"

Gaston and Kastor exchanged glances. Kastor murmured, "That's not been decided." Gaston snorted, "He has almost no telepathic ability. Such a shame."

"Anyone can be trained..." I began, realising that this lack of potential would be very bad news for Patrick. Gaston looked almost mournful, putting me in mind of the Walrus and the Carpenter in *Through the Looking Glass*. They had sorrowfully eyed the dwindling group of chattering oysters that had followed them, while tucking into the little fellows one by one. I pictured one of the little oysters carrying a reporter's notebook and phone. Kastor, picking up the image, could not resist a smile.

"Why yes, training is always a possibility," said Gaston, not at all put out by this allusion, "if we get them early enough, or they have your kind of potential. Sadly, in this case..."

"I think," said Kastor quickly, "that we just need Cassandra to focus on the twin."

"You want me to talk to him about life outside?"

"Yes," said Gaston, "That's all. You don't need to worry about anything else. You'll like him, I think. He's quite a charmer."

"Does he know about a possible switch?"

"We're going to raise that with him now," said Gaston, airily. "I've cleared it with the commercial centre, by the way. They're quite happy for you to give us some of your valuable time."

There was a silent knock on the door and we turned our heads. A man in his mid-thirties entered. He was dressed casually and gave us a winning smile.

"Hi, would it be convenient to talk now?" The accent was clearly American. Presumably he felt no need to show off his British intonation with this group. He closely resembled the intruder, although Patrick had seemed older, as well as more battered and dejected. Gaston got up, with an almost sunny expression.

"Yes, splendid. Cassandra, may I introduce you to Ryden

Asgard?"

Ryden took my hand, looking into my eyes with a gaze that was only a shade off being openly impertinent. He had dark, almost black hair and penetrating brown eyes. Hand shaking was not the norm at Binaries and I withdrew mine quickly.

Ryden continued his impudent staring. "Well, hi, Cassandra. Call me Loki, all my friends do." Gaston looked mischievously at Kastor, then back at this relaxed visitor.

"Adorable, isn't she. But I'm afraid she's taken, Ryden."

Ryden looked across at Kastor, signalling, *OK, no problem.*

"Cassandra has to attend to other duties for a while," said Gaston, airily, which I understood to mean that I should now leave them to discuss their secret plans. As I turned to go, he said "But if you could spare us a moment in an hour or so?"

I nodded unenthusiastically as I left the room, aware that Ryden's eyes followed me, sweeping over my figure with a careless insolence. More suitable for Helen, I thought as I left. I made my way to the main cafeteria. I felt that I should at least try to eat and fortify my strength for this discussion with the twin destined to usurp poor Patrick's life.

I was sitting at one of the café tables, disconsolate, when I felt Kastor coming near. He fetched a glass of water, joining me.

"I've only got a few minutes. Gaston's going over the final details with our protégé." We exchanged glances, agreeing that we had no liking for any of this.

"I don't want to be involved," I said. "Loki – that was the trickster in the Norse Gods, wasn't he? I suppose he knew all about the twin switch already."

Kastor nodded, resignedly. Silently, he transmitted confirmation of what I had inferred. Ryden had been brought over with this very purpose.

"So letting Patrick get into the grounds last night was a trap," I said, in a bleak tone. "As for briefing Ryden-Loki about London, I feel like giving him all sorts of wrong suggestions."

Don't even think about it, signalled Kastor, alarmed as ever about my disobedient streak. "There's more...," he said hesitantly, trying to ignore my sullen expression. "They may want you to establish a thought channel with him, perhaps answering phone calls from him, too."

"I don't want him in my mind," I said firmly.

"And God knows, I don't," said Kastor, fervently.

"Why is it so important, this switch?"

"Patrick was..." he corrected this quickly, "...is a good reporter, ferreting out stories, lots of contacts. The organization thinks Ryden will be extremely useful. His interests include what you might call spying, uncovering spies."

"And Patrick, what about him? Why not make him a spy for the Binaries, on the outside – I'm sure he'd agree."

"Yes, no doubt. But that isn't going to happen." His eyes said, *don't ask.* "I'm afraid I have to get back now, I can sense Gaston wondering where I am." He got up, downing the rest of the water.

"I don't trust this 'Loki'," I said, very quietly.

"From you, that's very significant," said Kastor who knew that my first inclination was to trust people. It was how my twin had tricked me. But my time with the Binaries had sharpened my sense of whom to trust.

"By all means, keep your wits about you," he said. "You're a far better telepath, but he's a schemer – and ruthless. It doesn't bother him in the least, taking over his twin's life.

Like Helen, we both thought silently. When Kastor left me, I sat with my uneaten sandwich, dreading the next few hours.

It was a Wednesday, when I'd normally have made my way over to the nursery. I helped in a visualisation class as an excuse to see Leo. He was growing up with little understanding that both his parents were living so near. He didn't call me Mummy, or any other name that showed he knew our connection. My ability to make images and tell stories made me popular with the children. I hoped that Leo would know, somehow, that the stories were mostly intended for him. When I took part in mind picture sessions at the nursery, I chose stories far from my daily experience and worries, remembering those I'd enjoyed as a child. I also took care not to show too much attention to Leo, including all the children in the stories I made up. But in my secret thoughts, I tried to send messages just for him. It was difficult to tell how much he picked up. He had already learned to conform to Binaries nursery life and constant conditioning.

Now, sitting alone in the restaurant, I tried to channel my son, sensing he was enjoying his lunch, with far more gusto than I was managing. I thought I detected a little smile of recognition, but Leo had become slightly embarrassed at my frequent visits to the preschool area. The other mothers rarely visited, unless there was a group event. Leo was already good at silent conversations, something that had to be conditioned from birth. I could do it, but not so well in a crowded room, with many people sending thoughts. This would mean, I reflected sadly, that Leo would be hypersensitive to the thoughts and noises of the outside world, conditioned like other Binaries children to prefer the cloistered world of the telepathic community.

These thoughts were interrupted by a signal to return to the surveillance centre. Gaston and Kastor were standing, apparently having a good old chat with Ryden, when I entered the room.

"Cassandra!" said Gaston, with exaggerated delight. "Excellent. Ryden is most interested in our little plan. I suggest you and he have a talk in one of the private lounges. C59 is free, I believe."

"Looking forward to it," said Ryden, with a studied politeness and none of the impertinent manner shown at our first meeting. I wondered if Kastor had made it very clear that he wouldn't tolerate any more of that. Ryden picked up a folder from the table.

"There's so much I need to get right," he murmured.

"There'll be more information from the subject, later," said Gaston. I deduced that Ryden probably saw his twin as merely a subject to be drained of data. This thought was placed so deeply in my mind that I was sure Ryden wouldn't pick it up. But I sensed he was clever and intuitive. I'd keep up my guard.

D.R.Rose

7

I stood outside room C59, wondering why Ryden Asgard had not responded to my silent knock. Eventually I decided just to enter the room, finding him bent over a large dossier, deep in concentration.

"Oh, hi," he said, sitting up and indicating a chair beside him. "Just the person I needed to see – I thought I knew all the basic stuff about London, but it's pretty terrifying, now I have to go in."

Not as terrifying as this experience had proved for Patrick, I thought coldly, in a deep part of my thought house. I moved the chair to the other side of the desk, saying that I needed to watch his mannerisms and way of speaking. I added, "Do you have a recording of Patrick speaking, to help us?"

He picked up my chilly, business-like manner but made no reference to it, assuming it was mainly to do with my being 'spoken for' by Kastor. "Sure," he said, switching on a machine on the desk, adding in careful English intonation, "I mean, yes indeed."

The recording was of two men speaking. I recognised Patrick's voice, just like Ryden's, apart from the accent. He was talking about the possible identification of a spy working as a parliamentary researcher. The other man seemed to be an informant, answering Patrick's eager questions with reluctance.

"One of our field workers," said Ryden. "I was sent some of the recordings in advance, just in case…"

"Quite," I said, not wanting to know how much preparation had gone into the trap set for Patrick Lynch. Ryden switched off the playback and repeated what we'd just heard the reporter say, with perfect intonation.

"I'll be OK in the professional role, but I'm more worried about meeting his wife and girlfriend, Marcie. I have to meet the wife – Lizzie - tonight. Any ideas about that?"

Remembering Kastor's warning that I shouldn't be obstructive or misleading, I suggested that Ryden should meet her first by taking her out for a meal.

"It could be easier than just arriving at the flat and having to improvise – he may have used a particular greeting. I mean, do you know if he kissed her when he arrived home?"

"Good point," said Ryden. "Patrick's been pretty forthcoming, but not in that kind of detail. Yes, meeting at a restaurant could work. I'll ask them to find one he hasn't mentioned as a favourite for outings with his wife."

"How are you going to get there? Does he drive?"

"Taxi, tube, buses," said Ryden shortly. "I don't drive, of course. We learn the basics at the Virginia centre, it's so important for the American way of life, but like you, we don't have cars or drive any distance. Luckily, it seems he also used a lot of taxis, especially after drinking – which is most days." I nodded, knowing that driving was a difficult task for the conditioned telepaths at Binaries: their heightened sensitivity increased the risk of distractions and accidents.

"And when you get home, you can say you're exhausted, head for bed?"

Ryden grinned. "Yeah, best not to alarm her with an amazingly improved sexual technique, on the first night."

I eyed him coolly. "What makes you think his performance was so modest?"

He shrugged. "Just guessing. We're always better at it, as you must be aware." He was picturing an image of me with Kastor, in graphic detail. I shattered that with a deft shot into his mind. He remained composed, still grinning.

"Oh, you're good," he said appreciatively. "Must learn to do that shattering thing."

I decided to move off this subject, speaking with a detached, professional air as we covered details such as the British way of making tea. I pulled the dossier towards me. "So much information," I murmured, turning the carefully indexed pages. "Have you checked if there are any birthdays coming up, ones you need to know?"

Ryden produced the journalist's diary, making me think of all the days that Patrick would no longer be concerned with. "He doesn't seem to have made a note of any. Of course, I know his wife's, and the girlfriend. I should be long gone by the time they come up." Seeing my look of surprise, he explained, "I'm planning to go on a reporting assignment overseas pretty soon. That's partly the point of this exchange."

"But you'll be keeping Patrick's identity?"

"Oh yes," said Ryden, a little too quickly.

He was hiding something and I hoped his telepathy was not up to sensing my doubts. He shrugged. "I'm hoping to land the job of foreign correspondent. Just occasional trips home."

I felt it unwise to be too obvious in dwelling on this subject. Turning again to the dossier, I examined a photograph of a blonde woman with short hair and sharp, intelligent eyes. I noted it was the girlfriend, Marcie Brown.

"When do you expect to link up with Marcie?"

"She's a reporter on another paper, mainly fashion, women's stuff. I'm thinking it may be time to tail off this affair. Bit of a complication for our plan." He grinned. "He was pathetically keen on her, so maybe I should assess her in person. I got the impression she's really good in the sack."

"She'll appreciate you, then," I said, in an innocent tone, but he narrowed his eyes and did not smile.

"Yeah, but we all have to make sacrifices. She probably knows him better than his wife does."

"Yes," I said, "It's going to be difficult enough just walking into his home. Women can be disarmingly perceptive, don't you think?"

He gave me a relaxed smile. "Some of them. I'm lucky I don't have to play the lover to you, out there. Although it would be a lot of fun."

Deep in my thoughts, I decided that he was one of the most unlikeable men I had ever met. But perhaps, seeing how I'd fallen for the bullying, arrogant Roderick in my former life, I shouldn't be too smug. Also, I didn't want him to tell Gaston that I was hostile to the project. In my superficial thoughts, I let him perceive a hint of wistful regret. It was important not to make an enemy of this ruthless twin. For the remainder of our meeting we worked through questions about London life. His confidence was disarming as well as arrogant. He had a code name to ask for if he needed to contact me by phone, but said he'd be unlikely to have to do that. He didn't mention telepathic communication, which was just as well, as I'd already decided to minimise any thought channel with him.

Back in our Askeys apartment that evening, I assumed that Kastor was working late at the surveillance centre. Ryden would by now have arrived at the restaurant to meet Patrick's wife. I secretly hoped that Mrs. Lynch would ask all sorts of awkward questions. I asked the kitchen to send up some eggs, tomatoes and cheese, rather than order a meal. It was ages since I'd made an omelette. Talking about the outside had made me nostalgic for home cooking. I was turning my somewhat overcooked omelette onto a plate, when Kastor arrived home. He signalled his surprise that I'd prepared it myself.

"It's always better cooked fresh," I muttered, defensively, as he eyed the leathery omelette with a burnt tomato slice peeping out.

"Hmm, yes," he said, "well that looks delicious."

"There's enough for two." I reached for a knife to divide it, but he signalled for me not to bother.

"We had sandwiches over at the centre. No, you just enjoy it. What is it, by the way?"

"OK, I know the chefs downstairs won't be worrying I could replace them."

I sat down at the small kitchen table. Kastor stepped behind me and slipped his arms round my shoulders.

"If you were a more... professional cook, well then you'd be just too annoyingly talented. Give the others a couple of things to excel at, Cass." He signalled that he would be getting on with some papers in his study, so that I could eat in peace.

"I'll make some tea in a few minutes, so we can talk," I called to him and he replied, "Yes, that'd be good." He looked tired, preoccupied, probably still upset about the Ryden-Patrick switch.

After the modest meal, I took a tray of tea into the living room. I selected a Liszt etude, *La Campanella*, on our music centre. It started slowly, with hesitant notes as if asking questions, moving onto faster, louder trills, finishing with a crescendo burst of anger. This was Patrick, when he realised what was going to happen. I replaced the disk with

Dvořák's *New World Symphony*, which was playing when Kastor came back to the apartment. He said nothing, drinking some tea and looking at me pensively. I was sitting calmly, but he could detect that my mind was fizzing with anger and anxiety.

"O brave new world, that has such people in it…" he murmured, knowing that I wasn't thinking how 'beauteous' they were in the Binaries world, very much the reverse. He got up and picked out another disk, replacing the Dvořák with a slow, solemn orchestral piece. It caused me to have an image of a march of sinister figures, moving through a dark, stormy scene. I looked at Kastor, questioningly.

"Rachmaninov's *The Isle of the Dead*," he said, "seemed more appropriate to your thoughts. I'm sorry, yet again, that you had to be involved in this. I know I said that many of us wanted things to change and then – this."

I closed my eyes, picturing a funeral procession bearing Patrick away, knowing that something much less ceremonious would have occurred in his case. I pictured him in his life outside, possibly no less likeable than his twin, but still not deserving to be simply wiped out for a devious Binaries plan.

"Don't try to think of his life," said Kastor, softly. "He was also involved in some very unpleasant stuff."

"And he never knew he had a twin. Was he really so lacking in telepathy?"

"Yes – and 'Call me Loki' has limited skills. Paradoxically, that makes him more likely to succeed in his twin's persona. He can pick up thoughts when he tunes in, but won't be distracted by receiving too much."

I asked about the assignment abroad that Ryden had mentioned. He spoke slowly, watching my reaction.

"They want me to work with him, if he uncovers more about an organization that we've been tracking."

This was what I'd dreaded. "No! Not outside?"

"Yes, outside, if necessary."

"You mustn't do it, Kastor, I've a really bad feeling about this."

Kastor sighed. "It might not happen. Ryden needs to check out the story and his informants first. Patrick exaggerated a lot when talking about it, he thought it might help…"

"…save his life?" I looked up to heaven. "Poor, deluded man."

"If Patrick uncovered as much as he claimed, Ryden will need a good telepath to work with. Like me."

"I think he has another agenda. I sensed it strongly."

"He's one of us, committed to this plan. He's been training for months."

I sniffed. "Sure – or 'yes indeed' as he's been learning to say. He's devious, unscrupulous. He showed not an iota of regret about his twin."

Kastor didn't want to comment on this most sensitive of subjects for me. He glanced at the cold tea languishing on the tray.

"I think we need something stronger?"

I smiled, cheerlessly. "There's a cocktail called '*Death in the Afternoon*' that might suit the occasion. Absinthe and champagne."

"I'll go down to the bar and get a couple of those," he said quickly, getting up without waiting for my reply and choosing not to comment on my darkly ironic request. He could have ordered room service, but I sensed he needed to be doing something, as an alternative to discussing Patrick's fate.

While he was fetching the cocktails, I stared through the large window overlooking the gardens of Askeys. In the darkness I could just make out a small light by the pagoda, possibly someone emerging from the underground station. I remembered Patrick's desperate run across the grounds. What had possessed him, to think he could enter this secret world so easily? He had unwittingly sold his soul – at least, his continued existence - just to get a story. I started humming a song, the words coming back as I hit the right tune:

" *You load 16 tons, and what do you get - another day older and deeper in debt... Saint Peter don't you call me, 'cause I can't go, I owe my soul to the company store.*"

And there was something about '*a mind that's weak.*' What was Loki's weakness, I wondered? He was arrogant, sexually predatory, quick on the uptake - but not in my class for telepathy. All that conditioning and training had probably made him good at empathy, but ironically without the feeling for it. This meant that while he could sense superficial emotions, he possibly missed deeper motives.

Kastor found me still at the window, swaying unconsciously to the tune of *Sixteen Tons*. "Interesting choice of song. Is that what you think of the Binaries?"

"It could be the organization's anthem, but they can't have our souls, I won't let them."

He folded his arms around me, looking out over my shoulder at the dark garden beyond. "I'm sure of that, at least," he said, while I thought sadly that my warnings about the future were no more likely to be heeded than those of the mythological Cassandra.

8

As the next few days passed, it seemed that Ryden Asgard had slipped into the persona of his twin Patrick with relative ease. He reported regularly to Gaston and Manes, but made no calls for advice from me. Manes occasionally asked me into his office to give updates on his progress and to check if I'd received thought messages from him. I sensed that Manes disliked him too, but he never made critical remarks. Sometimes he would make a deadpan comment, sharing a mental smile with me. He did not speak of Kastor's involvement and the mysterious assignment outside. I wanted to say, "Manny, please keep Kastor out of this," but realised there was no point. I was having disturbing dreams, seeing Kastor looking ill, imprisoned, sometimes dead. Aware that precognition was less accurate when the emotions were involved, I tried to believe that my vivid imagination was playing out in the nightmares. I didn't discuss them with Kastor, although if I awoke suddenly from one of these, I'd find him gazing at me with concern. But he didn't ask me to describe the dreams, nor attempt to share the images.

A couple of weeks after the Ryden-Patrick swap, I had a disturbing vision while sitting in the Askeys garden. I hadn't been thinking about Ryden, whom I always now referred to as Loki, since he seemed to suit the role of trickster. But suddenly I saw him quite clearly, sitting in a wintry park with bare trees. He was leaning back on the park bench, with a familiar arrogant pose. There was another man on the bench, bending towards him and talking in a nervous, hurried manner. I took in the scene, carefully shuttering my thoughts so that I could receive but not transmit. While doubting that Loki could channel me, it was wise to be cautious with all trained telepaths. I knew that this was something happening either now or in the near future and focused, tuning in to see if I could pick up what they were saying.

"It could be dangerous, if he suspects," the nervous man said.

"He doesn't suspect a thing. I promise you, he's been trained to follow orders. If they order him to come," said Loki, shrugging, "well, he'll come."

"So where do you suggest we act?" said his companion.

"Like I said, I'll give you the signal. Certainly, not in this country. They have field operatives everywhere."

Loki was speaking with his American accent and his companion had a middle European accent. Their voices were low, hard to pick up and the next part of their conversation was almost in whispers. I concentrated on this vision and any associated images. I saw bright sunshine, unfamiliar white buildings and narrow alleys. A few people were walking about, mostly in long, flowing clothes, while women in the scene had their hair covered. A Persian carpet floated past. At first I dismissed this, irritated at the way my mind conjured up stray images, but then reflected that this too was a clue. Flying carpets recalled *The Arabian Nights*, that must mean a country in the Middle East. I heard someone laughing and speaking in French. North Africa, I thought, they're talking about a country there, wishing I'd paid more attention to geography.

I focused again on the park bench and the two men. Their conversation was now inaudible, but I sensed they were talking about some kind of code. An image of a hangman's noose appeared. Execution, I thought, with a panic. Were they talking about executing this unnamed man, the one who would follow orders? I tried to be calm.

Perhaps it was to do with the code, a code to be executed like in computer programs? This signal, perhaps it would be in binary code – that would be logical, something that could be transmitted as apparently meaningless ones and zeros. But no further clue emerged and then Loki was getting up to go and the other man was just nodding, as though accepting – or memorising - whatever Loki had told him. The vision faded. I tried to recall every detail before opening my eyes. Kastor had not been mentioned, yet I sensed they had been talking about him. Or was that a faulty sense, triggered by strong emotions and fears for his safety?

That evening, I asked Kastor if he had more information about the mysterious assignment.

"Yes." His eyes darted away, avoiding mine. Clearly, he'd hoped to delay telling me. "I suppose you've picked up on that. It's going ahead, next week probably. I'm afraid that I shall have to go. There's a contact that they want me to interview, first hand."

I drew in a breath with a desperate sigh, as if he had told me he was going on a death mission.

"It's not dangerous," he said, taking both my hands. "Well, no more risky than other assignments I've had outside."

"It's a trap," I whispered. "Loki has arranged this, hasn't he?"

"Lots of people are involved. The information has been checked, double-checked. I'll only be gone a few days."

"What can I do, to persuade you not to go?" I pleaded. I started to tell him about my vision, but he stopped me.

"Please don't tell me. I have to go. It's a direct order."

"But that's what he said, '..*if they order him to come, he'll come*'."

Kastor was gripping my hands so hard that I signalled pain and he relaxed his hold, staring down at my white fingers. "I'm sorry, you're making me so tense. I can look after myself, you know. And you've certainly given me enough warnings." He looked into my now tearful eyes. "Please, Cassandra, I need you to be strong, to know that you're supporting me."

"Always," I said, "I'll do everything it takes to look after you."

"So, for the next few days, while I wait for the final instructions, you'll try not to talk like this again?"

"All right," I murmured, forcing a smile. "So would you like to eat, now, we could go to the restaurant?"

He looked embarrassed. "I'm sorry, I have to go back to the surveillance centre. Another meeting. But perhaps later, if you haven't decided to cook an omelette or something by then?"

He was looking at me so hopefully, wishing me to be happier. I couldn't help smiling back.

"No promises," I said, "you know I can't resist breaking a few eggs."

When he had left, I quite uncharacteristically poured myself a glass of wine. I almost never drank while on my own. I needed to dull my senses, because I couldn't convince him that I'd seen this terrible danger, out there, waiting for him to just walk into it. But after only a couple of sips, I started to wonder if there was anyone I could talk to, to help me get through this. An image of Theodora came to mind, with her candid, kind and knowing eyes. Of all the people I'd come to know at Askeys, Theodora was the one I most trusted to give a wise and unbiased opinion. I tried to sense if Theodora was in the mansion. She tended to work late on those endless assessments. Please be in, I thought, please be in your lovely, cluttered apartment and have time to see me. Theodora's face became clearer in my mind and there was a distinct nod and a signal, *"Yes, come and see me."* I hoped I was not mistaken, given my heightened emotions, as I left the apartment and made my way down to the next floor where Theodora lived.

The door opened as I approached. Theodora stepped out, watching with a concerned expression.

"I would say, an unexpected pleasure, but this is quite the reverse for you, is it not?" she said, ushering me into the hallway.

I glanced at the side table with its crowded collection of unusual objects and noticed the thought cup that had intrigued me on my first visit to Theodora's home. I had no need for prompts for the thoughts that currently preoccupied me.

Theodora followed my gaze, saying, "Perhaps another object interests you this evening?"

I was drawn to a large marble key, rather like a scaled up version of those on gateaux to celebrate 18th or 21st birthdays. This was no cake ornament, but a heavy, ornate key, inlaid with a detailed geometric design.

"Ah, the key," said Theodora. "Openings, prisons, secrets, codes – which is it, at this moment, do you think? Pick it up, Cassandra."

I gingerly lifted it, finding it even heavier than it appeared. Holding it in both hands, I saw that the design was Islamic, like wall patterns in a mosque.

"What does the pattern mean?" I asked.

"Like many Islamic art patterns, it portrays the meaning and essence of the world, in this case, a key, but it transcends objects. It is a spiritual representation, outside space and time."

"The symbols just repeat."

"Yes, to remind you that one can find the infinite, the essence of Allah, in these small, endlessly repeating forms."

"So it isn't a code, a way of undoing a lock," I thought, but as if I had spoken aloud, Theodora replied. "I see. I thought it was going to be codes. Although you've also those other things on your mind, prison and so forth."

"I need to find a code," I said, desperately. "But I don't know where to start."

"Hold the key for a moment and focus on it," said Theodora. "I'm going to fetch you a refreshing drink. You look exhausted and frightened."

I was grateful for her perceptiveness. Sitting on a small hall chair, I stroked the key, closing my eyes. The geometric pattern, circles entwined within scrolls, expanded in my mind, moving and re-arranging itself in further repetitive shapes. The ends of the scrolls could be seen as little rods, while the circles contained further tiny circles. Ones and zeros, like on my binary wedding ring. While at first glance it simply repeated these shapes, closer examination revealed that it was not totally symmetrical. For example, on one line it was 01000011, while on the next, 01100001 and after that, 01110011. *It's another ASCII conversion code*, I concluded with a smile. At the start of my strange adventure to find my twin, conversion codes were one of the clues to the location of Binaries.

When Theodora came back to the hallway, bearing two glasses and a jug on a tray, she found me in a more positive mood.

I looked up and asked, "Can I write something down? It's a code that I've just spotted."

Theodora set the tray aside and handed me a notebook and pen from a nearby shelf. She watched while I scribbled the three rows of binary digits. But when I tried to focus again on the key, Theodora took it from my hands.

"You've found one key to the code that you seek," she said, "but there's no point in trying to record it all. You just need to remember the principle. The words could be quite different in the real code. It's only a key, not the full solution."

"So should I just throw this away?" I held up the page from the notebook.

"No," said Theodora, "but be very careful where you store it. Don't show it, for example, to the surveillance teams."

"Including Kastor?"

"Particularly Kastor," she replied. "You're here tonight, are you not, because you can't discuss this with Kastor. And as for the rest of them, you don't know who to trust?" I nodded, and Theodora signalled "*Just so.*" Her questions were often rhetorical, requiring merely agreement. Placing the key carefully back in the array of objects, Theodora indicated the nearest door, her living room.

A fire was flickering in the grate and I took one of two comfortable chairs facing it, with a small table between, on which Theodora placed the drinks tray.

"This is a herbal tonic," she said, pouring a warm brown liquid into the glasses. "It also has a delightful taste, which is always a bonus with herbal ingredients."

I sipped and agreed it was delicious. Theodora nodded, indicating that this was exactly what she'd said, and took a long draught of it herself.

"Now," she said, "You wanted to see me."

I felt tears springing up again as I wondered where to begin. Theodora simply waited, staring into the fire.

"Kastor is going on a mission," I said, at last. "But I don't know much about it, just that he'll be going into some dreadful danger."

"You've had a precognition of this," observed Theodora. It was not a question. She was more aware of my unusual talent than anyone else in Binaries and also how much distress it caused me.

"Yes, but I know my fears could be affecting my perceptions. And I probably shouldn't be talking about it all. Kastor has asked me not to keep giving him warnings. It's obviously very upsetting to him. Because he doesn't have a choice, it's an order, he has to go."

Theodora sighed, still looking into the fire. The flames licked the coals, constantly changing the shape and colour of the glowing caverns being formed in the embers.

"If it helps," she said quietly, "you should be aware that anything you tell me will stay with me, not divulged to any one."

I trusted Theodora, almost as much as I trusted in Kastor's feelings for me. So I told her about how the intruder into our gardens had been eliminated to make room for his twin – and that the twin, Loki, possibly had a deceitful plan of his own. I described the vision of Loki and another man, meeting in secret in a park, possibly talking about trapping Kastor.

Theodora nodded as she listened. "Your perceptions are probably correct, but you have no evidence," she observed.

"Yes. This is an important investigation, with months of planning. No one wants to see problems in it. Ryden Asgard is trusted…"

"…as one of us, yes. I see the difficulty. Yet they should know enough about your perceptions to trust you, except for the issue about possibly clouded judgment. Kastor would think your worries are linked to your feelings. He hasn't been on such a mission since you arrived here."

"Well, he has been outside, but not on this kind of assignment and I've had no qualms or visions about those trips."

"Indeed," murmured Theodora, refilling my glass. "You're afraid, are you not, that if you confided in Gaston, or Manes, they might talk to this twin, Ryden? Or to someone else who might be involved with the danger you suspect?"

"Yes, I'm sure they would. And without evidence, they or he would just deny it and I'd seem foolish or worse, trying to compromise the mission, because I want Kastor to stay here."

Theodora contemplated the problem. "I've not been asked to assess Ryden Asgard. That's quite unusual, for such a mission. But I understand he was fully assessed in the Virginia Binary Centre. It would perhaps appear politically incorrect for us to question their abilities. Now he's in the field, I can't even suggest a short interview to help with any skills he may need."

I nodded, miserably. "He was very confident and had studied an enormous dossier. But I know there's something else going on – that vision about possibly deceiving one of us, Kastor I believe – and the other man asking where and when to 'act'. Do you think it could be a kidnap? But, why?"

"There are many reasons why other organizations would wish to use one of us, Cassandra. Think of your own skills, in remote viewing for example."

"But we wouldn't do that willingly, just for anybody."

"Pressures can be brought to bear," murmured Theodora. "Kastor has you – and a son."

I paled. "I think I'd have known, if I were in danger, or Leander."

Theodora did not reply, her thoughts about my emotional blocks in this case being eloquent enough.

"If I could find the code they were discussing, that would be proof," I said. "Perhaps if I try to access Ryden–Loki's thoughts?"

Too dangerous, signalled Theodora. Aloud, she said, "I've one suggestion. There's a computer expert whom I trust, a very bright young man. He may be able to help you with codes – perhaps, in the first instance, a code that you can use with Kastor, that only he'd be able to access, if he finds himself in trouble."

"Something deep in our minds." I saw the sense in this. "So that even if someone was able to penetrate Kastor's mind, it would be meaningless to them. I suppose there are telepaths who work against us, on the outside, who'd try to get at hidden thoughts?"

"Oh yes," said Theodora. "Natural telepaths, like you, may develop considerable skills without our training, or with alternative training. Some governments and organizations actively seek such people."

I stared into the fire, seeing images and strange constructs in the burning coals. An inferno of trouble and danger.

"This young man, the computer expert, does he work with Gaston?" Even with Theodora's recommendation, I was unwilling to trust him.

"Yes, occasionally. But I shall talk to him. He has a finely developed sense of justice. And I've found him extremely discreet."

I smiled at her gratefully. "Thank you. I think it's urgent, though. Kastor said the mission would be next week, but I feel it could be sooner."

"And if you feel that, it's almost certainly true. I'll contact the young man first thing in the morning and then, discreetly, contact you. His name is Joel."

"An Old Testament prophet," I murmured, dredging up a long forgotten Sunday School memory.

"Yes, and he has precognitive ability, which, as in your case, he can combine with remote viewing. You'll find him interesting, I believe, and sympathetic to your worries. You needn't tell him everything. That would be unwise, even though I believe he can be trusted."

I nodded. "I'd better get back. I don't think Kastor has returned, but he'd be even more concerned if he knew I'd been discussing…" I tailed off, awkwardly, feeling I'd been disloyal.

Theodora closed her eyes briefly. "Kastor is still in the surveillance centre," she murmured, "but surely he won't mind you making visits."

When I left, Theodora unexpectedly took my hand.

"You are very strong, Cassandra. Don't be afraid of your skills. They'll protect you more than you presently imagine."

I smiled shyly, hoping that this was true.

D.R.Rose

9

Theodora Sage was as good as her word. While I was listlessly going through some products the next morning with Simon Arbalest, I sensed that Theodora was calling me. I signalled an acknowledgement, explaining to Simon that I had to go to the assessment centre.

"If you could just give us a pointer," said Simon, "now you've whittled the choice down to these two? Should the company go for both, or...?"

I focused, seeking images. "This one," she said, indicating one of the boxes, "I'd advise giving priority to this." "Sure?" said Simon, since I'd been very distracted of late.

"Oh yes," I said, trying to appear more interested. "I can see this one flying off the shelves. If that's all for the moment, I really have to go." Simon reached for the phone almost before I left the room. He was thinking that even when I was in this kind of mood, I was rarely wrong.

Shuttering my mind instinctively as I passed near the surveillance centre, I made my way to Theodora's office. I was admitted to the anteroom immediately and offered coffee by one of the assistants. When I went into the office, I found Theodora talking with a handsome young black man, introduced as Joel Grigora. He had elegant features, like a classical statue, with a penetrating, serious gaze. He was probably a couple of years younger than me. I had seen him at morning meditations although we had never exchanged words.

"Cassandra. I've been hoping we'd meet," he said solemnly, with a deep emphatic voice. "I very much enjoyed the meditation you led a few weeks ago."

"Thank you – I've been too preoccupied lately to lead another."

"So I understand. Dr. Sage tells me you're worried about something and have had some precognitions."

I was unsure how much Theodora had told him. *Very little*, signalled Theodora. "So, you two should go into my private study for a chat," instructed Theodora.

He nodded courteously as Theodora directed us to the small study adjacent to her office. It was a book-lined room with heavy curtains and desk lights that looked as though they were converted from old oil lamps. The only concession to the technological age was a computer on one small desk. I was accustomed to the direct way in which telepaths gazed at one while communicating, but Joel's stare was particularly disconcerting. He sat silently, drinking the coffee, watching me. I detected no images, just his interested thoughts.

"You miss your son," he said, breaking the silence.

I realised with a start that I'd been thinking of Leo. "Yes, always," I admitted. "Coming from the outside, I thought I'd see him so much more."

"You'll have other children – two I think," said Joel, thoughtfully. "Don't worry about your son, meanwhile – I don't think he's in danger." He paused, studying me carefully. "However, I do see difficulties ahead for you. But much more danger for Kastor."

I bit my lip. "I know. I just don't know how to help. Theodora wondered if you'd have ideas about a code, one I could devise so that Kastor could contact me, if…" I paused. "I mean, when he encounters difficulties out there." Joel did not reply, his expression still grave.

"And I think people are seeking to harm him. I sensed a conversation about a secret code," I said, hesitantly.

"Ah," said Joel. "Shall we start with that?"

"I can't tell you anything about the mission, not that I know much."

"Yes of course. But we're speaking in confidence. When Theodora asks for my help, she knows it'll be confidential. You're very trusting, Cassandra, a good quality. Here, you've had to learn to be more cautious."

I felt I could trust this enigmatic young man. "I had a vision of two men talking." He nodded, as though he could see it too. "I think they were planning to abduct Kastor," I continued.

"Did you hear them say his name?"

"No, I just sensed it. It could be my imagination, worrying so much about his safety."

"Let's assume you were right. What did you sense about the code?"

I told him about the images suggesting North Africa after the men had talked about where to send the message and also that the code could be in binary.

"I know parts of North Africa," he said. "I came originally from Ethiopia. Tell me about this idea of a binary code."

I took the crumpled page from Theodora's notebook from my pocket and handed it to him. "This may not be connected. It just seemed likely that they might use an ASCII text conversion."

Joel turned to the computer and keyed in the numbers on the piece of paper. After a few moments, the translation appeared on the screen. "It's the letters C, A and S," he said.

"Cas – could it be the start of my name?"

"Possibly, only it could stand for lots of things. Close Air Support, for example. But you say the men were talking about a place?"

"Yes, one of them, our man, said it couldn't be in this country - too many field operatives."

Joel pondered. "A place called Cas, perhaps in North Africa. Well, there's Casablanca. Let's focus on that and see what comes."

I hadn't worked with someone sharing my precognitive abilities before. I projected the image of the carpet and white buildings from the vision of the secret conversation. He took this up, elaborating it, turning the images.

"You may be right – I sense Morocco strongly. But is this where your suspected kidnap will occur – or just where the message will be sent?"

I shrugged, helplessly. "Is there a binary centre there?"

"I don't think it's active any more. There were problems, I believe, leading to a relocation."

"I need something more definite," I said, "Otherwise Kastor won't listen to my warnings."

Joel looked solemn. "We may have to wait for more developments. This man in your vision, the one you say is one of ours, is he already in the field?"

"Yes." As I spoke, an image of Ryden/ Loki came unwillingly to mind.

Joel looked interested. "Oh, him. He's been in the language laboratory here. Let's focus on what he may be up to."

I felt frightened. Supposing Joel was going to go straight to Gaston about this? He responded immediately with a reassuring glance.

"I didn't like the look or feel or him, if that helps. Not a good type, limited abilities, but very cunning. And ambitious. Try thinking about him, now, in the field."

I hesitated. The last thing I wanted was for Loki to sense me probing his thoughts.

Joel smiled. "He's not like us, Cassandra. I believe you'll find him rather dense about detecting us, at this distance. I'll give it a try, if you're nervous. He found you attractive, I suppose?"

"Possibly," I said, knowing that "probably" or "for sure" would have been a more accurate answer.

"Hmm," said Joel, "so it's better I try, in case he'd be more in tune with you." He closed his eyes.

I sensed he was trying to locate Loki. After a few moments, Joel opened his eyes. "He's in a newspaper office, talking. Let's wait until he has a moment alone. If we're lucky, he'll be thinking about plans for this mission."

I sat quietly, drinking the rest of the coffee. Joel was very still, concentrating on the remote viewing. After a few minutes, he looked across at me.

"He's so pleased with himself. He wants to stay outside and is thinking about how that'll go. Ah, I caught an image of Kastor. He thinks he's cleverer than him, but something else - how he can trick him. Yes, this man is treacherous."

I sat on the edge of my seat, gazing intently at Joel. But now he opened his eyes and looking solemnly back at me.

"I'm sorry, you know how it is, so hard to keep contact. I'll try again later. This man needs to be watched."

"Ryden Asgard, posing as Patrick Lynch, a reporter." I wondered if Joel had already picked up those details.

"Just so," he said, reminding me of Theodora, as of course he would, being one of her past students.

"But surely he'll be under close surveillance already, on such a mission?"

"Yes, regarding the mission. Possibly not for his other plans. He's probably been specially selected, watched for a long time. They trust him. And his treacherous tendency, even if they are aware of it, they'd expect him to use it on the organization's behalf, to dupe others."

I sighed. We didn't seem to have got much further in finding evidence. Joel looked at me sympathetically.

"Don't despair. We can work on the code idea for you and Kastor, at least."

We discussed the possibilities. It would need to work on several mind levels, superficial ones, then deeper if those messages got through. The superficial images could be those than anyone in danger might be thinking. I thought of the hangman's noose and the guillotine that I'd sensed when the men were talking about a coded message.

"Yes," said Joel, "along those lines. A guillotine is good, just indicating that the person in danger fears execution. Then, on the next level, a door perhaps. Several doors, to mislead anyone able to read that level. And each door with a different knocker. Some leading to meaningless thoughts, but one taking you to the next level. I suggest the hand of Fatima on the important door. In Morocco this is a traditional protection against evil."

He shared an image of a brass hand hanging down, lightly holding a disc for contact with the door. "Protection of the hand, the hand of God," he murmured.

We talked about other levels, Joel advising me that Kastor and I must devise these, so that it would be our secret alone.

"With this type of code, one needs to make a complicated maze, with a coded barrier on each level, in case someone very devious is able to plunge right into the depths, to find the message."

"How do these devious people plunge the depths, as you put it?" I asked, very nervously.

"You and Kastor, I sense that you have very deep mind contact," observed Joel. "But that takes time and much trust to develop. The layers are very delicate and must be negotiated with care. If an aggressive telepath wants to get deep inside your mind, he or she doesn't care about causing damage, they just want to rip through the layers to find your secrets."

I went pale, thinking of this dark side to Binary existence.

"But that would be an extreme and ill advised approach," Joel added quickly. "It causes far too much damage. Fellow telepaths have an instinctive respect for the structures that allow our abilities. It would be like stabbing someone several times to get them to answer. Not productive."

"Do they use… instruments?"

"Some have been developed. We would never use them, but we can't control all the organizations interested in telepathy."

"Can we defend ourselves against that kind of attack?"

"Yes, with training we can strengthen the superficial layers, so that only extreme aggression could get through. Kastor, for example, will have passed through very advanced training on that."

"So he'd be all right, even if…"

"Yes, mostly, and of course he can attack in return, if it comes to it. He would be able, at the very least, to ensure that what they found in his mind was valueless to them, only then it could mean…." Joel tailed off, probably regretting he had said this much, seeing my growing alarm.

"It could mean," I said, continuing his thought, "that his mind was very damaged, too damaged for them to use it."

"No one would want that to happen. If you're right and for some reason they want to kidnap Kastor, they'd want his powers, not a damaged mind."

We both fell silent, contemplating the horror of any of us losing our abilities, of people wanting to damage them.

"I'm sorry," said Joel, very gravely. "I guessed this would be very upsetting for you, but you wanted to know how to protect him. I think we've made a start."

"I'll work on a code. I'll call it the execution code, because it is to protect him against execution – of him, or his abilities."

"Yes – that could be interpreted as just something about executing a computer program. So if you send me a thought message about execution codes, I'll know you need help."

"He's leaving for the mission very soon," I said. Joel reflected, then nodded. "Tomorrow?" he said.

"Yes, very probably," I agreed. It was so reassuring to be with someone who shared my troublesome talent for seeing glimpses of the future. Although I could tell he was much more focused and that was perhaps due to his more extensive training.

Joel looked directly into my eyes. "I can't tell you not to worry. But you'll find someone to help you – and Kastor - outside." He paused, then surprised me by saying, "Perhaps the code would be better for that person. It may not work for you and Kastor."

I stared at him, confused.

"Kastor's mind has been shaped and conditioned over many years," said Joel. "Sitting with you, I sense that yours is very different. With the many structural layers in his mind, such a code could take months to develop, and even then..." He looked at me gravely.

"So I've been wasting your time?" I faltered.

"Not at all. I think it was very important for us to meet, to talk this through. You very much needed to explore this code notion. Work on it anyway, you may need it for another purpose." He took my hand and pressed it, saying as we parted, "May the hand of Fatima be with you."

10

After lunch, which I scarcely touched, I went over to the nursery area. The supervising nanny was surprised at this unexpected visit, but was accustomed to my needing to see the children. My privileges had been granted at a high level. They had been told to make concessions for me, particularly since I'd had come to terms with the required separation from my son. Even so I knew the nanny would record my unscheduled arrival in these quarters.

The toddlers were playing in the nursery garden and I wandered amongst them, seeing that they seemed very happy and lively, well adjusted to Binaries life. I sat on a bench watching them. After a few minutes, Leo came and sat quietly beside me.

"Why sad?" he asked, looking up at my eyes.

Not yet three years old and so empathic. "Just tired," I murmured. "Let's go for a little walk," I suggested cheerfully. He looked hesitant, glancing at the nanny in the garden.

"It'll be all right," I said, sending a quick thought message to the nanny that I was only going to spend a few moments with him. The nanny looked disapproving.

"It's nearly time for their nap," she protested. I signalled that I'd be back very soon, taking Leo's hand and walking out of the garden with him. The nanny would report this, for sure.

Outside the garden, I walked quickly with Leo to the nearest underground station.

"Where going?" he asked, not averse to an adventure.

"For a little ride!" I said playfully. The young children were not allowed on the underground trains, a source of great interest to them, so Leo's eyes opened wide at the prospect of going on a train ride. At that time of day, there were few travellers on the system and none at the nursery station. I helped Leo climb into one of the cars and pressed the 'go' button. He was very excited as we travelled past the stations en route to the Askeys-staircase stop. He had never visited the mansion before. Entering the Askeys grand hall, I looked around nervously, knowing that a child visiting the house would attract great attention, but there were no staff around. As we emerged from the lift at the second floor, I whispered that he should be very quiet, it was a great secret.

"Quiet as a mouse!" I said, as we tiptoed across to the door of the apartment. He was happy to obey. This was a marvellous adventure.

Once inside the apartment, he ran around the rooms, looking at everything. "Your house?" he asked.

"Yes, this bit, mine and daddy's," I said, suddenly sadly conscious that he did not think of Kastor as daddy. He was only dimly aware that Kastor was his father, having met him so rarely. "I mean, mine and Kastor's," I added, for explanation.

I put on the Mozart sonata that I had played to him in the womb and he danced happily on the carpet. I wished there were toys for him to play with, trying a game of hide and seek instead. This was a pastime that I'd seen the toddlers enjoying in the nursery and he entered into it with enthusiasm, although his hiding places were of course very easy for me to find.

"Try making yourself invisible, Leo, like this," I said, closing my eyes and folding my arms. "You just close everything off and say "I'm invisible" to yourself."

"I'm in'isible," he repeated, unsure of the word, but catching the meaning from my thought image. When I pretended not to see him standing against the curtains, he was thrilled. In fact, it had taken a couple of seconds for me to spot him.

"More, do more!" he said and I glowed to see how quick a learner he was. When he seemed tired, I gathered him up to lie with me on the sofa. He nestled into my arms and I looked at his fair curly hair, lighter than Kastor's, and his long fingered hands. While he still had the cute button nose of a toddler, it was well shaped and would one day be long, enhancing the intelligence of his face, like Kastor. Pale wintry light from the window softly illuminated the sofa, with only the rustling of trees in the Askeys grounds to disturb them. We were soon both asleep.

I woke up with a start, finding Kastor standing there, looking at us. I sat up guiltily, trying not to disturb Leo. Kastor was not smiling, but he didn't appear angry at this flagrant breach of the rules. I gazed up at him nervously, willing him to understand that I just wanted a little time alone with our son. To my relief, he smiled and crouched down, looking from me to Leo, who stirred, possibly sensing that someone else had arrived.

"You look beautiful, like a picture," he said softly. "Mother and son, asleep on a winter afternoon."

"I know, I shouldn't..." I murmured, as he sat down next to me.

"The house nanny called me," he said. "I knew you'd be here." Leo was now fully awake, looking a little perplexed and perhaps worried that he was in trouble. Kastor awkwardly ruffled his hair, smiling at him.

"Hello Leander," he said, "Do you like our home?"

He nodded uncertainly. "Go now? Don't want to..."

Kastor smiled indulgently. "Not quite yet. Would you like to see my study?"

"Yes!" he cried, excited, then, carefully, "Yes, please."

Kastor took his hand and led him out of the room. It was the first time I've seen them together, without any of the other children or nannies around. I heard Kastor saying, "You'd like to see the globe, I think. Do you know what a globe is, Leander?" Then I heard him add, shyly, "I mean, Leo."

As father and son talked on the way to the study, I heard Kastor laugh and a responding chortle from Leo. Quietly, I went into the kitchen to see if we had soft drinks and biscuits. When Kastor and Leo came into the kitchen, knowing of course that I was there, I held out a plate of Jaffa chocolate and orange cakes. Leo's eyes opened wide with delight, taking one but looking up for permission.

"Just this once," said Kastor.

We went back into the living room and sat together on the sofa. Leo was now chattering away, quite at ease. Kastor looked over Leo's head at me. My eyes were wet. I knew someone would be on the way to collect our son. Within a few minutes, there was a silent knock at the door and we turned to greet a nanny, formally dressed in her cape. She looked primly at me, then at Leo.

"So there you are! Well come along, Leander, you don't want to miss story time." He jumped up and ran up to the nanny, hugging her. "Don't be cross with Cassandra, Nanny, she's from outside, not like us."

Seeing this grown up little boy trying to explain my odd behaviour, I wondered how much the nannies had said about this strange mother from the outside. I forced a cheerful smile. Kastor was sending me messages of support. I felt an invisible arm wrap round me. Overt physical contact was not appropriate at that moment, with the nanny standing sternly by the door.

"Of course I'm not cross!" said the nanny, firmly taking his hand. "We love Cassandra don't we, and Kastor, and all the grown ups who come to see us." She bent down and whispered something to Leo, who nodded shyly. Turning to us, she said briskly, "I'm sorry to ask, but could we just quickly use the bathroom, he needs..."

I started forwards. "Oh, of course. I'll take him." I was embarrassed to think that it hadn't occurred to me that Leo would be too shy to ask for the toilet, probably still working on his toilet training.

The nanny looked horrified, putting an arm around the little boy. "No!" she said abruptly, then, more calmly "We have our routines. I'll take him along there now." I indicated the door, standing back. Kastor just stared at the carpet. I detected embarrassment, confusion, also sadness, but no direct thoughts. When the nanny returned with Leo, she said something about needing to clear up and disappeared back into the corridor.

Leo marched up to us. "I did a poo!" he said proudly and I beamed encouragingly, crouching down to his level. "Nanny took me to your bedroom," he whispered in my ear. Kastor looked alarmed at the state the bedroom might be as a result of this visit, but then he bent down like me, kneeling beside his son, asking him what pictures he could make in his mind.

When the nanny returned after two or three minutes, she beckoned to Leo. "All done!" she said, "It was easier to clean him up on a bed – your bathroom is quite small, isn't it. I've put the towel we used in your laundry. So, come along now, Leander."

She opened the apartment door, as if to usher our son out hurriedly before he could be further contaminated by this experience. Leo held back, gazing at Kastor and me, sorry to have to leave.

"Say thank you," said the nanny. He nodded at us solemnly. "Thank you very much." But as he left, he sent a thought message, "Bye, mummy, 'bye daddy" and I longed to rush over and hug him. But I had to be content with just sending a hug, as the door closed behind them.

I collapsed onto the sofa. Kastor sat beside me. There was a rare glimmer of tears in his eyes.

"I can't imagine," he said, "what it would be really like, to have our child with us. It would be so natural for you – I try to understand."

"You're not angry?" I rested my head on his shoulder. "I just had to see him. I'm sorry you had to leave work to come here."

"I insisted," said Kastor, rubbing his cheek against mine. "They were just going to send a nanny over to collect him, but I wanted to see you both. It was wonderful, seeing you together."

Inwardly, I sighed with relief. I curved round him, happy at least that we'd been allowed to live together and that Kastor empathised so closely.

"Do you have to go back, now?" I asked, oozing seductive thoughts.

He smiled at these, holding me close. "I think this is more important." He slid his hand under my silk blouse, feeling my skin. "Much more important," he added, turning his attention to my hold-up stockings with lacy tops.

"This might be a Norwich moment," I purred, settling back on the sofa, so that my legs rested on his lap. He looked puzzled. "NORWICH," I pronounced carefully, emphasising the usually silent W, "You know, an acronym teenagers and soldiers once used. 'Nickers Off Ready When I Come Home. I've always wanted a chance to say that, ever since my mother told me boys used to write it on love letters."

"Love letters. I expect you got a lot of those. Are there any other cities I should know about from your past?"

"Just Norwich. The rest were countries I think, BURMA, Be Upstairs Ready My Angel, CHINA, Come Home I'm Naked Already...."

"I get the idea," he laughed, twisting me round so that I was lying on his lap again. "So you were thinking, bodies first today, minds later?"

Oh yes, I thought back, "Or both body and mind together," conjuring up a coquettish image so that we were transported into a Parisian nightclub scene and I was tickling him with a large feather boa. Laughing, we made out on the sofa as though we had no cares in the world.

A little later, but still well within surveillance centre working hours, Kastor was dozing on the sofa under a bedspread that I'd thoughtfully thrown over him. Meanwhile I was preparing a drink in the kitchen, wearing a long silk dressing gown. I came into the living room with a tray, watching him in his light, apparently untroubled sleep, but I'd sensed his deep tiredness and was glad to see him resting, just for a short time.

Suddenly I sensed the approach of Gaston in the corridor, then a silent knock at the apartment door. I put down the tray in alarm, wondering what could have prompted this most unusual visitor. I went into the hall before signalling for him to enter, thinking possibly he had come to admonish me about bringing Leander up to Askeys.

Gaston Ajax strode into the hallway, carrying a thick folder of papers. I detected immediately that Leo was not on his mind. Seeing me in a dressing gown, he looked mildly entertained and glanced into the living room. I was embarrassed to notice a few items of discarded clothing still on the rug by the sofa. I hadn't got round to tidying up, while Kastor was resting.

"Ah," said Gaston, taking in the scene with a knowing leer, "Both working at home this afternoon I see. Charming, quite charming."

"Kastor needed to rest…" I began and he waved a hand tolerantly.

"Of course, my dear, and who wouldn't want to rest with such a delightful companion? But I fear we shall have to wake him, just for a few moments."

He walked into the living room, where Kastor was already stirring awake. He seemed not particularly surprised to see Gaston, while I noted with dismay the look of grim concern that had returned to his face.

"Gaston," said Kastor, sitting up under the bedspread. "I was going to come back to the centre for the file, you needn't have bothered."

They communicated silently, Gaston merely nodding to me that perhaps I could be doing something else for a few minutes.

"But don't trouble to dress," he said, "I'm mortified to have disturbed your little idyll. We do want Kastor to be in the very best condition. I'm sure another work out will do him the world of good." My flash of anger was simply bounced off Gaston's shoulders with an amused shrug, but I left them alone. I reluctantly retreated to my bedroom and ran the ensuite shower to make it clear I had no intention of eavesdropping.

I had dressed in a simple tracksuit when I heard the door of the apartment close, denoting Gaston's departure. Quietly entering the living room, I saw that Kastor was sitting on the sofa, still wrapped in the bedspread, looking through the file. I didn't need to ask if it concerned his mission. He looked up.

"Just a reminder of the key points," he murmured.

"Will you have to take that with you?" I asked. It was a bulky file.

"No – Manes will be calling for it in the morning. We travel very light on missions, for obvious reasons."

Not obvious to me, I signalled, picturing the grim underworld of spies and treacherous strangers that I imagined he would be dealing with.

"It's just an interview," he said, but then tapped the folder thoughtfully. "I think I'll put this in my study for now." I understood that he wanted me to see it, when he had gone. "Just tell Manny that you'll give it to him later, he'll understand. And that you know it's secret, not to be examined."

I nodded, surprised at the clear thought message. He expected me to read it. He got up, wrapping the bedspread around him as if for modesty, although it could have been the chill in the room, now that the slight warmth of late November sun had left it. He took the folder into his study.

"I'll order a meal – would you like steak?" I called after him. He signalled, yes, great.

Neither of us spoke of the imminent mission while we ate. I was certain now that he would be leaving in a few hours, perhaps in the early morning. Otherwise, he would be there to greet Manes and would not have asked me to give him the message about the file. It merely confirmed my precognition of the timing of his departure. We drank some very good red Bordeaux, but less than a glass and a half each. This was not an occasion for blurring perceptions with wine. Kastor had also showered and put on a tracksuit. We were dining in the small elegant room off the living room, rarely used except for entertaining.

Kastor raised his glass. "Here's to us," he said.

I lifted my glass in return, "Who's like us? Damn few and they're all dead." The Scottish toast, that I remembered Mum using on occasion. He smiled faintly.

"I've thought of a code, that we could possibly use to contact each other while you're outside," I said tentatively. He narrowed his eyes.

"You think we need codes to communicate, we who can hardly get out of each other's minds?"

"But if you're uncertain of the people you're with, just a few images to alert me that we need a particularly secure channel."

I talked about the execution symbols, as a way into a code sequence. He put down his glass and laughed drily. But his face showed he appreciated these attempts to protect him. He reached across the table for my hand, holding it so that he could press his thumb into my palm, massaging it gently.

"All right," he said, "Just who have you been talking to?"

I blushed. "Well, only a little, to Theodora – and to Joel Grigora. I didn't talk about your mission, I mean I don't know enough to talk about it. I just asked how to devise a code, in case I should ever need one."

"Joel Grigora," murmured Kastor, "the mysterious and handsome Ethiopian." I detected a faint tinge of jealousy, or was it just annoyance that I had been consulting others about him?

"It's not like that… He's studied with Theodora, I met him in her offices."

"Hmm," said Kastor, but not with innuendo. "One of the lovely things about you, Cassandra, is that you are surprisingly unpredictable. You can appear very obedient, but really you don't follow rules at all, you just do what seems right, at the time." We shared a thought image of me leading Leander to the apartment.

"Well, I had quite an erratic upbringing, you know, outside. Not full of rules and conditioning, like yours."

"Yes," said Kastor, laughing, "I've gathered that, at least. And you're very adaptable. Here, you might've been trained to work in surveillance."

"Like Helen?"

He pondered on this. "I'm not sure – it's so hard to know how different you'd have been, brought up like us. With your precognition and remote viewing abilities, there could have been several alternatives."

I gave some rare thought to my twin, still presumed dead somewhere in the Caribbean seas. It occurred to me that Helen, if alive, could be much more useful to Kastor on the outside. I had no idea how to create a group panic and had never tried to inflict pain on assailants. I also considered what Joel had said about the structure of my mind being different, because of the lack of Binary conditioning.

"Joel said…" I paused, seeing Kastor's quick look of less amicable interest. "Well, when I was talking about making a code, he said that our minds would be very different, it might not work."

"You seem to have had quite a deep conversation."

"Yes, but Theodora trusts him, and I do."

"But you trust everyone. You tell me to take care, yet you just hurtle into things."

"OK, forget my idea of an execution code, but I'm right about the dangers out there for you."

Kastor got up. "I'll be very, very careful. And now, let's do something more relaxing."

Thinking of the distraction of domestic chores as relaxation, I started to tidy up the plates and dishes. He stopped my hand, laughing.

"No, not the washing up. We'll get someone up from the kitchens to do that. I was thinking more along the lines of sharing our dissimilar minds for a while."

"Oh," I said. "I think I've offended you. I shouldn't have talked to Joel without letting you know."

He took my hands and gazed into my eyes. "You can talk to whoever you want, whenever you want, so long as I'm the only one who gets inside your gorgeous, deep, intriguing, enchanting mind." *And body*, I thought, mischievously. Kastor grinned.

"Well, yes, that too, but here we're really only driven to jealousy on the matter of minds. Perhaps it's time we did some really deep mind exploring?"

Yes please, I signalled, taking a tentative little plunge into his. He swooped into mine so quickly that my legs nearly gave way, as a wave of pleasure soared through me. He grabbed my waist to steady me and whispered in my ear, "Norwich, I'll certainly remember that. We can make that part of our secret communications, for starters…"

11

We settled comfortably onto the large double bed, still wearing our tracksuits. Even so, it was a little cold and we retrieved the crumpled bedspread to lie beneath it. Just as I was about to speak, Kastor signalled for me to be silent. He sat up, looking keenly around the room.

"What?" I inquired, in thought only.

He felt around the bedside table, picking up items. Then he examined the wall behind the bed and triumphantly plucked something from it. He showed it to me, still signalling silence. It was a tiny metal disc, like an electronic battery, but with wires poking from the rim and a spot of adhesive on its back that had been used to stick it to the wall.

"A bug?" I signalled. He nodded. He dropped it into a glass of water and took it out of the room. I followed him into the kitchen, where he carefully decanted the metal receiver onto the draining board and crushed it with the handle of a knife. Then he opened the small kitchen window and threw it out. I was appalled at the idea that we were under surveillance in our own home.

"Do you think there are others?" I whispered.

"I don't know," he murmured, holding me very close and speaking softly into my ear. "I thought the nanny was up to something, it may be the only one. Someone's very interested about what we're talking about, tonight. She didn't have time to hide it well. I don't sense any other microphones, do you?"

I had never tried to look for bugging equipment, but closed my eyes, visualising our apartment and looking, in my mind, for any strange vibrations or other indication that something had changed. Finally, I shook my head.

Kastor nodded, but looked keenly towards the direction of the surveillance centre. "They know we speak out loud, mainly," he murmured, very quietly. "What are they up to, I wonder?"

I focused with him. An image of my execution code came to mind, just the start, with the fear of execution.

"Something about codes," I signalled.

He nodded slowly, then whispered again into my ear. "Cassandra, remember this. If you feel any code or communication from me from outside, you must ignore it."

I nodded, desperately, feeling guilty I'd discussed it with Joel Grigora. Had he betrayed me?

"This is disturbing," he admitted, still in a whisper. "But don't assume anything. It could just be that they don't trust…"

"…me?" I interrupted.

He frowned. "They know you're very worried, trying to stop me going. That could be all there is to it." He signalled that we should be very careful from now on. "Keep checking the apartment after I've gone," he whispered. "I don't think Gaston left anything, but who knows? This is an unprecedented invasion of our privacy."

We returned to the bedroom, where Kastor checked every inch around the bed. It seemed we had found the only monitor of our conversation. We sat quietly, our eyes locked in troubled thoughts. Then Kastor shrugged, shifting the mood. "What were we discussing, oh yes, mind exploration. Do you still feel like doing that?"

"Yes, if you do," I murmured.

Kastor smiled, taking my hands and saying softly, "No one can disturb us, doing that. We need to be very close to go into the mind." *But we don't need to touch*, he signalled, stretching out on his back, gazing at the ceiling.

"Mind exploring, it's different from plunging. You just take it a little at a time, moving very slowly."

I lay down beside him. "But surely, we've already looked into each other's minds, sharing images and so on?"

"Yes, but this is more structural. Like being an archeologist or an architect, looking at the forms behind the images."

"You've done a lot of this mind exploring?" I was feeling once more so much the outsider to the Binaries way of life.

"Not a lot," he said. "Certainly not with a lover. It needs complete, intimate trust and I've only found that with you. Sometimes they need to do it in the assessment centre, to fully understand how a telepath is developing, or if they're ill or injured. But even then, not to a deep level."

"Can it be dangerous?" I signalled nervously.

Not with you and me, he signalled back. He closed his eyes and told me to just try and explore the surface of his mind.

"Clear your head of all images," he said, "That's difficult for you, but you need to be thinking you're like a gentle probing instrument, nothing more. Imagine you've become a miniature explorer, able to travel within the body. Only you're not concerned with the structure of the brain, just its invisible network, the one we use to communicate."

"How do I go in?" I asked. "Through your eyes, ears – nose?" It all sounded very uncomfortable. He smiled at the idea of a tiny Cassandra travelling up his nose.

"Any way you like, but it isn't anatomical – you simply have to visualise yourself slipping into my mind."

I shut my eyes, transforming into a small underground adventurer, tentatively entering his world of thought. I felt his receptiveness, waiting for me, offering no obstruction. After a few moments, I could see a strange landscape, like an alien planet, dimly lit with a faint violet glow. The surface was smooth, a soft white colour, sparkling a little like a recent snow fall. I stroked it uncertainly, surprised to feel it give slightly as I moved across. There seemed to be no structures like doors or holes that would give entry to what lay below. I gingerly probed the surface, looking for a pattern, something to indicate the layers of the mind. I adjusted an imaginary small torch light on my head, such as those used by miners, to get a more detailed view of the terrain. Suddenly I felt a slight separation in the surface and gently probed within it, slipping down into a shallow chamber below. Kastor sighed, letting me slide fully into the cavernous space.

I looked around. This layer had many small columns, like pillars supporting the upper layer. Like a church, with a floor which appeared to be made of soft shiny tiles. The pillars were not stone or marble in appearance, seeming to shimmer slightly. On closer inspection they were made of hundreds of tiny entwined filaments, like transparent wires in an electrical appliance.

I could make out a few shapes, resembling chests or cabinets, in the edges and niches of the chamber. I tiptoed over to one chest, gently lifting the lid, feeling Kastor sense this but with no resistance. Inside there was a swirling mass of thoughts and images. A city landscape rose up and I smiled, recognising Norwich from the thought pattern and a dainty pair of knickers that floated up alongside the landscape. I felt a little laugh from Kastor, lying somewhere way above, or around me, I couldn't be sure. I remembered that I was not here to share images, softly closing the lid and probing the tiled floor. Around the edges of a tile, I felt a similar separation to the one experienced in the superficial layer. I slithered down, catching a column in the larger cavern below but hastily letting go, when I sensed a twitch of possible discomfort from Kastor. These structures were all alive, aware of me.

The next cavern was more brightly lit, with a pale green illumination around the pattern on the ceiling, a network of filaments just as in the pillars and the columns themselves glowed and sparkled, as though a current was flowing through them. The floor had illuminated pathways of various colours, tracking in different directions. I delicately probed between the pathways, finding the now familiar way of slipping further down. The caverns became more complex, with archways leading to further halls, while the columns were closer together, so that I had to slide this way and that to avoid clutching them by mistake. There were intriguing drawers, little doors and chests that I had to resist opening. These were carefully stored ideas, memories and possibly secret matters of his mind. I had no wish to pry.

"It's like my thought house," I reflected, recalling the way I'd learned to store thoughts in compartments within a mansion, on an island surrounded by a swirling sea of mental tides and emotions. "Only so much more organised and intricate." Descending further into this amazing labyrinth was now irresistible, despite a slight qualm as to how I'd be able to exit.

As I went further and further through the layers, losing count of how many I had passed, it became much harder to avoid touching the vertical, horizontal and diagonal networks of active mind channels. I sidled against them gently, with the lightest touch and sensed deep pleasure in Kastor as I tickled and tingled particular strands within the dense filaments. In these lower caverns, it was as if I were inside a crystal, with many glittering facets, gliding past transparent crystal columns that were soft and pliant, moving away slightly at the merest contact. I gazed around with awe, thinking "*I'm loving this, loving being surrounded by your mind.*" I felt Kastor's response, wordlessly, that he was in a trance state, aware only of the exquisite feeling of my subtle journey through the labyrinth of his psyche.

I came to a cavern that made me giddy, for the floor was now quite transparent and I could see hundreds, countless floors below, all softly illuminated by the pathways and now curving columns and supports, like a forest of crystal. I felt that I now might descend through several layers at once, into an infinite network that would absorb me into the constant motion of changing patterns.

"How do I get out?" I wondered, feeling, not for the first time, like Alice in Wonderland, about to meet a strange creature or perhaps even to suddenly enlarge and damage these lace-like structures. I glimpsed strange shadows between the columns receding into the distance and started to feel a little afraid. I was deeper inside Kastor's mind than possibly anyone had ever penetrated. Perhaps I was now exploring areas over which even he had little conscious control. Seemingly miles distant, I felt a response from Kastor, aware of me feeling I was becoming lost in his labyrinth. With an effort I composed myself, remembering that I also possessed powers of the mind. I radiated some of my thought strength, touching the columns with the electric force of one who could visualise and travel beyond the mind and body. While careful to make these currents slight, I felt a thrill as some of my power seeped also into the columns, perhaps adding to the protection he would soon need.

I became aware of Kastor being somehow with me, within his mind network. I felt his support, lifting me gently so that I could glide upwards. It became more like the ascent from a thought plunge, sliding effortlessly through layers that parted like sea waves, buoying me up onto the next level. When I reached the uppermost caverns, filled with their chests and cabinets, I paused briefly to slip a door with Fatima's hand into the space between two bookcase-like structures. I felt Kastor chuckle as he pulled me away, so that I was now flying through the network, feeling an incongruous breeze as though we were both soaring into the sky over a receding patchwork of countryside below, with lights twinkling from the filaments that now seemed like little roads and paths. With a feeling like a cork popping out of a champagne bottle, I landed in a shower of sparkling lights, but gently, on the surface of his mind. I rested on the smooth surface for a moment while I took a silent breath. Then with a whoosh I soared out of him altogether, lying apparently on a cloud, which quickly transformed into the familiar bed.

I opened my eyes, half expecting to still be in miniature, dwarfed by the enormous folds of the bedspread and pillows. The room was out of focus, shimmering slightly. Kastor was there beside me, eyes still shut, breathing deeply as though asleep. Picking up that I was looking at him, he slowly opened his eyes and gave a long, sensuous sigh. He lay otherwise quite still, like a carved statue of a god resting after a major feat. He gazed at the ceiling, occasionally shutting his eyes again. He was recalling the sensation of my journeying through his mind. I wondered if those myriad columns still quivering, gently, remembering my touch.

"Cassandra," he said at last, enunciating every syllable. I turned slowly so that I could watch his face, feeling a little uncertain of how my body moved, in this dimension, after the experience of being a mind probe. He glanced sidelong at me, not smiling outwardly but grinning widely in his mind.

"Do you remember when I told you that mental flying was almost better than sex?" he murmured. I nodded. "Well, this *is* better than sex," he continued. "I'd like to stay like this, with you, forever."

"I felt like Alice in Wonderland," I said, quietly. "All those towering arches and tunnels."

"You didn't see the good bits, then," he murmured.

I started to say, "It was all good…" I'd seen the strands of lights, the cabinets and the sliding floors and longed to discuss it all.

He turned towards me and touched my lips with his fingers, stopping the flow of speech. He shared an image of soaring into the night sky, weightless like immortal beings.

"Would you like to come inside my mind, like that?" I asked shyly, when we had descended into mere mortals once more, lying on the bed.

"Oh yes," he said, dreamily, but not making a plunge as I expected. "But for the moment, I think there's been enough exploring. It's exhausting, don't you think?"

"Well, yes," I admitted, acknowledging that I felt too weak to move much and he was clearly in much the same state.

"But, would my mind look so very different, if I could see it?" I wondered if Kastor could view his own mind structure, explore it in the same fashion.

"We can't see into our own minds in that way," he replied to this thought. "It's not unlike not being able to hear your own voice, as it seems to those outside us. You can have an idea of it; and we learn about general telepathy structures during training, but everyone's a bit different, obviously. Especially people like us."

I thought of Helen, writing about outsiders as talking potatoes, picturing that this meant there was just dense matter inside them; no illuminated caverns or streams of thought light.

"So what is my mind like?" I persisted, "You've glimpsed quite a lot of it."

With apparent effort, he turned and held me in his arms.

"Your mind," he said softly, "is beautiful, like a maze of enticing patterns. There are few definite structures. It's as if, without the conditioning, the layers are free to move around, like subterranean ocean currents. It's impossible to describe how exciting it feels just to slide inside, to feel all the thoughts ebbing and flowing around, with constantly moving treasures and ideas beneath and beyond the ocean, like sirens leading me in."

"Ooh," I said happily, "Sirens – and perhaps mermaids?"

"Probably, knowing you, yes there must be mermaids too," said Kastor, gazing intently into my eyes and I felt him float, very gently, over the warm seas of my mind.

"Well," he said, after a few seconds, "I can't see any mermaids yet, but I can't wait to find out, on my next exploration."

The night had moved on, with the moon shining in through the bedroom window, but we felt no urgency either to undress and go to bed properly, or to do anything else. Kastor was mainly silent, either looking at me or closing his eyes, trying to recapture the feeling of my sliding within his mind. As ever, I was full of questions and when he seemed receptive, I started to ask them.

"Am I the first to explore that deep?"

"I'd never allow anyone else to get beyond the first layer. It's almost sacred to us, this structure of the telepathic mind."

"But mind plunges, they seem to go a long way down, sometimes?" I felt shy even discussing it, it was like talking about physical sex.

"Yes, but it's different. When you plunge, you're still outside, in your mind. It still needs a lot of trust – consenting adults, if you like, but you're not examining the layers, just feeling the sensation of passing through them."

"All those structures," I mused. "I don't understand how I could plunge into your mind at all. Now I think I'll be scared of damaging the wiring, distorting the strands."

"They're not evident anatomically," said Kastor, giving up the idea of just enjoying lying there with me in blissful, united silence. "At least, not with current techniques. It really is 'all in the mind'. So when you plunge, given that the other person is receptive and wants you to do that, these invisible layers just separate."

"Hmm," I murmured, "but the structures felt very real to me. I could touch them, feel their substance."

"But only with your conjured mind probe – otherwise they're

invisible, intangible."

"I see." Mentally, I portrayed myself as a probe, not like a human form at all, more like a little torch with arms and legs, a cartoon figure. He laughed at this image, sending back a picture of getting married to the torch, wearing a demure veil but flashing on and off and dodging the confetti on the way from the church.

The phone by the bed rang and Kastor reached to answer it reluctantly.

"OK," he said, "I'll be there. Half an hour."

I knew it was the call to leave for the mission, but wondered why they did not just send a thought image of a clock, with his orders attached. "In case I was asleep, with you," he murmured in reply, "and not responsive to outside thought messages."

"Shall I help you pack?" I asked.

"Oh," he said carelessly, "that's all done. Standard case with changes of clothes, passport, all that stuff."

"Why didn't you tell me, that it would be tonight?"

He looked earnestly at me. "Well, one, because you obviously knew. There's no point trying to conceal much from you when you're curious, is there? And two, because I didn't want us to talk about it, especially tonight."

I sat up, knowing that we had only a few minutes left. "You mean, we both sort of pretended it was days away, yes, I suppose I went along with that."

Kastor went into the bedroom by his study, to dress quickly. I followed him in, unusually, not wanting to lose a second of time with him. As he dressed, I sent thoughts of protection and how he should be constantly on his guard.

"Thank you," he said, putting on his jacket, "I really do know how worried you are. That's why I didn't want to go over it all again this evening."

He slipped off his binary ring and handed it to me. "Please keep it safe. It wouldn't do for me to be wearing it on this mission."

I held it carefully, touching my own ring with it, then placing it on the ring finger of my other hand.

"And there's something else," he said, reaching into one of the tallboy drawers near his bed. He drew out a small velvet covered box, pressing it into my hands. I opened the box and pulled out two beautiful earrings. They were green crystal drops, held by a cluster of diamonds at the top. There was a white gold hinge between the diamonds and the crystal and I moved it to and fro, seeing the crystal glow with shifting shades of green in the light. I put one in my left ear, tilting my head so he could admire it, but held the other one, enjoying its colour in my hand.

"They're Lalique crystal," he said, proudly. "It was so hard to match the colour of your eyes. These are the closest I could find."

"I'll wear them always," I said, putting in the other earring, "Every day while I wait for you here."

"Manny will keep you in touch," he murmured, putting his arms round my waist. "Anything you need to ask. I'll be back very soon," he said, hugging me tightly.

"I'll depend upon it," I murmured. He glanced towards the window. He was being called.

"Cassandra," he said, still holding me close, "I just want to say, about today."

"I won't do it again," I said hastily, "Break the rules with

Leander, I mean."

"But you will," he said, smiling. "I was going to say, thank you for doing that, bringing our son here. I felt such a bond with him, with all of us being together. When I get back I want to see him again, with you, like that. Damn the rules, they don't understand do they? You coming here, making your home in this place, we're so lucky and I'm the luckiest of all. We can work something out, make changes."

I nodded, trying not to cry. I knew it wasn't that simple, that I would have to tread very carefully at the nursery for some time after the escapade with Leo. As we held each other, for a moment we relived the remarkable mind exploration and feeling of shared bliss.

"And that," he said, pulling reluctantly away, "will sustain me more than anything else while I'm outside. Thanks, by the way, for the door with the knocker."

"I didn't think you'd notice," I said, blushing at having deposited something in his mind. Kastor just signalled, *remember what I said, no codes*. Then he looked up, receiving a more impatient message from the surveillance centre. "*Au revoir*, Cassandra," he said quickly, walking away to the apartment door, without glancing back. I felt that if he had eyes in the back of his head, they would have been staring sorrowfully at me, wanting more than anything in the world not to leave.

12

The clock on the bedside table showed it was nearly 3 a.m. The witching hour, I thought, miserably, remembering old tales from the outside. I was wide awake, with no wish to go to bed and catch some sleep before the dawn. I felt the green crystal droplets hanging gracefully from my ears and went over to the antique cheval mirror in my bedroom, ordered when we had done the extension and other improvements to the apartment. I switched on a small sidelight, to admire the earrings in the mirror, tilting the mirror slightly so that the crystal glass sparkled in the soft light.

As I looked into the mirror, I saw a slight shift in the image, which blurred and readjusted to show, for a moment, a different reflection. I caught a glimpse of a woman my height, but with flowing dark hair, almost black, to her shoulders. The face was very like mine, but the nose seemed more pointed and the heavy make up gave her the appearance of slanting eyes. The reflection smiled briefly and I instinctively touched my lips, to see if I was smiling in the same way.

"Sister Cass," I heard in my mind, then the image faded and I was looking at myself again.

"Helen!" I thought with a start. In all the time that the mirror had stood in the corner of the bedroom, I had never sought my sister's image, nor seen any change in the reflection. "So, are you alive, or a ghost?" I thought, thinking of the hour, but the mirror remained just a sheet of reflective glass.

Turning with some disappointment from the mirror, I remembered the secret file in Kastor's study. I looked in the direction of the surveillance centre, trying to discreetly detect anyone thinking about me, but nothing came. Kastor was by now possibly travelling towards the private airstrip for his flight. I went into his bedroom and opened the door of the study that led off from it. I rarely intruded on this very private space, unless he asked me in. It was a small room, lined with bookshelves and cabinets, with a desk looking out onto the now dark gardens beyond. I smiled, recognising structures from those in his mind for storing thoughts. But there was no folder on the desk or lying anywhere within the room. While he had said that I'd be able to find it, I hoped he had not made this too difficult. I pulled down the blind at the window and switched on the green glass desk light. It was not that I thought that anyone was peering in, but after finding the bugging device, it seemed wise to be very discreet.

I sat at his desk, enjoying being in his comfortable captain's chair. I gently turned the globe standing to one side, thinking of Kastor and Leo playing with it. Then I focused on the file that he had been reading, trying to locate it within the room. It was definitely there, I detected, but out of view, possibly with other files. I looked at the bookshelves, noting a pile of documents but sensed it did not contain the file. I had a clear mental image of one of the cabinets. I span the chair round to locate this cabinet, getting up to pull open the upper drawer. It contained alphabetically tabbed files.

"Not in this one," I thought, "so it must be the drawer below." Opening it, I knew the folder was in there, starting to flick through the tabbed files that gave no clue, some having the names of places, possibly past missions, others indicating training or procedural documents. Then I noticed a tab labelled *'Norwich.'* "Of course!" I thought, smiling, drawing out the file. A glow of pleasure filled me as I imagined Kastor carefully writing the tab, laughing when he thought of my reaction.

The file was bound with a neat button and elastic ties, which I removed carefully. Taking care not to disturb the pages too much, I opened the folder on the desk and started to examine its contents. There were photographs, particularly of a man I'd never seen. I guessed he was the mysterious interviewee that Kastor had to see in person. The instructions seemed innocuous enough, with statements from people in the organization, travel details, an outline of information obtained from the doomed Patrick Lynch, with annotations that I assumed to have been made by Ryden and others in the surveillance centre. It all seemed to relate to uncovering a plan to penetrate the Binaries. I felt a chill, thinking of Ryden's possible additional agenda. But why would he want to help anyone threaten our organization? There was no indication of travel to anywhere in North Africa, let alone Casablanca. As far as I could see, Kastor would be going directly to the Centro Binario in Cadiz, in southern Spain, and the interviewee would be brought there.

I opened one of the desk drawers, looking for a notebook. Finding an unused one, I started to make quick notes. I took down names. I studied photographs and made quick sketches to remember their faces. I guessed that Kastor had been trained to assimilate all such information without needing notes, but I had less confidence in my memory. A photograph of an overweight, olive skinned man took my attention. An Arab in appearance, he was wearing a military jacket, with epaulets. I turned the photo over, noting the name, Abdul-Azim Samara. There was no other information, but I deduced that this man was closely involved with their investigation. He had a cruel face, despite smiling for the camera. When I gingerly focused on him, I caught an image of that Arabian scene with white buildings. It was similar to the scene that I'd glimpsed when visualising the meeting between Ryden and the other man in the park.

So, this man could be in Casablanca. I had no sense that he was a telepath, able to detect my interest. I could see him walking down a corridor, giving an order. Then I had a clear image of Kastor, being interrogated – not by this man, but nearby. I froze, remembering the dream of seeing him imprisoned. The image faded and I looked through the folder carefully, searching for the image of that contact of Ryden's in the park. There was no trace of him. That had been a secret meeting, outside the knowledge of the Binaries team.

When I had finished going through the file, I noticed with surprise that it was now 5 a.m. Now I felt tired, the lack of sleep making the pages hard to read. Carefully, I bound up the folder. Where to hide it? I couldn't put it back in the Norwich slot of the cabinet, for Manes might come into the study and he could guess that Kastor had selected that hiding place for me. So I went over to the stack of files on the bookcase, lifting the first two so that I could insert it below. The titles of the other two files showed that they concerned only procedures. The stack looked neat, just as Kastor might have left it. I picked up the notebook, switched off the light, then gently rolled up the blind.

It was still dark outside, with only a glimmering of dawn light beyond the trees. I tore out the pages I'd used in the notebook, replacing the book itself in the office drawer. Going into my bedroom, I looked around for a hiding place for the notes. After the episode with the nanny, nowhere seemed safe. Perhaps the cleaners would also have instructions to place bugs, search for evidence that I had been prying? I would have to memorise the notes when I'd had some sleep, then destroy them.

Meanwhile, my attention focused on the cheval mirror. I tilted the frame, noting the wood panelling behind the glass. There were three pieces to the panelling, lifting slightly with age. I felt delicately along the edges. One was a little loose. The few slim sheets of paper easily slipped into the space behind the panel. I'd need tweezers or some other very fine probe to remove them, but examining the panels now concealing the notes, I was satisfied that only a very diligent search would uncover them. Feeling very sleepy, I pulled off the tracksuit and threw it into the bottom of the wardrobe, too tired to fold it properly. Then I slid between the sheets and dropped off to sleep.

I woke to hear the phone by the bed ringing and drowsily picked it up, noting the time the bedside clock to be 9 a.m. It was Manes.

"I'm sorry to disturb you. I've been trying to reach you for a few minutes, but guessed you must be fast asleep."

"Oh, hello Manny, yes, sorry, it was so late when Kastor left, but

I stayed up to see him go, then I must've just dropped straight off."

"Did Kastor say something about a folder? Gaston brought it round, yesterday afternoon?"

"Folder, yes, of course. He said you'd call for it. I think he put it in his study. Do you want me to look for it?"

"No," said Manes quickly, "I'm in the building, I'll come over now, if that isn't too inconvenient?"

"I'll get up and make some coffee," I murmured, putting the phone down. I felt exhausted, wondering how long I would have slept without being disturbed: probably until the cleaner arrived at around 10. I slipped on my long dressing gown and went into the kitchen, where I picked up Manes' silent knock as the coffee filtered through. I signalled for him to enter, smiling wanly at him as he took in my dishevelled appearance. I had brushed my hair, but it was still springing untidily about my face, refusing to settle. He looked curiously at the earrings and I touched one, embarrassed that I had left them in. The sensitive Manes perceived at once that I had not wanted to remove this parting gift from Kastor.

"Oh, you need more sleep," he said, embarrassed. "It's just that we need the folder over at the centre."

"Of course – just go into the study. He didn't show it to me, but it must be in there somewhere." I handed him a cup of coffee, which he took gratefully as he entered Kastor's sanctum. After a minute or so, he called out.

"Cassandra, I can't find it. Didn't he say anything about where he was going to put it?"

I felt more awake, now the caffeine was surging through me. I went to the door of the study. "He explained it was very secret," I muttered. "I didn't want to know – I didn't want him to go, anyway."

"I know," said Manes, giving me a concerned look. I sensed no suspicion that he thought I'd been reading the file. I was surprised how easily I could conceal my interest, thinking that this was more in Helen's line, remembering suddenly the blurred image in the mirror. I stood at the door of the study, cradling the cup of coffee.

"I don't know, Manny. I guess he'd have put it somewhere easy to find, when you called. He knows I don't interfere with things in this study."

I projected helpful images about the desk, its drawers, the bookshelves. Manes looked around the room, focusing on the stack of files on the bookshelf. He plucked off the first and second files, then spotted the thicker file below.

"Ah," he said, "I think this may be it." There was no writing on the folder, but Manes scarcely needed that. He tapped the securing button. "Light blue," he muttered, "we use that for active assignments." "Oh," I said, genuinely unaware of this detail. Manes quickly opened the folder, just to double check. He did not have my ability to view inside closed files. Then he downed the rest of his coffee.

"I won't disturb you any longer," he said. "Go back to bed - I'll tell housekeeping not to come in until you call for them."

"Thank you, but I'm awake now."

Manes paused, despite in obvious hurry to get to the surveillance centre. "Please try not to worry. I'll be keeping a close eye on it all."

I closed my eyes briefly as I felt a strong image coming into my mind, of Ryden grinning and talking. Had he already met up with Kastor? I sensed he was explaining something, speaking plausibly but with underlying menace. I did not trouble to conceal this image from Manes, who looked at me sharply.

"What is it?"

"There's a change of plan," I said, opening my eyes. "Ryden is talking about a change in the arrangements."

"No - he can't do that – you're worrying too much, letting your emotions interfere…"

"Perhaps," I agreed, knowing it was futile to bring up all my suspicions of Ryden-Loki, especially in my exhausted state. "But you will remember, Manny, that he shouldn't be fully trusted?"

"He's one of us," said Manes, wearily. He walked towards the apartment door.

I signalled, "Tell me, if the plan changes, won't you?"

"It's best that you don't know anything about it," said Manes, now in full professional mode. "And Kastor will be home, before you've a chance to worry any further."

He left quickly, not wanting any more discussion. I remembered the microphone we had removed, hoping that no one else had heard our conversation in the living room. But emotional interference or not, I knew I was right about the change of plan.

13

I washed and dressed, ordering breakfast from the kitchens as I was in no mood for cooking. When it arrived, I took the tray into the living room and noticed the clothing still in disarray on the sofa and carpet. Quickly, I picked them up and dropped them in the laundry basket near the bathroom. When the housekeeping team arrived, I was sitting peacefully finishing off the breakfast on my tray. I switched on the television that we hardly ever used. I did not like to be reminded of the world outside and Kastor had little interest in it. In any case, the channels in our home were limited to films and documentaries.

When the maids had left, I tried to sense if any more bugging devices had been placed, carefully checking places where they could have been put. I sensed none, wondering if the bug left by the nanny had been simply to pick up the words exchanged before the mission. Now that Kastor had gone, my domestic conversation would presumably be of much less interest to the organization. Still, I needed to be on my guard, wondering what Gaston would do, when he realised we had removed the monitor. I thought angrily about Joel as the key suspect to have told the surveillance team that I was trying to devise a code.

Joel's face became clear in my mind, with a serious, searching expression. "Execution code," I snapped at him in my thoughts. He nodded, without apparent guilt or remorse about betraying me. "Meet me in coffee room 5," he signalled. His face faded before I could respond. "I should go," I reflected, "at least to confront him about this."

Surely Theodora would not have introduced me to someone who would betray such a confidence, I thought miserably. But in an organization where they stooped to bugging a bedroom, whom could I possibly trust? I changed into a work outfit and made my way across to the underground network. Walking through the corridors, trying to remember the location of coffee room 5, I was surprised to see Theodora Sage come out of a door directly in front of me. Binaries people were so good at tracking you down. I wondered if I'd ever be fully accustomed to it.

"Cassandra," said Theodora, "I could pick up your anxiety. Kastor left during the early hours, did he not?"

"Yes," I said, sending an image of the bugged bedroom and also of my suspicions of Joel. I thought that Theodora might have picked that much up, already, but she looked very shocked.

"That's disgraceful. I refer to the monitoring device. Your suspicions of Joel are unjust, I feel." She signalled that we should not discuss it further in the corridor, ushering me into a nearby doorway. This led to a small reading room that I had not previously seen. There were so many nooks and crannies in this large underground complex.

In the small room, Theodora looked at me with great concern.

"You are tired and very confused. You already know more than you should about this mission."

"Mostly what I have sensed. Kastor wouldn't discuss it."

"I'm not in their confidence on the fine details," said Theodora. "I know it concerns the very deepest levels of security, of protecting our organization. But why do you suspect Joel of being involved?"

"He was the only one, apart from you, that I discussed a code with. And I trust you, completely."

"I am glad, of that," murmured Theodora, still looking at me gravely. "For your safety is very important to me, Cassandra. I'd never put you, knowingly, in danger."

"But now, they seem to know all about my idea for an execution code," I blurted. Theodora glanced sideways, as if trying to pick up the secret world of the surveillance team.

"If Joel spoke to them," she said, slowly, "it wouldn't have been to betray you. Perhaps they asked him to help with a code in the field. He has special abilities in that area."

"If I go to meet him, as he's suggested, will they know, I mean will Gaston and the others know?"

"Keep your thoughts well shuttered. You and he, with your excellent visualising and rapid thought channels, should be able to communicate discreetly. Coffee room C5 is very private, used only by a select few – I don't think you'll be monitored, there."

"You trust Joel Grigora." I felt guilty now that I had seemed to be so accusing.

"Yes, but he also has to follow orders. If he talked to them about a code, it will not have been to endanger you."

He said I was also in danger, I thought desperately, looking into Theodora's eyes. She nodded. "Go and talk to him," she said softly. Then, in a normal voice, she added that we should dine that night, since I'd be on my own. "Come at eight," she signalled, sending an image of her antique clock.

I left the room, sensing, once back in the corridor, that Joel was already in the coffee room. Theodora gave me brief directions, smiling at my difficulty with finding my way around Binaries, after all this time. Coffee Room C5 was on the next level up, off a little used corridor. I silently knocked and entered. Joel was sitting as if in deep thought. The room was small with just four comfortable chairs and a small table with a tray of coffee. Apart from a picture on one wall and the porthole radiating morning light, there were no other features. It was obviously intended for private meetings, such as this. The picture seemed to be of a crystal forest. It reminded me of exploration of Kastor's mind and I guessed the artist had tried to convey something of a journey through this strange telepathic terrain.

"The tunnels of the mind," observed Joel. "But the eye cannot fully convey the sense of being within one." *No*, I signalled briefly, anxious to move on to my present worries.

"The code," I said, sending a flash of anger, quite a small one by my standards, but it nevertheless made him sit up abruptly, as if pricked by a needle.

"Ah, yes, I was asked to see them about making a code."

"So you gave them the one we'd talked about? After telling me you wouldn't discuss it with them?"

Joel did not seem particularly perturbed, indicating the coffee politely and pouring some out. "I told you that I wouldn't discuss your concerns with them, particularly about this Ryden, the trickster."

I sat down with a sigh. "But the code, you must have told them about it."

"They asked about suitable codes to be used on this mission. Apparently Ryden is most interested to know how to contact you. He hasn't established an effective thought channel?"

I shook my head. "Not as far as I'm aware. It isn't something that I've been encouraging."

"No, I imagine not," said Joel. "As you know, I also detected that he's treacherous. The key members of the surveillance team appear to be blind to that. So when they asked for a code, one that Kastor would use and one also that Ryden could use, I was very careful." I drank some coffee waiting for Joel to continue.

"We, that is, you and I, had talked about whether a code was in fact suitable for you and Kastor – because of the difference in your minds and the short time available. Also, I think Kastor wouldn't like to use one with you, am I right?"

I tilted my head, signalling that he assumed correctly. "We only got as far as the execution symbols, like the guillotine, before he closed off that discussion."

"So, Cassandra, I was puzzled why they should be so keen to have a code that perhaps you and Kastor hadn't even discussed."

"Our home was bugged." I watched his reaction, sensing genuine surprise, adding, "I don't know how much they'd have picked up."

"Surveillance, in your own home at Askeys, it's unheard of! Kastor might have been uncooperative over at the centre, when they started to plan this, but I don't know why they should've been so desperate to pick up ideas from your private conversations."

"In bed…" I said, flushing angrily. I sensed that Joel knew nothing of this intrusion, unless he was extremely good at hiding it.

"Had you mentioned our conversation to Kastor?"

"Not until last night. He was a bit annoyed that I'd been talking about him, I think."

"Just so," said Joel. "But I spoke to them only yesterday about this code. Before you told Kastor that we'd been speaking. So, I don't think they knew we'd had our chat in Theodora's study." Joel now gazed with a sincere expression, letting me know he was not holding back, "They asked me, what code Kastor might choose to open a thought channel with you."

I smiled, thinking of Kastor snorting derisively at the idea that we'd need such a thing. Our close and intense communication was unusual, even for Binaries.

"It's hard to imagine skills that one does not possess," Joel observed. "Our precognition, for example, is a mystery to most of our colleagues. I'm sure Kastor would find a way of communicating with you. He'd use a single image, I think, not a coded set of symbols. An image that only you two share."

"I'm not expecting him to try to communicate," I said cautiously, not willing to share any further private ideas. Theodora had said that they all had to follow orders sometimes.

Joel nodded, understanding. "As I thought. So I suggested to the surveillance team that Kastor would start a code by using something loving, like a heart or a flower. They were surprisingly receptive. Your relationship is wondrous to many of the residents here." He glanced at my green crystal earrings, smiling. "Kastor was not known to be sentimental, before he met you, but now he wears his feelings on his sleeve, as poets say."

I sensed that Joel knew the earrings were a very recent gift, specially chosen and kept hidden until the right moment. I looked down at my lap, shy under Joel's dispassionate gaze, aware that he knew that Kastor and I did not send thoughts of hearts and flowers to each other. Noticing my discomfort, Joel reduced the intensity of his stare, continuing, "But I also suggested that there'd be layers, something to signal there was an important message."

"So you gave them the idea of the execution code?"

"Not as such. You remember we talked about a hangman's noose or guillotine?"

I nodded. "Well," he continued, "I didn't suggest those images, but something more closely connected to a firing squad, or execution by an enemy. I also hinted at the use of binary numbers. But I sensed very strongly that they were very interested in codes between you and Kastor. There was someone in that room who, I felt, was going to share this information with Ryden."

"Who?" I couldn't believe that even Gaston would be this devious, and certainly not our friend Manes.

"Have you met the operation room officer, Tad Lemur?"

"Very occasionally." I tried to picture him. A youngish man with sandy hair, who seemed to take his work very seriously. We did not socialise with him, Kastor in any case keeping social contact with the surveillance team to a minimum, apart from his long standing friendship with Manes.

"Yes, that's him. He's closely involved with this mission. I believe he's in charge of contact with Ryden while he's on the outside."

"Lemur, such an odd name. Not that all the names here aren't odd."

"A cunning primate," observed Joel. "But also, possibly short for the lost land of Lemuria, somewhere between the Pacific and Indian oceans. It's strange how our names seem more apt, later, when we've developed. Tad always seems, to me, to be looking for something more, something he should have – but has been denied."

"And your name, Grigora? How does that apply to you?"

"It means 'quickly' – a grigoro is a fast man. I learn quickly, like you, but your first name was chosen by your parents, not by the sages here. It's rather surprising that your parents picked the name of a prophetess."

I pondered for a moment on this, giving rare thought to the parents who had not seemed particularly interested in me. Perhaps Mum had chosen that name as a secret way of acknowledging that she knew I was different, that this was why the Binaries had been so keen to buy one of her twins. Then she did everything she could to suppress any telepathic or precognitive abilities, including my name. I noticed that Joel was gazing at me, taking in these memories. It would have been good to discuss it with him. But I realised we should not stray too far from the urgent matter of codes.

"So this cunning primate, Tad, could easily tell Ryden about the code conversation?" I asked anxiously.

"It would be understood that he should only relay what he was told to – but yes, I sensed his keen interest. Tad would like to go on a mission outside, but spends most of his time in the operations room, where his skills are best used. That doesn't mean he's happy about it. Possibly, Ryden has promised him an opportunity, what do you think?"

I considered this likely, with a chilling sense of how Ryden's plan was unfolding. "You said you'd be watching Ryden, out there, when we spoke before. Do you have any inkling that Tad has passed on this code idea?"

"I sensed only that he wanted to - which means he probably has."

"So, have you told them to be careful about any codes they receive here?"

Joel glanced sadly in the direction of the surveillance centre, or so I assumed. "As a key part of the team, Tad was present the whole time I was there. He's a good telepath. It would have been too risky to try to send a message to one of the others, with him so near."

"Thank you for telling me this. I'm sorry I thought it was you, letting the cat out of the bag."

"The cat out of the bag…" repeated Joel, solemnly. "Interesting metaphor. Is that what they do outside, put cats in bags?"

I smiled, shaking my head. He went on, "But it's quite all right – you must question everything, think strategically. You <u>are</u> in danger."

"Not as much as Kastor."

Joel took my hand, rapidly sharing an image with me of an airport, of men watching, of possible kidnap – and my being involved.

"I'm not going anywhere," I said firmly, "Heavens no, unless…"

I thought quickly, if Kastor needed my help, I'd go outside. Joel shook his head, sighing.

"You're impulsive. But I'll try to help you, whatever happens next. And Theodora, she'll sort out the listening device in your home. The very idea!"

He closed his eyes, sharing thoughts of indignation with me. Then he stood up, indicating silently that he had to return to his work. He sent an image of the Fatima knocker as he left and the message, "The protection is with you."

14

I thought that I should at least look in at the commercial centre. Simon Arbalest was delighted to see me.

"Cassandra! Thought you wouldn't be in today – had a message from the surveillance people that you had something else on."

I sensed that he had little, if any, knowledge of Kastor's mission, as he excitedly explained that we had two new major clients.

"They've heard about the clever Lily West – but there's a problem."

I looked at him questioningly and he said that they were insisting on meeting me before entering into a contract on their business interests.

"Absolutely not," I said, "Not at the moment. I might consider meeting them later, in a few weeks."

"No, listen. We can arrange a meeting this Friday, at one of our London offices. It would only take an hour or so and we'll bring you straight back."

"Have you asked Gaston about this?"

"No." He shrugged. "Why should I? Gaston doesn't interfere with our commercial work and you'd be quite safe. We send people outside all the time."

"This office, is it anywhere near an airport?"

He looked very puzzled. "No – it's near London Bridge. Well I suppose the City airport isn't too far away, but we wouldn't fly. Just a quick trip in by car."

"I'll think about it, but on one condition. Don't tell Gaston anything about it, or any of the surveillance or security staff."

"If that's your condition, you've got it. Look, here's a file about the clients. They're only in London this Friday – if we can't produce you, they won't sign."

I took the file, but said, "I still need to think about it. It's not a good time for me. Kastor is away."

"*I see*," nodded Simon. "OK, but let me know very soon."

I was just about to leave when I heard some laughter from the next room.

"What's going on there?" I asked.

"Oh, a couple of our interns are playing with products. Would you like to meet them?"

"OK," I said, smiling. "Always keen to meet the students." It would be a welcome diversion to be with these relatively innocent young telepaths, I thought. He took me into the room. Two young women, aged no more than 18, were sitting at a table, surrounded by cosmetics and a few fashion items. With a start, I recognised one as Phoebe Star, the girl who had ended up in the Binaries when her twin had been killed. Phoebe gave me a delighted smile. Simon saw we knew each other, without asking questions. He introduced the other girl as Ashara.

"They're on a three month placement. They came top of the product prediction module in their course. Their reward is to do lots of work here."

"We love it," said Ashara.

"Do you get to keep any of these items?" I asked, looking at the pile of products.

"Well, sometimes they let us try them out," said Phoebe. "I want to work particularly with fashion." I picked up a pretty blue cardigan from the pile.

"Have you tried this?"

"Yes, I've identified it as a winner," said Phoebe, then adding more tentatively, "At least, that's how it seems to me." I held it, visualising it out in the field. "I believe you're right." At this confirmation, Phoebe smiled, proudly. Everyone knew that I was now one of the prized experts. I looked thoughtfully at Phoebe, wondering if in the three years since entering Binaries, she had come to terms with the strange life we now shared.

"It's good to meet you Ashara …and to see you again, Phoebe. I wonder, Phoebe, if you'd have time to talk with me some time this week?"

"Yes, of course," said Phoebe, while Ashara gave her a jealous glance. Noting this, I said quickly, "Ashara, it's just that Phoebe and I go back a long way. I'd like to catch up. I can tell that you too are very good at product prediction."

I signalled to Phoebe that I'd be in touch. It suddenly seemed important that I should do some one to one communicating with this young woman. Then I left them to carry on giggling as they opened packets and discussed which ones to try or discard.

I strolled towards one of the self-service restaurants, feeling I could do with some lunch. This was a good sign that I wasn't letting concerns about the mission stop me looking after myself. I joined a table where other Binaries were eating happily, occasionally sharing a trivial thought. It was relaxing to be with them. But when I went to fetch a dessert, I suddenly saw a clear image of a heart, entwined with flowers. I glimpsed a flash of Kastor's face, looking upset. Was this a trick, or was he trying to contact me? The image was quickly replaced with a view of a prison yard and I had to steady myself at the counter when I visualised a firing squad, apparently facing me. I took a plate of jelly and ice cream, the first item I saw on the counter, and sat down at a nearby empty table.

The image had faded, but I tried to recapture it, to glean its source. Kastor had said he would send no codes. Then, as I sat quietly, toying with the jelly on the plate, I heard a voice clearly, saying "Cassandra, Cass, please come." I saw the heart and the execution squad again. It seemed to be his voice, but someone else was involved: I was now very pleased to have discussed the unlikelihood of Kastor choosing a heart as a code image. The images faded and I ate the melting ice cream, carefully shuttering off any ideas of messages that he would use with me. I hoped that Joel had been as good as his word, not telling the surveillance centre of our meeting, remembering Theodora's comment about his keen sense of justice. If there was a devious plan to trick Kastor, Joel would not approve, I was certain of that. I focused on the thought house in my mind, placing optimistic, innocent ideas in the upper rooms, while storing doubts and the beginning of a strategy deep in its cellars. I sensed strongly that I'd be hearing from Gaston or someone in the surveillance team very soon.

I went to one of the coffee rooms, where I recognised one of the mothers who had attended antenatal classes with me. It was Agnes, Finley's mother. I had only seen her a couple of times at the nursery.

"Hello Cassandra!" she called. "I suppose we'll see you at the concert on Thursday?" Agnes had low telepathic ability, but Finley was developing with much higher skills. I had forgotten about this concert at the children's centre, where the nursery group would be performing a song early in the evening.

"Oh, yes, of course," I said, thinking that I'd rather not go to the nursery for a few days, wondering if I was due for a severe reprimand from the chief house mother.

"Finley and Leander are such great friends," Agnes said to her companions. "They're top of the class for picture transmission." I was surprised that Agnes had drawn attention to either of the children. It was not the norm at Binaries to show preference, even for parents.

"I'm looking forward to seeing all of them," I said carefully. "It's always a pleasure to see Binaries children." The others nodded, feeling a little wave of sympathy for Agnes, who could scarcely make any images and they sensed too, that Agnes had wanted them to acknowledge her connection, however small, with me.

When they left to return to their duties, I lingered, never able to finish a cup of coffee as quickly as most people. I touched my crystal earrings, thinking about Kastor and where he was at that moment. But I avoided trying to visualise him. There was nothing I could do, if he was in trouble. I would just have to wait for more definite evidence. An image of Gaston's face appeared, looking for me. He nodded in a friendly way and I gave a thought nod in return. He was calling me to the surveillance centre. *Here we go*, I thought, carefully checking that my thought house was in order and that all my guards were up.

With some surprise, I recognised the interview room with the black shiny panel: the one with the viewing screen where I'd been interviewed on first arriving at Binaries. *"They're really keeping an eye on me,"* I reflected, in a shuttered thought, as I smiled innocently and took a seat at the table. It was just Gaston and Manes, but I sensed two others watching from the other room, through the black mirrored wall. I felt a tingling in my neck as their attention focused on me. One of the watchers was unknown to me but the other seemed familiar. I put that aside while greetings were exchanged. Gaston nodded benignly, Manes with more concern. Gaston composed one of his more sincere expressions that did not suit the cynical lines of his face.

"I hope you managed to get some sleep. Manes told me you seemed quite exhausted when he called this morning."

"I'm sure it was a tiring night for all of us," I murmured.

"What lovely earrings," said Gaston, "Kastor is quite the romantic, isn't he?"

I smiled wanly, radiating thoughts of missing him.

"Yes, well, we were wondering if he's been in touch?"

"Obviously, it's a bit soon," said Manes. I nodded, waiting for them to introduce the subject of codes.

"So you haven't sensed him at all?" asked Gaston.

"Um, there was something just now, in the coffee lounge," I said tentatively. "But I think it was just my wishful thinking." Gaston prompted me to tell them about it.

"It's silly really," I said, "just a heart… and the idea that he's worrying about something. I promised I wouldn't try to contact him, to be a distraction."

"Ah," said Gaston. The hairs on the back of my neck practically stood on end as I sensed someone completely focusing on me in the room beyond. He has sandy hair, I thought, deep in the cellars of my thought house. Possibly that keen officer, Tad Lemur. Gaston was studying me closely, trying to probe my thoughts. I gazed innocently back at him, feeling certain I was now his match at keeping things concealed.

"But we want you to contact him, Cassandra," said Gaston. I noticed that Manes looked uncomfortable, studying some papers in the file in front of him. "You see," Gaston went on, "apparently Ryden has been trying to reach you. He appears to struggle a bit with transmission at this distance – seems to think you've been blocking him?"

Certainly not, I signalled, with appropriate indignation. "I've been expecting him to make contact, but there hasn't been anything, not even a phone call."

"Yes," said Gaston, a little hurriedly, "we're not suggesting you've been uncooperative, not at all." He smiled and I thought of crocodiles, quickly suppressing the image but I knew it wouldn't bother Gaston. "Fortunately," continued Gaston, "one of our surveillance officers, Mr. Lemur, has established quite good contact with him in the field. Ryden and Kastor are making good progress, but they need your help." I raised my eyebrows.

"I'm not trained in surveillance."

"No, but you're an excellent telepath – and with those other intriguing powers to see future events. They need to know what the subject is planning to do."

"Kastor can do that, surely?"

"Not like you," said Manes, looking up at me, but still with a troubled expression. I felt a chill, knowing they had something much more direct than remote viewing in mind.

Gaston sat back, nodding silently at the wall behind me to call one of the watchers in. A few seconds later, Tad Lemur entered the room. He had an attractive, open face but I sensed he was hiding his thoughts, now very grateful that I'd been tipped off by Joel. Tad sat at the table, smiling warmly.

"Hi Cassandra, such an honour to be working with you."

I nodded politely. Gaston beamed from one to the other. "Tad Lemur is one of our up and rising officers. Tad, perhaps you could explain what Ryden and Kastor would like Cassandra to do."

"Ryden, well, both he and Kastor, have been trying to contact you, asking you to come out to meet with them – and the subject."

"Really?" I said. "I thought I was just imagining things – it seemed far too early to hear from Kastor."

"But you have sensed something?" Tad asked, with a slightly disappointed air. *So it was you*, I thought, in a dark, hidden corner of my mind. I projected an image into one of my open thought rooms, of a firing squad and Kastor asking me to come.

Picking this up, Tad smiled delightedly. "Yes, Kastor has been asking you to come. The firing squad, that's nothing to worry about. It may just be a code, or something like that, between you?"

"Oh," I said, taking great care to shutter off all other thoughts. "Yes, but it was supposed to be very secret, just for us."

"No need to have secrets with us," said Gaston, "But Tad, we don't want to intrude on lovers' private messages, do we? You shouldn't have tried to pick that image up from her."

I touched one of my earrings, idly visualising a little heart as if unaware they'd be picking it up, before apparently recollecting myself and giving Gaston a cool look. I could tell he was remembering me, rosy cheeked, greeting him in my dressing gown at our apartment. Gaston had the grace to look slightly embarrassed as Manes coughed, meaningfully, beside him.

"The important fact is," said Gaston, wiping all such images, "that you sensing these thoughts from Kastor means that he is indeed trying to reach you. Tad, outline your plan."

"They've arrived at the Cadiz centre," said Tad. "The subject will be brought to them there. Our plan is to get you out there, just for a day, to help them in the early stages."

"No," I said firmly. "If Kastor wanted me to come, he'd have been more definite. If anything, he was just thinking about me. He wouldn't want me involved in this mission." Gaston shifted in his seat, with an air of irritation.

"You must try to disengage your emotions, Cassandra. It may be that Kastor was a little reluctant to have you involved, but things have changed. Tad has been in frequent contact with them both."

Tad was a good telepath, but I sensed immediately that this lie had caught him off guard. I guessed that he had only been in communication with Ryden. But I turned to him, radiating trust and good will.

The Execution Code

"Just to the Cadiz centre, you say?" I murmured, to raise his hopes.

"Yes – you'll be quite safe. Travel by private jet and then straight back."

Manes looked across at me quickly. "Well, not by private jet – unfortunately, we don't have one available on Friday." I sensed he had been arguing about this, before my arrival. Tad looked only momentarily disconcerted. "Oh, yes, sorry, I forgot. But we'd send an escort with you on a scheduled flight. First class, of course. You'd be met at arrival, shadowed every minute."

"Kastor wouldn't have it any other way," purred Gaston, "We wouldn't dream of putting you in any danger."

"Friday," I murmured. "I've promised to do some work on Friday morning."

"We can get that cancelled," said Manes, but I shot a warning thought across to him, replying, "No, I'd insist on keeping to that obligation. It concerns a very important, lucrative assignment. I've not been working well, worrying about Kastor. I need to do this."

Gaston and Manes exchanged glances, Manes sending a clear message that work for the Binaries at this level needed to be given priority.

"Very well," said Gaston, "Can you work around that Tad, arrange for her to fly out in the afternoon?"

Tad, ever helpful, nodded. "Yes, I can book a flight for her and the escort to Jerez. I could clear my commitments to be the escort."

"We need you here," said Manes, "as the main contact for them. We don't want you out of communication for a few hours, on a public flight." Gaston nodded in agreement and I sensed Tad's great disappointment.

"Possibly," said Gaston, noting Tad's eagerness, "We could

consider you being the escort to collect her, after she's seen the subject."

"I think I'd be the best person – I'd be able to sense any problems," said Tad, excited at the prospect.

Gaston nodded round the table, signalling that they were done. "So, just a couple of days to prepare, Cassandra. We'll give you some background information. Manes, can you see to that?" Manes nodded. I sensed he wanted to ask about this important assignment that was delaying their plans, but I signalled to him that we could discuss it later.

15

I waited until I was well clear of the surveillance centre before sending a quick signal to Simon Arbalest. He nodded, indicating he was free and I sent back an image of one of the private coffee rooms, picking one several levels below. G23, where I occasionally met up with friends. I was pretty sure I could find that. I didn't feel that the surveillance team was trying to track me. They were too pleased that I'd agreed to the Cadiz visit. I visualised Tad talking excitedly about the plan and saying he would try to contact Ryden and Kastor immediately. When I entered the coffee room, Simon had already ordered refreshments and greeted me with enthusiasm.

"You've been thinking about our proposal, for Lily this Friday?"

"Yes, just a very quick visit, it would have to be the morning. Would that work for you?"

Absolutely, he signalled. "We'll order a car to take you there, I'll also bring a couple of my best officers. I'll have any necessary briefing ready for you by tomorrow."

"I'd like Phoebe to come, for experience. She grew up outside, as I did. I'd like to mentor her."

Simon looked doubtful. "She's still very inexperienced."

"Just to watch, not to participate," I said. "I think she has potential. The journey would give me a chance to assess her a little." Simon started to shake his head, but I signalled that it was not negotiable.

"You know this is the first time Lily West will have been seen outside," I said. "That's my condition." He nodded agreement, with reluctance.

"One more thing," I said, taking a drink of herbal tea from the tray. "Don't say anything about this to the surveillance teams, any of them. They wanted me to go somewhere else on Friday morning - I had trouble persuading them. As far as they're concerned, it's just a commercial visit, very important to our income."

"Well, quite so," said Simon, a little puzzled at the secrecy, but happy at keeping things from the nosy surveillance team, especially Gaston.

"Particularly, don't mention Phoebe. Gaston or someone else would doubtless disapprove."

"You're a bit of a rebel," said Simon, with secret admiration. "You natural telepaths! You're not brought up to automatically obey everything, are you?"

"No," I said, smiling. "But that doesn't mean we're not loyal, or that we don't have complete commitment to Binaries work."

"That's what I like to hear," said Simon, thinking that Kastor was such a lucky devil to have found me, enjoying this rare conference alone in a social setting and thinking wistfully about how it would be to know me more intimately. He remembered too late to conceal this thought, but I grinned mischievously, radiating pleasure at the escapade and at our joint conspiracy. He'll do his best to keep all this from the spies, I thought as I left the room.

While Simon was attending to the arrangements, I signalled quickly for Phoebe to meet with me. The girl's face appeared in my mind, looking surprised and pleased. *Askey's Pagoda, fifteen minutes*, I signalled, adding a 'keep it secret' thought and Phoebe nodded. When I arrived at the Pagoda underground station, I sensed that Phoebe was already waiting just outside. I stepped out into the gardens, looking up at the windows of our apartment from which I viewed the pagoda so frequently. I walked around the back of the building, finding Phoebe sitting patiently, shivering a little in the December chill. When I told her about the prospective visit, Phoebe was thrilled, forgetting the cold.

"I thought it'd be good for you to see one of the outside commercial centres. Even I haven't been inside one. You'd just be an observer, of course. You might not be allowed to join the full meeting."

"No, I wouldn't expect that! But it would be wonderful – thank you so much for thinking of me! Ashara will be madly jealous..."

"Don't tell Ashara," I said quickly. "Just say it's a work task Simon has asked you to do. Don't even say it's outside, or to do with me." Phoebe looked worried. She had been in Binaries long enough to know that secret arrangements were forbidden. An image of her twin, the real Phoebe, sneaking out to have fun but finding only death, came unwillingly to mind. I nodded sympathetically.

"Don't worry, I'm not arranging anything dangerous for you. It's just that I made Simon agree to your coming and it wouldn't do for others to think they could go outside so easily."

"What's the meeting about?"

"New clients, who insist on meeting with me. We don't let them see how we work, as you know. But on this occasion, they just want to see that I really exist, I guess."

Phoebe nodded. She would have agreed to any condition to go on this trip. "There's another matter," I continued, "but I can't say more, yet. I need to trust you completely, Phoebe." I gazed into the girl's eyes, sensing only curiosity and a little concern about what she might be getting into. I felt she could be trusted. "It's because we both came from outside," I said, "and both lost our twins, before we had a chance to know them."

"You can rely on me," said Phoebe, remembering how we had talked about her entry into the organization, shortly after she had arrived.

"I'm working on something," I said, "and I think you could help. It would use your gift for styling, for one thing."

Phoebe looked delighted, thinking of a fashion project.

"Sorry to be so vague," I went on. "But let me know a good time to talk again, tomorrow or Thursday."

Phoebe suggested one of the library sessions, when they were supposed to be writing up projects. I fixed a time and place for the following day. I looked around the garden, pleased to note that there was no one else about. I felt strongly that Phoebe would be able to help, although it was more of a precognition than a structured plan. "You'd better get back," I said, leading Phoebe to the station door. "I'll signal if there's any problem about the meeting."

Phoebe took the train back to the commercial centre, while I made the short journey to the Askeys staircase. Back in the apartment, I closed my eyes briefly, trying to pick up if any more listening devices had been placed. Kastor would be better at this, but I sensed nothing out of the ordinary. In the bedroom, I carefully examined the wall behind the bed, noting the slight mark from left by the tiny microphone. I could not relax until I'd checked every corner of the room. Then I looked at the back of the mirror, sensing that the hidden notes were still there. I fetched a pair of tweezers and teased them out of the space behind the panels. I then placed the notes carefully inside a book on the bedside table. I sat on the bed, where my reflection from the cheval mirror showed me to be looking tired and pensive. The earrings sparkled in the glass and I smiled across at them. *Kastor,* I thought, *Kastor are you trying to contact me? I don't believe what they told me, but even so?* With a start, I saw Kastor very clearly in my mind, boarding an aircraft, being helped up the gangway. This is him leaving, I thought, sadly, it's just an after image. But Ryden-Loki wasn't with him. I looked again, seeing Kastor looked weary, drowsy and certainly not happy. The plane was a small one, smaller than I'd have expected for the flight to or from England. A newspaper floated past, with Friday's date.

"This journey is going to happen," I thought, *"He'll be making a trip from Cadiz."* Why should he be doing that, I wondered, if they wanted me in Cadiz with them on Friday? There was nothing in the mission notes about leaving Cadiz. I focused again, seeing Kastor sitting on the plane, slumped on a pillow, possibly taking a nap. He seemed to be unaccompanied. I had read in the mission folder that they were to be accompanied by a field officer at all times. Perhaps the officer was elsewhere on the aircraft? The image faded. I was too tired and the effects of too much caffeine were wearing off, leaving profound fatigue in its place. I tossed off my shoes and suit and crept under the bed cover, feeling that all would be clearer after a bit of sleep.

At first there were no dreams as the need for deep sleep engulfed me. Then I became aware of being in a room, somewhere warm, with bright sunshine pouring in.

"Terrible mix up," I heard someone say. It was the god Loki, with a beard and the garb of a jester. "Flight has been redirected to Casablanca. We'll have to bring her over from there, but..."

"But what?" said a man, who turned, showing the face of Kastor.

"We can't trust them, not since the centre collapsed. But she'd trust anyone, wouldn't she? I mean, they could spin her a tale and she'd go off with them."

"There'll be an escort..." said the figure I thought was Kastor.

"Hah!" said Loki. "Easily dealt with."

"She wouldn't agree to come."

"Already has, old boy!" Loki produced a flagon of wine, pouring Kastor a generous glass. "There's nothing for it, we'll have to get over there, intercept them." Kastor pushed the wine away and Loki started laughing, ripples of laughter that shook his body. I woke up, feeling the alarm of rousing from a nightmare. I told myself that this was just worry about Friday's journey. It was seeping into my all too vivid imagination.

It was early evening and quite dark outside. I sat up on the bed, looking round the silent room. I saw a glimmer of light in the cheval mirror, wondering if it was reflecting something within the room or a light from outside. But it appeared to come from within the mirror. I put on the bedside light and went towards it cautiously, staring at the dim reflection within and thought of the last time my twin had seemed to briefly appear.

"Sister, sister Cass," I heard, softly, from within the mirror. "You keep calling for me, you know," the voice went on. "You have to come through." The woman in the reflection held out a hand. I instinctively lifted mine to touch it.

"Helen?" I asked, uncertainly.

"Yes, it's me."

"You're a ghost?" I was not particularly afraid, after all I'd witnessed at the Binaries of the strange ways of thought and other dimensions.

"No, Cass, I didn't die. A boat, I got away. Too boring to talk about now. What is it, that keeps you calling me?"

"I'm not," I said, puzzled. But I reflected that I'd been thinking more of Helen recently: how she would manage an outside mission, how she would protect myself against hazards in the nasty world of spying. Helen tilted her head, smiling at me.

"Come through, then we can talk. It's OK really, I know it's hard to trust me, but that was just a one off, the awful thing I did. It's a very private space in here, I can only share it with you."

I hesitated, pressing my hand against the glass, wondering at the way the reflection followed my movements but not precisely. I thought of *Through the Looking glass,* and decided that this must be an Alice dream. I felt the glass melt away as I pushed my hand through, finding I could now feel a narrow space on the other side. Helen helped me step through. On the mirror side, we both looked rather blurry, insubstantial.

"It's all right, you can step back whenever you want."

"Where are we?" I looked round at the space, which was in darkness, with no structures visible.

"I'm not sure," said Helen. "I think it's a twin space, just for us. I discovered it the other day, when you saw me. I can't cross your way though, not that I'd want to find myself deep in Askeys, right now."

"You look different."

"So do you," my twin retorted.

"Is that a nose job?" I asked, peering at Helen in the strange mirror gloom.

"Just clever make up and lots of facial toning. I had to lie low for a while, obviously, but I didn't want plastic surgeons mauling me, especially the ones recruited in back streets. But I can tell you my adventures another time, it's you that's been calling."

"The call of the twin," I murmured.

"Yeah, I was a complete bitch, playing that trick on you, trapping you in Binaries. I owe you, big time. I reckon that's what this way of communication is about, a way of balancing one's misdeeds. And there are several of mine that I can't ever put right. But I can help you. Just tell me what you want me to do."

I would have stood back, to examine Helen more carefully, but found the space was very restricted.

"Cosy, isn't it," observed Helen. "But not for long chats. So spill the beans, sister, is it something to do with Kastor?"

"Yes," I said, thinking, either this is a dream and it doesn't matter, or it really is Helen and she could possibly help. "He's gone on a mission, but it's a trap. There's an ambitious telepath from Virginia, I think he's getting him kidnapped." Helen nodded, as though not in the least surprised.

"What does he look like?" I sent an image of Ryden-Loki.

"Nasty," agreed Helen, "although not unattractive."

I told her briefly about the twin swap and how Patrick had been eliminated.

"I didn't mean that to happen to you," Helen said quickly. "You believe that now, don't you?" She looked utterly miserable. I picked up her deep loneliness, living outside our community. "But no time for my remorse now," said Helen, "Go on."

I told her what I knew – after all, this was some kind of dream venue. Helen looked very concerned when I informed her that they'd arranged for me to go to Cadiz.

"And you saw Kastor getting on a plane, on the day that you were supposed to be meeting him?" I nodded. "How did he look?" asked Helen. I said, very tired, he had to be helped onto the plane. Helen shared a thought, that he was possibly drugged, urging me to try to visualise that plane again. Together we shared the image, looking round at the passengers.

"Is that him, this Ryden trickster, at the back?"

"Why, yes," I said, "so he is going to be on the plane."

Helen focused on the Ryden figure. "Don't worry. I don't think anyone but us can pick up stuff in this space." She appeared to be probing deep into Loki's thoughts. "I can't be sure, this is all obviously a bit distorted by the mirror. But he isn't just after Kastor – he wants you as well."

"Kidnap us both? Why?"

"Two telepaths for the price of one, maybe, more likely a much higher price for you two treasures. Well done, by the way, for doing so well here." Helen projected images of me as Cassandra alias Lily West and the popular member of Binaries, also the proud mother of a gifted child, all without apparent rancour. "Yeah, I was very jealous when I sensed how well you'd adapted. Gaston told me, too. But I've had time to reflect – I now think you're doing it for both of us. Anyway, no time for us to kiss and make up, you really do need my help."

I nodded, "But what can you do – where are you in the real world, anyway?"

"Living with a rich man, of course," said Helen with a smile. "This one's OK, a bit possessive but then he's an Arab, Faisal. I'm Jasmina Thorpe, English mother of Arabic extraction, American father somewhere in the States. Faisal's a bit telepathic, you know how they can be rather mystical. It helps me feel almost at home."

"And you can travel?"

"Yes of course. Dotes on me, I'm good at that. He wants us to marry, but I'm not sure about how his mother would take that. Anyway, to the point, Cass, you must not go on this trip to Cadiz. I assume they've an identity for you, a change of look?"

"Well, in the morning I'll be Lily West" – I told her about the unusual visit to the London offices. "I'm guessing I'll be less flamboyant for the Cadiz trip. Long bob, glasses, lots of beige."

"I'm going to take your place," said Helen, in a matter of fact tone. "Just give me some clues about your persona for the trip, as soon as you know for sure."

"How can you possibly do a swap? I'll be escorted the whole time. I've thought of getting a young student, Phoebe, to help me escape, but now I'm thinking it wouldn't be fair to involve her."

"No, that's a good plan. We may need a diversion. I'm thinking of a switch in the Ladies – they usually send male escorts. If there's a woman, a judo expert like me for example, we'd need a distraction to keep her clear while we swap over."

"Even if we manage that," I said, "what are you going to do in Cadiz?"

"Play it by ear. In your vision, Kastor was going to Casablanca. Any other clues?"

"Well, I dreamt that Loki – that's what I call Ryden – was laughing about a plane having to land in Casablanca and a woman who'd trust anyone. I guess he was referring to me."

"He doesn't intend anything good for either of you, that's for sure. There's a market in telepaths, perhaps they just want you as extra leverage on his cooperation, or vice versa. In any case, if he's trying to sell you or Kastor, he's vermin." She glanced sideways. "There's someone coming, got to go. Talk again, early morning."

She vanished and I was back on the other side of the mirror, looking at my own reflection. I sat on the bed, wondering if it was just a strange dream. Then I looked at the bedside clock. It was 7:30pm, giving me just time to get ready to go to dinner with Theodora.

16

Walking towards the door of Theodora's apartment, I wondered how much to tell her about these developments. Theodora was too perceptive to miss much, so I decided I'd just see whether Theodora wanted to discuss my concerns. The door opened slowly as I approached and Theodora peeped round it, smiling. I could hear singing coming from within the apartment.

"Flower duet?" I asked, and Theodora nodded. "You're getting better at recognising pieces," she said approvingly. "This one from Lakmé is particularly suitable for girl twins. You've been thinking of twins, have you not?"

I nodded, realising that Dr. Theodora Sage was, as usual, a step ahead of my thoughts. I paused at the hall table, since selecting something from the collection of objects had become a regular introduction to an evening with Theodora. My attention was drawn immediately to a bell. It was made of mirrored glass, twinkling in the light. Theodora signalled for me to pick it up. I hesitated, as the singers were still working through the duet. As I paused, the song ended. When I lifted the bell and gently shook it, there was a sweet ringing note.

"Calling, announcing, the beginning of a new phase," murmured Theodora.

"Apt as always," I said, putting it down. "What were they singing about, in that duet?"

"It translates as a scene with jasmine entwined with a rose on a river bank of flowers. It ends with the laughing flowers calling each other, *'nous appellent ensemble'*."

"Ah," I said, "Jasmine and Rose, getting in contact."

Theodora looked sadly at me. "You've been dreaming, perhaps, of Helen?"

"Yes," I acknowledged. "A very strange dream. She was called Jasmina – a funny coincidence." I hesitated, knowing that there were few coincidences in telepath world. "Anyway, she said she wanted to help me."

"It's time for her to do that," observed Theodora. "The way we grow up forms a network. We can feel each other's presence, we know when one of us is suffering or calling for help. It's one reason why we like to stay together, away from outsiders. It gives strength, but also makes obligations."

"When I was just an unknown on the outside, she didn't feel… obligated to me." I still felt the painful disappointment of realising that the twin, whom I'd so long yearned to meet, wanted only to take my place outside.

"Just so. But Helen acted impulsively, thoughtlessly. I'm sure she deeply regrets it, especially now you're within the network, assimilated into our community. Do you feel that?"

I nodded. "But this Ryden-Loki, he planned the switch with his twin and I don't think he feels any regret at all."

"No." Theodora shook her head with some distaste. "But come through and see what we have for supper. Shall I put on on some more music?"

I signalled that I'd like that, following my hostess to the small dining room. The table was elegantly laid, with cold meats, salad and a tureen that I hoped contained new potatoes. Theodora selected a piece on what appeared to be an antique record player. She used modern media, but preferred older casements. I was startled to hear *La Campanella* start playing. I had not listened to this since the day that Patrick had been interviewed. Theodora looked at me keenly.

"I'm so sorry," she said, "I was thinking of bells, but this reminds you of the fate of Ryden's twin." I nodded, but indicated we should let it play to the crescendo of anger at the end.

"There are very few twins that grow up together in our organization, for obvious reasons. It's hard for you to understand that this separation is, for us, complete. We don't need the other version of ourselves. Such callousness as Ryden has displayed is rare, but who knows what would happen if we all met our twins?" I nodded, sitting at the table. Theodora did not put on any further music when the Liszt piece had come to an end. For a while, we were occupied in serving up the light meal. I was glad just to be with my kind mentor and friend. But the forthcoming trip to Cadiz loomed heavily in my mind. It was relaxation enough not to have to shutter my thoughts.

"Tell me about this trip, the one they've asked you to do," said Theodora, "I'm rather astonished at this proposal."

"Have they told you about it?"

"I just picked that up from your thoughts.

"They say Kastor's been asking for me – but he hasn't."

Theodora observed me, silently.

"And there's another traitor – a young man in the surveillance centre, Tad Lemur. At least, I'm pretty sure he's involved in this plot of Ryden's. Perhaps there are others involved, maybe even Gaston…"

"Gaston, no, he's loyal. He's extremely able, but can be very dense, sometimes, when he's pursuing something. Like a ferret, or a fox after a prey - he just sees the prey."

"And who is the prey, in this mission?"

"They've been trying to pin down someone for a long time, a dealer in telepaths. One who recruits, but also has no scruples. Our organization has benign aims, even if you find its methods sometimes ferocious. Others are much more threatening."

I did not ask how Theodora knew so much. In her role, she must be assessing spies and such daily, I reflected, seeing Theodora raise her eyebrows at this thought, but not denying it.

"I think they want Kastor and me, both of us."

Theodora did not respond to this, gazing into the middle distance as though deep in thought. Then she returned to an earlier topic.

"About Gaston - he didn't know about the unpardonable intrusion of that listening device."

I wondered how she could be so sure, then corrected the thought, for Theodora of all people would know if Gaston was lying.

"Kastor thought it was the nanny, the one who came to our apartment." We shared an image of the nanny, standing primly at the door.

"She's young, pretty," mused Theodora. "Easily led, I imagine."

"Should I try to tell Gaston?"

"It's best if you just focus on this unfortunate mission. I shall deal with the matter."

"Perhaps she was just punishing me, for bringing Leander here." Theodora shrugged as if her motive were of no importance and asked me if I'd like some more potatoes.

"There's an interesting dessert – licorice sorbet."

"I love licorice!" I meanwhile helped myself to more of the first course.

I had not had such a good appetite for days. "And it's funny,

I've been absolutely craving licorice lately. Black thoughts, leading to wanting black sweets, maybe."

"And how are you feeling in the mornings?" asked Theodora, gazing at me.

"Oh, a bit nauseous. It's all the worry."

"I think not, although of course you have been worrying."

I suddenly realised what Theodora was getting at.

"Oh, no, I couldn't be."

Theodora smiled enigmatically. "It would explain one reason for your thoughts being all over the place." I tried to think when I had last had a period. I was rather erratic with those, as with so many things.

"Well, I'm a bit late, I just thought…"

"No need to check on that, just yet," said Theodora. "We have to get you through this week, first."

I instinctively felt my lower abdomen, there was no bump, but now I focused, it seemed very likely that I was pregnant. Perhaps twins, I thought, aghast, but Theodora appeared to be concentrating on the meal. When she looked up, it was to prompt me to speak more about the Cadiz trip.

"I'm going to try to give them the slip, at the airport," I announced.

"I see," said Theodora. "Is that where Helen may be able to help?"

"Yes, she said she'd come…" I suddenly felt very foolish. This could all be a dream, with Helen dead, just a ghost, giving me false hope. I had not meant to think about the mirror, but it came unwillingly to mind.

"Ah!" said Theodora, greatly interested. "You've had mirror

contact. I wondered. That's very rare, you know. Almost like magic, is it not?" I nodded, mentioning the tiny space where we seemed able to communicate.

"An illusion of the mind," murmured Theodora, "but that doesn't mean you weren't in communication. Did Helen say you called her?"

"Yes, but I'd only been thinking that she'd know what to do."

"Just so. Interesting. I knew she was alive, of course." No point in asking how Theodora knew this, but I waited for her to say a little more.

"She'd be angry, extremely angry, at this threat to you and Kastor. These are things that transcend the other matters, her jealousy of your outside life, her wish to taste it. She may have found, at last, a true purpose for her anger and abilities."

"So, you think I can do it, elude them?"

"Don't you?" Theodora got up, fetching the dessert from the trolley where the china dish containing the sorbet nestled on a bed of ice. It tasted divine and I could have eaten a bucket of it.

"You're still lacking a little confidence about your powers. Now is the time to lose those fears, Cassandra."

"It's Helen who'll need powers, if she goes in my place."

"And you, how will you leave the airport? Supposing there are still field operatives around?"

"I'm not sure," I faltered. I had just assumed that if all went well, I'd hide in the Ladies toilet for a few minutes, then catch a taxi back to the Binaries.

"You must use all your persuasive powers and your ability to melt into the background, like during invisibility exercises. And don't come back to Binaries straight away. You need to hide somewhere."

"For how long?" I asked, seeing a major flaw in my plan. Gaston's operatives would be able to find me in no time.

"Not long, I think. These traitors, particularly Ryden, will soon show their hand. Then the misguided directors of this mission will need you, desperately."

I thought, I'm frightened, no, I'm terrified. Theodora looked at me sympathetically, but with encouragement to keep a level focus. She intimated that I'd find more strength, once I was on this dangerous journey.

"Will it be safe to try to contact you, from outside?" I asked.

"Yes, by Friday evening, things will be much clearer – don't you feel that?"

"I can't see anything clearly."

"Tonight," said Theodora, "try to dream of events in a few months time, or later. That will help, catching glimpses of the future – to confirm you have one."

This was not totally reassuring. But Theodora was now reaching for a pot of peppermint tea, to conclude the meal. She had quietly put on the burner under the kettle while I was devouring the licorice dessert. While we drank the tea, Theodora put on Mozart's sonata duet for two pianos. "Twin power," she murmured. I thought of facing Helen across two pianos, playing at concert level.

"I have every faith in you," said Theodora, as I left, "although the piano playing may take a little longer to perfect."

I ran a bath, feeling it would help me sleep, although I certainly felt tired enough already. I listlessly checked the bedroom for microphones, deciding to trust Theodora's word that the bugging would not happen again. When at last I felt ready for bed, I took the notes from the hiding place in the mirror frame. I leafed through the sketches of the photographs I'd seen. Helen, if she reappeared in the mirror, would want all this information. But sleep overtook me, the notes slipping from my hands. I was dreaming when I sensed an interruption from outside the world of sleep. The dream was quite pleasant. I was playing on a seashore with Helen, then playing with two little girls. Gaston swept by, followed by a crowd of chattering oysters, but he was ignoring them. I was surprised also to see Marcie Brown, the mistress of Ryden's twin, strolling along the beach, holding a camera and whisking off her scarf to give a stylish wave. Then I saw a sunny villa, overlooking the sea. It was time for tea, I realised, seeing a table laid and a bell being rung to indicate it was ready. I heard Helen's voice.

"Cass! Wake up!" The cups and other china on the table rattled, leaping in the air. I became aware that the voice was within the bedroom, as I woke blearily and saw a glow within the cheval mirror. I glanced at the clock: 5:30 am. But I got out of bed, walking towards the mirror.

"At last," I felt the reflection say, urging me to come into the space behind it. I looked round, seeing the notes lying on the bed and floor. Hurriedly, I picked them up before stepping into the mirror.

"It's the middle of the night," I murmured to Helen, when I stood beside her. In the darkness, neither of us could see much of the other.

"Oh, sorry, I forgot about the time difference. Faisal has just left for work. It's the best time to talk, before the staff come in."

I was holding the notes, wondering how I'd managed to bring them through the glass. Helen looked down at them, pulling a torch from a pocket: she was more organised than me. We were amused to see that the notes were in mirror writing, backwards. But Helen was interested in the sketches.

"This man, the one you've noted may be in Casablanca, Abdul-Azim – can you conjure up the image of his photo?"

I could, mentioning that he seemed to be involved in the kidnap plot, as far as I could sense.

The Execution Code

"Yes," agreed Helen. "They need to get you both to Casablanca. I don't think the flight will be redirected there, though. You'll probably be travelling British Airways. I can't think why they'd change a scheduled destination."

"So Ryden-Loki will simply lie about that, to get Kastor to go there?"

"Kastor wouldn't be fooled so easily. They'll have to drug him, Cass."

"And drug you too, once you arrive?"

Helen snorted, derisively. "Well, they can have a try. Forearmed, and all that. But we need to check a few details. I've booked a flight to Heathrow – it will be Heathrow, won't it?"

"Yes, I believe so, but I'll contact you later – they'll probably give me more details today."

"I'll arrive in the morning and hang around in the first class arrival lounge. You must try to signal me, when you are nearing the airport. Any ideas for a good image to send?"

I thought and projected a toilet, flushing. Helen grinned, nodding. She went on, "And signal again, when you're approaching the check-in. I'll let you know which Ladies toilet I'm hiding out in. Now, we'll need two identical wigs – can you fix that?"

"Yes," I said, having no idea how I would justify taking two wigs. I hoped that Phoebe would help with that.

"And make up. Don't worry about clothes, I'll simply switch with you. Guess we're still pretty close in size. You do look a tad plumper, I'll wear something loose."

"Thanks for saying I'm fat," I said, "actually, I may be pregnant."

"Me too!" said Helen. "Not sure yet. It could be awkward,

Faisal really wants children, but… well we don't have time to talk babies. Hell, they'll be even keener to nab you if you're carrying another telepath. This makes it even more important. Anyway, you must find the flight time for me and other details about this trip."

"After the switch, I'm not sure how to get away from the airport."

Helen sighed. "Too bad we didn't train together in surveillance. You just walk away, keeping your thoughts shuttered. Oh, and you'll need money. That was my big mistake, when I first got out of Binaries. I'll bring a wad, don't worry. Faisal is very generous. I've told him an old school friend is ill in London. Now I can tell him she's pregnant, he'll understand that. Women looking after their women-folk."

"I may need to hide somewhere."

"Well, you're the one who really knows the outside. Try and avoid our mutual acquaintances though, it could give them a heart attack."

We giggled at the thought of a door opening, with someone fainting away at the sight of the ghost of Cassandra. But Helen pulled herself together, glancing to the side.

"Got to go in a minute, I sense someone approaching. Do you think I can take these notes?"

"Perhaps they'll vanish, when our reflections return to normal?" I said. Neither of us understood how this phenomenon worked.

"Worth a try, better not leave them in your apartment at Askeys – you'd have to destroy them anyway." I found I could not hand them to Helen, so dropped them into the narrow space in which we stood.

"I think they can't leave this space, now, unless I take them back with me."

"Leave them there. No one else can enter here, I know that at least."

Her reflection abruptly faded and I shot back through the mirror, reeling slightly and losing my balance. I glanced back, seeing my reflection tumbling onto the floor. Then I went back to bed, setting the alarm for 8 a.m. I felt a wave of nausea, wondering how I'd missed the tell tale signs of pregnancy before. I was glad that Kastor did not know. He would have worried even more. Despite Theodora's advice to try to dream of the more distant future, I had a vivid dream of Kastor in a cell, looking ill. I saw Abdul-Azim, facing Kastor across a table, demanding information, and making threats. I woke in a sweat, deciding I might as well get up, even though the alarm clock had a good hour before it sounded. I was due to meet Phoebe that afternoon, after going to the surveillance centre for the promised information about the trip. I can try to sleep after that, I thought, dressing in the darkness of the December morning.

17

When I arrived at the surveillance centre at 8:30, I went to Manes' office, finding him already hard at work, surrounded by papers. I sensed that Gaston was not around.

"Gaston's been summoned by Theodora," said Manes, looking up at me wearily. "Would you like coffee?" I said yes, then felt a bit sick and said I'd prefer chamomile tea. "My stomach is upset, I think it's the worry," I said, carefully concealing thoughts of pregnancy. He was in no mood to try to probe my mind, nodding sympathetically and ordering the tea. He pushed a slim folder towards me.

"The basic details are in there – flight and so on. You'll be given a wallet with a passport and necessary documents. Your name out there will be Sylvia Smith."

"I thought it might be Rose," I said, thinking of the Lakmé duet. Manes smiled, pointing to a line on the first paper in the folder. "Sylvia Rose Smith, you're right, as usual. You and Kastor, you're so clever."

"Unlike this mission, which doesn't seem clever at all," I said drily.

"I don't like it either. Gaston is hell bent on it, so are others. But I promise you'll be there and back in a jiffy. Kastor…" He stopped, sharing a thought with me about what Kastor probably really thought about all this. I looked around, trying to sense if Tad Lemur was nearby.

I did not try to conceal this from Manes, nor my disquiet about him, which was acknowledged with a tight nod.

"Tad's in the language lab, brushing up his Spanish. He's very keen to make a success of his first mission outside – if we let him go, that is."

"What's the Cadiz centre like?" I asked, feeling it would be futile and dangerous to talk about Tad.

"You'll like it – it's up in the Sierra Mountains, between a couple of lovely villages. There are stunning views and the food is wonderful. Pity you can't stay longer, really."

"And Kastor is there, with Ryden, right now?"

"Yes of course," said Manes, giving me an odd look.

The tea arrived and I sipped it, leafing through the folder. I told Manes about the trip to London Bridge on Friday morning.

"I see," he said. "They must be very important clients."

"So I understand," I said with genuine disinterest. "I suppose I'll have to go straight to the airport, from there? But I think Simon Arbalest will be going with me. Will he have to go the airport, too?"

"Oh, no, we'll have to send a separate car to collect you from the office. Another complication." He looked very tired.

"I'm sorry, Manny, but I couldn't put this one off. And my escort for the trip, have you arranged that?"

"Yes, I've picked a couple of good officers – and a reliable driver from a firm we use. Only one of the officers will go with you to Cadiz. Let me see, Gregory Bonmot and Mikhail Pavel. Mikhail will be the one going with you, he's OK."

"Good." I was secretly relieved that both were men, which would make it easier for the switch in the Ladies loo. Bonmot, I thought, noting the French pronounciation: Theodora had once mentioned that name to me. Manes was not his usual friendly self, obviously distracted by the pile of papers and arrangements to be made.

"Look, just take the folder into my private study, that door over there. I've got so much to get through – but do come back with any questions."

I picked up the folder and the tea, thinking that none of them were seeing the likely consequences of this mission. They were all just too busy planning it.

The folder gave very little information, just the code name of the subject and minimal background. Returning it to the preoccupied Manes, I considered the background information on Patrick and the mention, in Kastor's folder, of Patrick's girlfriend, Marcie.

"Any more news about Marcie Brown?" I called out, making Manes look up with a trace of irritation.

"No, she's no longer involved. Why?"

"Just a feeling," I murmured. Manes looked more interested. Feelings and hunches were always given careful consideration at Binaries. I had an image of her doing some kind of photo shoot with models abroad, which I shared with Manes, without mentioning the beach dream.

"Could you just check where she is right now?" I said. "Just for me, I mean. And if she's planning a trip?"

"You mustn't contact her, Cassandra," he said, also picking up that I wanted him to look into this discreetly.

"It's just a thought," I said casually, sending an urgent signal that I was begging him not to share this query with Gaston or Tad, or the agents in the field. "I don't know why it may be important, Manny – it's a big ask, but if you could keep it between us, look into it yourself?"

I looked at him pleadingly, sending hopefully subtle reminders of his close friendship with Kastor and now with me. I was fairly sure no one was snooping on our conversation, with so much to attend to that morning. Manes eyed me curiously, sensing mainly my compassion for the discarded girlfriend.

"I've got a million things to do…" he began, but I could be very persuasive. I secretly called it one of my 'Helen skills' as I could never make anyone bend to my will in the outside world.

"All right, I'll make a discreet enquiry." And tell no one, I signalled, asking him to let me know, later. He nodded, wondering what this was about. He owed it to Kastor, to put my mind at rest at this difficult time.

I walked away from his office, now getting a clearer image of Marcie, arriving in a plane somewhere hot and sunny. I felt sure that this woman was going to be involved with the events surrounding Kastor and Ryden. Distracted, I was surprised to find I was face to face with Wayland East, overall head of administration at Binaries. I rarely saw Wayland, whose duties kept him busy at our centre and elsewhere.

"Cassandra, how very good to see you," he said, in a confident, oily tone. I nodded politely, returning his greeting silently. "We're extremely grateful for your help on this mission," he continued. "I can't tell you why it's so important, but trust me, this one could make real progress for our organization."

"I'm very nervous," I said, which was nothing less than the truth.

"Of course, but have no fear!" said Wayland warmly. "I've been speaking with Gaston Ajax this morning, about how your safety is paramount. You look a little tired, my dear, I hope you're going to get lots of rest before the journey?"

He was eying me with a little too much interest, reminding me of his resemblance to a pervy teacher at school.

"I don't want to let any of you down," I murmured, in a demure tone.

"Nor will you. So keep up the good work, don't worry – Rome wasn't built in a day, you know, no need to lose sleep." He nodded benignly, stopping at a door in the corridor. I sensed he had deliberately intercepted me, to give me the benefit of his clichés and authority. I rewarded him with a grateful smile. It was important that they all thought I was innocently committed to their plans.

Then I made my way to the commercial centre. It was always a more cheerful place than the surveillance department. Phoebe and Ashara were busy testing themselves on products that had already been examined and tried in the field. Simon Arbalest greeted me with his usual good humour.

"My secretary's got all the bumpf for you, for Friday. I'm so grateful you're doing this."

I thought about telling him about the separate cars, but reflected he'd know soon enough. The least I said about my airport trip, the better. I looked through the information and the neat check sheet prepared for me. I was rather looking forward to dressing up as the dashing Lily West again. Platinum wig, snazzy specs and an expensive dress and jacket. I thought I'd have to compromise on the high heels, though, planning to take a more comfortable pair for the change at the airport. It occurred to me that I might need to make a run for it at some stage.

Phoebe was waiting for me punctually at 2 p.m. in the study room by the library. There was another student there, so I suggested in a business like manner that we should find a place to talk about products, where we wouldn't disturb others. By tacit agreement, we went to the Pagoda station stop again, sitting in a secluded part of the garden. I spoke briefly about the Lily West meeting, but soon moved on to the topic of greater interest.

"I was wondering, if, after the meeting you'd like to come onto the airport with me, so we could talk more."

"Oh, yes please!" said Phoebe, delighted that her visit outside would be extended.

"I may need your help with something. It wouldn't be dangerous at all, but I need to trust you, Phoebe." The girl nodded eagerly, despite a feeling of disquiet.

"You mustn't talk about this with anyone, at least not for a few days, until I get back."

"What is it?" asked Phoebe, now rather alarmed.

"Well, I'm planning not to go on this air trip. I sense grave danger there for me, Phoebe, you know how some of us can be very aware of that." She nodded and an image of sensing that her own twin was in trouble, just before she was killed on the outside, came to the surface of my mind. Yes, I nodded sympathetically, just like that.

"So I've found someone who's willing to take my place on the trip. We need to arrange a swap, exchange clothes and so on."

"But your escorts wouldn't be fooled by a replacement, surely?"

"She looks very like me."

"Your twin!" said Phoebe, in wonderment. I nodded.

"It's a huge secret, Phoebe." The girl gazed at me, understanding this only too well.

"What would you want me to do?" she asked, finally.

I explained that we'd need wigs and possibly a diversion, while we made the exchange. "I need to change anyway, so I'll make an excuse to go into a toilet on the way to the check-in. If you say you need the Ladies too, you could come in, keep watch. The escorts will be waiting outside – they're both men."

"I could help with make up, too, to make sure you look identical," said Phoebe, warming to the escapade. "I can get you a couple of wigs from the drama department, I've a friend there."

"Great. We'd need two identical long brown wigs."

"OK. But your twin, won't she be in this grave danger, if she goes on the trip?"

"She's better at looking after myself, you know, trained in surveillance. And she really wants to do it. She has her reasons."

Phoebe nodded. "After the swap, what will you do?"

"Hide in the loo until the coast is clear. You could really help by sending some sort of image to let me know when you and the other escort have left. One will go with my twin to the check-in. He's going to travel with her. The one with the Russian name, Mikhail something."

"I'll send an image of a wig, with wings," mused Phoebe, practising the mind picture.

"Excellent, I knew you were very talented. So if anyone picked that up, they wouldn't think it was anything more than a 'bon voyage', something like that."

We fell silent, contemplating this adventure. I realised that we should not be away from the centre any longer.

"You'll be quite safe, Phoebe. You'll just go back in the car with the escort and report, if asked, that all went well."

"The real Phoebe would want me to do this. For another twin from the outside."

I felt tears coming, as I worried about involving this young student. Picking this up, Phoebe took my hand.

"I'm on the case – I'd better get over to the drama centre straight away. How shall I get the wigs to you?"

"Oh, just pop them in your bag, the one you'll bring with you to the meeting. I can't think why you'd be searched, but you could always say you were thinking of a wig project."

We both laughed at the idea. No one was ever surprised at the strange products of interest to the commercial students.

Phoebe left me sitting in the copse near the pagoda. I felt very tired, thinking that I should just go back to the apartment and get some extra sleep. But an image of a heart shot into my mind, followed by a grim march to an execution block. Tad again, I thought grimly, shuttering off the additional thought that his images were very shallow and all too predictable. But something else was coming through, a series of binary numbers. Oh, please, I thought with exasperation. I guessed, in a deep closed part of my mind, that Joel had talked to them about Kastor and I agreeing on a binary code. I shan't even bother to note it down, I thought, but the numbers kept repeating, as if being typed onto a page:

01010011 01100001 01100110 01100101

01100011 01101111 01101101 01100101

01001011

The numbers appeared slowly, as if someone at the other end knew it would be hard to decipher the message unless it was carefully transcribed. I took out a notebook to record them, trying not to confuse the ones and zeros. I turned in the direction of the surveillance centre, projecting the thought that Kastor had contacted me. Time to go and give them the good news, I thought, moving towards the underground station.

The centre was buzzing with activity. Gaston was standing, talking to a group of field officers, while Manes and Tad were examining a folder of information. Tad looked up.

"Hi, Cassandra, it's all going well. They still won't let me be your escort, sorry about that." I smiled, not approaching them. Let them work for this stupid message, I thought secretly. Manes and Tad now looked up at me, curious about why I'd come.

"What's up?" asked Manes.

"I think I may have just had a message from Kastor. Of course it may be nothing, but…"

"No," said Tad eagerly, "we haven't heard from them today, so anything you gleaned would be good. What was the message?"

"Oh, the coded images and then a lot of binary numbers. It was hard to note them down, but I had a go."

I proffered the page from the notebook. Tad grabbed it, turning to a computer and typing the figures into an ASCII converter.

"You did well," said Tad, approvingly. "I believe the message was: 'Safe, come, K'. See here, a capital K is different from lower case in binary. Everything has a code."

"Safe – come - K," repeated Manes. I picked up a glimmer of doubt. I guessed he'd never received such a message, let alone in binary, from his friend and colleague when out in the field.

"I'm guessing he had to keep it as short as possible," said Tad, persuasively. "I mean, it's hard enough to note down just this short sequence."

"I noticed the end sequence was the same for the two words," I said. "So that was the 'e'?"

"Yes, well, he knows you're a brilliant mind reader," said Tad. "Few of us could retain the image that long, to get it all down."

"It helped that it seemed to keep repeating," I said, with as much innocent enthusiasm as I could project.

Tad grinned. "This is great. It means Kastor knows you're

worried about coming – but he's reassuring you." I noticed that Manes thoughts were shuttered, as he looked thoughtfully at us both.

"Well, this is good," murmured Manes, "so we're all set, then."

I nodded, letting him know my thoughts were shuttered, too. Manes tapped a folder on his desk.

"Just a couple more items to brief you with," he said casually, "but it can wait. You look tired. I can drop this off later at the house, go through it with you."

"Great," I said. "I do need to rest."

I left them and returned to Askeys.

18

Back in the apartment, I changed into casual clothes and examined my wardrobe for what I would wear on Friday. I decided on the outfit for the change at the airport and put a few other items into a travelling bag, including comfortable shoes. There was no need to rush. I still had Thursday to make the preparations, but who knew what the next day would bring. Also, there was that concert at the children's centre in the evening, I thought, with foreboding. I imagined a row of nannies, up on the stage, all glaring at me or pointing an accusing finger.

"This outsider," I imagined the head nanny saying, "is threatening the essential education of our children. Are we going to allow this?"

"No," chorused the audience, all turning to focus on me intently, with killer rays. I shook myself free of these thoughts, knowing that this was not a vision of the future, just my way of dealing with possible unpleasantness. Like the White Queen in *Through the Looking Glass*, upset about a brooch pinprick before it happened.

"Oh, Kastor," I thought, "I wish you were really contacting me." I tried to locate him, picturing his face, but nothing came. Perhaps he knew it was unwise, possibly he also knew of Tad's messages? I hoped so, but by now he must have been informed that I had been ordered to come. A silent knock at the door interrupted this reverie and I sensed it was Manes. "I've just come about the briefing," he said, unnecessarily, when I signalled for him to enter.

I took him into the living room. I was uneasy about microphones, despite Theodora's assurance. If Gaston had not ordered the bug, then it could be someone working without official knowledge. I shared this worry with Manes, who nodded understandingly. *It wasn't us*, he signalled. Then, also silently, he let me know that he'd found out what Marcie Brown was doing. She was leaving that evening to do a photo shoot in Morocco. He asked, again not out loud, if I thought Ryden was still interested in her. *Oh yes*, I signalled, with an image of Ryden-Loki finding Marcie an attractive bed mate. Manes smiled at this uncharacteristically lewd image from me. *Perhaps he'll arrange to meet with her*, I suggested in return but he shook his head. *Unlikely, with this difficult mission*, he thought. *Where in Morocco*, I asked, as if just vaguely interested and he thought back, *Casablanca*. I nodded.

"This is very helpful," I said aloud, looking through the slim folder he'd handed to me.

"Yes, well, just a couple more background details. You'll only be with the subject for an hour or so. I've arranged for a flight back that night. I know you won't want to hang around – unless you want to?"

"No, Kastor will be busy and preoccupied, it's best I just come straight back."

I offered Manes a drink, which he refused, saying he was going to dine out. As he prepared to leave, I asked, "Has Kastor contacted you, directly, today?"

"No, but that wouldn't be unusual. Tad and Ryden are doing the liaison. Ryden has been in touch, says all is well." But I sensed a strong thought that Manes was worried. The coded message from Kastor was odd behaviour for him.

"I'd like the flat checked thoroughly for any possible microphones or other devices," I said.

"Of course," said Manes, looking directly into my eyes, seeing the flash of anger. "We haven't got to the bottom of this, yet – I'll get a team over this evening, in an hour or so, if that won't disturb you?"

"Great," I said. "I'll eat at the Askeys restaurant."

When he left, I went into the bedroom and stared at my reflection in the cheval mirror. I touched the glass thoughtfully: it was hard, impenetrable. My communication with Helen through it was just a construct of the mind, as Theodora had hinted. But I focused on trying to contact my twin. After a few seconds, I saw the reflection shift, becoming Helen. "Not now," whispered Helen. "In the early hours, like this morning." The image vanished. I sighed. I hoped Phoebe had made good progress with the wigs and meanwhile, I'd have to wait for further communications.

I returned to the apartment after dinner, just as the surveillance team was leaving. An officer I knew only as a nodding acquaintance took me aside.

"We found another bug, under your sofa. It does look like one of ours, but it wasn't done with our authority. We'd never spy on residents of Askeys."

I paled, thinking of romping with Kastor on the sofa.

"How long has it been there?"

"Hard to say – but it would only pick up for around a metre or so of that point."

"So, not in the bedrooms or dining room, just in this area of the living room?"

I blushed, thinking of an unknown enemy snooping on Kastor and me, enjoying listening to our private moments.

"Kastor and I, well, we thought the bedroom microphone was the only one. He said he could usually detect them."

"Possibly it was put in after he left. Whoever it was may have acted after they realised you'd destroyed the other one."

"But who would do this?" I said desperately.

"Mr. Ajax has ordered a full inquiry. We'll be interviewing the cleaning staff, catering, anyone who'd be able to come in here without drawing suspicion."

"We don't have surveillance cameras inside our apartments, do we?" I asked, although surely Kastor would have known about those, I reflected immediately.

"No, but we do have surveillance in the corridors. Basic security for intruders. All that's being checked."

"A nanny came here, the other day, but she was only alone in the bedroom for a short time."

"A nanny?" said the officer with surprise. "It would need very little time to put one of those things up. Not very powerful, but they'd pick up pillow talk, if you'll excuse me saying that."

"Well, it's hard to believe a nanny would do that. I shouldn't have mentioned it."

"I'll put it in the report, anyway. They're pretty busy over there at the moment, I can't tell you when it'll get full attention – but meanwhile, the apartment is clear. And this check will hopefully scare off anyone who's been snooping."

I saw them to the door, looking round the apartment after they'd left. A bug under the sofa was bad enough, but at least they hadn't been able to hear conversation in the bedroom, or when Kastor and I had our last dinner together. Or the whisperings from the mirror. I set my alarm to 5:15 am, so as to be ready for Helen. I went to bed early, sleeping soundly and with unmemorable dreams. When the alarm went off, I sat up and put on the bedside light, watching the mirror. The time ticked slowly round to 5:30 and I saw a glimmer of light appear in the mirror. It was Helen with her torch. I tossed aside the bed covers and went up to the reflection, slipping through the now permeable glass as before.

"OK Sis, how's it going?" asked Helen. I confirmed the flight would be from Heathrow, also telling her about the wigs and the escorts.

"Good, anything else?" I told Helen about the false code from Kastor, transmitted by Tad, it seemed.

Helen narrowed her eyes, murmuring, "Ryden's either useless at long distance thoughts, or thinks you'd only be reassured by a message from Kastor."

"And there's another bit of info that could be useful. I've sensed that the girlfriend of Ryden's twin will be around – Manny checked it out for me. I think he hasn't told anyone. He couldn't understand why I was interested, except maybe compassion for a wronged girlfriend."

"The mistress," corrected Helen, remembering this detail from the notes. She asked me to share an image of Marcie Brown, nodding with interest when I said she'd be in Casablanca on Friday.

"You say she's very intuitive, that could help. Also, she could be ready for a bit of vengeance."

"She may be deeply in love with him, wanting to help him," I cautioned.

"I'll be able to sense all that. It seems likely that Ryden, and his gang, who we don't know much about yet, will be aiming to get you and Kastor together in Casablanca, for the kidnap. It's a pity I can't fly there directly, but I'll have to go through with the impersonation of you first. And avoid them trying to knock me senseless if they spot me."

"I haven't sensed Kastor at all, do you think they've already got to him?"

"Hmm, possibly," said Helen. "He's too sharp not to pick up on all this – and that Tad sounds pathetic as a secret agent, even if he is a good telepath. Ryden-Loki, he's clever, I suppose he could have persuaded Kastor all's going well though – the Cadiz centre is a nice place to be, maybe they're just relaxing, preparing notes for the interview."

"They could have made him ill – a bout of food poisoning, something to keep him in the medical centre there, what do you think?"

Helen smiled. "I think that's just what I'd do, so a definite possibility. The bastards, I can't wait to get at them."

"But you'll be careful…"

"Cass," said Helen earnestly, "I've been on the run for nearly three years and they haven't caught me – I've learned a lot about being careful."

"OK, so here's to Sylvia Smith, secret agent."

"Twin power forever," said Helen, as we shared possibly the first sincere feeling of our bond since our adventures to find each other had begun. "Check with me same time Friday morning, for all the last minute stuff."

We both left the narrow space, returning the mirror to its normal state. I selected an audio book for the player on my bedside table, something I enjoyed on the nights that Kastor slept in the bedroom by his study. It was a story about telepathic aliens and their threat to humans. "What nonsense," I thought, as the voice on the disk lulled me back to sleep, "they really don't have any idea, what it's like to be a telepath."

In the morning, I found the very thought of breakfast made me retch. I also noticed that I was going to the toilet more frequently. I gingerly felt my nipples, looking for another sign of pregnancy. There was now no doubt. I put this matter out of my mind, for I needed to concentrate on rescuing Kastor. Over at the Binaries centres, I helped Simon Arbalest with a product problem, taking the time also to talk to Ashara and Phoebe. I was especially attentive to Ashara, not wanting to appear to favour Phoebe. As I left their room, I caught an image of a flying wig and smiled. Ashara was busy, focusing on her work, so

Phoebe also gave me a little nod. The wigs were in the bag.

Gaston caught up with me as I was walking down a corridor later that day.

"My dear Cassandra, you look much more rested. I understand all the plans are now in order, but I'm sorry it'll be such a tiring day for you. The Cadiz centre people are all keen to meet with you, of course. Your fame has spread, even there."

"Have you heard from Kastor?" I asked.

"Me? I'm not involved in those communications. But don't worry, I understand he's been able to get a message through to you?"

I nodded. Then he startled me by saying, "I expect I'll see you at the concert, tonight?"

"Children singing – I wouldn't have said that was your ideal way of passing an evening," I replied.

"Oh, we all try to support our young telepaths. I fathered a child in the States, which increases my interest in how our Binaries develop."

I opened my eyes in surprise, but he did not elaborate. "See you later, then," he said, but paused before turning to march off. "Oh, and the other matter, the disgraceful bugging of your apartment. I have the report on my desk. As soon as this mission is sorted, I'll be coming down hard, very hard, on whoever was responsible."

Good, I signalled. I watched him march off, thinking about him as a father, never seeing his child. I wondered, secretly, about the mother. In a secret corner of my mind, I pictured Gaston in a loving relationship. *No*, I reflected, *just can't see it.*

The concert was due to start at 5pm, after the youngest children had finished their tea. I sent a thought signal to Leo, wishing him luck, but sensed he was preoccupied. Learning his part, I thought to myself. At the appointed time, I made my way to the small hall attached to the children's centre. Several residents and staff were already seated, examining the programme. It looked depressingly long, with contributions from every age group. I knew I shouldn't show particular interest in Leander, wondering how it would look if I left early. With my heavy commitments on Friday, it would be not so unacceptable. I saw Agnes and a friend from the assessment centre and went to sit with them. They were only three rows from the front, but the end seat was free.

When the nannies and junior teachers came on to introduce the programme, I looked nervously up at them. The young nanny who had come to the apartment was on the end. I was grateful that none of them looked in my direction. I guessed that I had been one of the main topics of conversation there, since I'd taken Leo over to Askeys. The toddlers' contribution was charming, a series of simple dance movements and a tuneless song, but their finale was to produce a joint image of a cake with a cherry on the top. The image was not very clear, some of the children obviously thinking about different colours or types of confection, but the audience clapped enthusiastically. As the older children came on, I was astonished at their abilities – playing instruments, singing some verses silently, and reciting poems with images. A couple of them had marked telekinetic skills, moving objects between them that were too heavy to be shifted by a breath, unlike the feathers in the toddler class.

When the interval came, I went up to the refreshment table. I felt the back of my neck tingle, turning to see the young nanny standing there.

"Are you enjoying the concert, Cassandra?" asked the nanny.

"Oh, yes, they're a credit to you." I reached for a glass of lemonade.

"About the other day, I should have been more sensitive. We talked about it, back here, and I realise I may have seemed cross, or too strict."

The Execution Code

"Not at all." I smiled. "It was just a crazy impulse, you know. I didn't mean to upset routines."

"Well," said the nanny, drawing me to one side, away from the others pushing to get a drink or snack, "I thought you'd like this little drawing, that Leo did yesterday." She produced a colourful scrawl on a piece of white paper, with attempts at circles and splashes of brown and yellow, with a pink blob at the top.

"Oh, thank you," I said, examining it. "What's it supposed to be?"

"He said it was you," said the nanny warmly, taking the paper back. "See, here, this blob, I think that's your face."

"Oh yes," I said, "a good likeness." We laughed and the nanny said, with nervous shyness, "I'll just pop it in your bag, shall I, so you can put it up in your apartment?" I had a shoulder bag, hanging open as one didn't need to worry about pickpockets at Binaries. The nanny slipped the paper in and moved away, smiling.

I watched her return to the other nursery staff, thinking it was kind of the nanny to think of this little gesture, attributing the young woman's nervousness to doing something quite out of the norm for Binaries. But as the nanny went to take her seat, a strong arm gripped her and I saw Gaston stooping, saying something menacing. I moved forward to defend the nanny, who had only acted out of kindness. But Gaston held up a warning hand. Two security officers, a man and a woman, appeared from nowhere and took my shoulder bag.

"We need to check this," said the woman, "It won't take a moment."

Looking round, I spotted Theodora and Manes sitting together in the middle of the hall. I signalled to them urgently. Meanwhile, the officers took my bag out of the hall. Gaston had ushered the nanny in the same direction. The incident had attracted little attention, with most people either still taking refreshment or looking for their seats. Theodora and Manes came over, looking concerned. I quickly explained.

"She was just giving me one of Leander's drawings. I don't know why Gaston's being so nasty about it." Manes looked thoughtful, saying he'd check what the officers were up to. Theodora took my arm, suggesting I sit with them.

"I don't think it's the drawing," murmured Theodora.

"I'm going to find out," I said, jumping up. "It's my bag, after all." Before Theodora or anyone else could stop me, I ran in the direction that the officers and Gaston had taken. I weaved my way through groups of children and gushing adults, seeing a door at the back of the hall.

I opened the door, hearing angry voices and the nanny's plaintive objections. "I don't know what you mean," she was sobbing, "I didn't put it there, I swear." I followed the direction of the voices, finding a small room with Gaston towering over the nanny, while the two security officers stood sternly by. I stood in the doorway, trying to interpret the scene. This was obviously something more serious than a child's scrawl. Even the Binaries didn't have rules about not having a child's picture on your wall. Gaston looked up at me. He was blazing with anger, but not, I sensed, directed at me.

"Is this the nanny who came to your apartment on Monday?" he asked.

"Why yes, but…"

"And did she just now put something in your shoulder bag?"

"Yes, a drawing, but why all the fuss?"

Gaston stood up, flicking a finger at one of the officers. He came forward, holding something in his palm. I looked, seeing a tiny disc microphone with little antennae, like the one we'd found in the bedroom.

"Cassandra, my dear," said Gaston, directing the female officer to hold the nanny securely, "I believe we've found at least one of the culprits for the disgraceful bugging incident." The nanny was in floods of tears, terrified. "Take her away, I'll deal with her in the detention centre."

I went over to the nanny, who avoided my eyes. "Did you do this?"

"No," she blurted, "Of course not." I knew she was lying. She was trying to hide her thoughts, but not effectively. I saw an image of Tad Lemur, smiling winningly from his good looking, deceptively open face. I was sure Gaston would have also picked this up. He glowered at the nanny, calming himself before turning to me.

"Stay out of this, Cassandra. I'll make sure you get a full report."

Manes was sitting quietly at the back of the room examining the contents of my bag, looking very troubled.

"Yes, most unfortunate," Gaston said, in a manner quite different from his thoughts, "but it's best for you not to be involved. We'll look into it all. I'll talk to you tomorrow."

I wanted to say, but I'm leaving for London at 7:30 am, and then flying to Cadiz, so how can we talk? But I realised there was no point in staying. Gaston walked with me, back to the door into the hall.

"It seems to be a case of misguided and overzealous surveillance," he said, very quietly. "Nothing for you to worry about. The poor girl must have thought she was helping Tad, while of course doing quite the opposite. He's quite a heart breaker, I fear."

"So he doesn't know about this?" I asked, equally quietly, sending a very doubtful thought alongside.

"It's unimaginable," said Gaston, briefly, with a thin smile. "But be assured, I shall find out how she got hold of those devices. May I suggest, now, that you sacrifice the rest of the concert and go back to your apartment? We really don't want people asking you all sorts of stressful questions, particularly before your trip."

"What about my bag?"

"It needs a detailed check, just to be sure. Are there any items you especially need, for a couple of hours? I'll make sure a reliable officer brings it over to the house, as soon as the examination is completed."

I shook my head. I had items such as tissues back in the apartment and there were no keys: we didn't use them at Askeys. I went back into the hall, then quickly to the exit, signalling briefly to Theodora, who nodded sympathetically. *"I'll be in touch,"* she sent, silently. When I emerged into the tunnel leading to the station, I was surprised to find a guard waiting.

"We've orders to escort you back to the house," he said. "Just to be on the safe side. Gaston said you've had a nasty shock."

Normally, I would have been indignant, but the microphone in my bag had shaken my confidence. Who knew what else had been organised to keep an eye on me, or worse?

19

When I finally reached my home, the guard checked the apartment quickly and declaring it safe, left me alone. I felt tense and put on all the lights, racing from one room to the other, looking for any signs of disturbance since I had left that morning. How long had that microphone been in my shoulder bag? I took it everywhere, but was fairly sure I had not left it lying around on a lunch or coffee table. Still, supposing the unknown listeners had heard my conversations with Phoebe? I trembled, sitting on the sofa, wondering if after all my assurances, I had lured that girl into something far more dangerous.

    I was not hungry, but made some toast as I'd missed dinner. After all, I reflected, I'm eating for two now, or possibly three. I directed my thoughts to the concert hall, sensing only applause. Perhaps the evening performance was ending. An image of a cell in the detention centre came unwillingly to mind. The nanny was being taken out for her first interrogation. She looked very frightened, as well she might. I had no idea what the penalty was for bugging telepaths in their homes, but guessed it would be very severe. I closed off the image, not wanting to see the poor girl being bullied or worse for information. Tad Lemur was behind this, I felt sure, but would he be cunning enough to elude firm suspicion until the abduction of Kastor had been completed? So many questions, I thought, deciding to check my packing for the next day as a distraction. I would be taking carry on luggage only, so reluctantly put aside liquid cosmetics and scent. While I had no intention of going on the flight, I'd need supplies to go into hiding for a night or two and felt I should prepare for flying, just in case. I hoped Helen would remember about the money, so that I could possibly check into a hotel near the airport.

When I'd exhausted the diversion of packing, I sat on the bed and wondered if it was too early to retire for the night. Then I heard a silent knock on the door. I signalled 'enter' and heard a polite cough from the hallway.

"It's Arthur, Miss Mason."

I went out to greet the head of household staff at Askeys, to all intents a butler, always smartly dressed and sombre in manner. He was rarely seen on the upper floors, especially in the evening. He handed me the shoulder bag. "I thought I should bring it up myself, seeing its personal nature."

"Thank you Arthur," I said, but he still hovered. "I'll be all right, now," I assured him.

"Yes, I hope so, Miss Mason, but I just wanted to say that I'm appalled, deeply shocked, at the listening devices placed in your apartment. It's being investigated at the highest level."

"Good," I said. Arthur lingered, clearing his throat.

"You may be a little reassured to know that a member of the catering staff has been, ahem, dismissed, pending further action."

"I see. Did this person plant both the bugs that were found?"

"As I understand it, the person has only admitted to placing one in the living room, under the sofa. The crime took place yesterday morning." Yesterday, Wednesday. I felt relieved, I had only seen Manes in the apartment and we'd communicated the important facts silently.

"So, not earlier – that is good to know," I murmured.

"Yes, indeed. The other device, the one in the bedroom, is still being investigated."

I nodded, adding, "Possibly, that one was placed there on Monday." Arthur shook his head, indicating the horror and shame.

"This has never happened before. I shall speak personally to all the staff, to ensure they understand the stringent penalties."

"I hope this'll be an end to it. Thank you so much for troubling to bring the bag and tell me about the other matter."

Arthur bowed and left. I hoped he was right about the timing. It was very good news to know that my evening with Kastor, and oh, Norwich, might not have been overheard after all. And the bedroom, with its mirror, was several metres from the living room – surely well out of detection range.

I made a drink to take to bed and set the alarm for 5:15 a.m. I guessed that the detention centre would be busy, now with two culprits to interrogate for the bugging. Perhaps they would cancel my trip, I hoped, if this plot involved several people. So I was relatively calm when I finally dropped off to sleep. When the alarm went off, I was dreaming that I was back in Aunt V's flat, looking at the watercolour of the beach scene with the two little girls playing. Aunt V was speaking excitedly, something about mythology and, incongruously, Gaston was standing with her, with an unusually cheerful demeanour. Remembering this dream as I awoke, I thought that I must be feeling a lot better to have such an apparently innocuous, if surreal, set of images. I got out of bed, putting on slippers as the cold of the morning filled the room. I had left the window slightly open and went over to shut it, looking out at the silent, dark parkland. Askeys seemed safe and homely, in comparison with what I'd be facing today.

I stood in front of the mirror, waiting for Helen. When 5:30 a.m. passed with no sign of her, I felt a panic. Supposing Helen was unable to travel, or to use the mirror that morning. Or possibly she'd already left for the airport for an early flight? Then I saw a glow in the mirror and my sister's reflection gazing back at me. I slipped into our space.

"Sorry, Cass, Faisal lingered to say goodbye. I told him it was just a couple of days, hope we're right."

I told her about the bugs and the incident with the shoulder bag. Helen looked alarmed.

"Wow, you've got someone really worried! I suppose you think Tad is behind this?"

"Yes, but obviously it's hard to know whom to trust, right now."

"Just as well, then, that I've made a change to the plan. I'll be coming to Heathrow, but I'll give the escort the slip at the check-in. Basically, I've booked a flight to Casablanca. I've managed to contact Marcie Brown – she's great! I'll be booking into the same hotel."

"But maybe I could have tried to slip away, to save you the journey?" I was worried about these complicated arrangements.

Helen gazed solemnly. "No disrespect Sis, but how much experience do you have, getting rid of escorts at airports? It won't be easy, but I can do it. Trust me on this."

"How did you reach Marcie?"

"Found out when she was flying, saying I was someone from a major fashion house – and paged her at the airport. We're going to meet up as soon as I arrive there, some time in the afternoon."

"I don't know when Kastor will be taken there." I thought of my vision with the newspaper flying past.

"Try and focus on that for me. I reckon they'll take him to the old centre, the one that was taken over. It's in Casablanca, I know how to find it. Obviously, I'm going to try to get him out, but first we'll need to deal with Ryden. When I don't arrive in Cadiz, he'll be panicking and, as we know, he'll have travelled from there with Kastor."

"Yes." I closed my eyes, trying to refocus on that image of the plane, trying to find a time. "Possibly mid-afternoon, I think, it's the best I can do."

"OK," said Helen, "Maybe Ryden was planning to get you both

on the flight, suitably drugged to be compliant. He'll have to be on that plane."

"And I detected a conversation, where he was talking about my flight being redirected to Casablanca. It was only a dream, but it felt very real."

"Right," said Helen. "I don't have good precognition – wonder if the training beat it out of me? But I'll trust your instincts. Ryden-Loki will be desperate to find you in Casablanca. Possibly he'll send someone to meet the flight. I'll be ready."

Helen was in her element. But I was still worried whether the hidden microphones had compromised our plans.

"Supposing someone eavesdropped on my conversation with Phoebe?" I said.

"You said the nanny was caught putting it in tonight. I reckon that was a desperate measure. Someone's very anxious about any plans or misgivings you may have. You've probably shown your reluctance for the mission a bit too clearly."

"And perhaps Tad is less confident than he seems about the pathetic messages supposed to be coming from Kastor."

"Yeah, that too," said Helen. "Anyway, to details. I think your flight would be around 2 p.m., with a stopover in Barcelona. Ryden won't know you're not on the flight until after departure, but he's probably taking a private jet to Casablanca, so he won't wait if he knows or suspects you're not going to be joining him. I've managed to find one of the few direct flights to Casablanca. It takes 3 and a half hours, leaves around 1:30 p.m. It'll be tight, but if you get to the airport in good time, I can catch that flight and be away before they realise what's happened."

"I'll keep the meeting short."

"Bring a different coloured jacket – probably you'd better give me a different wig too. Your blond Lily West one will do. Just in case

Mikhail goes looking for me. And you must make sure you look different when you leave the airport."

"OK."

"Got to go in a couple of secs, have a taxi waiting for the airport. Oh, another thing, don't wear jewellery, it'll complicate the switch. Or wear something you don't mind losing."

I touched the crystal drops, thinking I wouldn't want to lose those. "Fine, so good luck, see you at Heathrow."

"First loo you come to, after arriving at the terminal," said Helen, disappearing.

I shot back into the bedroom. I carefully removed the earrings and put them in their velvet box, at the back of one of the dressing table drawers. Then I changed my mind. I'd wear them for the Lily West meeting, for luck and confidence, and ask Phoebe to look after them. It would seem plausible that I wouldn't want to take them with me. I was far too awake to go back to bed, taking a shower and dressing as Lily West ready for the day ahead. Then I sat on the bed and tried to calm my mind, to see if any vision would come. After a few seconds, I saw Ryden-Loki. He seemed to be in a restaurant area, chatting agreeably and looking very smug. Cautiously, I tried to focus on where Kastor was. He wasn't at the breakfast table, so I mentally imagined my little camera, roving around the centre. An image that seemed to be the medical wing came into focus, and a man being helped to sit up bed by a nurse. I concentrated, not worried about being picked up. I was getting so good at channelling at long distance. The man was Kastor, looking pale and drowsy. The nurse was speaking, but I couldn't pick up the words. It was to do with a journey. Something about Kastor feeling much better by the afternoon. They're preparing him for Casablanca, I thought bleakly.

20

At about 7:15 a.m., Simon Arbalest let me know that the car was ready to take us to the office at London Bridge. Arthur ushered me to the front of the mansion, where the car was waiting. Phoebe was already sitting in the back next to Simon, looking excited. I was also pleased to have a journey, wishing that the Lily West meeting was the only one I needed to worry about. As we drove towards London, we talked about products and the ones that the new clients would be most interested in. Simon said they had wide ranging business interests, so we'd play it by ear, but there was an understanding that this meeting was only to meet Lily West, not to test me. All the same, he'd given me detailed briefing notes on their companies and I always liked to be fully prepared. It was not just about feelings and intuitions, I explained to Phoebe: clients liked to see that you knew something about the history of their products, such as those that had succeeded or failed in the past. We drove through the City of London, Phoebe avidly looking through the car windows at the sights, while Simon Arbalest pointed out a few.

"Cassandra knows London much better than I do," he murmured, "So do correct me if I get something wrong."

"It seems an eternity since I last saw it," I said. "We'll be stopping near Borough Market, Phoebe, that was one of my favourite places to meet a friend for lunch and buy some good food."

"I suppose we won't have time for lunch," said Phoebe sadly and Simon and I exchanged a sympathetic glance. Binaries life was comfortable, but hardly varied enough for the young. Phoebe stole a look at me, tapping her bag, without sending any thought messages that she might not be able to conceal from Simon. He looked quickly at her.

"What's that, Phoebe? You certainly have a large bag with you. I hope you haven't stashed it with products."

"Phoebe's kindly brought a spare wig along," I said quickly. "I'm not sure whether to ditch the blonde one later." He nodded, accepting the explanation. He had been informed that I would be travelling on to a meeting abroad after our session I had a different handbag with me, not wanting to use the tainted shoulder bag. There was also a small carry-on bag for the flight, which we'd agreed Phoebe would look after until the other car arrived to take me to Heathrow.

As we drove across London Bridge, I felt a pang of regret for having no contact, for so long, with my city. It was a grey December day, but London was built for poor weather, shining in the morning light and drizzle. I told Phoebe how they used to put the heads of executed criminals on London Bridge, sometimes for doing little more than upset the monarch.

"I've always wanted to visit the London Dungeons," murmured Phoebe, whose visits to London had been few before entering the Binaries.

"We'll see what we can do, another time." I was ever optimistic that the Binaries would one day be able to engage more with the world outside. The car drew into busy Borough High Street, stopping by a quaint old wooden doorway with wrought iron trellising in small windows on each side, like something out of a Dickensian story.

"This is Charles Dickens territory – also Chaucer, and the Canterbury Tales," I whispered to Phoebe.

"Quite an adventure," murmured Simon, who made fairly frequent visits to London, but not for sightseeing. We got out of the car, Simon leading us through the elaborate doorway into a small cobbled courtyard. There were a couple of business signs indicating law and architect offices, but Simon took us round an L-shaped bend towards an over-sized door. He tapped the ornate knocker and I thought briefly of the Fatima hand knocker in a closed part of my mind, hoping it was giving some protection to Kastor.

The courtyard was quiet, but we could still hear the hum of the rush hour traffic outside and a cacophony of voices. I was now unused to all the noise, but found I could close off easily. Phoebe looked more uncomfortable and Simon had a tight, controlled expression as he tried to shut off the extraneous sounds. A receptionist opened the door and we were ushered into the offices and to a meeting room. While I could tell that the receptionist had telepathic ability, all of us were speaking aloud. Like ordinary humans, I thought with a smile. A middle-aged man and woman, both very smartly dressed, were waiting in the room. I had checked that I was looking the part of Lily West in the car, but still felt nervous. I was wearing a tailored lime green jacket and a black dress, with expensive high-heeled shoes. My blonde wig was shaped into a fashionable cut, set off well by glasses that had a hint of green in the frames.

The male client stood up, smiling and introducing himself in an American accent as Leo Garston, while Simon quickly said to the woman, "And you must be Jeannette Summers, a pleasure to meet you both at last." He introduced himself and me as Lily, then asked them if they'd mind having a student sit in with them. When they looked doubtful, Phoebe quickly said she'd like the chance to look around the offices. The receptionist, appreciating her tact, took her out of the room. The remaining four of us settled around the small conference table. Leo Garston, who I warmed to partly because his name reminded me of my son, expressed his gratitude at the rare honour of meeting Lily West.

"You're quite a recluse." He looked at me appreciatively as I did my best to radiate confidence, attractiveness and a suitable air of mystery.

"Lily works best away from all this. And whatever works for Lily is good for us," said Simon.

"Where did you train?" asked Jeannette in an east coast drawl, clearly less susceptible to my appearance.

"Bristol University, for my basic degree, then masters in product design and business studies here in London," I said. I knew Lily's curriculum vitae off pat and three years had been added to my alias's age to give her time to have done all this – I was still only 21. "But my main experience comes from working free lance, before we formed this company."

Jeannette Summers reached into a large briefcase, bringing out a couple of boxes with colourful labelling. One was a package for a set of make up, the other appeared to be a kind of toy. Neither was familiar. I looked at Simon, questioningly: this meeting was not supposed to get into product detail. He suggested to me silently that we should just see where this was going. Retaining my helpful smile, I studied the two prospective clients carefully. They did not appear to have telepathy, but I sensed the woman was hoping to trick me. I focused my mind, closing off all external thoughts, just in case they had any ability to detect them.

"I know this is just a 'getting to know you' meeting," said Jeannette, "And your market performance speaks for itself, Miss West, but we were wondering what you'd have to say about these two products from our range."

"Your fees are much higher than we usually pay," murmured Leo Garston, "I guess we're just being cautious."

Simon poured some coffee, looking a little anxiously at me.

"I work mainly from detailed studies of products and performance data," I murmured, picking up the toy box and seeing it was for an electronic robot. "Are these new products?"

"You tell us," said Jeannette Summers. "We'd just like to hear anything that comes to mind. Obviously, we don't expect a full assessment."

I turned the box to read the specification. I was getting a clear image of this one having been on sale. Simon sat quietly, knowing that I would not reveal how I assessed products. The last thing he wanted was for the company to be linked with telepathy or occult arts.

"I've heard you're called the 'prophetess' because you're so good at saying when a product will do well," said Leo Garston.

I smiled. "I'm just very good at it. Of course, I use a bit of intuition, but it's mainly a lot of hard work and knowing the markets well."

"So?" prompted Jeannette, "Just on your intuition, then, what do you have to say about the little robot?"

I took out the robot. "I haven't done much lately with toys," I murmured, "but I think this one has been on sale, perhaps two or three years ago. There was a problem with it, wasn't there? It rings a bell, somewhere, did you have to withdraw it?"

Leo Garston drew in a breath, and whistled. Jeannette Summers stared at me hard.

"It was never marketed here in the UK."

"No. The packaging is wrong for here, although markets are becoming more international. Robots are always popular, but I'm wondering, maybe a safety issue caused concern?"

Jeannette took the box and robot away from me, trying to hide her disappointment. Clearly I had been spot on.

"I can't imagine how you'd know that."

"Just an informed guess," I said. "I wouldn't dream of using it as the sole basis of advice to you. I follow product withdrawals of course, but can't remember them all."

Leo Garston proffered the make up box. "OK, any thoughts about this?"

Again I examined this new box, taking out its contents. I looked at the ingredients and the neat styling. "Hard to say, there's so much make-up on the market."

"New or old product?" asked Jeannette.

I felt the woman's animosity, sensing she was the main decision maker on this deal and that she had argued against the prospective contract for Lily West's services. I tentatively radiated persuasive thoughts. "OK, I think this is new, not yet on sale."

Jeannette Summers raised her eyebrows. "I don't see how you can be sure."

"I'm not," I said, untruthfully. "But that's what I think."

"And you're right," said Leo, "You're very impressive, Miss West."

"How will it do on the market, do you think?" said Jeannette, sitting back and eyeing me. Simon was about to speak in protest, but I was ahead of him.

"Oh, I think that's a matter for when we've got an agreement to work with you," I said, smiling sweetly. "I couldn't possibly come up with a snap judgment, now."

I sensed Simon's relief and looked around at them all. "If you could excuse me for a few moments, perhaps you'd feel more comfortable talking about me if I left you for a short time?" I didn't wait for their approval, getting up and strolling confidently out of the room. I asked the receptionist for directions to a toilet.

I was touching up my lipstick, wishing I didn't feel so nauseous – I shouldn't have had the coffee, not with this morning sickness – when Jeannette Summers came into the Ladies room. I nodded to her politely, but deduced that Jeannette had come in on purpose to speak to me on her own.

"You're a mystery, Miss West," said Jeannette, standing beside me as we looked into the mirror. "Tell me, are you a psychic?"

I turned to face her. "Would that bother you?"

"Plenty of companies use psychics or astrologers. I just like to know what I'm dealing with."

I sighed. "Miss Summers," I began, but Jeannette interrupted, saying, "Actually, it's Mrs. Summers. You didn't pick that up, then."

"Sorry," I murmured. I had become unaccustomed to married titles, since Binary women retained their single names and form of address. "And in answer to your question, I wish I were a psychic. There's so much I'd like to know about my future, just now. I'm simply very intuitive, but I've worked at it. My mother was slightly psychic and it didn't do her any good at all. I believe in checking things out, like I suspect you do."

Jeannette stared and I sensed suddenly that she was worrying deeply about something. What was it, I wondered, cautious about trying to pick up too much from this woman's mind.

"You are at least a bit psychic," said Jeannette. "I should know, I've been to a lot. Mostly fakes."

"Often people go to those who claim psychic powers because they've lost someone, or are searching for someone – does that apply to you?" I said, before wishing that I'd held that back. In my mind, I saw a young boy, about five years old and Jeannette's anxious face, holding a photograph. *Careful*, I thought, *don't say any more*. Jeannette had lost some of her hard businesswoman manner.

"Our son disappeared, five years ago," she said, quietly. "I just keep hoping he's still alive, that someone's looking after him."

I put away the make up bag and took Jeannette's hand. "I'm so sorry. I felt a deep unhappiness – I do pick up people's feelings, it's why I need to work mainly alone."

"Cut the crap," said Jeannette, her eyes a little tearful. "This is just between us, nothing to do with the business deal. I know you're psychic. Just tell me, can you sense anything about my son?"

I felt the woman was sincere, not trying to trap or betray me. "I don't want you to think that's how I work," I said, cautiously.

"No, Lily, I know you're superbly qualified and I know it wouldn't look good for you to be implying you had special powers. But I said, cut the crap. I won't say a word."

I was still holding the woman's hand, my head reeling with a succession of images. This search had dominated Jeannette's life. I focused on the photograph of the boy, imagining him growing older. Then I had a clear view of this boy as older, sitting in a small classroom, putting his hand up eagerly to answer a question. Was this a future vision or the present? I decided it was now: the boy was out there.

"He's alive, I think, a bright boy, about 10 years old and doing well, in a school. I do hope that one day you'll find each other." I let go of her hand. "I've never done that before, tried to find someone's son," I murmured.

Jeannette took a tissue from her bag and dabbed her eyes. "Thank you, Miss West. That's what I wanted from you. I suppose there's no point asking you to help me find him?"

"I can't. Well, not yet, anyway. I don't want to develop this psychic stuff, please try to understand. I have to focus on the company. It could affect my work."

"I promised I wouldn't say a word and I won't. But now you know a key reason why I wanted to meet you in person. Those results you've achieved – I knew you had to have some special ability."

"I think there are genuine psychics, mediums who could help – you should go on trying to find the right one."

"I shall. Thank you, I appreciate what you've just told me. You can't imagine…"

"I've got a son," I confided. "I don't see much of him, it's complicated. So I understand in more ways than you may imagine."

When we returned to the meeting room, the two men looked up expectantly.

"Simon says Lily has to get back," said Leo Garston. "Do you have any more questions?"

Jeannette picked up the briefcase, putting the boxes back inside. "No, we're done."

"We'll wait to hear from you, then?" asked Simon.

"What? Oh, the contract, no, I reckon we can sign up now. Hire her Leo, she's fantastic."

Simon beamed, getting out some papers. I went in search of Phoebe. It was only 10:30, so we should be at the airport by noon, maybe a little later if the traffic was heavy. I felt shaky after the intense conversation with Jeannette. When I had visualised the boy in the classroom, I had felt something else very strongly: they were communicating telepathically. That boy was possibly in a Binary centre, or a Binary school. Was he one of those 'rescued' after birth, when his abilities were detected? I scarcely liked to think about it. I was now a member of an organization that bought babies, stole children, liquidated people who got in the way. And now I had to try and rescue one of their best performers, who had possibly been involved with all these activities, directly or otherwise. I thought of Kastor's kindness, feeling I would surely have sensed a cruel streak in him, a willing agent in the less savoury side of Binaries. I touched one of the crystal earrings, hoping he would not come to harm in the hands of more ruthless players.

D.R.Rose

21

The car to take me to Heathrow was waiting outside. The two security officers were sitting in the back. It's like being a dangerous prisoner, I thought, being escorted to another prison. But Simon was radiating delight.

"Well done Lily. Thought we couldn't pull it off, for a moment there. You won round Jeannette – she was the sticking point." I nodded, smiling wanly. I did not want to discuss this. Phoebe was standing uncertainly by the car. I spoke cheerfully, beckoning her in.

"You'll come to the airport with me? I'll give you the low down, if Simon is OK with that."

I signalled to Simon that I wouldn't reveal too much, just talk about those products the clients had cheekily produced to test my acumen. He nodded, waving me off. Anything Lily wanted was OK with him, after securing a very lucrative contract. I asked Mikhail Pavel to sit in the front, so that Phoebe and I could be in the back. In any case, this was advisable. Even with tinted screens, they did not want either of us to be recognised on the outside. Once settled, I took off the earrings, putting them in the velvet box I had brought along.

"Please look after these for me, I wouldn't want to lose them on the trip. And maybe I should change the wig now, get into character?" Phoebe carefully took the box and produced a wig in a plastic bag from her large holdall. I wrapped the blonde one in the same plastic bag and dropped it into the carry-on case. I pulled my hair back and donned the brown bob.

"It needs adjusting," said Phoebe, giving me a hand.

"We can do more at the airport. I'll keep the clothes as they are, I think. Maybe just change the shoes." I took off the pretty Kirkwood designed shoes, admiring the sculptured heels as I slipped them into the travel bag. Then I talked lightly about the meeting and how I'd been made to comment on products. Phoebe opened her eyes wide, knowing how risky this would have been, with clients who had no idea how we worked.

"It was a close thing," I admitted, "Not recommended. But they signed up, so Simon is pleased. Do you think you'd like to work in this field?"

"Oh yes," said Phoebe. "Do we get many fashion clients?" I nodded, smiling. "It's one of the hardest areas though. Difficult to disengage our own feelings about what we'd like to be wearing."

Mikhail asked if I had all the documents for the trip, unnecessarily. The Binaries were always well prepared. I said I was not looking forward to it as I'd never enjoyed plane trips. We talked about the Cadiz centre, which Mikhail had visited and I sensed he had a particular interest there, perhaps a girlfriend. I did not detect that Mikhail was involved in the plot about Kastor. Manes had carefully selected these officers, I reflected, sharing at least some of my worries about the mission. They'd soon be even more worried, I thought, in a closed sector of the thought house in my mind.

As we drew into the airport, Gregory Bonmot suggested that Phoebe should stay in the car.

"I need the loo," she said quickly. I appreciated the way she could improvise with such convincing innocence.

"Sorry," she added. "I know I should have used the Ladies at the office."

"Actually, I need the loo again too," I said, "So we'll go together, then Gregory can escort you back to the car."

I had flashed an image of a flushing loo about half an hour before, signalling Helen. While Gregory or Mikhail may have picked this up, I was fairly sure that Helen's quick response of a similar toilet went unnoticed. Gregory nodded reluctant agreement to the toilet trip, seeing he had little choice. "You can leave your holdall, though," he said, as Phoebe lugged it out of the car.

"No way. Women's stuff," she said, knowing he'd be too embarrassed to press the issue. As we entered the departures terminal, I flashed an image of a flushing toilet, directed at the nearest Ladies. There was no response, hopefully because Helen was being careful. Then I saw an image of a mirror, a face looking out. It was a signal from Helen. "We can wash and brush up there too," I murmured.

"Check-in won't take long," said Mikhail, "You'll be in the First Class lounge and it'll be easier to do your make-up and so on there." He wanted to get me safely onto the flight with minimal time in the crowded departures area.

I gave him a cool look. "I have to get out of Lily West and into Sylvia Smith before check-in. It's vital I start to act in character and look the part."

"You look great to me already," said Gregory.

"You're a man, you wouldn't understand," said Phoebe pertly, who had noticed that Gregory had good physique, with a face that tried to look stern but betrayed his susceptibility to young attractive females. There were gay Binaries, but Mikhail and Gregory were not among them. As we approached the nearest women's toilet on the left, I sent another image of the flushing loo, receiving a flushing noise in exchange, which I hoped Mikhail detected as also produced by me. "I'm quite desperate, must be all the coffee," I muttered, in explanation.

Gregory stepped up to the door leading to the toilets. "I'll just check it out," he said, preparing to go in. Phoebe rushed to his side, radiating female indignation. "You will not!" she exclaimed. "That'll draw attention, won't it,... Sylvia?"

I nodded. "You go in Phoebe, check if it's empty." Gregory had to content himself by fetching one of the cones used to close off toilets while they were being cleaned. Phoebe went in. She signalled a flushing loo and received the image back from a cubicle. There was one other woman in there, washing her hands. When the woman left, Phoebe followed her out and nodded to the others. *All clear*, she signalled. Gregory put the cone firmly in front of the toilet door, while Mikhail stood by, amused.

Phoebe and I entered and I noticed that Phoebe was effectively shuttering her thoughts. *"You're doing great,"* I signalled, as we went to the cubicle where we knew Helen was hiding. Helen emerged and Phoebe looked happily at us both, knowing she could not comment on how alike we were and how pleased she was to get us together. She had no idea, of course, of our checkered past history. While Helen and I rapidly changed clothes and shoes and adjusted the wigs, Phoebe used a cubicle and paused before flushing it. The security officers were standing near enough to hear such sounds from the loos. Phoebe ran some water into a washbasin while I passed over a change of jackets for Helen to tuck into the carry on bag, along with the passport and tickets. Helen also slipped in her ticket to Casablanca and some other items from her bag. She put a wad of cash and the passport for Sylvia Smith into the bag I would be taking. It wouldn't do for Helen to go through airport security with two passports: she already had her own, as Jasmina Thorpe.

I looked towards the door, sensing the men's impatience. "Hurry up Phoebe, they're waiting for us," I said, for the men's benefit.

"Just a minute," replied Phoebe, stepping back into a cubicle. When Helen and I indicated we were ready, Phoebe flushed the loo and ran water into one of the sinks again. She looked expertly at our faces, approving the make up. With a last look at Helen, full of concern and good wishes for the next stage, I stepped into the cubicle. I donned a shocking pink beret, because Mikhail wouldn't be looking for a flash of this bright colour, if he tried to find me in the airport.

Phoebe went out first, followed by Helen. "Sorry to keep you waiting, boys," said Phoebe. Gregory removed the cleaning cone.

"Just in time," he muttered, "I saw the real cleaners coming down the hall." Gregory took Phoebe's arm. "Time to get back to Binaries," he said.

"Has anyone told you look like Daniel Craig in the Bond films?" she asked and Mikhail snorted. Gregory said no, but was flattered and I guessed that he was looking forward to the trip back with Phoebe. Then I could no longer hear them as they left the departures building, while Mikhail anxiously propelled the woman he thought was Cassandra towards the First Class check-in. Meanwhile, I felt a cold sweat of fear as I hid in the cubicle. I had to wait until Phoebe gave the signal that they were drawing off in the car. Mikhail was a pretty good telepath, so I also took care to shutter my thoughts. I hoped Helen would be able to fool him, correcting this thought to knowing that Helen was more than his match.

I guessed that Helen might try to induce a panic to ensure she could check in without Mikhail being right behind her. Within a couple of minutes or so I heard a great commotion outside. Someone yelled that there was a bomb, others screamed and there seemed to be a stampede, presumably passengers rushing for the nearest exit. I heard one of them saying they'd heard an explosion. I was keeping my thoughts too contained to be able to visualise Mikhail, but imagined him whirling about in alarm, trying to see where 'Cassandra' had gone. With any luck, Helen would be on her way to the Casablanca check in.

Airport security officers were checking the now cleared area and one looked into the toilet where I was hiding, standing on the toilet seat. All was quiet, with no signs that cubicles were occupied.

"Anyone in here?" he called, but was satisfied it was empty and that any woman in there would have probably joined the stampede to the exit doors by now. As he left, I breathed out. But I felt a rising panic when I realised that Mikhail would delay checking in while he searched for 'Cassandra'. Perhaps he was waiting outside the airport or wherever security officers had herded the crowd of passengers. Hopefully, Phoebe and Gregory would not be stopped from leaving the airport. Also, this noisy hoard would hardly be an ideal environment for telepaths so Mikhail would be hindered from detecting either Helen or me.

It took around half an hour for no source for the alarm to be found. "Someone panicking - it happens," I heard one of the security officers saying from near the Ladies toilet. Then, I sensed Helen calling me from the mirror. I stepped out of the cubicle cautiously, seeing my reflection change to Helen. I did not dare to try to enter this mirror. Supposing someone came in, when I was only half way through? *Calm down*, I told myself, *it's just an illusion of the mind*. Helen spoke quickly, from her reflection.

"Tell him you've checked in, Cass, send a message, he's thinking about what to do. I'll do the follow up."

I focused, thinking of Mikhail until I had channelled him. I hoped my voice would ring clearly in his mind. Persuasively, I signalled, "It's OK, Mikhail, I've managed to check in. You go ahead, see you in the lounge."

Helen nodded and disappeared. While I looked at my own reflection, bemused at this amazing twin communication network, another woman came into the toilet. I bent over the sink, washing my hands, so that the woman just glimpsed a figure and without another thought went into one of the cubicles. As soon as the cubicle door closed, I walked quickly out of the toilet, trying to be invisible as I slipped out of the terminal. "Blend into the environment," Helen had advised. I remembered playing this telepath game with Leo.

A quick image of a flying wig came to mind, which meant that Phoebe and Gregory were driving away from the airport. With the pink beret in place, I hailed a cab from the taxi rank and got in. I was breathing very rapidly. "All right, love?" asked the cabbie, looking at me with concern. "Oh, yes, there's been a commotion in there," I said. The cabbie was still looking at me expectantly. Finally he said, in a irritated tone, "Where to, then?" "Oxford," I said, "The Randolph

Hotel."

As we sped along, I channelled Mikhail, seeing him looking very worried and speaking to a clerk at the check-in.

"I'm travelling with someone, Sylvia Smith," he said, "She may have checked in just ahead of me?" The clerk replied, "Oh yes, Mr. Pavel, Sylvia Smith has just checked in. She'll have gone straight to the lounge. The Fast Track route is just over there. Have a good flight."

Cautiously I signalled quickly, "Mikhail! See you in the lounge."

When we were well away from the airport, I took out a handbag mirror, wondering if any mirror could serve for our special twin communications. Sure enough, a flickering image of Helen appeared, already on the plane. I remembered that the timing for the Casablanca flight had been tight. She raised a glass of champagne and winked.

22

As the taxi travelled towards Oxford, I checked the roll of bank notes that Helen had given me. More than enough for a few nights at the Randolph. But as I sat back, trying to enjoy the rare experience of seeing England outside the Binaries, it seemed very sad to be visiting Oxford without seeing my aunt. I focused briefly on the surveillance centre, sensing no concern about me yet. Mikhail had not realised that Helen was long gone, nor reported in to his superiors. On impulse, I asked the driver if he had a mobile phone I could use. I decided to adopt an American accent, which seemed more appropriately furtive, if the driver should be asked later about passengers.

"I've lost my phone and need to contact a friend, a local call," I said, plaintively, with a little girl lost look that was not far from reality. The cabbie started to say no, he never lent his phone, so I produced a £50 note.

"I know it's a cheek, but this might cover it?" He handed over his mobile and closed his window to give me some privacy for the call. I tried to remember the number. It had been a long time and I had only phoned Aunt V on a few occasions. But with the address, directory enquiries were able to give me the information. I agreed for the additional charge to be put through. Fifty quid for an enquiry and call that would scarcely cost two or three pounds was generous enough, I thought. The phone rang and I tapped my foot, willing my aunt to be there and to answer. After five rings, I knew the answer phone was not on, which was hopeful. Finally, I heard Aunt V's voice.

"Hello?" I smiled at the familiar clipped tone Aunt V preferred when answering calls.

"Hello, is that Veronica Myers?" I said, in an American drawl.

"Who is this?" demanded my aunt.

"Oh, Miss Myers, I'm sorry to call out of the blue, but I'm a friend of Cassandra. I mean, I was a friend, before the tragedy. It's just that I happen to be coming to Oxford today and wondered…"

"A friend of Cassandra," repeated Aunt V, without further comment.

"I don't know if she ever mentioned me, Sylvia Smith? I heard so much about you, Aunt V. She was always talking about you. It would be so good to meet you, just for a few minutes – I'm sure you're very busy."

"I'm in the middle of writing a paper," said Aunt V, "but I'd like to meet any friend of my niece. Would you like to come round this afternoon?"

"Oh, thank you, wonderful," I gushed. Aunt V asked if I knew the address and I just stopped myself saying of course, murmuring instead that I knew it was in the Woodstock Road. I ended the call and tapped the window for the driver to take his phone back. When he opened his window, I also asked to be taken to Woodstock Road instead, knowing it wasn't far from the hotel. "Got hold of the friend, then," said the cabbie, while I wondered if he had been able to hear the whole conversation. He may also have been puzzling about my accent, which didn't sound authentic even to me. It didn't matter: I rather wanted the Binaries to find me, after I'd seen Aunt V. The taxi drew up and I tipped generously, as I thought fitting for an American visitor. I approached the familiar door of the house, seeing a curtain twitch in the ground floor window. Aunt V had been looking out for this strange friend of her niece, having never heard of her before. When she came to the house door, she opened it cagily.

"Good afternoon," she said, then gasped. "Cassandra!"

"Hello, Aunt V," I murmured, entering the house quickly. My aunt staggered back, holding the dado rail on the wall behind her. She seemed to have lost the power of speech and I stood there, radiating calm and friendliness, before gently taking her arm and leading her into the flat, whose door stood open.

"Sit down, it must be a shock," I helped her into a chair.

"I went to your funeral," said Aunt V, finally being able to speak.

"It was premature," I said. "Shall I make you some tea?"

"Wait," said my aunt, "you were seen, falling."

"It was staged. I'm not dead, Aunt V, not a ghost."

She was recovering from the initial shock, staring at me, taking in a slightly fully figure but the same innocent, enquiring face, albeit with a lot more make up. I took off the wig and shook my own hair down. "I've so wanted to see you, all this time," I said.

"And I you," she faltered. "I've always wanted to see a ghost, it's almost a pity. But I'm delighted you survived that accident – or I suppose you arranged that?"

"Long story," I said, not wanting to give the further shock of Helen's impersonation of me, just yet. Aunt V pulled myself up from the chair and gave me a big hug.

"Well, I imagine you'll be wanting cheese scones, as well as tea? Come through to the kitchen and try to explain yourself."

I smiled happily, following her into the kitchen.

23

I wondered how long it would take Mikhail to sound the alarm. Perhaps he had wanted to savour the first class lounge for a while, persuading himself that I was just doing some shopping. He would have heard the rumours about the mysterious entrant from outside who didn't always obey orders. But over in Cadiz, Ryden would be waiting anxiously for me to arrive. It was good that his long distance telepathy was very poor, so if he was at the airport, without the Centro Binario officers to help him, he would have to rely on conventional phone calls.

I didn't dare to try to sense what was happening in Casablanca, Cadiz or in the Woodstock surveillance centre. As I relaxed with a restorative cup of tea, I could smell the aroma of newly baked scones, almost ready to be taken from the oven.

Aunt V sat primly, with a stern expression.

"So, where have you been all this time?"

"You know the Binaries, how I met Kastor," I began.

Aunt V gave me a startled look. "Have you been there, have they been holding you? I thought something like that would happen, but then, after your marriage and the accident…

"It's very secret Aunt V," I said slowly. "You must promise not to tell anyone, anyone at all, including Dad."

She nodded. "I know how to keep secrets. And now I've got you back, I wouldn't want anything to threaten you." Her expression softened. I was now the only close relative she had left. "I think I'd rather die," she added quietly.

"Well, I <u>have</u> been in the Binaries." I watched her reaction. It was less full of astonishment than I'd expected, but this location clearly had occurred to Aunt V, after recovering from the shock of seeing me apparently return from a dramatic death. She filled a teapot with hot water, eager to hear the rest of the story, but as she prepared the tray to take it through to the living room, she saw me suddenly jump up, as if I'd heard a noise outside. Aunt V heard only the normal traffic, with possibly a car drawing up outside the house: not surprising, since there were other flats in the building.

"Oh!" I exclaimed, looking in the direction of the entrance to the flat. I had sensed Gaston, of all people, approaching. I had been thinking of Theodora, wondering if I should send the promised message that I was safe. This seemed to have been enough to alert the perceptive Dr. Sage. The outside doorbell to the flat rang and I briefly considered telling my aunt not to answer the door. But there would be no point if it was Gaston and his officers. Aunt V put down the tray.

"Are you expecting someone?"

"Sort of," I said, nervously. "I think it'll be all right, though." My heart sank as I regretted involving her. Why had I not just stayed at the Randolph, as in the earlier plan? I followed her into the hallway of the flat, standing at the entrance while she opened the outer door. Gaston stood there apparently alone, but I sensed there was at least one other man outside, probably the driver of his car.

"Good evening," said Gaston, radiating charm. "Dr. Veronica Myers? So sorry to disturb you, but I wondered if Cassandra was visiting."

Aunt V looked back tensely at me, noting I looked afraid. It was too late to say I wasn't there, as Gaston beamed across at me.

"Ah Cassandra, there you are. Theodora told me about your visit and I wanted to come myself. We're all delighted to know you're safe."

"And Kastor?" I asked, while Aunt V looked bemused at me and back to Gaston.

"We need to talk about that," said Gaston in a conversational tone, "but for the moment, may I come in, just briefly?" He smiled warmly again at Aunt V. I noted with irritation that she seemed to find this menacing man attractive, having become quite flustered and demure. Thought power, I reflected, grimly.

"Yes of course," said Aunt V. "Cassandra only got here a short time ago, she was just about to tell me…"

"I haven't had a chance to tell her anything, yet," I said defensively, shooting thoughts of protecting Aunt V, an innocent in all this, across to Gaston.

Gaston murmured, "Yes, yes, such a rare chance to catch up," as he strode into the living room. He looked around, appreciatively.

"A charming room, but tell me, are you the Veronica Myers, author of '*Mythology and 18th century manners*' ?"

Aunt V almost simpered, smiling shyly. "Why yes, how astonishing that you've read it, hardly anyone else has."

"My dear lady," said Gaston, still gazing about the room, focusing on the bookcases. "I read and devoured it – a masterpiece of research. Many years ago, I had an interest in the topic myself. I wonder, could it be possible, that you've heard of Colin Winstanley?"

"Winstanley – you? – the author of '*Threatening themes in the sub-mythological culture of the Enlightenment*'? Why certainly, but many of us thought he was using a pen name. It was the talk of the seminars at one time, the fact that he never appeared to deliver a paper or discuss his work…"

Gaston smiled modestly. "I am Colin Winstanley, at your

service." He bowed and then looked towards the kitchen. "But is that scones I detect, in danger of over cooking?" Aunt V looked round anxiously and dashed to rescue them.

Alone with Gaston, I was speechless at this revelation, which was just as well as he only wanted to communicate with me in thought.

"Kastor is in danger, as you suspected," he signalled. *"We must get back urgently to arrange his recovery."*

I signalled that my suspicions were the reason that I'd slipped away from the airport. He said silently, he'd like to know later how I did this, but that meanwhile help was under way and suspects had been arrested. I was eager to find out more, but Aunt V returned from the kitchen, with the tray now loaded with tea and scones.

"Cheese scones," breathed Gaston, "A favourite of Cassandra's and indeed mine."

"Well, you must have some," said Aunt V, smiling with flirtatious interest. My aunt was not so old really, perhaps a couple of years younger than Gaston Ajax. Both in their forties, both unattached, but the idea of her having a relationship with Gaston was too absurd, too dangerous to contemplate. I hoped that I had shuttered this thought, but Gaston was smiling fondly at Aunt V. He went over to the bookcase while Aunt V put the tray down on the table and started to pour cups of tea. Within seconds, Gaston drew a slim volume from the shelves. He held it, stroking the cover.

"I'm deeply flattered you possess a copy of my poor attempt," he murmured, but Aunt V was looking with great surprise at how quickly he had found it amongst the many books.

"I recognised the binding," he said, picking up this thought, "but it's so very long since I saw it. I had to put all these studies aside, when I started a very different career."

I thought, I'll say, and a complete change of personality as well, but Gaston had settled into a chair, opposite Aunt V, who had just handed him a cup of tea and one of her famous scones. I helped myself to the remaining cup of tea, feeling like a gooseberry with these two erstwhile research colleagues. Aunt V had started to talk enthusiastically about mythological themes, while Gaston laughed and chatted back. He seemed a different man.

"Sadly," said Gaston after consuming a scone and most of his tea, "I have a driver waiting outside. Unfortunately there's a serious matter that Cassandra and I have to deal with. But I wonder, dear Doctor Myers, if I may call again, in a few days? It's so rare, to find someone of your calibre – and still looking, if I may say, as elegant as when you presented your thesis in Oxford?"

"You were there?" gasped Aunt V, "But why didn't you come to speak with me?"

"I was very shy," said Gaston, while I tried not to snort derisively.

"I'll take some tea and a scone out to your driver," said Aunt V, preparing to go into the kitchen to fetch another cup.

"No need and no time, tragically," said Gaston. "We really must be going." He stood up, his eye falling on the watercolour of the beach scene and Aunt V's fanciful depiction of me playing with another little girl. "Yours, I think," said Gaston, "How talented. Cassandra and her twin."

I sent him a warning shot, transmitting that my aunt did not know about Helen. Gaston gave me an indulgent look, while Aunt V raised her eyebrows questioningly.

"But more of that another time, Doctor Myers," he said, with great reluctance, ushering me towards the door.

"Do call me Veronica," said my aunt, "and I'd be delighted to see you again." I picked up the holdall that I had tossed onto a chair when she arrived in the flat. I wished that Aunt V and I had telepathic contact.

"I'll try to contact you soon," I said quickly and Gaston nodded benignly as we took our leave. Aunt V stood at the door of the house, watching me and this attractive scholar getting into the car.

"Look after my niece," she called out, as Gaston was shutting the car door. "As if my life depended on it," replied Gaston, radiating friendly, protective thoughts.

In the car, as we sped away towards Woodstock, I was silent, trying to make sense of this encounter between Gaston and Aunt V.

"I only noticed the name today, when we were checking the address," said Gaston, dreamily. "But I should have known. There are so many interesting aspects and connections with you, Cassandra. Your aunt is delightful. We so rarely have the chance to meet people on the outside, especially those we deeply admire."

I nodded, dumbfounded, but found the courage to say firmly, "She knows nothing about all this. You won't do anything to harm her?" He said nothing, so I added, "Will you?"

"Of course not," he replied, "I can understand your misgivings, but give you my deep reassurance. I really do intend to see her again."

"For interrogation?" I muttered, with a flash of anger.

"Not in the way you imagine." Gaston smiled to himself and I caught an image of an affectionate meeting between the two aging students of the Enlightenment.

Before I could say any more, he switched the topic, returning to the melancholic manner to which I was accustomed.

"I was wrong, Cassandra, about this mission. I'm mortified. But now, we must rescue Kastor."

It seemed safe now to try to visualise Kastor and I gasped at the image I gleaned, of him slumped in what looked like a prison cell.

"He's in a cell, looking very ill," I said. Gaston nodded grimly.

"You must tell me everything that you've sensed. We found out about the plot but the traitors at Binaries knew little of the details. Tad was the main player of course, but it would appear that Ryden was aiming to make him the scapegoat. He was in on the abduction of Kastor but not the full reasons. Unfortunately, Ryden has been very cunning. He persuaded the officers at Centro Binario that everything had to be treated with extreme secrecy, including the private flight he arranged to Casablanca."

"So why has Kastor been detained? You can't imagine that he was part of this plot?"

Gaston looked uncharacteristically uncomfortable.

"I regret to say that we were not in time to stop the flight. Ryden had cut off contact with the centre."

"But surely Kastor wouldn't have agreed to get on the plane?"

"He's been ill, with food poisoning – someone got at his food. Botulism. They obviously wanted something that would act reliably fast. It was administered during his trip to Cadiz. We've caught the culprit - at least the Cadiz team have detained him - but we haven't yet reached Kastor. He was still very unwell, but Ryden insisted on the importance of the meeting he'd arranged and over-ruled the doctor and nurses. Again, I regret that we gave him full authority for this mission, so they got him as fit as they could and obeyed Ryden's orders. If he is in a detention cell, it's in Casablanca."

"And Ryden Asgard?"

"Still on the loose, but we've been getting confusing thought contact from out there. It almost seemed as though you'd travelled to Casablanca yourself."

"Intriguing," I said, with no intention of revealing Helen's role.

If Gaston suspected my supposedly dead twin was in Morocco, he showed no sign, continuing, "This plot has been planned for a long time. It's remarkable that someone with Ryden's limited skills managed to do it. He's clever, of course, with good adaptation to our ways. We're quite vulnerable when dealing with one of our own. The conditioning is powerful. Treachery is almost unknown."

I shrugged, since there was little point in bringing up all my forebodings and ignored prophecies. But remembering that Theodora had said Gaston could be trusted, I told him about the conversation I had detected between Ryden and another man.

We had reached Askeys, the car drawing up on the forecourt of the mansion. We lost no time in getting over to the surveillance centre, where there was an atmosphere of extreme anxiety. I tried to sense Kastor but could not pick him up at all. Perhaps he was already dead, or at best deeply unconscious.

Manes rushed up to me, his face a picture of misery.

"I tried to stop the plane…"

"I know," I said. "Just tell me what I can do to help."

"We didn't get much out of the catering assistant and nanny, who planted those microphones in your apartment. Tad had been playing them both. He told them that this unusual surveillance was needed to check on you, as, er, someone not reared in our community."

I shrugged indignantly at this.

Overhearing this, Gaston added, "Yes, quite amazing what women will do for love. Such a shame that Mr. Lemur won't be with us much longer. He'd have been a persuasive field agent."

"Cassandra didn't fall for his charms," commented Manes. "She warned me about him, too."

"Ah, Cassandra," said Gaston, with something near to wistfulness. "And it seems that you've managed to recruit your wicked twin as well? Of course, we knew she hadn't died. But she has at least been living quietly these past few years."

I blushed. I should have known that Gaston would be onto that part of this escapade. Theodora came to my defence. It seemed that all the senior staff were in the surveillance centre - and no wonder.

"Helen is trying to redeem herself by helping in Kastor's rescue. I'm sure that Cassandra will now want to tell us the plan."

"She'll be arriving in Casablanca, if not there already," I admitted. "It was her idea, to help."

"Let's hope she wasn't involved in the plot," said Gaston ominously and Theodora put up a hand to stop me attacking him. "She couldn't make things much worse," he continued, unabashed.

Manes came forward again. "An unknown informant contacted the Centro Binario and told them about the abduction. It may have been Helen. Filipo – he's my opposite number there – rang me early this morning. As Kastor had become seriously ill, there didn't seem urgency in cancelling the flight. Unfortunately…"

"Yes, yes, it's a disaster," snapped Gaston. "But what would be helpful now is for Cassandra to try remote vision to get more information."

"We're working on the idea that Kastor would have been taken to the prison and secret police headquarters," said Manes. "Which happens to be on the site of the old Binary centre in Casablanca."

"So pretty impregnable," I commented.

"Yes," agreed Manes. "But at least we know the broad design. Filipo is sending over a boat with some officers, but it won't be easy."

I groaned and suddenly felt very dizzy. All the pressures and exertion of the day had taken their toll. I fainted.

When I came round, I was lying on a couch in the surveillance anteroom. Theodora was sitting on a chair next to me. She made me drink a glass of water.

"I'm going to take you back to Askeys," she said. "Don't worry, all our best people are working on getting Kastor back. But you are exhausted and need to rest."

"Just for an hour or so," I said plaintively. "I know I can help. Abdul-Aziz, he's a key person in this plot I think."

"No more talking," advised Theodora. She nodded to a couple of security guards, who picked me up as though I was light as a feather to carry me out of the room. Theodora followed us, glancing back at the surveillance centre where sounds of phones, printers and urgent orders showed that the team were on the case.

24

Back at the flat, I was deposited on my bed, while Theodora ordered a herbal restorative and filled the room with a Brahms lullaby, played on a guitar.

"It'll be all right, you'll see," said Theodora, putting the herbal drink on the bedside table. As the lullaby soared into the room, she sat on a chair beside me.

"Rest and let us do the worrying. Certainly the surveillance team deserve that, as do I. I knew of your concerns, but felt that your anxiety and condition might have exaggerated them."

My condition, I thought, suddenly remembering my pregnancy. Binaries had all sorts of superstitions about pregnancy, since so few of them had direct experience. Even the all-knowing Theodora.

I sipped the drink. "Helen..." I began to say, but she lifted an elegant hand to interrupt me. I noticed the sparkle of her rings. Even in emergencies, she was dressed as if going to a grand reception.

"If she contacts you, tell me at once. She will certainly try to contact Ryden and we need to know."

"She could end up like Kastor, in prison," I agreed miserably. From Gaston's acerbic comment, I guessed that Helen would be considered all too expendable. No rescue for her.

"I doubt that very much," said Theodora. "She's very resourceful, as you are only too aware. Now, I won't go until you close your eyes and get some sleep."

Perhaps it was the herbal mixture, but when I closed my eyes I fell asleep very quickly. I didn't hear Theodora leave.

A strange ringing woke me up. In the darkness of the bedroom, I fumbled for the phone, but heard only the normal buzz of an inactive line. Then I spotted a light in the cheval mirror. I sat up and put on the bedside light. Helen was gazing at me from the mirror, looking irritated.

"Buck up, Sis! This is urgent. I had to project a bell ringing and that's not easy, you know, at this distance."

I stepped over to the mirror and slipped into our secret space.

"You look awful," Helen observed. "Bad day? Wait until you hear about mine."

"Just tell me, if you know how Kastor is," I said wearily.

"He's on his way to Cadiz," said Helen triumphantly.

"So he's OK?" I felt a wave of relief.

"Not exactly, Cass, but I'll get to that. At least he's out of that awful prison."

"Do they know at the surveillance centre?"

"Of course. I couldn't do it all on my own," Helen snapped sarcastically. "Although they'd never have been able to storm the building, it's too well defended."

"And Ryden?"

"Oh, he's tied up with something," said Helen mischievously. "OK, if you're awake now, I'll tell you how I did it. But you look as though you need to sit down. Go back and sit on the bed, I can talk to you from here and this time, we don't need to worry about eavesdroppers. The surveillance lot will have to know all this, anyway."

"Should I fetch them?"

"I don't think they can see me in the way you can," said Helen. "Remember, it's a mind construct. Between your mind and mine."

I obediently slipped back onto the bed, facing the mirror.

"So," said Helen. "First of all I checked into the same hotel as Marcie Brown and got in touch with her. We met up for a drink and I hinted that her old boyfriend, Patrick, had a fling with me, then dropped me. Just as he had done to her. I said I'd found that he would be staying at the hotel…"

"How?" I asked, receiving a sneering glance from Helen.

"I just did, OK? Surely you know how our surveillance works by now. It helped that I knew Ryden would be travelling as Patrick Lynch. It was the best hotel in Casablanca, so highly likely to be his choice in any case."

I nodded and promised no further stupid questions.

"Anyway, when I told her the awful things Patrick had said about her – too clinging, too demanding - we agreed to play a trick on him. For Marcie to pay him a visit for old time's sake, you know, because she was still so sweet on him. But it wasn't what he expected, especially when I showed up in his room as well. He had just taken a shower, getting ready for some fun with Marcie, when she arrived and pretended to be very eager. Then she introduced her friend Jasmina – yours truly – and said that maybe he fancied a threesome."

"Didn't he have work to do, like selling Kastor to Abdul-Azim?"

"I was too late to stop that, Cass. It happened before I reached Casablanca. But his telepathic abilities were so feeble, that I could tell the handover had occurred. Also that Abdul-Azim was none too pleased to receive someone who looked too ill to function. But let me get on with the story."

I couldn't help smiling at Helen's enthusiasm, despite my increasing concern about Kastor.

"So we got him quite drunk and tied him down onto the bed posts with some of the belts and scarves from Marcie's photo-shoot. I managed to slip a sedative into his drink while she wasn't looking, to make him even more compliant."

Of course, I acknowledged silently. I wondered if Helen was thinking about how she sedated me, to get me into Binaries. She was too busy relating her adventure.

"Marcie wanted to untie him afterwards, and I promised to do that while she went back to her room to go to bed. She has an early shoot tomorrow morning. But naturally I didn't release him, because having Ryden nicely secured was what I wanted."

"Did you hit him?" I asked. I would also not have been surprised if Helen had given Marcie a little dose of the sedative, to make sure she felt like an early night and not check up on the aftermath of their punishment of Patrick.

"A little discipline was indicated," she said briskly. "I took his phone, wallet and watch as well. Only for surveillance purposes, obviously. Also, I wanted it to look like a visit from a couple of prostitutes, who had robbed him. And to stop him making any calls. Naturally I disconnected the hotel phone and snapped the jack, so even if he got free, he wouldn't be able to call for help. He was fast asleep by this time, thanks to the barbiturates."

"So he's still there, tied to the bed?"

"Well the next thing I did was to contact Abdul-Azim. Or Colonel Samara, as he's known in the secret police. Great that you found his number in Kastor's file. Ryden had pretended that the plan was to kidnap Abdul, take him over to Cadiz and interrogate him there. But Abdul-Azim thought he'd purchased a prize telepath."

Helen related how she'd made an appointment with the Colonel, using the persona of a KGB agent who was also after telepaths – and willing to pay any price to get Kastor.

"I called myself Dr. Viga Blavatksy," she said proudly. "For once, I was very grateful to Binaries for all that language education so that I could do pretty well in Arabic and Russian. Abdul-Azim was alarmed to know that the KGB was interested in his intriguing 'package' and that we knew all about the transaction. He reluctantly agreed that I should come over, leaving my other operatives outside the prison."

"And Ryden?" I queried.

"Oh, wait," said Helen impatiently. "When I arrived in the colonel's office, I sensed Kastor was being tortured. I couldn't get any response to my thought messages. He was in a bad way. So I insisted on inspecting the 'package'. I told him that Patrick Lynch, who also used the name Ryden Asgard, was well known to us for selling fakes. And that Ryden was a skilled telepath himself. It seems that Abdul-Azim had no idea that Ryden had these talents, thinking him just an agent. Anyway, it wasn't easy, they had me at gunpoint at one stage…"

I looked alarmed.

"Don't worry, Sis. I gave the guard such a shot of pain that he dropped the gun. He thought I'd touched his hand with some clever KGB technique, and backed away. Meanwhile, the colonel had told me that they had started interrogating Kastor. He said that telepaths were mutants, an insult to Allah and that trading them was all they deserved. You can imagine that I wanted to kill him when he said that."

I nodded, glad she had restrained herself at that point.

"So we went down to Kastor's cell. Oh, Cass, it was awful. You're going to have to know. Their doctor was using a mind probe on him. He'd only just started…"

"A mind probe?" I exclaimed, aghast. "What, one of the banned instruments that can damage the mind?"

"The same," said Helen, grimly. "Well I got that stopped immediately. I said no agency would be interested in damaged goods and I pretended that my wristwatch could be used to detect telepathic talent. That it gave out a nasty buzzing sound when the person had little or no ability, or when the wrist tattoo was a fake."

"They fell for that?"

"With a nifty projection of that sound into their heads," smirked Helen. "Anyway, then I said that Ryden was the real telepath and they should take him instead. Switch Kastor over to the hotel. I had to work on convincing Abdul-Azim so that he thought that Ryden had tricked him, but he agreed. He was suitably outraged when I mentioned that I'd checked out Ryden and he'd been 'relaxing' with some prostitutes at the hotel, when he thought the deal was done and dusted."

She paused and I noticed that she too looked tired. It was the early hours of the morning in Casablanca.

"What's next – oh, I gave Abdul-Azim my watch so that Ryden could be tested. Then I ordered them to take Kastor on a stretcher out onto the street, Rue des Rêves. I signalled to the Centro Binario squad that they could collect Kastor from Rue des Rêves and that I'd arrange a commotion to make that easier."

"Fire alarm?" I queried, stunned at Helen's resourcefulness. Theodora was right.

"Yeah, seemed the easiest. And I told Abdul-Azim that it would be OK to try out the mind probe on Ryden. As a 'proper' telepath, it wouldn't be so dangerous on him, I advised."

I raised my eyebrows.

"It's what he deserved, Cass! Nothing compared with what the Binaries would do to him for such treachery."

"So it went off OK," I murmured, thinking of Kastor on that stretcher and seeing an image of him being lifted into a white van, while a siren sounded within the prison complex.

"Then I had to get back to the hotel, change back into Jasmina clothes, you know, hijab headscarf and so on. I wore your Lily West wig and a tight dress for the meeting with Abdul-Azim, just to distract him. I had stowed the clothes change in a bin on the Rue des Rêves. I slipped past reception and waited until the security police, along with Abdul-Azim, came to inspect Ryden. I made the wrist watch make a lovely ringing tone when he held it over Ryden's tattoo, who was coming round but very drowsy. After that, I arranged for the Cadiz boys to collect Abdul-Azim on the street outside the hotel."

"How?"

Helen chuckled. "Oh, funnily enough, he had a nasty turn. Became pale and sweaty, with a chest pain radiating down his left arm."

"A heart attack," I commented, recalling Helen's nasty range of skills.

"Yes, he was a candidate for one, right age and overweight. The ambulance that arrived to collect him was of course arranged by Centro Binario."

"You're amazing," I said, "I couldn't have done it."

"I expect you could, with practice. Although without my years of that severe conditioning, you might not want to."

"What are you going to do next?"

"Check out from here, as early as I can," said Helen. "Even with Abdul-Azim out of action for the moment, I don't fancy my chances with the security police and he could have arranged an arrest, once he had Ryden. Luckily the Binario squad got him before he could find out that Kastor didn't make it to the hotel."

"Get some rest," I advised. "I need to go over to the surveillance centre to find out what is happening to Kastor."

"Yeah, this is not sensible behaviour for someone expecting twins," she agreed. She smiled warmly at me. "I'm sorry I couldn't get to Kastor before the mind probe was used, but it was only a few seconds."

"How many seconds, do you think?"

"Oh, five or so," she murmured. I knew it was probably more but appreciated this kind lie.

She put her hand up to the surface of the mirror and I touched it with mine.

"Thank you," I said, as her image faded.

The clock showed the time to be 3 a.m. One hour ahead of the time in Casablanca. I hesitated for a moment before signalling Theodora, but she responded immediately and the phone rang. I guessed she wanted no confusion in our communications, especially as I was in such a tired and anxious state.

"Kastor is now at the Cadiz centre," she said. "And you should get back to sleep, now that Helen has briefed you." No need to wonder how Theodora knew.

"I couldn't sleep. I must find out more, I'll go over to the surveillance centre."

"Just as I anticipated you would wish," said Theodora in a resigned tone. "We'll go there together. I'll see you in 10 minutes."

I dressed in a tracksuit, splashed my face with cold water and waited for Theodora's silent knock.

25

The atmosphere was tense in the Binaries surveillance centre. I sat by Manes' desk, silently, trying desperately to sense Kastor and receive a response. I refused offers of refreshments, watching the phone between gazing into the far distance, focusing my mind on the warm night in Cadiz.

At last, Gaston came into the room. "Our people have Kastor, as I gather you know," he said. "As well as Colonel Samara, who will be interrogated today."

"Thanks to Helen," I said softly.

He glanced at me sharply. "She could have been one of our best agents, had she not chosen such a devious course. But yes, she has done her duty for once."

All in the room sensed my misery, that I was aware that Kastor's condition was very poor. They tried to smile cheerfully at news of this success, to have at last found him. Manes was communicating with Filipo by thought, nodding and sending congratulations. He turned to the others. "He's been seen by the medical team."

I sniffed sullenly at this news, with little confidence of medical help. "I need to go over there," I said aloud.

Gaston seemed about to forbid this, but a nod from Theodora

silenced him.

"We'll travel to Cadiz tomorrow. Gaston and I will go over with you," said Theodora.

"Take Clea," said Manes, who had finished his short burst of thought exchange with Filipo. Dr. Clytemnestra Foucoe was the senior psychiatrist, known as Clea by those on friendly terms and Clyppie to those who had grown up with her, like Kastor. I shrugged. This doctor had not even known that I was not my twin, when I first tumbled into the Binaries. How could she help Kastor?

"Dr. Foucoe has a lot of experience with those of us who've been harmed, outside. She'll assess him, Cassandra," said Theodora, picking up my cynical thoughts. "You must get some more rest. Nothing else can be done for a few hours."

Gaston was unusually subdued. He felt responsible for having promoted the mission with Ryden, using his authority to quash objections. He sensed my deep anger, knowing it was justified.

"A jet's on its way here, to be ready for a flight as soon as it can be arranged. I'll contact you all." He left the room, brooding as he walked away.

Theodora travelled back to Askeys with me. Neither of us spoke. I was moving like an automaton, my thoughts full of the day's events. Of course I was relieved that Kastor was in safe hands, but perhaps it was too late. I had received an image of the mind probe, unintentionally sent by Helen, in her shock at seeing it being used on Kastor.

"A mind probe," said Theodora, "how very wicked." We had reached the Askeys staircase stop and she helped me out of the train carriage, then went with me to the door of the apartment.

"I'm OK," I said wearily. "Thank you for coming back with me."

Theodora ignored this and entered the apartment with me.

"Straight to bed," she ordered. "One of the staff will prepare your suitcase for the journey."

I lay down on the bed obediently. She disappeared into the small kitchen, returning with a mug of hot malt chocolate.

"I need to pack as well," she said, leaving the room. As she closed the bedroom door, I thought I heard Theodora send the message, *"Helen did well, today."*

I smiled, looking across the room at the cheval mirror. I tried listlessly to see if I could channel Helen, out there in Casablanca. After a moment or two, an image appeared of Helen smiling, making a thumbs up sign. I hoped that meant she was on the way to the airport. Thank you, Helen, I murmured, drinking the mug of cocoa before settling back into the bed, feeling sleep overpowering me.

I woke when I sensed someone moving about the room. Blearily I looked and a chambermaid smiled back at me.

"Sorry I woke you. I've packed your case, but you may want to check if there is something special you need."

I remembered that my earrings were still with Phoebe. I would have to signal Phoebe to get them sent over to the house. I took a quick shower and, when the maid had left, sent the message about the earrings. Then I went over to the cheval mirror. There was no response and I turned with disappointment to pick up my handbag. A faint buzz from within made me look inside and pick out the powder compact.

"Hi there Sis," said Helen from the compact mirror. "I'm waiting for my flight back to Abu Dhabi. It was all OK, had to give a massive bribe to reception as apparently the secret police had asked about me, for some reason."

She grinned mischievously. "Oh, and I left a message for Marcie. Told her that Patrick had been picked up by the police, in case she asked about him. I said it sounded like he'd been too curious a journalist. Anyway, Marcie was good value. Quite intuitive too. Wasted on Patrick-Ryden."

"Do you know what they did with Ryden?"

"Not much. Their doctor used the mind probe on him. I think he used it for at least half an hour."

I thought, in a closed part of the mind, that Helen might have advised that.

"Theodora said you did good," I said, to shift the subject away from mind probes.

"I miss her," said Helen sadly. "I miss all of you. What a mess I made. They'll never let me back, of course, not even after my dare devil rescue of Kastor."

"You don't know that…" I began but she made an angry 'huh' sound.

"Trust me, I know them. But at least, maybe, I'll be off the death list for a while."

I didn't know what to say, but let my eyes meet hers thoughtfully as I said, "I'm going over to Cadiz this morning, to see how he is."

She closed her eyes, in uncharacteristic remorse. "If only I'd got there a few minutes earlier. But honestly, Cass, it really was only a few seconds. And Kastor's mind is strong, you know that."

Tears sprang into my eyes, as I gave a plucky nod.

"Keep in touch," I murmured.

"It's all done by mirrors, as they say," she said, winking. Then her image faded.

I finished dressing, choosing jeans and a light sweater for the journey. A breakfast delivered to the apartment filled me with nausea. I just drank the orange juice and pushed aside the coffee. Sitting on the sofa in the living room with dawn slowly filling the room with grey light, I tried to channel Kastor, depressed at the lack of response. While I sat quietly, another image came to mind, a discussion in the medical centre. Dr. Foucoe was talking about me with Dr. Philips.

"So you don't think that Cassandra should go to Cadiz?" Dr. Philips was saying.

"No – their relationship is too intense. It'll be very distressing for her and what can she do to help him?"

"Too intense," repeated Dr. Philips, thoughtfully. "Possibly because she was brought up on the outside. She's adapted well, but..."

"But there are many things she doesn't understand, yes?" said Dr. Foucoe, whose accent I now knew to be due to her early upbringing in eastern Europe. "He'll almost certainly need to go to St. Anthony's. It may be better if we help her to forget him."

I shut the scene off, angrily. The image of the dark fort where St. Anthony's was located filled my mind. It had haunted me as where I would be taken, when I was first imprisoned at Binaries. There was no way I'd let them take him there. Too intense, indeed! I felt strongly that my feelings for Kastor, and my ability to communicate with him, were exactly what he would need to recover. I was still fuming, wondering if that was the opinion of the other Binaries who would accompany me to Cadiz, when there was a shy silent knock at the apartment door to announce Phoebe. I invited her in, offering her coffee from the breakfast tray, which Phoebe eagerly accepted, also eyeing the toast so I was pleased to let her have that as well. She handed over the velvet box and while I was putting in the earrings, I gave her a very brief account of how Helen had reached Casablanca safely and helped in Kastor's escape. Our secret, I emphasised. I didn't say I had visited my aunt, just that I'd been collected and brought back to Askeys safely. Phoebe asked if Mikhail had returned. I had forgotten all about him. I focused on the airport for a second.

"I think everyone has overlooked that – he's still there!"

We both giggled guiltily before Phoebe said she'd contact Gregory to sort it out.

"I wish I could come to Cadiz," said Phoebe wistfully.

"If I have to stay a while, perhaps Simon Arbalest will let you and Ashara come over to do some commercial work with me."

"That would be wonderful!"

"Yes, well, don't raise your hopes. I'll do my best," I promised. There was another silent knock at the apartment: Theodora had arrived. She nodded politely to Phoebe, raising her eyebrows just a little. Students were rarely invited to the house. The girl left quickly, embarrassed, despite my explaining about the earrings to Theodora – as if Dr. Sage ever needed explanations.

"I've sensed that there's a lot of worry about Kastor's condition," I said, when we were alone.

"Just so," said Theodora, "But you'll be able to help him, don't you think?"

"Yes, I'm sure of it, but I don't yet know how."

"One thing at a time," said my wise friend. "This is where your growing strength will be needed."

"I couldn't have done what Helen managed, out there."

"And she couldn't have done it without knowing her connection with you – and her great debt to you." Theodora smiled, gazing into the far distance, as far possibly as Cadiz or even Casablanca. She then gave a nod and said, "Yes, Cassandra, I believe these actions will almost completely exonerate her, free her from the threat she's been living under."

"Almost?" I queried.

"Well, so long as she does not try to return. Our rules are very firm."

"She misses us, she said, but I don't think she wants to come back here."

"Do you not?" said Theodora enigmatically, having sensed rather the opposite from my mind. "But for the moment, we need to leave for the air strip."

She got up. A security officer entered the room and picked up my suitcase. I wondered what horrors awaited me in Cadiz.

26

While we were waiting in the library for the news that the minibus had arrived to collect them, I was surprised to see Joel Grigora enter the room. He communicated silently with Gaston but when I heard a hollow laugh from the security chief, I looked up from my reverie about Kastor.

"His 'execution code' that he deceived us with, so unwisely, has proved quite prophetic – for him and Ryden," Gaston transmitted to Joel.

The Ethiopian nodded gravely, glancing at me, aware that I was now following their exchange. I felt a chill, realising that there would be no reprieve for Tad and wishing I had never contemplated such a gloomy code. Perhaps there had been an element of prophecy in it, since both Joel and I shared this unusual extension of telepathy. Gaston noticed the glance and came over to me.

"Your compassion does you credit, Cassandra, if misplaced in this case. Tad Lemur acted extremely foolishly and with callous intent for Kastor or yourself. But we shan't be making him face a firing squad."

"*No?*" I signalled, noticing that the others were studiously looking at travel documents and to avoid appearing to eavesdrop on this.

"No," said Gaston, sitting beside me and speaking very softly. "We have places where we can put those who've injured us to hard labour, building new facilities and so on. He'll be executed, if you could put it that way, from any further role in the organization. He'll also undergo a programme of...," he paused, seeking a word, "re-education. If he doesn't respond, other measures may have to be considered."

"And Ryden, what will you do with him?"

"We're still trying to find him," said Gaston. "We've found no trace, but he must be still in Casablanca." I focused for a moment, trying to pinpoint him. He was not responding to any thought messages, so I switched to distance viewing. In my mind, I roamed through Casablanca, using his facial features and particularly that arrogant smile. I sensed only the vague idea that he was still there, but no location.

"Do you have a map of the city?" I asked and Gaston narrowed his eyes, appreciatively.

"Have you tried this type of remote viewing?"

"No, but I've just thought of it. I could try, if you give me a map."

Gaston nodded to Manes, signalling the request and Manes came over with a folder of documents, pulling out a map of Casablanca. A steward entered to say the bus was ready, but Gaston indicated for the others to get on board, while he gave me the map. I spread it out on a small table and composed myself. I had never tried such indirect communication, but the mirror construct with Helen had given me confidence with unusual techniques. Gazing at the map, I visualised the streets and buildings, probing for any trace of Ryden-Loki. Gaston sat quietly, watching me. After a minute or so, I pointed my finger at a place on the map. "He's here, I think."

Gaston looked, murmuring, "The university hospital."

I closed my eyes, visualising the hospital. "Yes, he's in a hospital bed, but he looks different. He's smiling..."

"No difference there, surely?" said Gaston, but I went on, "No, not his normal smile. It looks idiotic, like a baby smiling at nothing in particular, with eyes unfocused. I can't sense his mind at all – do you think he's drugged?"

"No," said Gaston thoughtfully, "I think he's been wiped."

Wiped? I paled and said, "You mean, like they've done to Kastor?"

Gaston had stood up, to communicate the news of Ryden's likely location to the surveillance and security teams, but turned back to me with an unusually kindly look.

"Kastor is damaged, but not like this. There's much hope, don't despair." The steward came back into the library, signalling that the bus had to leave. Gaston took the map and ushered me out of the room.

On the bus, I heard him talking to Manes and communicating with the surveillance team.

"It seems we can add divining and dowsing to Cassandra's exceptional range of ability," said Gaston.

"Nothing surprises me about Cassandra," replied Manes, "but I wish we'd paid more attention to her fears about this mission." Gaston nodded, solemnly. He said quietly, "Yes, a severe lesson for me, for all of us. Let's hope it isn't too late." I picked it up, despite the near whisper, from his thoughts.

Dr. Foucoe and Dr. Philips were sitting together, also conversing in a low serious tone. The senior doctor in Cadiz was recovering from the mild dose of botulism and they now knew that Ryden had engineered this, so as to ensure the doctor was unfit on Friday and unable to protest about Kastor being loaded onto the plane for Casablanca.

"He thought that it would just be attributed to the doctor picking up the illness from Kastor," murmured Dr. Philips.

"Yes, without realising that botulism isn't infectious – you have to ingest the toxin."

"He must have brought it with him from the States. Travelling only by private planes, his luggage was less likely to be searched diligently. I suppose they've searched his belongings, in his room at Cadiz?"

"I spoke to the nurses," said Dr. Foucoe. "Nothing relevant was found."

"He'll have disposed of it, probably en route to the airport. He'd have wanted the blame to rest with Tad Lemur, who admitted he'd given a vial of it to the catering steward on the plane going from here."

They shook their heads while contemplating these events. Treachery on this scale was horrifying to them. They had been brought up to understand that their enemies were outside the organization, the people who either thought they were freaks or mutants, or useful for espionage, to be exploited by force if they got their hands on them.

Theodora sat with me, talking about mind exploration to distract me from worrying too much. She explained that Dr. Foucoe would undertake a very gentle mind exploration of Kastor, to examine how much damage had been done.

"Is he speaking, showing any sign that his mind is still there?" I asked desperately.

"I don't know," said Theodora, "but it would be quite normal after… torture or even brief use of an illegal probe, for him to be unable to transmit or receive thoughts. Think of it like a fractured leg – it needs to heal before it can move properly again."

"And when Dr. Foucoe does the mind exploration, will she be able to start the healing?"

"It's a very slow process. Usually the first stage is to encourage rest, complete cut off from the outside world and our realm of thought."

"I've been inside Kastor's mind," I said shyly, thinking of our last evening together. "Not just plunges, he let me explore."

"Of course," said a smiling Theodora, "That's just what I'd expect of you two. None of us have done that with Kastor. So you know his mind better than anyone."

"So perhaps I should be the one doing the exploring, this first look?"

Theodora looked towards the two physicians, deep in conversation.

"When the mind's been injured, it's a delicate and dangerous matter. When you and Kastor were in this close contact, I imagine he helped you to move back through his mind, to leave it?"

"Yes," I admitted, blushing slightly at the blissful feeling we'd enjoyed.

"But in his present state, he may not be able to help you, to leave, I mean."

I considered this, the possibility of being lost in Kastor's damaged mind. "I'm not afraid," I said, eventually. "I think I may be the only one who can truly help."

Theodora eyed me thoughtfully. "We'll see, but you must listen to the doctors' advice. They've handled such cases and know the risks."

We sat silently as the mini-bus drew into the private airport.

The journey took a couple of hours, with a short drive to the Cadiz centre once we landed. In other circumstances, I would have loved the scenery as we drove along the modern motorway and up the narrow mountain roads in the sierra. A small, subdued, welcoming party greeted us. Gaston and Manes were soon in hushed conversation with Filipo and others from the surveillance team, while Julieta, apparently one of the most senior leaders at Cadiz took me, Theodora and the doctors to the medical wing.

"We've restarted his botulism treatment," she said as we walked down the corridor, "but that isn't the problem. He'll soon be free of most of the severe symptoms from the toxin. He's able to speak a little, but Dr. Foucoe advised complete silence, so he's in a protective tent." She smiled encouragingly, noting my determined expression. "It's a pleasure to have you here, Cassandra. I'm sure it will help Kastor, to have you visit him."

We entered the medical wing and a nurse took us to an isolation area. Through a glass window, I saw Kastor lying on a hospital bed, surrounded by what looked like a transparent igloo, formed of hexagonal plastic panels with a network of sparkling filaments holding the plastic shapes together. While the doctors discussed the patient, Julieta explained that this contraption was protecting Kastor from outside sounds and telepathic contact.

"Can I go in, briefly?" I asked. Dr. Foucoe was called over. It was clear that she didn't want me to be involved before they had assessed Kastor's state. But when I persisted, she relented.

"Just for a moment, but don't try to communicate with him. We'll observe - it'll be interesting to see if he responds at all."

It is as if they are talking about a rabbit in a laboratory, I thought irritably, but I didn't want the psychiatrist to change her mind by responding provocatively. I nodded agreement, and a nurse lifted a flap of the igloo tent. There was a small chair next to the bed and I sat on it uncertainly, gazing at Kastor, who did not appear to have noticed my arrival. He was lying quite still with his eyes closed. The arm nearest me was lying with the hand palm side up, as though waiting for someone to put something into it. I glanced nervously at the watchers through the window before gently touching his hand. I felt Dr. Foucoe's irritation. Did this slight contact count as communication in her book? Cautiously, I moved my thumb, pressing it slightly into the centre of his palm, just as he had done to mine so often, particularly when I needed reassurance. The rest of his hand was cradled in mine. As I kept up the gentle pressure I sent a thought, as secretly as I was able. *"I'm here,"* I signalled, *"I'm safe and I'm with you."*

Outside the tent, I sensed Dr. Foucoe ordering me to come out. But I continued sitting there, willing him to make the slightest response. His face showed nothing, but his fingers moved to wrap round my thumb and curved to cradle my hand in return. Then the hand relaxed, returning to its former position. Dr. Foucoe was now standing at the tent flap, beckoning me to withdraw and I got up reluctantly. Outside the room, I said, "He responded to me, he knew it was me."

"It could have been merely a reflex," said Clea, dispassionately. "Were you also trying thought contact?"

"Not consciously," I said, gazing at the psychiatrist innocently. "But our level of communication is, as you know, deep. Or as you'd say, intense." Dr. Foucoe's eyes flickered, sensing that I had picked up some of her earlier conversation back at Binaries. But unabashed, she maintained her view that I should now leave, to allow the initial assessment to be done.

"But I can stay and watch?" I said. The psychiatrist shook her head.

"No, he'll be quite safe, but it might distress you. Please, I must insist. You need refreshment after the journey. I'll tell you all about it, later."

I let myself be led away, reluctantly. It was true I was tired and also felt a slight return of appetite, now that I'd seen Kastor. A buffet had been laid out in one of the surface buildings, looking out onto the mountains. I looked around for Manes and Gaston but Theodora reported that they were visiting the detention centre.

"Helen managed to deliver them a great prize. Ironically, it's one of the subjects the Cadiz centre has hoped to interview for some time. He may know the major dealers in this repulsive business."

I nodded, letting Theodora see an image of Helen, giving me this news. But just as I was enjoying the buffet, I heard a piercing scream, knowing it was Kastor. The others did not appear to have heard it, except for Theodora, who looked up at me anxiously.

"What are they doing to him?" I asked in alarm.

"They'll be doing a very superficial examination – but even that may be extremely painful, in his current condition," said Theodora quietly. "They have to make an assessment, to gauge the treatment."

"I'd like to see the special probe, if that's how they'll do it."

"They wouldn't use one of those," said Theodora in a shocked tone. "The examination will involve just trying to enter the first level or two of his mind, as you did when you explored Kastor's. But I'll see if they have a photograph of a mind probe. It helps to have a good image of the enemy, does it not?"

"I know what it looks like, but a detailed picture would help me to visualise the damage."

Theodora nodded, going off to talk to Julieta. I flinched, having to sit down, when I felt another scream of agony from Kastor. After talking to Julieta, Theodora came back to me and said a picture would be brought to my room, where she insisted that I should now go, to get some rest and try to be patient.

27

My room was on the first floor of the villa, overlooking a hillside. Rain had fallen since our arrival, glistening on the grass and rocks with the return of the winter sun. A giant rainbow arched in the sky and I tried to see this as a good sign. Closing the blinds to the window, I curled up on the bed and dropped off to sleep. When I awoke, I saw that someone had delivered a tray with a jug of hot water, some tea bags and a plate of dry biscuits on the far side of the room, near the door.

I noticed a slim folder by the tray, opening it to find an image of a mental probe, with some background information. It worked by disrupting the delicate network of filaments, destroying the partitions and floors of the telepathic mind, with the aim of accessing the deep layers below. Apparently this could also damage the neural network of the normal brain, but it was estimated to require at least ten minutes to penetrate the upper layers of the mind, sending high frequency electromagnetic impulses through the columns of filaments. There were different kinds of probes, apparently, like fire arms and some could cause more intense damage in a short time. I closed the folder, deciding it was time to talk to Dr. Foucoe about the extent of injury to Kastor's telepathic structure. I went across to the main part of the centre.

Hearing voices and a melée of thoughts coming from one of the communal rooms, I pushed open the door. Dr. Foucoe was holding court with a group of the Binaries from Woodstock and Cadiz. Theodora was sitting pensively to one side of the room, looking up when I entered.

"So, I could only reach the surface, but that was bad enough," Dr. Foucoe was saying, "There are cracks and deep fissures. I could see into the first layer but it was piled with debris. It was too painful for him for me to probe for more than a few seconds." A warning thought from Theodora made her pause, looking towards me. I stood, ashen faced, at the entrance to the room. Julieta came over, taking my arm and bringing me into the group.

"Cassandra," said Dr. Foucoe, awkwardly. "You were so closed off, I didn't realise you were there. I'm so sorry, the damage does seem severe. It's important to be honest with you."

"What can be done?" I asked.

"It'll improve with rest," said Dr. Foucoe, "but I advise moving him soon to St. Anthony's, where we have a specialised unit. The deeper layers are probably OK, so he'll recover some function."

"Some," I repeated, in a shocked tone. "But apart from rest, what treatment will you be able to give?"

"He'll need constant attention," said Clea Foucoe, "so that when he starts to receive or transmit thought, we can ensure that the channels start reforming correctly."

"So it's watch and wait, basically," I said. "Can I see him now?"

Julieta, at my side, emanated sympathy. "He'll be exhausted after the initial exploration. Perhaps later tonight, or tomorrow morning. Yes, in the morning would be best."

Clea nodded. They all turned to the door, sensing the approach of Gaston and Manes. "How is he?" asked Manes, but the others thought, almost in unison, *don't ask.*

Manes looked sadly at me. "He has a good chance, Cass, now that he's safe with us."

I tried to smile, sensing the wish of all of them for me to feel more confident. "Meanwhile," said Manes, "Gaston and I were wondering if you could help, with an interview?" I caught an image of Abdul-Aziz, deep in the detention centre and shook my head. I did not want to be near the man who had ordered Kastor's torture.

"You wouldn't have to be in the room - we have a viewing chamber," Manes continued. "Gaston's with him now, he's been very keen to given information. But he's holding back, we need your perception on how to unblock that. Just any ideas that come."

"Since you can't see Kastor for a while, it would be a distraction," said Julieta, persuasively. "I'll come and sit in the viewing chamber with you."

Theodora approached. "I think you should do this, Cassandra. Exercising your abilities could help to build up your strength."

"I have to go over to Casablanca," said Manes. "Two of us need to collect Ryden."

"You're going to bring him here?" I asked, alarmed.

"You won't need to see him," said Manes. "We've been in touch with the hospital. He's in a much worse state than Kastor. We can't leave him there - he's a charity case, so they've done scarcely any investigation. We don't want them to try to contact authorities in the States or in London. Or to be intrigued by his tattoo."

I shrugged. "All right, take me to the viewing chamber. I'll follow advice, for once." Theodora smiled enigmatically as Julieta and I left the room.

Walking towards the room where Gaston was interrogating the colonel, I felt nervous about seeing him in the flesh. Helen had provided sufficient additional images for me to feel that I knew him quite well already.

"He was sedated for the journey here," said Julieta, "and woke up in the medical centre, thinking he was in hospital, being treated for a heart attack. He was talking about devils, images in mirrors. Now we've made him think he's being held by the Central Intelligence Agency, with dire consequences if he doesn't help us."

I nodded, amused at the idea that the Binaries could be seen as a branch of the CIA. "I suppose it's been a lucrative trade for him," I muttered.

"Oh yes, all his deals are for large amounts of money," agreed Julieta, "but this trading of telepaths is a new venture. That's why he didn't know what a mind probe could really do, how destructive it would be to his... merchandise."

We stepped into the viewing chamber. In the room beyond, a tired Abdul-Azim was speaking rapidly, with occasional prompts from Gaston, whom I was entertained to note had a convincing American accent for this interrogation. Sensing our arrival, Gaston nodded to a guard in the room and left his prey to come to speak to us.

He noted my lethargy, showing rare concern. "Thank you for coming over," he said sombrely. "Our subject's given us details of several his bank accounts. Officers are working on transferring all the funds. We know he has more, he's hoping to conceal those from us. But he's holding back also on his contacts. He believes that once we have the money, we'll release him – and fears for his life if he gives us more information." I sensed the futility of the colonel's fears, reading the cynical thoughts in Gaston's mind. This particular cockroach would not be checking out of the Binario hotel.

"I'll switch to more general questions," said Gaston, "while if you sense anything at the back of his mind, his deepest fears, his secrets, anything at all..."

"I know," I said, "I'll try." My normal compassion was greatly reduced in this case. Julieta and I took seats in front of the screen, visible only as a framed mirror in the room beyond. As Gaston and the colonel continued their conversation, I focused on the unpleasant man, seeing him growing up as a boy, training in the militia, walking pompously through corridors. Then I saw him having a furtive meeting with Ryden and reported this. Julieta signalled to Gaston, but he wanted more: who else had Abdul-Aziz been meeting with? I saw a sunny city scene, with the colonel sitting at a table in a pavement café. A man in a beige suit was leaning towards him. They were negotiating, smiling but both also with busy thoughts, calculating their terms of agreement. I turned my inner camera to the man in beige, sun tanned but not an Arab. A can of soup floated by, ridiculous, I thought, then I said suddenly, "Baxters." The maker's name wasn't visible on the tin, so I didn't know why I'd come up with that particular brand.

Julieta looked at me keenly. "A tin of soup? But what...?"

"No, not the soup, that's just a clue. I think his name is Baxter." Try that, Gaston, I signalled and he nodded appreciatively. Abdul-Aziz started at the name, sweat breaking out on his forehead. Gaston pursued the connection, while the colonel blustered that it was more than his life was worth to say more. He wondered what traitor in his own network had revealed the contact to these agents.

I tried to get a first name, concentrating on the man we now could call Baxter. Perhaps the colonel had never known it. The connection was too indirect to probe further. I closed my eyes and was surprised to see some sausages appear and a flask of beer. It was a German style of tankard. I said aloud, "Frankfurt, try Frankfurt." I could now see a beer cellar, with Baxter wearing a dark suit. A woman was sitting in their group and Baxter was talking, pointing to his companion. He had just the trace of a Continental accent but I couldn't place it.

"Anna will see to the transfer. Anna Brandt knows all about these valuable assets. She knows how to make them see sense and do the work we need them for."

The colonel was nodding, eyeing the attractive companion. She had yellow blonde hair, plaited around her head in a traditional Bavarian fashion, but her clothes were modern, tight and well tailored. I projected the image and name, but then I saw another image. It was the god Loki, amorously embracing this woman in a snowy scene with frost sparkling on overhanging trees. I shared this image with Julieta, puzzled why this had come strongly to mind. Binaries were always well versed in mythology. It was a strong element in their culture, when they discussed tales from ancient times when telepaths were valued and understood by fellow humans.

"A lover of Loki," said Julieta. "He had many, but this snowy scene calls the frost giantess to mind, Angrboda. They called her the herald of sorrow."

I was pleased, sensing that I now had the clue to the woman's real name. "Anne Guburda," I exclaimed as the name came into my head. "Not Brandt, that's just a field name."

Julieta looked pale. "Anne Guburda," she whispered, her shock turning to fury as she spoke, "she was one of us, thought to have been killed on a mission." Gaston had meanwhile reduced the colonel to abject terror, asking him about his meeting with Brandt and Baxter. When Julieta relayed the Guburda name to him, he looked very startled. He glanced at the large mirror, quickly averting his gaze. I thought about those devils in mirrors that he had mentioned. Perhaps Helen had projected a suitably terrifying image.

"How could you know, even Ryden didn't know...," the colonel spluttered. Then, looking around the room desperately as if there were a chance to escape, he whimpered, "Brandt warned me, if I spoke only one word about her, she'd give me a horrible death..."

"A dilemma," said Gaston, nonchalantly. "You tell us everything and we'll ensure she never gets to you, or we let you go, but inform Brandt that you've betrayed her." He got up from his chair, signalling the guard to take the prisoner for a comfort break.

"I'll give you a few minutes to think about it. Your choice seems quite simple, but we're not unreasonable. Consider your options, Colonel, and we'll have another chat."

Gaston came into the viewing chamber, his face dark and furious. Julieta was no less angry.

"I can't believe it," said Julieta, as they exchanged thoughts. Turning to me, she explained, "Anne Guburda was one of our best agents, she was last posted to the German centre. Her death in the field was mourned, but all the time, she was planning to betray us."

I thought about Helen, secretly deeply relieved that all she had done was to try to live an outside life, even if had meant killing a husband and causing our mother's death. I had been in Binaries long enough to know that treachery against the organization was the worst of all crimes. While I was musing on this, Gaston and Julieta were urgently discussing how to manage the new lead. The woman posing as Anna Brandt needed to be found. She would have learned by now of the failure of the abduction, although probably not in detail. Neither Ryden nor Abdul-Aziz would have had the opportunity to notify their contacts.

Gaston beamed at me. "Brilliant, quite brilliant. You never cease to surprise me. We'll be able to work on this now. We'll get the codes for his contacts out of him, then we can start to trace Guburda."

"I'd like to stay a little longer," I said. "I loathe being near him, but sense he needs to be really, deeply afraid to tell you the final details."

Gaston looked at me with admiration. "This isn't a kind of work that appeals to you, but if you sense that, you obviously have a great gift for it."

"A one off," I said, "for Kastor and all of us threatened by the plot."

The colonel had been brought back into the interrogation room, his mind full of how much he needed to reveal to ensure his release. I sensed he was determined not to reveal any accurate details of how to reach Anne Brandt. While Gaston winkled out vague information, I thought of Helen generating one of her panics, with her now long dark hair blowing about her face. This screen between the rooms was like one of our mirrors, a special place for twins to work through. Focusing carefully, I projected an image onto the mirror in the interrogation cell. Abdul-Aziz was facing the mirror, concentrating on Gaston, but looked up when he detected movement in the dark glass. He went white, gripping the desk in front of him. Gaston glanced round at the glass. He sensed that I was projecting something fearful in it, but the image was for the benefit of the colonel alone. Abdul-Aziz saw the face that he had last glimpsed at the prison, the mysterious KGB agent Dr. Blavatsky. Helen's face, distorted into a devil mask. The demon's eyes blazed with unnatural red irises, seeming to dart rays at its victim.

"Save me from this devil!" he cried, jumping up from the chair, only to find himself restrained by two guards. They held his head, forcing him to go on looking at the mirror.

"You can be saved only by telling everything. Allah is displeased with you, very angry." The voice was heard only in his mind, of course, but appeared to come from the she-devil in the mirror. Abdul-Aziz looked at Gaston, who sat silently, gazing at him sternly. Gaston had picked up my message into the man's thoughts, saying quietly, "I can't save you from this vengeful angel. I advise you to obey."

"Angel?" gasped the colonel, looking at the image, now seeing wings unfurl behind the face. Helen would be proud of me, I thought, as I added this detail. "Abdul-Aziz," said the voice in his mind, "For the love of your departed mother, for everything you hold dear – it's time to show you truly believe, to redeem yourself…"

"And then," he whispered, "I shall be let free?"

"Of course," said Gaston, with a smile. "Then we'll ensure this will be at an end, you'll be safe from this vengeance…"

The colonel started to talk, rapidly, switching from English to Arabic and with spatterings of French. Julieta made quick notes, being more fluent than Gaston in Arabic. I maintained the image, fluttering in the mirror, while the terrified man now told every tiny detail that he knew. When Gaston signalled that they had enough, I let the image fade, slumping exhausted onto the bench in front of the viewing screen. Julieta signalled for someone to come to collect me.

"I have to stay here, to follow up on these leads," she said softly. "But you must rest. There'll be a good dinner waiting when you've recovered, you must be hungry?"

I felt starving, the hunger that follows an enormous physical effort, although I had only been sitting in a room. I was taken to a quiet chamber to lie down. It was a soothing place, illuminated with gentle blue and violet light. I was given a milk drink, like a lassi, then I slept dreamlessly until sensing that someone was standing beside me. It was Theodora. "A good day's work, was it not?" she said, smiling, indicating that dinner was served.

28

Eating a meal with the friendly crowd of the Spanish centre, I noticed that Manes and one of the Spanish female field officers were missing, already on their way to Casablanca. Despite the shocking news that Anne Guburda was probably the main agent in the plot to steal telepaths from their organization, the mood was elated, with excited discussion of how this threat could now be controlled. We ate in a terraced room overlooking the mountains, with a clear starry sky above. Gaston, arriving late for the dinner, nodded towards me with respect. The meal was concluded with music and a flamenco performance, but I was in no mood for joining the dancing that followed. Theodora recommended that I return to my room and accompanied me back to the villa.

"You can see Kastor tomorrow," said Theodora, sensing what was uppermost in my mind. *Why not tonight*, I thought sullenly and Theodora responded at once with, "Or whenever you feel it would be best. I'll tell the medical unit staff to let you come and go just as you wish."

I nodded gratefully, but Theodora added, "Take great care, Cassandra. I know you want to explore the mind damage, but perhaps all he needs, for now, is to sense you near."

"Will he sense me?" I was worried that he couldn't even receive thoughts.

"He has all his other senses," said Theodora, raising my

eyebrows that I had seemingly forgotten that communication between humans was possible without telepathy. "He can see and hear you, feel your touch. But don't expect too much." She then left, with little confidence that her protégée would heed advice.

I tried to sleep again, but dreams of devils and surreal images disturbed my rest. In the early hours of the morning I found myself wide awake. I looked at the clock at my bedside. It was nearly 3 a.m. The villa was quiet and I turned my thoughts to the medical centre, of Kastor lying beneath the protective igloo tent. Dressing in a tracksuit and soft-soled shoes, I opened the door of my room and padded down the steps of the villa. There were two exits, one leading to the outside, a formal Spanish garden, while another door led to the tunnels below. A guard stepped across my path in this subterranean corridor, but seeing who it was, he moved aside with a polite acknowledgement. When I asked for directions to the medical unit, he signalled for another guard to take me there. Theodora's instructions to the staff had been thorough. There was no indication of surprise at this pre-dawn visit to Kastor.

The patient was awake, staring at the ceiling. When I came into the room, telling the nurse that I just wanted to sit with him for a time, he turned to look at me, managing a smile.

"Cassandra," he said slowly, as if each syllable was painful to utter. "I can't even talk properly," he murmured, in frustration.

"You don't have to speak," I said, lifting the flap of the tent and taking his hand, before sitting in the chair beside the bed. He held my hand tightly, closing his eyes.

"I've lost it," he said miserably. "All the telepathy, all the empathy." He pronounced the words slowly, in a bitter tone. I knew that if he could think clearly, he would be sending images of this closed, frightening state.

"It'll come back," I said. "I'll help, make sure." He turned his head away as if to rebut this idea, to let me know it was hopeless. I asked the nurse to go out of the room for a moment, to allow us some brief moments alone.

"Dr. Foucoe tried to explore your mind," I said, tentatively, seeing him grimace in memory of the pain. "But Kastor, I need to look too. I'll be more gentle than she'd know how to be."

He shook his head. "No, too dangerous. Can't help you get out." He closed his eyes again, keeping hold of my hand.

"I must do it Kastor," I said, like a firm nanny with a reluctant child. "Please, just the surface. I can't sleep or rest until I know... and when I've seen it, I can start the cure." He muttered inaudible protests, but I gazed at him, moving round the bed when his head turned away, so that I could look directly into his eyes.

"I'm going to try, whatever you say," I said, in a determined tone, "So you may as well try to help."

He sighed resignedly. While his memories were confused and hard to access at present, he had a clear idea of how stubborn I could be. I returned to the chair and told him to keep looking at me. "Don't speak," I said, "Just concentrate on letting me slip in. I'm becoming smaller, like that little torch character when I explored before." I knew that he could not see this image, clear in my mind, but I spoke soothingly, reminding him how easily I had entered back in our apartment, with his complete trust. I felt that I was travelling behind his eyes, letting them fall shut as I waited, trying to sense when he was ready. Still holding his hand, I felt my grip relax as I miniaturised completely, landing on the mind's surface.

This was a very different terrain from the sparkling, snowy surface I had seen just a week previously. The surface was a dull, pale green colour with lumps like hardened snow strewn about. It was uneven and I noticed a large crack near where I had landed. The edges were sharp with a cragged appearance. Holding onto one of the snow lumps, I looked down into the crack, into the chamber below. It glowed slightly but this was mainly from broken ends of filaments, waving hopelessly, as if seeking their connectors. I turned my gaze to the stricken surface, looking for a relatively undamaged area. Sharp points projected here and there where the floor had sunk round the columns below. It was like a bombsite covered with a large dusty canopy of thick debris. I had seen bad skin wounds and this was similar, like a pock marked area of lacerated skin, with patches of different, unpleasant colour, where greenish fluid oozed out, hardening the lumps of snow. It was as if a cheese grater had moved over this pristine surface, ripping and shredding its integrity. I thought of the mental probe, with its rotating antennae, slicing through the invisible tissues of the mind.

Kastor moaned quietly as I tentatively moved towards a smoother area. I sensed that he was trying not to cry out, remembering how painful even this slight contact must be for him. Wherever I stepped, I laid a transparent layer of protective thought, like a clear sticking plaster. I stroked each Band-Aid into place, having no idea if that was what was really needed, but it felt healing to me and that would have to suffice. Mostly I had to crawl, with no confidence in the ability of the surface to withstand even the slight weight of my probe persona. I felt Kastor flinch, creating a tremor across the mind, making me slip and slide, with little to hold onto.

The jagged peaks from the damaged columns gave little electric shocks and were obviously very tender to Kastor, whose groans echoed around the space whenever I touched one. I wrapped little pockets of foam around each sharp crag, an imaginary foam that I projected as a healing white substance, such as those used on severe skin wounds or burns. It made the slow traverse of the surface easier, but I decided I had seen enough for this visit. I started to focus on leaving, standing up unsteadily to try to propel myself back into reality. But as I did so, I slipped and felt my little probe feet sliding into one of the natural partitions of this upper layer. Before I could regain my balance, the partition gaped open and I dropped into the chamber below. I landed on a surface like broken glass and Kastor screamed with agony.

I stumbled up, dusting off the glass that I knew could not really harm me, although it felt real, like falling into a pile of shattered windows. I looked round aghast at the damaged cavern, which had seemed like a serene Norman church on my previous visit, with neat glistening pillars and a smooth tiled floor. Now it appeared like a building site, where excavators had swung to and fro with heavy axes and hammers to clear the place. Chests and other pieces of furniture had fallen over, spilling little thought traces. I stepped cautiously over to the nearest chest, heaving it back into position at the edge of the chamber and picking up the fragments of thought and carefully replacing them. But Kastor was now moaning constantly. I had to leave, but how was I to do it? I looked up at the gap through which I had fallen.

"Help me Kastor!" I called, realising in a panic that only thoughts could be clearly transmitted here and that he was unable to receive them. I looked around desperately for somewhere to get a foothold, to climb up to the upper layer. The floor, even where the glass had not accumulated, seemed fragile and every step seemed about to open a fissure, with the risk of falling into the next cavern. There were little circular dents, as though punched by a fiendish office hole puncher that had attempted to crush a thick wad of paper, seeking to incise the edges. Sitting on a relatively firm area near the thought chest, I calmed myself, focusing on how to escape. The ceiling of the cavern too high to reach even if I stood on the chest. I looked for possible materials to make a kind of ladder. In addition to the fragments that seemed like glass, there were more solid lumps, possibly the protective coating of the damaged columns. I gently prodded one of the larger lumps, sensing that this at least seemed not to cause greater pain to Kastor. I guessed he was trying to control the impulse to yell and scream, while he recovered from the exquisite agony of my fall into the cavern. Gradually, I rolled a few together and placed them on top of the chest, which stood just below the furthest point of the gap into the surface layer.

After what seemed hours, I had made a sufficient heap to be able to stand on, but still not enough to reach the gap. A few filaments were hanging down next to the gap, partially detached from their column. I looked for filaments with no glow, sensing that these had been rendered inactive by the damage and would probably be the least painful. Clambering to the top of my precarious mound, I took a breath and grabbed a couple of these filaments. Then, when my grasp felt secure, I pictured myself like Tarzan, swinging through the jungle and took a leap upwards. It was enough. I reached the edges of the gap, swinging through, but when I released the filaments, letting them spring back into the lower floor, I slid backwards. I was in danger now of falling head first through the gap again. Desperately I clutched onto a sharp crag that I had wrapped in one of my Band-Aids, near the gap.

Kastor shrieked as my fingers pressed through the thin coating, touching the live connections within. My sudden wave of remorse was useless to him. He could sense only a painful, agonising invasion, perhaps like someone twisting a hot lance inside him. I coated the crag with my healing foam, feeling his pain, but also knowing my departure was now urgent. With a force of will, I imagined my probe as the slimmest of flexible shafts, able to float up, so that I could visualise myself ejecting from his mind. At first I simply wobbled, like a cotton thread that would just curl up and fall to the ground, but I persisted, remembering how Kastor and I had soared into an infinity of stars. With a jerking sensation, I felt the surface receding and for a moment I could see Kastor lying on the bed beneath. I tumbled down to earth, finding myself back in my own mind, but then losing all sense of the room around me.

When I awoke, I was lying on a couch in a small room leading off from the single ward where Kastor lay, under the igloo tent. Faces came into focus and I saw, first, the angry visage of Dr. Foucoe. Theodora was standing there too, as well as a couple of nurses.

"What on earth did you think you were doing?" said Clea Foucoe, letting me feel all her fury. "Do you have any idea, how dangerous…"

Theodora spoke with quiet authority. "Not now, Clea. No real harm has been done."

"Is Kastor all right?" I signalled, looking quickly at his outstretched form beneath the tent. *No thanks to you*, Clea shot back, but

Theodora merely nodded.

"He's just glad that you're safe," said Theodora. "It's extremely difficult to leave a mind when the owner cannot help you. Kastor would have done anything to assist your departure."

"To relieve the pain, alone," said Dr. Foucoe, glaring down at me.

"You were found unconscious, lying on the floor by his bed," said Theodora. She did not need to remind me of her warning about attempting a mind exploration.

"I had to know," I said feebly, trying to sit up but feeling very weak. One of the nurses helped me. When Kastor had started groaning and then screaming, the nurse had quickly entered the ward and sent for help. She had guessed from my trance like state that I was engaged in mind exploration. They had waited until Kastor was able to speak, to tell them that I had left his mind. It would have been hazardous to us both, to try to move me while we were still connected.

"Heaven knows how much this will have retarded his recovery," said Clea, a little calmer but still furious. Now able to sit unaided, I swung my legs down in a determined manner and appeared to be about to go back into Kastor's tent.

"Oh, stop her, for pity's sake," said the psychiatrist, exasperated, signalling to the two nurses, who stepped to bar my way. I glanced round at the group, noting that Clea and Theodora were in their nightclothes, Theodora in a colourful Chinese silk dressing gown, while the psychiatrist was wearing a simpler long pink robe.

"I'm sorry to get you out of bed," I murmured contritely. "I suppose it must be nearly time to get up."

"It's 3:30," said nurse who had found me. "I came back into the room just a minute or so after you asked to be left alone."

Clea turned my glare to the nurse. "Disobeying express

instructions," she rapped, but Theodora urged calm. I looked puzzled that so few minutes had passed and Theodora said softly, "In the mind, the illusion of time is not needed. No real time, that is, the passing of the hours that seems real to us, passed while you were in there."

Dr. Foucoe looked impatient, as well as tired. "Perhaps we should all now get back to our beds and leave the nurses in charge." She turned sternly to me. "But I tell you this, Cassandra. Now you've trespassed into his mind, you know how serious his condition is, no?"

I nodded, feeling tears coming, but not wanting to give the angry psychiatrist this satisfaction. "He needs urgent transfer to St. Anthony's," continued Clea. "I shall arrange that in the morning."

I felt a wave of anger, turning to gaze at Clea. "No, that's not going to happen." When the psychiatrist glanced around at the others, seeking their disapproval of this stubborn statement, I felt a surge of strength, the anger mutating into formidable power. A minor tornado seemed to be blowing around the group.

"Hear this," I said. "He stays here until I say so. And he isn't going to the dark fort. I know how to enter and leave his mind now and he needs me to do it."

Clea, despite the blazing force field that I had created, stood firm, gazing at me indignantly. "So, you're adding medicine to your skills? This is too much, really too much. You don't have the first idea..." There was a murmur from the igloo tent, and they turned to see Kastor gazing at them, trying to speak. The psychiatrist signalled quickly to one of the nurses, letting her know that a sedative would be needed. "You've exhausted Kastor with your meddling, your wicked disobedience," she said, but Kastor beckoned us over. One of the nurses pinned back the flap, so that they could communicate more easily.

"Cassandra," he said, with obvious effort, "... stay here, stay with me."

"You surely don't want her trying that again, that agonising probing?" said the psychiatrist.

I nipped through the flap, taking his hand, wishing my regretful thoughts could reach him but my face said it all. He looked up me, nodding that it was all right. Gazing at Clea, he said, "I must stay… she must stay. She can help me, I know it."

He gripped my hand tightly, so that my fingers hurt, but I didn't care. I looked at the others defiantly. "So that's settled then," said Theodora, yawning. "It's time to return to our beds, is it not?"

29

On the following morning, I made my way to the medical unit at about 11 a.m. I was determined to carry out my plan to keep Kastor at the Centro Binario for at least a few weeks and to attempt further mind explorations. Tossing and turning after returning to my room in the early hours, I had visualised the damage and practised different ways of applying healing in my mind. I knew how the structure should look and surely it was better to try to encourage it to heal that way, than follow the 'watch and wait' policy, while those crags and crevices hardened into permanent twisted remnants. My approach to the injuries seemed instinctively right and living at Binaries had taught me to trust instincts. When I entered Kastor's wardroom, Dr. Foucoe was discussing his chart with Dr. Philips and nurses. Dr. Philips and at least one of the nurses greeted me with a friendly smile, but Clea Foucoe's expression was severe.

"So, Cassandra," she said, in lieu of a more polite greeting. "I hope there'll be no repetition of your exploration in the night – or the tantrum." The others looked embarrassed, but my eyes flashed steely resolve.

"I've worked out a regimen," I said. "I don't want to interfere with your treatment once telepathy starts to return. I know you're the expert on that - but I want to be closely involved with the early stages, in the weeks he stays here."

"Weeks!" exclaimed Clea. "Absolutely not. What are your

qualifications for thinking you know how to do this?"

I hesitated. "Well, I've studied the brain in psychology, I know about mental processes. And I was in the St. John's Ambulance Brigade, so I've had a lot of practice in dealing with wounds."

"That's all very well, for the physical sphere," said Dr. Philips, diplomatically, seeing that Clea was too flabbergasted to reply. "But what do you know about curing the telepathic mind?"

"I just feel that I can," I said, losing a little of my defiant manner. I looked towards Kastor, apparently dozing within the igloo tent. Dr. Foucoe had recovered from her indignation sufficiently to argue the points. "Cassandra," she began, in a more measured tone, "we understand that you want to help him. And you can, by visiting him and sitting quietly. He's quite able to sense you in the ordinary way."

"How could I visit him, if you send him to St. Anthony's?" I demanded.

"Well, occasional visits would be possible," said Clea, in a reasonable manner, although I read clearly from her mind that once Kastor reached there, my chances of seeing him again were slight. I also sensed that Clea thought this would be for the best.

"In my experience," she said authoritatively, with a disdainful sneer at me, "it could take years for even partial recovery, with recovery of the telepathic skills often severely hampered by the damage. Before you arrived, I was discussing the unfortunate likelihood of deep damage."

I sensed she had exaggerated the findings of her very brief exploration of his mind. She picked this up, flaring with anger again.

"Cassandra – your exploits in the night could have done untold harm, with your inexperience and inept handling of the delicate mental fabric."

"I know his mind a lot better than you do," I protested, although

I had not intended my voice to sound so much like a sulky teenager.

She turned to the others. "Perhaps our poor Cassandra is succumbing to a similar mental complaint to that of her sister," she said menacingly.

'*Mentally unstable,*' was the clear thought that she transmitted and I flinched, for this touched on one of my deepest fears.

"You are angry Clea, and I'm sure we can sort this out," said Theodora, sending her a stern thought. Expression of strong emotions was not the norm for the carefully brought up Binaries.

"We find that cautious medical management is best in these cases," said Dr. Philips, smiling kindly at me in an attempt to restore peace.

"Why don't you try surgery?" I asked, thinking that the crags and loose filaments seemed more like broken bones than a disturbance of physiology, which the mind might be able to repair without intervention.

"I suppose you did surgery, in your St. John's Ambulance brigade?" asked Clea in turn, with heavy sarcasm.

"I was brilliant at slings and splints and very good at bandaging."

"I stand corrected," said Clea, even more sarcastically, sweeping my eyes round the group. "I hadn't realised that you'd also trained in such... advanced surgery." The small gathering in the ward sensed the approach of Gaston and Theodora. They came into the ward with an innocent air, although I knew they would have picked up the argument.

Dr. Foucoe turned to the new arrivals for further support. "Please, Gaston, Theodora, you must make Cassandra see sense. Now she's demanding to be in charge of Kastor's treatment."

Gaston smiled benignly at me, as one who currently could do no wrong in his eyes. "Your alternative being...?"

"Immediate transfer to St. Anthony's, where he'll get the

necessary conditions to start the mending of his mind."

"No!" I said. "I won't allow that."

"She's unqualified, impetuous and clearly too distressed to think clearly. And she's an arrogant outsider," declared Dr. Foucoe.

Theodora approached her, radiating calm and not rising to the normally unpardonable insult of calling one of the Binary community an outsider.

"But I recall that you, Clea, have always maintained the need for greater contact with the outside, for more recruits with that experience, for us to be able to work alongside one another."

"I wouldn't call Cassandra an outsider, if I were you, Dr. Foucoe," said Gaston with a menacing glare. He was less forgiving than Theodora. "Nor arrogant," he added. "I, for example, am extremely arrogant – and it takes one to know one." He looked meaningfully at Clea, before continuing, "Clearly she feels very passionately about this. And I've learned recently that her feelings are to be trusted."

I was astonished to find that I had an ally in Gaston, but now Theodora ushered us into the corridor, murmuring that this discussion should not be held within earshot of a patient, even if he was in a protective tent and apparently asleep. Clea reluctantly followed us out, while Dr. Philips had obviously decided to stay out of it, lingering with the case notes in the ward and asking one of the nurses about Kastor's fluid balance and continuing recovery from botulism.

"I acknowledge your psychiatric ability, Clea," said Theodora, "and I'm sure Cassandra does also. This case is quite unique, though, is it not?"

"In what way?" demanded the psychiatrist.

"For one thing, Kastor was suffering from a debilitating infection that may have affected his responses to attack. For example, without this weakness, his training in resistance to probing could have worsened the effects of an artificial instrument, by resisting too much. We train for attacks by other telepaths. For another thing, the attack was savage, but very brief. We have an eye witness account." Dr. Foucoe raised her eyebrows. She had not been made aware of an eyewitness.

"The account was received by Cassandra, who is an expert remote viewer, as you know," continued Theodora smoothly. "But there's a third matter, perhaps most important of all." She paused, assuring the attention of the group. "Kastor's bond mate has rights to influence the way he's treated. And Cassandra is exceptionally gifted, with powers that even we are only just beginning to understand."

"Powers," sniffed Clea. "Perhaps if these talents had been developed within our community, from an early age, she'd know better how to use them. As it is…"

"As it is," interrupted Gaston, "I'd say that if Cassandra thinks she can help with the healing, she's almost certainly right."

"This is ridiculous!" said Clea, feeling outnumbered. "Are you now saying that she's some kind of magic healer? This is the kind of thing that gives telepaths a bad name, outside, the idea that we're dabblers in necromancy, occult arts…"

"No, no," said Theodora, calmly, "Not magic, sadly. It would be a fine thing if we all had magical ability. But I think it may be best if I talk this over further with you alone, Clea, without the others?" The psychiatrist, who was outranked by Theodora, felt she had no choice but to nod agreement and they strolled away from the ward. This left me standing awkwardly with Gaston.

"Clytemnestra is a strong woman," murmured Gaston appreciatively, "but not very flexible. Perhaps we could have a quiet talk about this, Cassandra, if you'd lend me a little of your time?"

He took me to the Spanish garden, formally laid out in the old Arabian style, like the rose gardens of the Alhambra. I was trying to adjust to this much more benign Gaston Ajax, suppressing a thought that it might have something to do with his friendship with my aunt. He indicated that we should sit on a marble bench, overlooking a little fountain with a repeating inlaid marble pattern surrounding it.

"It's brave of you to stand up to medical advice," he announced, after we sat down. He was looking into the fountain, as if far away in his thoughts. I felt it would be best to wait until I had heard more. I already knew that my mind mending ideas might be foolhardy.

"A long time ago, I sustained a vicious mental attack," he continued. "I was captured on a field mission. The interrogators included a rogue telepath, who knew exactly how to damage minds. The injuries were different from Kastor's but I too lost all my telepathic and empathic powers."

I looked at him gravely, trying not to show too much compassion, which I felt would irritate him.

"When I was rescued, a watch and wait policy was applied to my treatment. Gradually, with the help of the doctors and other therapists, I recovered much of my ability."

"I see," I said. "So you're saying that's the right approach."

"Wait, no I'm not saying that," said Gaston, with annoyance, as if he had just remembered that I was sitting there. I resolved to stay silent.

"I was treated for a time at St. Anthony's, if you can call it treatment. It is a remote place, but the weather isn't always as dire as in your mental image." I realised that I had been picturing the dark fort, with heavy rain falling and little light penetrating within.

He tilted his head slightly, taking in my image. "It's a place of exile for many, few come back. I'm a rare exception. Your fear that Kastor would never leave there is justified."

I sat, solemn, pondering on this. He turned to me, his dark clever eyes roving over my face. "Theodora called you extraordinary and she's never wrong in an assessment. But extraordinary people have a difficult path. Your twin was very able, but her upbringing may have been wrong for her. We've seen its effects and the way she chose to use her skills." I gazed back at Gaston, not reacting outwardly at the reference to my twin.

"In your case, it seems to have been better to grow up on the outside. It's made it very confusing for you, discovering all these talents so late, but perhaps maturity helps. It may assist in making the right choices. It's only just beginning, for you, this exploration of the range of your telepathy." I allowed myself to nod, just slightly.

"If you think you can do mind surgery, I suspect that you can," he went on, "but it may help you to know another argument in your favour." I nodded expectantly.

"If you allow the psychiatrists and physicians to have their way, Kastor will gradually return to something like his old self." He looked away, into the distance, while we both contemplated the 'something like'. "But he'll be more like me, than the Kastor you knew."

I lowered my eyes, glad that no response was required, such as *"Oh no!"* or, untruthfully, *"Well, that would be OK."* He smiled sardonically. "Yes, quite, I know I may seem a monster to you. Cruel, ruthless, a certain crudeness, all that."

I wanted to say, *"But you were kind and charming to my aunt,"* but felt silence was still the correct policy.

"You've been in Kastor's mind," he said, ignoring my thoughts of Aunt V. "You've seen the flexibility and endless interconnections of the structure before the injuries. And now, you've seen parts that have hardened, broken. Left to heal on their own, they will form different, more inflexible constructions. Like mine."

I nodded, my eyes filling with tears. He glanced away, sensing for a moment my memory of Kastor's groans and screams while I clambered over the damaged structure.

"The difference between what happened to me, and that

inflicting Kastor, is you. I had no one prepared to make those dangerous journeys, to care enough to fight for an alternative management."

I turned, so that he would not see my anguished expression. In twenty years time, if the prognosis were the same as with Gaston, Kastor would be a ruthless telepath, with little compassion and much reduced empathy. That was what made Gaston so effective in his work, his dislocation from worrying about feelings. Although I was beginning to suspect, particularly since his meeting with Aunt V, that were deep levels of empathy that could be brought back to life. I closed that thought off as securely as I was able, knowing that the last thing Gaston wanted was pity or to be patronised.

"You may not use this information," he said, "I'm sure you understand why." He waited for a nod from me before continuing, "But perhaps it will help you in sustaining a position, the one you decide is right." He stirred, as though our one sided chat was now over, but I silently asked him to wait a moment.

"I shall not share what you've told me with anyone," I said, "but I wonder, does Theodora know all this?" Gaston laughed, lifting the melancholic demeanour of his features.

"You should know by now, Cassandra, that Theodora knows everything." Then he got up and walked away, without looking back.

30

It was nearly noon and I wondered if it would be wise to return to the medical ward. I wanted to see how Kastor was after the ordeal in the night. I tried to sense if Dr. Foucoe was there, waiting to argue with me again. My mind was full of the conversation with Gaston, increasing my determination, as he knew it would, to stick to my resolve and try my mind explorations. Remembering my panic when I could not leave Kastor's mind, it was also a frightening, lonely prospect. Suppose I did all this and the mind still hardened into a Gaston-like structure, or what if I could not repair the particular filaments that influenced his feelings for me? Coming closer to the unit, I began to think that my plan was quite mad, as well as dangerous. When I reached Kastor's room, a nurse stood up to greet me.

"May I see him?" I asked cautiously.

"Yes, of course," said the nurse, "but Dr. Foucoe has ordered that a nurse must stay with you at all times, for your own safety."

"Could you pull me out of his mind, if I were lost inside it?" I asked.

"No, I don't know how to do that," admitted the nurse. She smiled uncertainly, having heard of the fierce force field I produced when Dr. Foucoe had announced the transfer to St. Anthony's. She did not want to provoke a mini tornado from me.

"Well," I said, "by all means stay in the ward, but not close. I need privacy to try to communicate with my husband." Husband was not a word used by the Binaries and the nurse looked shocked. "I meant to say, my bond mate," I said contritely. I had no wish to further antagonise the clinical staff.

I stepped up to the igloo tent and lifted the flap. Kastor's eyes were closed, but opened immediately when I took his hand.

"Well, hello," I said, smiling and sitting on the chair beside him.

"Hello, bond mate," he said, managing a slight smile. I wondered how much he had heard, since the tent was supposed to cut off sounds. Perhaps the flap, not secured very well, allowed him to hear quite a lot, including some of the earlier row with Dr. Foucoe.

"Does it still hurt, to talk?" I asked.

"Cassandra, it hurts to talk, think, feel, imagine. Basically, it all hurts."

"Did I make it worse?" I asked nervously.

"I don't know. It feels different though. You didn't just explore, did you? What did you do, exactly?"

"Well, I tried to ….patch it up a bit."

"Ah," said Kastor. "So, Doctor Cassandra, what are you going to do next?"

"They don't want me to do anything. They want to watch and wait."

"And you, naturally, want to disobey?"

"Not if it'll make you worse," I said quickly. There was a hint of humour in his eyes that cheered me. But then his eyes clouded and I put both my hands round his, watching his face anxiously.

"Is it the pain – oh, don't speak, just nod."

He awkwardly shifted himself up the pillows and the nurse rushed to help, adjusting them so that he could half sit in the bed. When the nurse moved away he stared weakly at me.

"I'm a wreck," he said, bitterly. "And that's not just my opinion. In the night, when you were all round the bed, I think I said you should stay with me."

I nodded. "And I will stay." He closed his eyes, seeking the words and I could feel the effort of dragging them out.

"But that may not be right for you," he said, finally. "To stay with a hopeless invalid. It's all right, you know, I won't hold you to any promises."

"I don't recall promising to obey you," I said, "Unless I missed that bit, as the ceremony was in French."

"So you don't know what you agreed to?" asked Kastor. "I wish I'd known that earlier."

"It wouldn't make any difference," I said nonchalantly. "I'd probably do the opposite anyway, but one thing is sure – I shall stay with you."

Kastor was trying to laugh and I thought delightedly, that a sense of humour must be one of the things governed by the mind, so perhaps that was recovering.

The nurse was busy outside the tent but she also kept looking at her watch. I stepped out of the tent and asked if the nurse was waiting for her replacement.

"Well, yes," she said. "It's supposed to be my lunch break. But we're very short staffed, now the other serious patient has arrived."

"Who's that?" I asked innocently.

"Oh, a man from Casablanca. He's in a very bad way."

Ryden-Loki, I thought. I didn't want to see him, rather dreading his recovery. Then I thought of Gaston saying that Ryden had been 'wiped' and how Helen had said that the probe had been used for a long time on him.

"Look," I said, "Theodora has also given orders that I should come and go as I wish – and I'll be all right here, why don't you just go on your lunch break?" I could be very persuasive, when I chose. Now, I filled the nurse's mind with thoughts of lunch and getting away from this claustrophobic room. The nurse finally agreed.

"OK, thank you," she said. "If there's any problem, just press this buzzer." I nodded, urging her to get off and have her break. When the nurse had left, I closed the door of the room, rather disappointed that it could not be locked. I went back into Kastor's tent, who had been observing this performance with interest.

"I'm not at all sure I'm safe with you, Doctor Cassandra."

I took off my shoes, climbing up onto his bed. "Move over," I ordered, "there's hardly any room." I ignored his protests, making him shift over. Then I lay down beside him. He smiled, clearly finding this contact a pleasant sensation, but I detected no emotion. Sensing this, I bathed him in mine, willing him to feel just a little of it. After a while, I murmured, "I need to come inside your mind again."

"What? Didn't you have enough, in the night?"

"It's these early days that are so important, for the healing."

"No! – it was agony and you nearly couldn't get out."

"I know what to do now," I persisted. "If the replacement nurse comes, she'll just think we're having a cosy sleep. That's very good for you, you know."

"Sleep? You're waking me up quite… effectively," he said, turning on his side and moving his hand across my body.

"Good," I said, holding his arm still. "Now, I'm only going to come in very quickly, just on the surface."

"No-o," he moaned, "Please, I'm a sick man."

I gazed into his eyes. "And you want to be better, don't you? We don't have much time, Kastor, I promise I won't slip down like last night. I've worked out where to start, this time."

He sighed. "I'm too weak to resist." I wished I could communicate by thought, but this would have to do. I murmured that he just needed to remember the trust that we shared and gradually felt him becoming receptive. Then my miniature investigator travelled into his mind, this time as a probe with more sensible footwear, with little rubber snow chains attached.

I landed gently on the surface, noting that the transparent bandaging and healing foam were still in place and that the damage certainly seemed no worse than in the night. Taking care not to go too near the jagged holes, I worked across the surface, applying foam and bandaging to any sharp or tender looking areas. Kastor groaned occasionally, but I found that there were several undamaged areas that I could tread on without disturbing him. It occurred to me that possibly the intact plates of the surface might eventually spread over the smaller holes. I visualised the pattern of the plating, remembering how the smooth surface had seemed to give a little in particular areas, like fault lines under the sea, when I had explored his uninjured mind. Carefully, I pushed ridges of the healing foam along the intact areas, until they were perched precariously on the edges of damaged plates, but still in line with the original formation.

When I had coated every sharp point and foam filled every puncture hole, I stood back to admire my work. Kastor was very quiet, hopefully because it was less painful. Finally I peered down the largest jagged hole in the surface, shining my torch into the chamber. My pile of column cladding, perched on the chest, was still intact, but I would need a safer means of escape, if I explored that cavern on my next visit. I strung some transparent bandaging carefully across the edge of the hole, sticking several together so that they could hang across and provide a kind of rope ladder into the chamber. I reasoned that if it would still be there on my next visit, it might be safe to use it. It did not occur to me to question how I was able to generate these healing materials within someone's mind. I was just aware that I could. It's an illusion, all this structure, I told myself, and making illusions is one of my special gifts.

When I was satisfied that I had made some improvements, encouraging the sentient building blocks of the mind to get on with reforming the correct patterns, I decided to leave. I focused on ascending, soaring upwards and this time there were no mishaps. I popped out of his mind and then felt myself back within my own. Kastor stirred as he felt my head move from its seemingly unconscious state, lying on the pillow beside him. The room was out of focus. I moved my head from side to side, trying to adjust to being back in the real world. I turned, to find Kastor gazing at me.

"I suppose that hurt a lot?" I asked, nervously.

"Yes. But not as much as last night." I moved my head to rest on his chest again and he cradled me in his arms, possibly wondering at why I wanted to bother with what Dr. Foucoe obviously thought a pretty hopeless case. I looked at my watch. Scarcely any time had passed, like on my last venture. I slipped off the bed, despite Kastor trying to still hold my body close to him. I was sitting on the chair putting on my shoes when the replacement nurse arrived, surprised to find me there. But everything seemed to be in order and I explained that the other nurse had only just left. While the nurse was checking various items on trolleys, I whispered to Kastor, "I'll be back later. I think at least twice a day at first, then adjust according to how the healing is progressing."

"Do I have any say?" he murmured.

"Well," I said, "it looks like it's me or the dark fort of St. Anthony's. But of course it must be your decision." I left the ward quickly, not wanting to run into Dr. Foucoe or before Kastor had a chance to respond.

31

In the end, it was Ryden who was urgently transferred to St. Anthony's. It was agreed that there was little point in a mind exploration, which would also be extremely dangerous as it was evident from his state that his mind was now, mostly, a gaping hole. There was also considerable brain damage from blows to the head and possibly the mind probe being switched to progressively higher settings, where it could also disrupt normal brain tissue. Dr. Foucoe enthusiastically related all this to me and also advised that I should see him before he was taken away.

"It will help to give you closure," she said, "as well as understanding the great care that Kastor will need to get well, although his injury is mild compared with that of this loathsome traitor."

I was curious, as ever, so reluctantly accepted Clea's advice and went to the detention area. I was shocked to see the transformation in this once handsome, self assured young man. His mental age was judged to be less than one year, perhaps 10 or 11 months, so he mostly crawled around on all fours, occasionally hitching himself up proudly to a semi standing position, but falling over if he was encouraged to try to walk. He bawled when he was hungry, opening his mouth wide and yelling until food was put into it. When not needing a nappy change or feed, he was relatively easy to manage, grinning amiably at nothing in particular and making gurgling sounds.

He could manage a few words, 'No' being his favourite, soon with a marked Spanish intonation, and the nurses thought his "Nanna" was quite sweet, although it was applied to more or less anything he wanted. 'Nanna' was one of the first words learned by Binaries, in their communal nurseries.

"Will there be any recovery?" asked one of the nurses, spooning some food into him and hoping he would not throw the bowl on the floor again. Clea was in the room, while I stayed outside by the viewing window.

"Perhaps a little," said Clea Foucoe. "We'll scan his brain regularly at St. Anthony's. Possibly there will be some minimal recovery there. But with no connection with the mind…"

The nurse nodded, sagely. "He was a very bad man. But he doesn't even know that, now."

"Such cases are very interesting to study – and rare," murmured the psychiatrist. "His life certainly won't have been wasted. He'll be contributing to science."

Coming out of the room, she explained that they had devised experimental methods at St. Anthony's of looking within the mind without the peril of having to enter it. It was extremely painful for the patient, but, reasoned Dr. Foucoe, Ryden would have little memory of each attempt. It would come up fresh each time and he would be given a special feed or cuddly toy to hold afterwards. Viewing him through the inspection window, I had noticed that being put down into his bed, with restraints to stop him rolling off, seemed to upset him. Dr. Foucoe commented that he was unaccountably afraid of leather belts and anything resembling a scarf. I could have enlightened her about his experience with Helen and Marcie, but we were not on good terms after my insistence on mind exploring. Still, she could not contain her enthusiasm about the research opportunities. She declared that it would be fascinating to examine the parts of the mind cavity that could be made to react in this way, with appropriate stimulation.

With such an interesting victim for her research, Dr. Foucoe accepted that Kastor should stay at the Centro Binario, not least because Theodora had suggested that my unusual technique could mean an additional research paper for the psychiatrist. Within a few days of Kastor's arrival at the Cadiz centre, he and I were the only Woodstock Binaries left in residence. It was a much smaller centre than the one I was used to, with very limited entertainment, but much more freedom to go outside. For the first week, I scarcely noticed my surroundings, with my frequent visits to Kastor's bedside and increasingly rigorous mind explorations. When I could see obvious improvement after three days, I increased the frequency of entering his mind to three or four times a day. At first he protested, but gradually had to admit that he was sensing an occasional, if unclear, thought. While still very painful, it seemed a modest price to pay for the return of any of the telepathy that had been the central focus of his life.

As to his feelings for me, he admitted that he found them confusing. He remembered loving me before the injuries, but he found it hard to recall any shared images and experiences or to sense my moods and feelings. Mainly he saw me as alternatively kind or strict. He also said he liked my attractive body. I was pleased at first, but this proved to be the first major problem in my healing regimen.

I had become increasingly adept at traversing the damaged areas, turning to the tangled or broken filaments when I had repaired much of the tiling and roof structures of the two upper caverns. I was thrilled to find that layers beneath that were scarcely damaged, the main difficulty being the loss of connections with the outer layers where thoughts were expressed and stored for regular use. Some parts of the second cavern down remained no-go areas because of tangles and pieces of furniture that had fallen on each other. I devised a clever way of repairing the filaments, sensing that recovery would only accelerate when I had managed to re-create the flowing network of pulses around each chamber. The healing foam stopped what looked like inflammation, but did not appear to encourage re-growth, so I conjured up thin transparent tubing, of the same type and texture as the transparent coating of the columns. The tubes were open at one side, so that I could thread around fractured filaments, encouraging the ends to touch. This was particular agony for Kastor.

After a couple of sessions of this, he said he wanted a couple of days' rest from any exploration. "It's torture," he moaned. The senior nurse in the unit, Sister Isidora, took me aside and suggested that at this stage of recovery he needed a good balance of physical sensation. She'd seen cases of mind damage before and the only thing that calmed the patient was sex. I blushed, saying that surely this would be inappropriate, in a hospital ward.

"No, it'll make him more agreeable – to what you're doing to his mind."

"Has he been... asking for sex?" I said tentatively, wondering why this had not come up before.

"Oh yes," said Sister Isidora, with a sexy intonation enhanced by her Spanish accent.

"But I don't understand why he didn't tell me, I'm his bond mate, after all," I said, feeling both puzzled and guilty. The truth was that I was finding the repairs increasingly fulfilling, looking forward to each new journey inside Kastor's mind. I'd hoped that despite the pain, he found the improvement and shared experience equally exciting. Hadn't he always said, it was mainly my mind that attracted him?

The ward sister smiled. "No, he doesn't want it with you, not until he's much better. He needs, how you would say, sex therapy. Just sex, it doesn't matter who with. We can arrange this for you both."

I was stunned. "Well, why can't I do it?" Sister Isidora looked equally shocked. "Because you are a senior telepath. It wouldn't be respectable! And you his bond mate!" She held out her arms in a gesture of disbelief at the very idea.

"Does this often go on, sex therapy for patients?"

"Not often – but it's just a physical thing. We can ask for volunteers."

"Volunteers?" I exclaimed.

"Oh, si, for Kastor that will not be a problem. Then, he can just ask for sex whenever he needs it, without the embarrassment of making you do this."

"You think he hasn't asked me, because he's too embarrassed?" I felt lightheaded, glancing around for somewhere to sit down. Isidora looked more serious, gazing at me kindly. "And there's the baby. You haven't told him yet?"

"How did you know?" I had noticed a little bump emerging from my pelvis, but had managed to keep the morning sickness to myself. It was getting worse, but I always breakfasted in my room and there was no pressure to go to work or keep to a routine.

"I'm good at spotting pregnancy," said Sister Isidora. "So, perhaps you are about 12 weeks now?"

I thought back, maybe I was 7 or 8 weeks when Kastor had left for his mission, but that was just over two weeks ago. But I had missed two periods, it was hard to be sure. Plus I had the idea that it was twins, which would make me bigger than my dates. I did not share the twin idea with Sister Isidora. The nurse was horrified that I had not had a pregnancy test or seen a doctor. She arranged for Dr. Fernandez, now recovering from his attack of botulism, to see me on the following day.

"Meanwhile, you must be very careful. The baby is the most important consideration, no?"

Oh yes of course, I thought in a closed part of my mind. I should have known that Binaries babies had high priority, far higher than the mother. "It's perfectly safe to have sex in pregnancy," I said firmly, "And I don't want any volunteers having sex with Kastor, absolutely no! I'll talk to him."

Isidora looked appalled, not bothering to shutter the thought that this English Binary was very stubborn. She was confirmed in this when I said, "And Kastor must not be told I'm pregnant. He'd worry." The sister felt sad for me, knowing from experience of cases that Kastor, at present, was not concerned much about my feelings. She did not know that I had been brought up outside, which would have helped to explain my resistance to something quite normal for Binaries, particularly the younger ones. Physical sex was not a basis for a relationship in their community, just an appetite.

I went into Kastor's private ward, now seeing more significance in the side room with its couch. Perhaps they had chosen this suite with particular care, knowing he would need the couch as part of his recovery, if not transferred to St. Anthony's. And St. Anthony's, I thought with shocked realisation, must be a writhing hotbed of mind damaged men and women having sex with volunteers, each other, anyone to hand. Why had Kastor never mentioned this? Kastor was lying peacefully on his bed and seemed to be dozing. He still needed to sleep for short periods, several times a day. I turned away, going in search of one of the coffee rooms to mull over this latest revelation of Binary life. I was pleased to find Julieta there, normally too busy to take a formal coffee break. I tentatively raised the subject. Julieta knew my background and looked sympathetic.

"So, a nurse has been talking to you. You see, Kastor wouldn't want to bother you about it, perhaps he'd also worry that you wouldn't understand."

"I don't understand," I said flatly. "Does it seem so odd, that I don't want other women having sex with him?"

"No, of course, in a passionate relationship, not odd, when both partners are in telepathic communication. But it's not so unusual, when the man is damaged – or has special needs. Think of your King Henry VIII, he always took a mistress when his wives were pregnant."

"And when they weren't pregnant... but that was nearly 500 years ago!" I gasped, suddenly thinking, *does Julieta think I'm pregnant too?*

"Oh, sorry, yes of course I knew you were having a baby," said Julieta, "I sensed it, when you first arrived. Many of us have that ability, you know that." She gazed more intently at me, murmuring, "Perhaps two babies? Oh, twins, that would be wonderful. But I'd also say, sentient already. Definitely one – or hopefully two – of us."

"But Kastor doesn't know. I've asked Sister Isidora not to tell him."

"Why?" asked Julieta, puzzled. Pregnancies, particularly bearing likely telepaths, were a huge cause of celebration in Binary communities.

"He's not well enough yet. I want him to feel it, feel good about it," I said, on the point of tears. Julieta came to sit nearer.

"Kastor will recover, you're seeing to that. But at the moment, he's not susceptible to emotion. This is very hard for you. He knows he's lacking it, it must hurt him. He wouldn't want to be using you."

I was now crying, feeling the strain of the past two weeks: the plotting, deceit, violence, deaths. And now my lover had been asking for sex, behind my back.

"Will it seem outrageous, if I insist that I provide this service?" I said.

"Well, yes," said Julieta, "But you are English. We make allowances." She was smiling and I had to laugh too. The whole situation was so bizarre.

I went back to my room and sat on my bed, staring at the mirror in the wardrobe door. I wondered where Helen was at that moment. Busy with her life with Faisal, possibly on the run again? No harm, I thought, in trying to reach her anyway. In my mind, I called for Helen, while staring intently at the mirror. I smiled with relief when the reflection shifted and I saw my twin looking back at me.

"Cass! How's it going?" I came close to the mirror and my twin saw my tear streaked face. "Oh, not so well," said Helen, "I thought as much."

I started to give her the news, that Kastor was slowly recovering and that they now had the information to break Anne Guburda's network, but although whistling with surprised horror at who had been behind the kidnap of telepaths, Helen stopped me impatiently.

"Try and come through, into our space. You look terrible. Faisal's at work and I was just trying on some new clothes." I pressed my hand on the mirror, meeting the hand of the reflection. The mirror still felt hard but I closed my eyes and thought of Alice going through the looking glass. When I opened my eyes, I was standing in the dark space behind the mirror, with the blurry form of my twin beside me.

"It's Kastor – he…" In a rush of words, I told Helen about the mental fabric repairs and the current dilemma of sex therapy. Helen nodded sympathetically.

"I know now how peculiar and unfeeling that must seem to you. But Cass, it's not a big deal in Binary world. I've been a volunteer myself." My eyes opened wide, picturing Helen slipping into bed with damaged telepaths. "It's not like sex with ordinary humans," Helen continued. "When telepaths lose their senses, it's as if they can't tap into emotions at all. They can be quite violent, not at all concerned with your feelings." I thought of Roderick trying to bully me into sex, but Helen, picking this up, shook her head.

"No Cass, not like Roderick – he enjoyed being sadistic and also being on the receiving end. But these non-sentient telepaths, they don't enjoy it. They just want to briefly forget the feeling of lacking everything important to them. They don't want the other person to be feeling anything for them, either."

"I think I understand," I said uncertainly, "but there's also the pregnancy – I think a lot of people here know about it, even though I haven't said a thing. And that seems even more shocking, that I'd agree to do this… service, while pregnant. With twins."

"Twins!" squeaked Helen. "Like we thought! Mine have been confirmed - the obstetrician did a scan. What about that, both of us. Faisal wants us to get married, but he'd probably want me to live in some compound, with female relatives. But sorry," she paused, seeing my distress, "I'm being insensitive. I suppose you're thinking, why can't he wait, while you get on with these amazing mind repairs."

"It seems to be working, but it's terrifying too. I have to really concentrate to get out."

"And while you're wearing yourself out on this, he's just asking the nurses for sex," said Helen. "OK, this is what I think. Give it a go, see how you feel about it then."

"Everyone will be shocked, disapproving," I murmured.

"Who cares about them? We're the wonder twins, Cass. I never wanted more to be back there with you."

"Oh, and about that, you've been forgiven, well almost. You can't come back to Binaries but you don't need to worry about death threats." I also told Helen about Gaston meeting up with Aunt V and Helen exclaimed in amazement.

"No kidding! Well if anyone can drag out his deeply hidden feelings, she might just be the one. Does she know about me?"

"Not yet," I said, "I was only with her for a few minutes." Helen turned her head, saying she'd heard someone and had to go. As her image faded, she called, "Go for it Sis. Contact me again. If it's early morning we can throw up together."

I was back in my bedroom, seeing a normal reflection. But I felt a lot better. Right, I thought, putting on set of easily removable clothes: if this is what Kastor needs, I'd better get on with it. With this resolve, I headed back to the medical unit.

32

I found Kastor awake, sitting by his bed, trying to read. "I still can't concentrate," he said, putting the book aside. I looked towards the side room, working up the courage to bring up the subject of sex. Normally, Kastor would have picked this up immediately, but he gazed at me blankly, just seeing that I was worried about something.

"The nurses think you should be having… sex therapy," I said, blushing.

"Oh," he said simply, then, "They shouldn't have told you."

"Well, I'm up for it, would I do?"

Kastor rolled his eyes, looking grim. "I don't want to impose myself on you, not in this state."

"Nonsense, why ever not?" I stood up and looked more meaningfully towards the side room. A nurse came into the wardroom and I turned to her.

"Could you give us a few minutes privacy, we need to…"

Sensing my thoughts immediately, the nurse looked shocked. "I'll fetch Sister," she said, dashing out of the room. The senior nurse appeared within a minute.

"*It's not for negotiation*," I signalled, "*I insist.*" Looking towards Kastor, who was watching us, wishing he could pick up the thought transference, Sister Isidora sighed. "You English...," she said, as though that explained everything. "*Very well*," she signalled at last. "*But you've been warned.*" She officiously drew a screen across the entrance to the side room and silently told the other nurse to leave.

Once in the side room, Kastor got up onto the couch uneasily and I joined him. The couch was narrow, so we were inevitably in close contact, but Kastor turned his head away.

"You don't understand. I don't want it with you."

"Well, I thought we'd do a little mind healing, first."

"That counts as foreplay, does it?" said Kastor, looking at me with a thin smile. With his body so close to mine, his face showed a surge of physical desire. I would have been pleased, had I not sensed that he was trying to suppress it.

"These are my terms - mind exploration first, then sex." Seeing that Kastor was increasingly uncomfortable with me lying with him, I slipped off and sat at the end of the couch. Kastor closed his eyes, feeling the pain of not being in touch with me by thought.

"Cassandra... please. It's probably just a phase in my recovery. They can get volunteers, I promise it would mean nothing to me."

I gazed at him, with a stubborn look that stirred his memory, reminding him agonisingly of our life together at Askeys.

"There's a kitchen assistant, one who brings my meals – she'd do. Quite pretty." He reeled back as I shot a fiery glance. Good, I thought, he can feel that, at least.

"Did I say pretty, I meant plain. Very plain. Scraggy, hideous in fact," said Kastor, weakly.

"Has she indicated willingness?" I demanded, trying to picture this woman, who I felt I must have seen coming through the medical unit.

"Er, yes," said Kastor carefully. "She mentioned it this morning. I expect the nurses spoke to her."

"But you haven't... done it... with her?" I said angrily.

"No, I haven't. Why are you being like this? It's quite normal treatment."

I folded my arms. "Well, here's how it is. If you have sex with this kitchen girl or any... volunteer, they'll wish they'd never been born, and so will you."

"I already wish that," said Kastor and I felt a wave of compassion. Kastor now looked as though sex was the last thing on his mind and I detected his confused wish to try to pacify me.

I moved up the couch, lying sideways, with my back wedged uncomfortably against the wall. "Let's see how we both feel, after I've been in your mind," I said. He sighed, tilting his head back to gaze at the ceiling.

"I didn't know you had this cruel streak," he said plaintively.

"I want my Kastor back," I said, quietly. "If that's cruel, so be it."

I signalled, *let's get on with the mind entry*, before remembering he couldn't pick this up, so I said it aloud. He nodded, with no energy for resistance. I focused and travelled into the now familiar caverns. The mind's surface was healing well, with many areas showing a sparkling snow appearance and almost no jagged points sticking up. I busied myself in the chamber below, having found a way of moving the storage cabinets back into place. I used little balls of column material that avoided the effort of heaving and pushing. I adjusted my splints on the filaments, now untangled on this level. When I emerged after seemingly having been there for ages, I felt exhausted and stiff from the awkward posture in which I'd left my body. Kastor also looked tired from the pain of the experience.

"So, would you like sex, now?" I was not at all in the mood, but I had promised. I curved my arms around Kastor, thinking how much I had missed him. He pushed my hands away and rotated me efficiently to lie beneath him on the narrow couch. "I'm just going to have to forget that it's you," he said brusquely and I thought it was the most unromantic statement I'd ever heard.

"By all means," I said sarcastically but he didn't appear to be listening. He didn't look at my face, his eyes closed, his whole being intent on this purely physical activity that required no thought and lessened his mental suffering. He tore at my clothes and grabbed me fiercely. I suddenly recalled Roderick's bullying ways and I recoiled. I felt an ache beneath my womb, remembering the fetuses within. I twisted away from him, sitting up angrily.

"Now what?" he said. "Oh, you're waiting for me to say please or thank you, I suppose. Well, thanks for nothing. Is that what you want me to say?"

I slapped his face hard and he looked bemused.

"We can rule out sex therapy as a career for you, then," he said, rubbing his face.

"You didn't have to be so cold and impersonal about it," I said, glowering at him so that he flinched. "You used to be so sensitive. Anyway, you should be more careful with me, now…"

He looked puzzled. I seized his hand and placed it firmly on my little bump. His expression changed to shock and horror.

"You're pregnant? Why didn't you tell me?" He looked in the direction of the wardroom, as if expecting one of the nurses to come in and chastise us both. Then he sat up, adjusting his hospital pyjamas, wide awake and furious. "This is so disgraceful," he murmured. "It'll be the talk of the centre. How could you – what made you possibly imagine this was appropriate?"

"Oh don't worry, they'll just blame the outsider," I said

scornfully, slipping my feet back into my shoes and closing my track suit top. "Your mind is looking a lot better, incidentally, not that you seem to need it any more."

He gazed at me, looking more upset than I'd seen him since the injuries. I sensed he was trying to conjure up images, fighting to reach the damaged upper layers of his mind. He closed his eyes at the pain, trying to ignore it, forcing thoughts to somehow reach his consciousness. But I did not feel conciliatory.

"If it's just sex services you want, you might as well ask to be transferred to St. Anthony's," I thundered. "And then you can bonk away to your heart's content. If you had a heart," I added, pitilessly. "It's twins, by the way - and they'll be fine. I know that's all any of you really care about. Why, maybe I can have several sets, so you can all stop stealing people's babies!"

"Please, stop it. I can't bear it," he shouted, turning away. I sprang round to look at his face and was astonished to see tears running down his cheeks.

A nurse had run into the room, hearing the raised voices. She pulled the screen aside. She saw the tears, pausing to signal that this was a very good sign before leading Kastor back to his bed, where he turned away from us both.

"I suppose that's at least a result," the nurse said, with no indication that she approved. "Do you understand, now? You should leave, he needs to rest."

I felt confusion mixing with my anger. This sex therapy, at least with me, didn't seem to make Kastor either calmer or more agreeable, but then what did I really understand about these alien people. Admittedly, we hadn't got as far as sex but I'd hoped that lying together would have helped, for starters. I pictured the kitchen assistant, greeting him with a pert "Ola, Senor Kastor, and 'ow would you like your sex today?" noting his contented grunts afterwards for later entry in the ward report, then leaving to carry on delivering breakfasts. I won't have it, I thought fiercely, feeling at the same time remorse for telling Kastor to transfer to the dark fort. Perhaps he will do just that, I thought, with a slight panic. I went to his bedside and gingerly took his hand. The nurse stood by, signalling for me to simply go. Kastor pulled his hand away, burying his head in the pillow. "I'll come back later," I said and then turned and left the room.

Dining later with the other members of the centre, people were polite and showed no sign they'd been discussing my actions. But I felt their thoughts and ate silently. Filipo came over and said he'd arranged for Phoebe and Ashara to come over. I'd forgotten that I'd asked for them to stay briefly for commercial experience and tutorials with me.

"They'll be here tomorrow. Perhaps that will help you to take your mind off... other things." I nodded, grateful that I could feel his sympathy. They were all so kind, I thought, trying to be tolerant of my deviant behaviour. They had arranged to see a new film after the meal, but I excused myself and went back to the medical unit. A nurse was sitting by Kastor's bed. She stood up, unsmiling, when I entered the room. "You shouldn't stay long," she said briefly, leaving the ward. I took my place on the chair, waiting for Kastor to acknowledge my presence. He turned his head, not meeting my eyes.

"I've asked for the transfer to St. Anthony's."

"Oh, no, Kastor, I didn't mean it."

"It's for the best. You need to get back to a normal life, normal Binary life that is. Or perhaps you want to leave. I'll understand, everyone will understand."

"They wouldn't let me. I'm too valuable, now," I said, thinking both of my abilities and the twins.

"As if anyone could stop Cassandra," he said wearily, but with the hint of a smile. "Please, let me do this. I may get a bit better, you've done wonders, I can feel that. But I can't sense your thoughts, emotions - that's just additional torture. And after what I nearly did to you today, I don't want to be reminded, by seeing you."

He lowered his eyes, as if that would wipe the memory. He remembered mainly all his senses being overpowered by lust without the slightest trace of emotion for me. I gathered this much from his confused thoughts, trying not to cry. His training made him shocked and humiliated at going along with my plan, especially while I was carrying twins. "How could you think of letting me... treat you like that?"

"So it's all my fault," I said, bitterly.

"Cassandra, don't you realise, ... I really didn't care who you were, in those moments. That's what I've become, so perhaps this will convince you to stop dreaming about the old Kastor." He added, with an air of being done with this conversation, "Anyway, now we can forget each other, that's what we both need."

I burst into tears. He frowned, wondering if he should reach for my hand, tentatively touching it. "I'm so sorry," he said, "I am forever having to apologise to you. What we had was wonderful, but it's over. Please don't make it more painful – I've made my decision."

"Now and forever, that's what you promised," I blurted through my sobs. He sighed, saying nothing. I stared at him fiercely. "I'll veto your request. I don't care how long it takes, I'm going to make sure you come through this, back to health." He breathed deeply, watching me.

"Don't you want me to go on? I've made such progress," I pleaded. "I mean, if it's just the sex, I could try to be OK with... volunteers."

He rolled his eyes, making a small dry "hah" sound that could have been an attempt at laughing. "I'm not sure if I ever want sex again," he said, "It seems to have been good aversion therapy."

"Thank you," I said disdainfully. "That makes me feel great, I must say."

"Well," he said, taking care with his words, "I wouldn't want a pile of dead kitchen assistants and other volunteers cluttering up the hillside. I've been lying here, remembering us together before all this. I think those memories will be quite enough, for now – and better for the local death statistics." I laughed, despite my distress. "I wouldn't kill them," I said, narrowing my eyes. "Not all at once, anyway."

"Are you really willing to stay?" he said, hesitantly. I gazed deeply into his eyes, feeling a twinge of response and my heart soared with hope. In answer to his question, I shook my head. Kastor appeared devastated, before I replied, "No, not willing to stay here, at any rate. We're going back to Askeys, I'll arrange it. Perhaps in a couple of days."

"You won't take no for an answer, I suppose?" said Kastor, looking happier than at any time since his arrival in Cadiz.

"No, we'll go back and take it one step at a time." I was about to leave the room when I paused, looking at his contented face. "We'll continue with the mind work, then?" I said.

"Whatever you say," he murmured. "What's a bit of pain, when you have Cassandra looking after you."

Dr. Foucoe was not happy with my request, but now that she was travelling frequently to St. Anthony's on her research project with Ryden, she reluctantly agreed that if Kastor was really becoming sentient again, his care could be managed at the Binaries.

I arranged the return journey before going to greet Phoebe and Ashara. "I've suggested you should make some trips into Cadiz, to see what's in the shops," I said, pleased at the girls' excited response. They would be going outside with a field officer and two Spanish students. "Julieta will be your supervisor, as I'll be going back to the Binaries on Friday. I'll expect a very detailed report." Phoebe and Ashara nodded eagerly and I left them planning their trips. I knew the Binario staff would enjoy having them there and the girls would have a good time. They might even improve their Spanish, I thought, since the male students could definitely described as fit.

It was noon before I had time to visit Kastor. He was sitting anxiously, obviously waiting for me. Perhaps he missed me, I thought, seeking empathic contact but I sensed only swirling fog.

"I couldn't sleep," he admitted, "Are we really going back?" I nodded happily, asking him if he felt up to a mind entry. "I'm very tired," he said, "but yes, please, let's continue." I noticed that the igloo tent had disappeared. He followed my glance, saying, "I felt I wanted to catch more of the outside noise."

"There's still a lot to do. I'm going to try to sort out the second level, do you think you could stand that?" I knew that working on the filaments would be especially painful.

"Would it make a difference, if I said no?"

I smiled and prepared to slide into his mind.

After fixing some filament splints in the columns that I had worked on before, I glanced at the tangled wiring to the side of the chamber. I assessed that it was not so much broken as needing gentle untangling, so that the filaments could spring back into position. I knelt down, wondering what was on the floor below, as it didn't look like normal tiling. While concentrating on my task, I sensed, in the far distance, that Kastor was becoming drowsy. We both knew the importance of staying alert, even if he could not yet help to eject me from his mind. Sleepiness, while I was within his mental fabric, would affect me as well as him.

Stay awake, Kastor, I thought urgently, moving to the stepladder up to the next cavern. But he was feeling very relaxed, happy to have made up with me and with the prospect of going home. I felt the cavern shudder a little as he started to drift off. A wave of sleep passed through the chamber, like a current from the River Lethe in the mythological underworld. I felt my eyes closing, fighting to stay conscious. I had heard of the dangers of being trapped in the unconscious mind. My body outside would stay in a coma indefinitely. Fearfully, I stepped back to the tangle of filaments, looking for somewhere safe to stand, so that I would not slip down into lower chambers. I remembered the shadows I had seen on my first exploration of Kastor's mind back at Askeys. They had been lurking in the corners of the deep layers. I froze with terror, feeling the approach of nebulous creatures who would suck me into the depths.

I slumped onto the pile of filaments, longing to join Kastor in sleep. He wants me in his subconscious, I thought, trying to focus. He wants me to drift down there, absorbed by the currents of hidden thought, so that he'd never need to fear me leaving. "Kastor, wake up!" I called, but only his subconscious was aware of me, recognising our deep connection, sending siren calls to lure me into blissful union. Sirens, I thought, shaking myself awake, remembering Kastor had spoken of these within my mind. I pushed against the filaments, hoping that the pain would stir him, but sensed only a numb acknowledgement of the pressure as the impending sleep anaesthetised these sensitive strands.

Then I felt a hard, cold object where I had moved the filaments. I looked down, seeing the doorknocker shaped in the hand of Fatima. The door must have fallen over during the attack, also protecting the layer beneath. I mustered all my strength to clear the area round the knocker, surrounded by small bits of debris. The brass hand lay there, looking a dull greenish colour in the dim light of the chamber. I grabbed it and banged on the door, screaming for Kastor to wake up. After several knocks, I felt the river of sleep starting to recede. I sprang up, sensing I had little time and scrambled up the stepladder, nearly slipping on the floor of the upper cavern, with its recovering surface. *Hand of Fatima, be with me*, I thought, visualising Joel's grave face, with little confidence that anyone outside Kastor's mind could assist. Normally I would wait until I reached the surface, but I transformed my probe into a rocket, able to roar through the gap in the next layer, which had not yet healed enough to close properly. Gasping, I felt myself leave the mind, but the impetus of the rocket shot me far above the centre. I jetted into an infinity of telepathic thought, milling around Centro Binario. I sensed several people feeling the jolt of my presence, looking around in bewilderment, seeing nothing. But at last I started to descend, shooting back into my own mind and at the same time tumbling from the chair, falling unconscious.

When I came to, the Sister was standing over me. I was lying on the couch in the side room. Dr. Fernandez was there as well, looking concerned.

"Is Kastor all right?" I asked, thinking of the rapid exit and how the fragile state of the healing structure might have reacted.

"He's fine, fast asleep," said the doctor. "He asked about you too. He sensed something went wrong. He's getting more sentient by the day."

I nodded with relief. "He became very sleepy, while I was in there."

"And you felt you'd never be able to leave," murmured Dr. Fernandez. "You're very brave to even attempt these journeys. We couldn't have rescued you. It would be as if you'd left your body for ever."

"Now and forever," I said thoughtfully, but the doctor didn't know how significant this was for us. He looked at me more sternly.

"You were supposed to come to see me, this morning."

"I'm sorry, I completely forgot."

"You've been trying to forget this pregnancy, while looking after Kastor," said Sister Isidora. "We can examine you now, if you feel OK?" I glanced into the wardroom where I could see Kastor's silent form, sleeping. "I suppose so," I said reluctantly, obediently undressing and positioning myself for the internal examination that I knew was coming.

When the examination and a quick real-time scan were over, the doctor smiled. "You're 12 weeks pregnant and we could both sense your babies. Just faint at the moment, but definitely twins, and likely to be highly telepathic. As we'd expect."

"Congratulations," said the sister, beaming.

"It's all a bit much, right now," I said, trying to conceal my selfish thoughts about how the attention would now inevitably focus on the excitement of Binary twins, with me as their 'carrier'.

"So, after this adventure, you must have a siesta, like Kastor," said Sister Isidora.

"Actually, I'm starving hungry," I said and she replied, "Good, some lunch and then rest". The atmosphere in the dining room was much more friendly than on my last visit. Baby news travels fast, I thought, or perhaps they're just glad this nuisance from the outside will be leaving very soon. It turned out that the Binario members were mainly excited that Anne Guburda had been tracked down and captured.

"Thanks to you and your sister," said Filipo.

"Phoebe helped me, too," I said, "but was sworn to secrecy."

Phoebe looked up proudly and I signalled that she shouldn't say much. The Spanish centre was more lenient than its namesake in Woodstock, but involving younger members in a mission was not normal policy and I didn't need any more disapproval of my wayward conduct.

33

When we had travelled back from Cadiz and settled into their apartment at last, it seemed we had been away for years. Only a month, I reminded Kastor, who slept in his study bedroom for the time being. I had relentlessly continued with the mind repairs before our departure. Kastor was not sure if he was receiving thoughts, but seemed much happier as he was finding it easier to sense feelings.

"I suppose you're going to go on torturing me, with these trips in my head," he murmured, waking from his rest after the journey.

"Perhaps not today," I said, "after being hours on a plane. Do you think it affected you?" The pressure of the air cabin was supposed to be potentially hazardous to injured minds.

"No, I just feel very tired and happy to be back. To be back with you."

I got onto the bed, lying beside him. "We'll just let your subconscious get on with the mind repairs, then. I didn't realise, until I was nearly trapped in it, that it's teeming with strange shadowy beings."

"I'm sure they all love you," he said, shifting the bedspread so that it could cover me, while we remained decorously separated by the duvet. Neither of us had mentioned sex since my attempt at therapy of this nature.

"And you?" I whispered, cuddling up to him. "Does the conscious Kastor feel anything for me?" He nuzzled me drowsily. "Cassandra," he murmured, "I think I'm going to fall in love with you all over again." I smiled hopefully, but he made no move to touch me further. I watched him fall asleep again, before quietly leaving his room.

Over the next few weeks, Kastor followed a routine of visiting the training centre to exercise his slowly returning skills. A special room was provided so that he would not have the humiliation of learning with the children or teenagers. Occasionally he would visit the assessment laboratories for a check on his progress. I returned to work in the commercial centre, coming back to the apartment with the sad feeling that Kastor would just greet me politely, as though I were a long staying visitor that he had to put up with. Or a therapist, I thought, coming to give him some mind repairs. Theodora counselled patience, reminding me that his recovery was astonishing and a tribute to my ability. He was having to concentrate on learning to use telepathy anew. He would not discuss the mission, his escape or our time in Cadiz. He seemed to want to forget all about it.

"But he appears to have forgotten about me, as well," I confided to Theodora when we met for a meal.

"Of course he hasn't forgotten you," she said. "But it's hard for him, needing so much help and not being able to communicate fully with you. Your impatience," she added, "is one of your faults, is it not?" I acknowledged this with a sad nod.

Christmas had come and gone at Binaries with little celebration. It was seen mainly as a festival for the children, along with important calendar dates in other religions that allowed parties. Seeing the little pile of presents around the tree, I had asked if I could get something special for Leander and the senior housemother had explained that there could be no differences between the children. Several adults attended the present opening and helped the children play with their toys. I was beginning to think that Leo had forgotten me too, when he came up shyly and sat beside me.

"*Hello Mummy,*" he said in his thoughts and I smiled warmly. Aloud, he said, "Can I see the globe again, one day?" I wondered whether another visit to the apartment would do Kastor good, reminding him of that rare family moment we had shared. I asked for permission and the senior housemother was sympathetic, knowing of Kastor's injuries. She suggested that as a great treat, Leander could be allowed to visit with a couple of his friends. A nanny would bring them over and stay with us most of the time, but might be allowed to leave us alone for a brief period. I decided to make this a surprise for Kastor, ordering suitable food and borrowing a few toys from the assessment centre.

So on a crisp January day, when Kastor returned mid afternoon to the apartment, he heard sounds of merriment and opened the door cautiously. The children were running around playing hide and seek and the nanny and I were pretending to find it hard to find them. The children stopped when they saw Kastor, accustomed to politeness with adults. But after recovering from his surprise, he joined in and was soon giving piggyback races to Leo, Finley and Astra.

After tea, I whispered to Kastor that Leo had asked to see the globe again and he nodded, quietly taking Leo by the hand and disappearing with him into the study. If the nanny disapproved, she gave no sign. That she might be feeling the opposite was shown when she suggested that Finley and Astra come with her to visit the pagoda. She nodded significantly to me as she ushered them out the door, signalling that she would return in about half an hour to collect all the children. I put my head round the study door, pleased to see father and son deep in conversation, Leo's eyes shining with pleasure at this indulgence. I suggested that we could listen to some songs in the living room. I fetched some fruit juice and Leo sat between us on the sofa. Leo tried to sing along, missing words and mispronouncing others.

I could tell that Kastor was enjoying the unusual family experience. When the nanny called to collect Leo, he whispered, "Come again?" and I nodded. To Kastor he said, with solemnity beyond his years, "Better soon, get better soon, Kastor." I was surprised, for no one had told Leo about the events of the past weeks and I would have been astonished if Kastor had confided in him in the study. Our son must have picked up the difficult thought transference and general lack of images coming from his father.

After Leo had left, Kastor and I remained on the sofa. I was remembering our frolic after our son's previous visit, but Kastor was sitting with a forlorn expression.

"My son is a better telepath than I am, now," he murmured.

"It'll come back all at once, when the mind is fully repaired, that's what Theodora said," I replied. I moved closer to him, willing him to remember our former intimacy. He turned, asking me what I was thinking about.

"Oh, Norwich, things like that."

"Norwich?" he said, puzzled. I looked into his eyes: perhaps this was a memory he'd lost. The therapists had explained that his brain memory was intact, but without the intricate mind connections, memories had lost much of their meaning for him. He was searching to link up the connotation. Finally he said, "Ah, knickers off ready." I smiled with delight, suggesting I could do just that, but his expression changed to shock.

"What are you talking about?" he asked. I bathed his mind with loving feelings, since if these could work on ordinary humans, surely he would react to them?

"No, Cassandra, I don't want sex with you," he said, although I detected, perhaps too optimistically, that he was trying to shake off the desire creeping through his mind.

"Would you rather, with someone else?" I said, hesitantly.

"No, there's no point without a proper range of feelings," he said, "or images. It's not that I don't feel love for you, please don't think that."

"I could try to make it fun," I said. "I mean, we could pretend that you've just come home and I'm the maid in a tight little uniform, bending over doing the dusting, and you could surprise me…" At this he smiled at last, putting his arm round me and interrupting the flight of seductive fancy.

"I haven't forgotten why I fell in love with you before. But seeing Leo today – it made me realise how much I've lost. It may never come back. I'm just grateful you're staying with me, this ruin, for as long as you can stand it. I don't want to spoil it with a repetition of - that physical assault on you."

I sighed, resting my head on his shoulder and wishing my healing efforts were more effective. His mind seemed almost restored, with lights moving down the filaments and the coatings of the columns now sensitive to the touch. But there was a sluggishness about it, as if everything was operating in slow motion. Lately I had turned to the thought chests and cabinets, carefully piecing together fragments of thought and feeling that had shattered in the attack. It was rather like assembling little jigsaw puzzles. When the last piece was clicked into place, the whole would glow slightly. I added a little healing foam, to help it stay together. The Norwich memory had shattered into tiny pieces, a difficult jigsaw challenge. So, even with a delicate binding, I could understand why it still meant little to him. Kastor now mostly enjoyed the explorations of his mind, with me gently slithering here and there. He also needed it, becoming impatient if I delayed our sessions or tried to change the routine.

"It seems selfish to say he's happy enough to just go on, endlessly, like this," I said plaintively to Theodora, when I had left him after mind work one evening and slipped out.

"While you have the stark choice to carry on or leave him?" asked Theodora.

"Yes, I should never have tried to give him sex therapy," I said, knowing nothing could be concealed from Theodora, who might also sense I was longing to talk about it. "Now he doesn't want physical contact with me at all. It's not just concern about the pregnancy."

Theodora was silent for a while, watching me blush at discussing this.

"Perhaps you need a short trip outside," she murmured, "so that Kastor can remember that he needs to consider your feelings more, even if he can't sense them clearly."

But where, I thought and Theodora said quickly, "Why not visit your aunt? You had only a few minutes when you were hiding out on that Friday." An image of Gaston floated between us.

"Ah," smiled Theodora, "I believe Gaston has visited your aunt again, but I'm sure he wishes her no ill will. Quite the opposite. In any case, he wouldn't interfere with you visiting. He has the highest opinion of you and knows the difficulties you must be experiencing, helping Kastor back to health."

"You've discussed it?" I asked, not liking the idea.

"We go a long way back, we don't need to discuss very much," said Theodora. "He perhaps told you of his own traumatic experience?" I nodded.

"Just so. Contact your aunt and arrange the visit for two or three days. You'll need to be a little disguised and avoid walking around in Oxford, would that be too great a restriction?" I thought not, warming to the notion of spending time with Aunt V and also curious about her meetings with Gaston.

I did not discuss the planned visit with Kastor, knowing he would argue that he needed my daily mind explorations. On the morning of the trip, with a car arranged to take me straight there, I thought it was time to try to contact my twin again. I rose at 5:30 a.m. and called to my twin through the cheval mirror.

Helen quickly appeared. "Cass! Wondered if you'd given up on me. What's up?" I stepped through into our space and found myself pouring out the misery of my relationship with Kastor.

"He was always quite prudish about these things," murmured

Helen. I thought about what Kastor had said, that she had proposed a liaison with him. Picking this up, Helen smiled grimly. "Yeah, well I was a lot more active in those matters than he was. But that was then, another life, Sis. You have to be patient, I suppose you've already been told that. Hard for us. But he's probably set on leaving all that stuff aside until he's the man you met at Blenheim. Men can be very proud."

I found it painful to be discussing Kastor and told her instead about visiting Aunt V.

"Lucky you!" said Helen. "I'm thinking of leaving Faisal, to be honest. He's OK but I've got a hankering to live on my own for a bit."

"Have you enough money to buy a place somewhere?"

"Yes – another home by the sea appeals."

"Me too," I said. We shared an image of a small house overlooking the sea, with our twins playing happily on a nearby beach.

"You can use the money in the Swiss account, the one you gave me the key and details for," I added. "And the bracelet, I haven't collected it yet."

"Hang on Cass," said Helen, "That's yours, at least Lily's. I've enough for a modest home and new identity. But don't rush into something. Are you really thinking you may leave Kastor?"

"I don't know," I said. "They seem happy to give me more freedom, these days, knowing how things are."

"I should think they'd be deliriously happy with you," said Helen, "They'll have made a bundle on sucking in all that colonel's money and you bring in loads in your own right, as Lily. I reckon you can state your terms, remember that."

"I'll think about the house, maybe France," I mused, but knowing it would not be as easy as Helen implied. They'd trace me anywhere; and why would they agree to my living outside?

We looked back into my bedroom, suddenly sensing that someone was coming near. Helen vanished and I slipped back, to see Kastor standing at the door.

"What are you doing?" he asked, looking curiously at the mirror.

"I was talking to Helen," I said, feeling honesty at this moment was best, even if Kastor could not do this type of communication.

"And that's how you plotted to save me," he said, coming over to me and staring at our reflections. The mirror accentuated the differences between us, I looking strong and a little defiant, he slightly stooping, his face uncertain and grave.

"I knew it was Helen, coming into that cell in Casablanca. She was amazing. Another few minutes and I'd have been going the way of Ryden." My reflection beamed proudly, but Kastor's remained solemn. "It might've been better if it had been later," he said, "Look at me now, making a star like you be my nurse maid."

I turned and hugged him, despite sensing he wanted to move away. "Don't ever say that again," I said fiercely. "You're nearly whole again, it won't take much longer." He shrugged, gently releasing himself from my arms and turning to leave the room.

"Don't go Kastor, I've something to tell you."

He paused and said, "I forgot how much you like getting up in the night. Can't it wait?"

"I'm going to visit Aunt V for a couple of days. I saw her briefly on that Friday and…"

"…and you've arranged to see her, without telling me." Kastor looked even more dejected. "You can't go, Cass, I need you here. You know that."

"You don't need me in your mind so much now. And perhaps we both need a break from each other."

Kastor sat on the bed, staring at me, wishing the images and other telepathic aids would come to him. "I can feel you're fed up with me, I understand that," he said, morosely. "This is just the beginning, you'll feel better not having me as a duty. Then you'll leave for good."

I gazed at him sadly, feeling the wave of depression in his mind. Sitting beside him, I tried to take his hand but he clasped his hands firmly together, staring ahead.

"You need to think about all this on your own," I said, before remembering that thoughts might still be painful to him, aggravating the scars in his mental fabric. "Your mind is all right now, it just needs something to set it firing again. It's confidence, mainly, that you need."

"Well thanks for that, Doctor Cassandra," he said bitterly. "And of course you must go. I don't really care, or care about anything any more." He got up abruptly and strode out of the room.

I looked at my wardrobe containing the disguise waiting to be put on, hesitating about the trip. But it would only be a couple of days and I'd make sure that Theodora and others knew he needed extra support. Convalescent patients are always the worst, I thought, and I'm no nursemaid. Not a very good one anyway, that's obvious enough. When breakfast was delivered to the apartment, I took a tray into Kastor, who was sitting up in bed idly turning the pages of a book.

"I'm sorry I was so mean about your trip," he said, in a flat tone. "I'll be fine of course. Give my regards. If I could be myself, I'd come with you."

"You can!" I said, "I'll make a call, I don't think there'd be a problem. Aunt V would adore to meet you, I talked about you a lot in those Blenheim days."

"No, I'll stay here. I'll be fine, don't worry. You're right, I need time to ponder on my interminably slow recovery."

"It's an amazingly fast recovery," I countered. "I'll call you and keep signalling, you have to unblock sometime." Kastor turned his attention to the breakfast tray as if dismissing me and said nothing more.

Both Theodora and Kastor were right. I felt a lot better once I'd left the Binaries and was sitting once again in my aunt's flat. She had cleared her diary so that we could spend time together and was eager to talk, having heard of the twin switch from Gaston and wanting me to fill in details.

"You appear to be getting on very well," I said with a knowing smile.

"He just seems comfortable here. We have the academic research in common and he's shown me how to share images. I'd no idea I could do that!"

Aunt V seemed quite girlish, discussing him. After my talk with Gaston, I was much less nervous of his motives. Perhaps he wants a liaison, like Manes with Poppy in Woodstock, I thought. I was fairly confident that Aunt V's telepathic skills would not stretch to picking this up, despite having Gaston as a tutor. The idea was surreal, but not beyond possibility. When Aunt V had finished updating me about this new relationship, she asked about Kastor. I explained about the mind damage and the strain this had caused. I also mentioned the pregnancy and the son I so rarely saw.

"I was very happy in that strange world, before Kastor was injured," I said, while my aunt was still reeling with my account of life at Binaries. Gaston had been very discreet about that, but I felt that my aunt could be trusted with these revelations. "But now, I just seem to depress him more."

"A couple of days without you will probably work wonders," she said encouragingly. "Meanwhile, I hope you won't be bored, not being able to go out."

"It's all right, I'm looking forward to perfecting scones and getting to know you again," I said. "In any case, I'm used to being confined."

The Execution Code

I telephoned the apartment several times, but Kastor did not answer. At first I thought he simply did not want to make me feel guilty about the trip. I signalled to Theodora and Manes but had already asked them to look out for him and received no responses from them either. I tried not to worry. On the second night of my stay I had a vivid dream. At first I was in the familiar caverns of Kastor's mind, which the dream quickly altered to be more like a Gothic castle, full of archways and mysterious staircases winding up narrow turrets. At a desk in the corner, a scribe was bent over some documents. He had grey shadowy robes, like the ghost of a medieval monk. I noticed two other robed men in a corner, who appeared to be mending the wall carvings. A woman, similarly robed, approached. "We've been waiting for you. The missing key, you have it?"

She led me to another desk, which contained a screen showing many images. It was fascinating to be able to walk into the images and explore them. One in particular, a beach scene, attracted me. I strolled on the sand, looking up at a sunny sky and then at Leo and other children playing happily with rock pools. "They're all twins, mummy," said Leo, pointing at the children. Nearby, I saw Helen wearing a sun hat like in the picture on the postcard she'd sent from Antigua. Gaston and Aunt V strolled by, dressed in black and purple respectively and talking amiably. A crab nipped my foot and I lifted it, only to see that the crab was alerting me to Kastor, buried in the sand with only his face showing. There was a sand model of the Askeys pagoda resting on his stomach.

"Where's the key?" said a chatty oyster, bouncing on the pagoda so that it crumbled over Kastor. He seemed asleep but opened his eyes, gazing at me.

"You have it, give it to them!" he cried out. I protested that I didn't know about this key, but they all started to shout, demanding it. I awoke with a start, looking around the room as if this mysterious key would appear.

I sat on the bed, focusing on the Binaries and Kastor. At last I sensed him, apparently sleeping. But another image moved into my mind, of that ornate key that I'd seen in Theodora's apartment. Then there was an image of Leo, holding up a drawing of a key and finally Theodora, nodding, telling me that I needed to act, but on what? I rubbed my eyes and seeing it was 3 a.m., tried to sleep again. Once more I descended into the gothic chambers that represented Kastor's mind. There were several shadowy robed figures in the cavern now, pointing at connections and opening chests or cabinets. They must be his subconscious, my dream self told me. I wandered amongst them, seemingly invisible to these beings. Then an old man sitting on a throne like chair looked straight at me.

"We must have that key, now," he said sternly. The woman I had seen before glided across.

"Don't be afraid," she said, "you just need to turn it and then we'll do the rest."

I looked around desperately: I could see no key. Then I heard a voice say, "In your pocket." I felt inside the pocket on the smock I was wearing and pulled out a large key, shining in the dim light of the cavern. As I looked at it, it started to grow until it was almost too heavy to hold. It was simply designed, like a key for locking a shed, but with intricate markings on the shaft. I held it firmly, as it seemed to be trying to slip away. I looked around for a lock, knowing in the strange logic of dreams that I had seen no lock or keyhole on my explorations, but would find one here. The group of subconscious workers followed me as I moved across the cavern to where a passageway led off to another part of the castle. I came to a wooden door, shaped to fit the pointed arch around it. There was a knocker shaped like the hand of Fatima, but with little jewel-like eyes that stared at me expectantly. The key was now incredibly heavy and I had to muster all my strength to lift it to the large keyhole in the door. Once it was in place, I felt the beings around me urging me to turn it.

"It's stuck," I said irritably, "or the wrong key."

"Turn it anyway," said Helen cheerfully, having unaccountably entered the cavern, or was it just my reflection speaking to me, from a mirror in a dim recess?

I grasped the key, pushing and pulling and finally just willing it to turn. With a creaking sound, I felt the key engaging with the lock and now I could move it with greater force, making it revolve once and then again. The door flew open and a gale blew in, knocking me over. I flew with this wind, soaring out of the cavern and over the coast of France, just as I'd seen it from the plane. Feeling exhilarated, I woke up.

"I'm so glad I found the key," I murmured and I suddenly saw Kastor's face in my mind, gazing at me. *I found it*, I said silently, *they're working on it all now*. I fell back to sleep, with no more memorable dreams disturbing me until I heard a ringing noise in the flat.

Aunt V brought her in a cup of tea, smiling cheerfully but I sensed she was concerned about something.

"I've just had a call from Gaston," she said. "He said you needed to come back this morning, that you'd understand."

I cast my mind across to the Binaries. I glimpsed Gaston and Theodora standing in conference and saw also that there was a group of people around Kastor, lying on an examination couch. I jumped out of bed, alarmed.

"It's Kastor, I shouldn't have left him Aunt V, he was so depressed..."

"I'm sure it's all right," said my aunt soothingly. "I'll make you some breakfast. Gaston said a car would be coming for you."

Travelling back to Binaries half an hour later, I tried to sense what was going on. Perhaps they were preparing to send Kastor to St. Anthony's; a worrying thought. Surely he was too well for that to be considered? Unless he had harmed himself. I picked up images of him lying somewhere, soaking wet, then being carried into the underground tunnels. With my anxiety, my precognitive and remote viewing skills were not obeying me, clouded with emotion and my fears. I looked tensely out of the car windows as it drew up at Askeys.

34

Theodora was waiting for me in the hall. "The break did you good," she observed and in response to my unspoken anguish about Kastor she added, "I'll take you to him now. An extraordinary thing has happened." She wouldn't say more, radiating calm as we travelled along the underground railway. But when we were walking along the corridor to the medical unit, she started to explain.

"Kastor was lost without you. Yesterday evening, we found he'd left the apartment and we couldn't at first locate him. It seems he'd just gone into the grounds, walking aimlessly. He was out there for hours."

"It was very wet yesterday, he must have got drenched." I was picturing my forlorn bond mate wandering like King Lear in the storm, not caring if the elements did their worst with him.

"Yes, he did. Then when he was exhausted, he crawled into the pagoda. He lost consciousness."

I hoped this was not leading to the news that he was seriously ill. *No*, signalled Theodora, continuing, "He was in a kind of trance, nothing anyone could do would wake him. He'd sustained slight hypothermia from the cold outside, but that was easily dealt with."

I turned to look at Theodora, noticing how tired she seemed. I guessed that several people had sat up all night with Kastor, trying to revive him. We were nearing the entrance to the medical unit and I heard a babble of voices, picking up many thoughts from within. They did not sound too upset, I thought with relief.

"You had a dream or two in the early hours, did you not?" said Theodora and I nodded, puzzled, sharing the image of the key.

"I knew a key would be involved in this," murmured the perceptive Theodora Sage.

We entered the unit and approached the room where all the noise was coming from. So many people were standing, talking and laughing that I could not sense what all the fuss was about. Then I saw Kastor, sitting on a hospital bed, smiling and nodding to those around him.

"*He's telepathing!*" I thought, with a surge of joy. I cut through the group to stand beside him and he looked up, grinning.

"My amazing Cassandra, you found the key," he said, sharing the image and several others in his excitement.

The clinical staff made everyone leave the room except me. I sat on the bed with Kastor and gazed into his eyes, sensing a torrent of thoughts and emotion. For a long time, neither of us felt the need to speak, euphoric to have rediscovered our close communication. Then Kastor shyly stroked my hand, as if he had only just met me and was tentatively testing how I would respond.

"I just wanted to die," he said, "It all seemed so pointless, and with you gone…"

"Your subconscious must have called me," I said, "They were adding the finishing touches to the repair."

"I told you they loved you, even if I'd started to lose hope that you could ever love me again."

"I never stopped loving you, nor ever will," I said firmly. "I shouldn't have left you alone."

"It seems to have been necessary," said Kastor. "I needed to lose consciousness, of my own volition, for my subconscious to be able to tell you what was needed."

"All that time in your mind, you'd think they could have given me a hint."

"Not without absorbing you. And then, I'd have had you in those deep layers, but would have lost you out here."

I looked at the clinic door, where a nurse was peering in us. "Do you want to stay here, resting, or go back to Askeys, for a bit of mingling?"

"Cassandra," he said, with a wide grin, "I don't need to answer that."

Later as we lay happily in our apartment, Kastor spoke dreamily, fighting back a tidal wave of images to focus on the present perfect moment. "I didn't think I deserved to ever make love with you again, after Cadiz."

"It wasn't so bad, I overreacted. Even in a damaged state, you seemed to be enjoying me being there."

"Please don't speak of it after today," he said, "but yes, I understand now why you wanted to be my... sex therapist. And why you were so angry when I couldn't respond to you emotionally."

"I was the emotionally dense one. I should have been more sensitive to what you were going through," I said guiltily.

"But you were right. I wake up in a sweat sometimes, thinking about it – and that kitchen assistant…"

"What about her?" My eyes were now sharp. He laughed.

"Well, how it would have meant her certain doom, she and all the other volunteers. It's not a good thing to have on your conscience, just to satisfy the libido." He projected an image of me as a Valkyrie, storming through the sierra, laying waste to young women and tossing their knickers to the winds.

"I wouldn't really have harmed them," I protested, "but I'm glad you've remembered about Norwich."

"That and so much else," he said, pulling me towards him.

"Are you sure you're up to all this therapy, so soon?" I murmured, "We need to keep your strength up."

Exactly, he replied silently. He signalled that we should make a simultaneous plunge into each other's minds. For a moment the deepest levels of our subconscious beings were united, something that most other telepaths in their community would have deeply envied.

After the dramatic and near loss of Kastor, everything changed. The discovery of the plot at the heart of the Binaries sent shock waves round the international branches of the organization. Review by the Board had two contrasting effects. On the one side, they agreed never to be so trusting again about schemes devised with so much secrecy. Surveillance was increased, with even more conditioning of the infants and children to make them averse to the type of treachery exhibited by Ryden and Anne Guburda, and those they had duped into assisting them. On the plus side, as far as I was concerned, calls for reform and relaxation of rules for loyal Binaries were at last heeded. Especially those who had taken risks in the field. This meant that Kastor and I could apply to move to another centre and to live nearby rather than within the complex. We had to wait a while until we could plan this. I had my twin pregnancy and Kastor needed time before he was ready for work again.

Six months after the ordeals in Casablanca and Cadiz, we relocated to the French Binaires centre, with our newborn twin girls and to my deep delight, young Leo. After much debate, we had been allowed to use the Lily West Foundation money, and the Swiss account left by Helen, to build a villa to accommodate our needs, including a nursery for our children. They would still have conditioning and supervision by nannies, but I was thrilled to have achieved this enormous concession. The villa had a small garden and strip of private beach, which abutted farmland belonging to Binaires. Helen's twins, born outside of course, were allowed to join us. Helen had left Faisal but seemed to have found a more lasting relationship with a wealthy businessman in Scotland. Helen was quite happy for her babies to be brought up in the Elam-Mason household and to receive the modified Binary training that had been agreed. She was reluctantly considering whether she and Alexander would have a child and bring him up in their home, in the odd way that I seemed to favour, having them running around the place.

Helen was permitted to visit, but not to enter the Centre Binaires. Her first visit was in the autumn of that year, only a few weeks after her twin boys had been born. The incongruous sight of Helen wheeling in the babies in a double buggy made even Kastor smile. As soon as she was inside the villa, she gratefully handed the babies over to the nanny. She seemed scarcely to notice as they were carefully taken down to the nursery in the converted cellars.

"Glad to get away from all that mothering stuff," she muttered, although even outside she had employed a nanny, so she was hardly a typical single mother. Her new man, Alexander, seemed quite content for the twins to be adopted by Kastor and me, along with a carefully documented cover story, in the event that he would ever want to see them.

"It's not likely," said Helen breezily. "He's very ambitious and not interested in us having children at present. Not ever, if I have anything to say about it."

"You'll miss them," I murmured. It was so strange to be face to face with Helen after all this time. She was heavily made up for the journey and with her now red hair, few would have spotted our resemblance, except of course me.

"No, I won't," she protested, "but I am missing a stiff drink after that air trip. Very good of the Binaries to let me use a private plane, by the way. I'm sure some of the crew suspected that my real name wasn't Jasmina, but they were all too polite to say so."

Kaotor and I exchanged a glance. He was standing with a disapproving air, remembering Helen's misdeeds. A silent prompt from me made him speak.

"So, hello again, Helen. I haven't had a chance to thank you for rescuing me in Casablanca. That was very brave."

She shrugged but her eyes, as expressive as mine, showed unusual sadness. "You of all people know that I had to do it. And was nearly too late."

"You're going to use your real name outside, I gather," he said, abruptly changing the subject.

"Yes, why not? Alexander understands that I had to change it after leaving Faisal. I'm still using Jasmina's passport though, as there's no point going through all the applications until I've married Alexander."

"Binaries are helping with that?" I asked.

"Oh, yes. Gaston has been in touch, sardonic as ever."

I smiled, visualising the taut phone conversation between them. Possibly one that wouldn't be used for training purposes.

"I've got passports for the boys too," continued Helen, "in case you ever need to travel with them." She rummaged in her carry-on bag and handed them over. Then she collapsed into a chair.

"Am I ever going to get that drink? And where is this private beach?"

A few hours later, our strange family party was sitting on the beach, enjoying the late afternoon sun. Two nannies took charge of the babies, while Leo ran happily about. His friend Finley had been allowed to visit and I could hear them planning a sand fort. Helen relaxed in a deck chair watching them.

"So proud of my little babies," she murmured. "I'm pretty sure they'll be good Binaries. I can already sense their latent abilities. This is the best place for my twins, without a doubt."

She adjusted her sunglasses and leaned back in the deckchair.

"Have you forgiven me, Cass? I won't blame you if you haven't."

"Yes," I said, truthfully. "Not quite what I'd planned in going to look for you, but I am so pleased to have found you. We'll always be very different, thanks to you being taken at birth, but I can see now the ways in which we are alike."

Helen laughed playfully. "Yeah, we're the wonder twins. And I'm sure there'll be more adventures ahead. If you're up for that?"

She gave me a cautious, uncertain look. When I gave her an equally cautious nod, she grinned. Kastor was in the sea, out of earshot. So I took the opportunity to ask her for more details about the rescue. Helen transmitted images of the various stages, including her disguise as the formidable KGB agent Dr. Blavatsky and the scene with Ryden in his hotel room. When she conjured up a thought image of the unfortunate Ryden, tied to the bedposts and all but naked, I held up a hand.

"Enough! Ryden will never recover. Dr. Foucoe has presented a research paper about him and the effects of mental probes."

"Good that he's some use, after all," said Helen without a trace of remorse. "If he'd been successful, you could have ended up like that too."

It was a chilly day, even for Southern France, but that was not the reason why I shivered. My current happy family life was never going to be normal, or completely safe. My attention was drawn to Leo and Finley, now preoccupied with the sand structure they were creating. I looked with concern at Leo's thin beach clothing, as he tipped buckets of sand and shaped them. Just a sand castle, but the shape reminded me of my image of St. Anthony's on its desolate rocky island. He was already more a Binary than I ever was. He'd stay with us until starting at Binaries boarding school in two years' time. Meanwhile he went across for training to the Centre Binaires via the underground tunnel that connected the villa with the Binaires farm, a security precaution insisted on by Gaston. Otherwise, the household appeared to the outside world to be a fairly conventional well-off family. Kastor and I left the home on occasion to do work projects for the Binaries or Binaires. Kastor still had a study and separate bedroom, his adaptation to relatively normal human life being a meandering process, where he sometimes begged for solitude. He had also insisted on a cook, despite my intention to perfect my omelettes. Today the cook had prepared the picnic for us to eat on the beach and was laying it out under a canopy.

"Leo, what have you done with your jacket?" I asked anxiously.

"Nanny said I mustn't get it dirty again," he called back, signalling that he wasn't cold.

"Well that's all right then," said Kastor, now wrapped in a beach towel after his dip in the sea. "But who can beat me to the picnic?" Leo and Finley jumped up, running after him and I smiled happily. In my mind, the Flower Duet chorus started to play and as the voices and notes soared up, the image with its music was caught by my fellow telepaths, expanding it into a lyrical entwining of jasmine and roses.

So Helen and I, after all our trials, had found different happy endings but our connection was now secure and our perilous adventures, for the time being, concluded.

§§ THE END §§

ABOUT THE AUTHOR

D.R. Rose is the pen name of a writer who lives in London, England. She started writing stories when she was nine. She is the daughter of an identical twin.

Now read the final part of the story, THE BINARY CONVERSION. In this darker and intriguing tale about Cassandra and her strange companions, they have to leave the French branch of the Binaries when rumours of baby stealing spread in a nearby village. Her attempts to reform some of the ruthless practices and cold relationships of the community are complicated by dangerous mind exploration, temptation to have an affair and a search for two lost children. She visits the grim psychiatric hospital in Scotland and causes havoc in insisting on different ways of managing patients, having to go on the run to avoid being imprisoned and put on trial. Cassandra discovers how much she has changed while trying to change the others. This fast moving story also explores the implications and challenges of their alternative world, if it could possibly exist alongside ours.

Available as a Kindle e-book and Amazon paperback.

Printed in Great Britain
by Amazon